P9-DBM-160

"I just want to feel safe."

She took in a deep breath.

Ben held up a hand. "Since I'm on duty anyway, I'll try to make a pass through this neighborhood every hour or two. But I can't promise anything. I could be called away for emergencies. If anything at all bothers you, if you hear a noise outside, a sound you can't identify, dial that phone."

"Yes, sir." At his stern look she managed a smile.

He started toward the door, with Rebecca trailing him.

Just as she reached for the handle, he turned. "Lock this when I..."

Their faces were nearly brushing. He breathed her in, and the scent of her filled his lungs. His heart. His very soul.

He leaned close just as she leaned forward. That was nearly his undoing. For one breathless moment he simply stared at her, fighting an almost overpowering need to hold her. To kiss her.

The sudden blaze of heat had him by the throat.

Very deliberately he took a step back.

RAVES FOR R. C. RYAN'S NOVELS

REED

"4 stars! Ryan's latest book in her Malloys of Montana series contains a heartwarming plot filled with down-to-earth cowboys and warm, memorable characters. Reed and Ally are engaging and endearing, and their sweet, fiery chemistry heats up the pages, which will leave readers' hearts melting...A delightful read."

—*RT Book Reviews*

LUKE

"Ryan creates vivid characters against the lovingly rendered backdrop of sweeping Montana ranchlands. The passion between Ryan's protagonists, which they keep discreet, is tender and heartwarming. The plot is drawn in broad strokes, but Ryan expertly brings it to a satisfying conclusion."

—*Publishers Weekly*

MATT

"Ryan has created a gripping love story fraught with danger and lust, pain and sweet, sweet triumph."

—*Library Journal* starred review

"Ryan, aka author Ruth Ryan Langan, takes it to the next level in the first book of her new Malloys of Montana series...Fans know that hot Montana men are Ryan/Langan's specialty (the

McCords series, anyone?), so get cozy in your favorite reading nook and enjoy!"
—B&N Reads Blog

"The beguiling first novel in the Malloys of Montana contemporary series from Ryan (a pen name for Ruth Ryan Langan) depicts the lure of the mountains as a Chicago lawyer falls for a handsome rancher...Touching and romantic, Ryan's portrayal of a city slicker falling for a cowboy delves into the depths of each of their personalities to find common ground in their love for the land. Readers will eagerly anticipate future installments."
—*Publishers Weekly*

"4 stars! With tough, sexy cowboys set against the beautiful, rural landscape of Montana, Ryan's latest is a must-read."
—*RT Book Reviews*

THE LEGACY OF COPPER CREEK

"Solidly written romance. Rich, layered, vulnerable characters in Whit and Cara, coupled with strong chemistry and intense heat between them, proves Ryan does the contemporary Western love story well."
—*RT Book Reviews*

"What a perfect ending to a series...I love this story."
—SillyMelody.blogspot.com

"If you're looking to lose yourself in a fictional family that will steal your heart and pull you into the thick of things, this is the book for you. *Copper Creek* is where a wayward soul can find a home and have all their dreams come true."
—MommysaBookWhore.com

THE REBEL OF COPPER CREEK

"A winner. Ryan writes with a realism that brings readers deep into the world she's created. The characters all have an authenticity that touches the heart."
—RT Book Reviews

"An awesome story."
—NightOwlReviews.com

THE MAVERICK OF COPPER CREEK

"Ryan's storytelling is tinged with warmth and down-to-earth grit. Her authentic, distinctive characters will get to the heart of any reader. With a sweet plot infused with family love, a fiery romance, and a bit of mystery, Ryan does not disappoint."
—RT Book Reviews

"Full of sexy cowboys and a western feel that is undeniable...A well-written fun story that I really enjoyed."
—NightOwlReviews.com

COWBOY

on my MIND

R. C. RYAN

FOREVER

NEW YORK BOSTON

This book is a work of fiction. Names, characters, places, and incidents are the product of the author's imagination or are used fictitiously. Any resemblance to actual events, locales, or persons, living or dead, is coincidental.

Copyright © 2018 by Ruth Ryan Langan
Excerpt from *The Cowboy Next Door* copyright © 2018 by Ruth Ryan Langan
Rocky Mountain Cowboy copyright © 2018 by Sara Richardson

Cover design by Elizabeth Turner. Cover photograph by Rob Lang. Cover copyright © 2018 by Hachette Book Group, Inc.

Hachette Book Group supports the right to free expression and the value of copyright. The purpose of copyright is to encourage writers and artists to produce the creative works that enrich our culture.

The scanning, uploading, and distribution of this book without permission is a theft of the author's intellectual property. If you would like permission to use material from the book (other than for review purposes), please contact permissions@hbgusa.com. Thank you for your support of the author's rights.

Forever
Hachette Book Group
1290 Avenue of the Americas, New York, NY 10104
forever-romance.com
twitter.com/foreverromance

First Edition: June 2018

Forever is an imprint of Grand Central Publishing. The Forever name and logo are trademarks of Hachette Book Group, Inc.

The publisher is not responsible for websites (or their content) that are not owned by the publisher.

The Hachette Speakers Bureau provides a wide range of authors for speaking events. To find out more, go to www.hachettespeakersbureau.com or call (866) 376-6591.

ISBNs: 978-1-5387-1115-6 (mass market), 978-1-5387-1114-9 (ebook)

Printed in the United States of America

OPM

10 9 8 7 6 5 4 3 2 1

ATTENTION CORPORATIONS AND ORGANIZATIONS:
Most Hachette Book Group books are available at quantity discounts with bulk purchase for educational, business, or sales promotional use. For information, please call or write:

Special Markets Department, Hachette Book Group
1290 Avenue of the Americas, New York, NY 10104
Telephone: 1-800-222-6747 Fax: 1-800-477-5925

To those families who, by blood or by choice, form an unbreakable bond. And to my own beautiful family, who fill my life with so much love and laughter.

COWBOY

on my MIND

PROLOGUE

Haller Creek, Montana—Fifteen years ago

A wicked wind blowing down from the Bitterroot Mountains assaulted the horse and rider.

Mackenzie Monroe dismounted and knelt at a fresh grave site.

His eyes were fixed on the names etched on the wooden cross that marked the final resting place of his wife, Rachel, and nineteen-year-old son, Robbie. A year earlier they'd been killed in a head-on collision with a cattle hauler on the interstate. He had planned on replacing the temporary grave marker with a fine piece of marble. Now there would be no time for that.

The bitter cold froze the tears on his cheeks as he touched the bottle of pills nestled in his pocket that old Doc Peterson had prescribed to help him sleep.

"There's no joy left in my life, Rachel. The pain is too deep." His hand rested on the mound of earth, now covered with snow. "You and Robbie were my reason for living. You know how I've loved this place. But now, without the two of you, all I see is a future of endless work and misery on this godforsaken land."

This land.

He'd been born here, as had his father and grandfather. Not that it mattered anymore. It was dirt and grass and sweeping vistas. But the people who mattered most were gone.

He got to his feet and swept off his hat in a courtly gesture. "I hope you'll forgive me. But I can't go on like this. I pray there's truly a heaven, so I can join you there."

Pulling himself into the saddle, he turned his mount in the direction of his ranch in the distance.

Once in the barn he unsaddled his gelding before turning the animal into a stall with fresh feed and water. From a rusted old truck he retrieved a bottle of cheap whiskey he'd bought while in town. Though he wasn't much of a drinking man, he figured if he swallowed the entire bottle of pills and washed them down with enough whiskey, he'd never wake up.

Leaning his weight against the barn door, he latched it and headed toward the house. While he walked, he began writing the note in his mind. He would try, in simple terms, to explain why he couldn't live with his pain. He would leave his message on the kitchen table, where it would surely be found by Otis, Roscoe, and Zachariah, three characters who had, through the years, attached themselves to Mac and his family. It had been Rachel's tender heart that had brought this diverse group of strangers into his home. She'd never once considered turning away anyone with a sad story.

Otis Green had witnessed his family wiped out at the hands of a crazed firebomber and had fled their tenement on the south side of Chicago, a man broken in body and soul.

He showed up one day on the Monroe doorstep, a black man, city born and bred, completely out of his element in cattle country but seeking a better way of life and willing to do whatever necessary to earn it. Rachel welcomed him like a long-lost relative.

Roscoe Flute, an itinerant cowboy and handyman, came to fix a generator years ago and never left. It was Rachel who'd learned that he'd sold his horse in order to pay for a cheap room in a motel. When the money ran out, he had nowhere left to go. In exchange for a warm bunkhouse, he kept every piece of equipment on the ranch humming.

Zachariah York was a successful rancher and retired lawyer who'd been living alone on his family's neighboring ranch until Mac found him lying in a meadow, where the old man had fallen from his horse and broken his hip and was unable to get up. Mac and Rachel hauled him to the clinic in Haller Creek before taking him home, where Rachel had insisted on nursing him back to health. Months later he was still living here, insisting that he wasn't ready to go back home and live alone.

Otis and Roscoe were up in the hills with the herd. Zachariah was slow-moving these days. Though his hip had mended, he wasn't ready to take on ranch chores yet. By now Zachariah had helped himself to a sleeping pill and wouldn't wake until nearly noon. Mac figured, with those three otherwise occupied, he would be long dead before anyone could find his body, thus resisting any attempt to have his stomach pumped.

Through his fog of pain, he shrugged aside a twinge of remorse at the thought of leaving his three housemates to fend for themselves. He hoped the profit from the auction of his ranch and outbuildings would afford them a comfortable retirement. The note he intended to leave would designate them equal beneficiaries of his estate. It would be his last gesture of goodwill before departing this world.

How he yearned for just one more of Rachel's sweet smiles. For the infectious sound of Robbie's laughter. His heart ached for the loss of the joy they had brought to his life.

Tears misted his eyes as he mulled the proper wording of the letter he intended to leave behind.

I, Mackenzie Monroe, being of sound mind...

He shoved open the back door and stepped into the puddles of melted snow on the floor of the mudroom before stopping in midstride.

Puddles? Snow? He'd been gone for hours.

Who could have done this?

From the kitchen he heard the sound of muffled voices.

By heaven. Intruders. Thieves.

Taking aim with his rifle, he kicked in the kitchen door to confront the villains. He stared in stunned surprise at the sight of three filthy boys. One was at the table, devouring a chicken leg. One was standing at the open door of the refrigerator, drinking from a carton of milk. One stood at the counter shoveling cold beans into his mouth.

Runaways. Dirty, ragged, scruffy boys. Their clothes were thin, with no sign of parkas or gloves or boots. In fact, one was barefoot. One was wearing a pair of Robbie's boots that had been stored in the mudroom. And one had drawn a checkered tablecloth around himself for warmth.

Surprise, pity, fear for his safety warred within him.

In some small part of his mind he watched as their heads came up sharply.

The boy seated at the table jerked to his feet and took aim with a kitchen knife.

Survival took over.

"Drop it or I'll drop you where you stand." Mac's voice was colder than the snowstorm raging outside the door.

The boy looked to the taller one, who nodded and stepped in front of the other two. The knife clattered to the floor.

"Now you'll tell me who you are and what the hell you're doing in my house."

His words were greeted by sullen silence.

"All right." He pulled his cell phone from his breast pocket. "You can tell it to the sheriff."

"No way." The tallest of the three swore a blue streak and reached out a hand in an effort to snatch away the phone. Seeing Mac make a swift turn, his rifle aimed clearly at his heart, the boy lifted both hands over his head. "Hold on. Don't shoot. I'm Ben Turner. These are my brothers, Sam and Finn."

Mac sized up the two younger boys before returning his attention to the tallest, who had positioned himself to protect his brothers. "What're you doing out on a night like this? And where the hell is your family?"

"Our folks are dead. They died six years ago, when I was six." The boy exchanged a look with his brothers. "Sam was five and Finn was four."

"Where've you been living since?"

Ben shrugged. "All over. We've been separated and living in foster homes. Our"—he swore again, using words Mac rarely heard except from an occasional world-weary wrangler—"caseworkers keep saying they'll find a way for us to be together, but we know it's never going to happen."

The middle brother nodded. "Those"—the boy mimicked his older brother's choice of coarse language—"say whatever they want, and keep on moving us around. We know they're lying. They've been lying since the day they took control of our lives. I overheard one of them telling my caseworker we were too old and ornery to ever be adopted, and it'd be a cold day in hell before they'd ever ask any family to take on all three of us."

"So we decided to run away," Finn put in.

"Shut up, Finn." The other two glared at him.

Seeing the youngest boy shivering uncontrollably, Ben squared his shoulders and dropped an arm around him, drawing him close. "Okay. So he's telling it straight."

Sam darted Ben a look of shock and anger. "You said we wouldn't tell..."

Ben put a hand on Sam's arm. "It's okay." He turned to Mac. "We made a pact. Nobody's going to separate us again. We figured this was a good night to run. No freakin' fool's going to follow us in this snow."

Sam nodded. "Especially way out here in the middle of this piece of..."

"That's enough." Mac's voice had the desired effect of shutting him up.

Ben again shoved the other two behind him, sending a clear message that he would do whatever necessary to protect them. "If you let us go, I promise we'll be on our way and won't bother you again."

Mac lowered the rifle and nodded toward the window. "In case you haven't noticed, that's not just a storm raging out there. It's a blizzard. I don't know how you made it this far, but you won't survive an hour in this kind of deep freeze. Especially dressed like that."

The two younger boys looked to their leader.

Ben lifted his chin like a prizefighter. "So, what're you going to do? Tie us up until the"—he let loose with a string of swear words—"law can come and take us back?"

"I said that's enough of that kind of talk. I won't have it in my house."

Needing time to think, Mac walked to the mudroom to

hang his parka and hat on hooks by the door, before setting aside his rifle. He sat on a bench to nudge off his frozen boots. Then he surprised them by walking into the kitchen and turning on the stove.

"First, let's deal with hunger. Mine and yours. The quickest thing I know how to make is scrambled eggs." He pointed to the refrigerator. "Sam, bring me that carton of milk and a dozen eggs. Finn, there's bread in that breadbox. Put some in the toaster. Ben, since you already started on that chicken, cut off enough to fill a platter."

While he turned eggs in a skillet, he pointed to a cupboard. "There are mugs up there. Fill them with milk and stick them in the microwave. When the milk's hot, add some of that chocolate. It'll take the chill off our bones."

The boys did as he said, and in short order they were seated around the table, eating their fill of chicken, eggs, and toast, and drinking mugs of hot chocolate. Afterward, they piled their dishes in the sink and waited expectantly, to see if the man in charge would now call the law.

He surprised them by saying, "I don't know about the three of you, but I'm too tired to deal with anything more tonight. Come on. You can sleep upstairs."

They followed him up the stairs and peered inside when he opened a door.

Ben spoke for all of them. "So, what's the trick?"

"I'm fresh out of tricks. Go to sleep. I'll figure out what to do in the morning."

As they stepped inside, seeing two narrow beds covered in matching plaid quilts, Ben shot him a look of suspicion. "Who else will be sleeping in here?"

"Just you three."

The boy's eyes narrowed. "Who usually sleeps in here?"

"My son, Robbie."

"Yeah? And where's Robbie tonight?"

Mac absorbed an arrow straight to his heart. "Robbie's dead. For tonight, it's yours. But only for tonight," he added with a growl. "So enjoy it while you can."

He pulled the door shut and listened as the voices within began an intense debate.

With a muttered curse he descended the stairs, too keyed up to think about sleep now. What had just happened here? How had all his carefully laid plans gone south? He didn't want to deal with any of this. Not three angry delinquents who were mad at the world. Not a call to the authorities in the morning. And not another night of pain and anguish over his terrible loss and the emptiness of his life. How much more should a man have to take? Were the Fates having fun at his expense?

After washing the dishes and tidying up the kitchen, he made a pot of coffee and sat at the table, mulling over his options.

He knew what Rachel would have said about this. He could hear her voice inside his head, soft, coaxing. Hadn't she always had a soft spot in her heart for the downtrodden? The lost? The outcasts of society?

But Rachel wasn't here now. And he couldn't even cope with his own troubles, let alone those of three foul-mouthed runaways.

These three were trouble. With a capital *T*. And thankfully, not his problem.

He drained his coffee and made his way up the stairs. When he tried to open the door to Robbie's room, he found it blocked. It took plenty of time and a lot of sweat to wrestle aside the dresser the boys had placed against the door.

He stepped inside, expecting to find them gone out the window. Instead they were in a dead sleep in one small bed, tangled up around one another, obviously too exhausted to be roused even by his noisy entrance. Despite the fact that there was a second identical bed, they'd been unwilling to separate for even that small distance.

Then he noticed something else. The blanket had slipped from the shoulders of the oldest brother, Ben. The tough guy. The leader. The boy's back and shoulders were crisscrossed with scars that could have only been made by repeated whippings.

The sight of it had his hands clenching into fists. What sort of monster would beat a helpless kid? How much pain and fear had this boy endured in his young life?

Mac glanced at Robbie's picture on the dresser. It had been taken when he'd been about Ben's age, dark hair slicked back, wearing his best shirt and tie, standing proudly between his loving parents, smiling broadly for the camera. In his lifetime, the boy had never had a hand raised against him. He'd known only pride and unconditional love from his mother and father. Like most innocents, Robbie couldn't have conceived of a lifetime of pain and abuse.

Mac's heart contracted painfully.

He let himself out and walked to his room at the end of the hall. Inside he stored the bottle of pills and the whiskey in a file cabinet in his closet before locking it and heading back downstairs.

He poured himself another cup of coffee and walked to the window, staring out at the raging storm. Even if he got phone service, there was no sense calling the authorities. The roads way out here would be impassable for days.

In the meantime, he'd just have to hold off on his own plans. Not that he intended to change his mind about anything, he told himself. But for now, he'd just watch and listen and see how much more information he could pry out of those three hoodlums upstairs.

What kind of hell had they been forced to endure? And what had such cruel treatment done to them?

Damnable troublemakers couldn't have come into his life at a worse time.

Mac thought about the ever-present hole in his heart that would never heal.

Now, it seemed, he would have to bear his unbearable sorrow while he found a way to deal with these wounded young hellions. He hoped to heaven a new day would help clear his mind and show him a path through this latest challenge.

"Ben." Sam and Finn shook their oldest brother's shoulder until he stirred. "Wake up, Ben."

The boy rubbed his eyes. "What's wrong?"

"Last night you said we'd be up and out of here before the old man could call the cops."

Ben sat up, shaking aside the last dregs of sleep and spouting a litany of curses. "Why didn't you wake me sooner?"

"We just woke up." Sam glanced at Finn, who nodded in agreement. "I guess it's 'cause this is the first time we've been warm and well fed in so long."

"Yeah." Ben glanced at the dresser. "It looks like the old man figured out what we were up to."

The three brothers stared at the heavy piece of furniture they'd dragged across the room to bar the door. It now stood to one side at an odd angle.

"Jeez. Now we're in for it," Finn muttered.

"Yeah. I'm sure he's made a phone call by now." Ben swung his feet to the floor. "May as well go downstairs and face the music. Just remember. If we see a chance to run, we grab it. Agreed?"

The other two nodded and followed their leader down the stairs.

In the kitchen, bacon sizzled in a skillet, and Mac flipped pancakes onto a platter. He turned. "About time you three got up." He nodded toward the table. "Sit and eat while it's hot."

Seeing Ben remain standing, his younger brothers followed suit.

"You thinking this will ease your guilt when the law comes for us?"

At Ben's question, Mac filled three glasses with milk. "Nobody's getting through these roads today." He pointed to the curtain of snow falling outside the window. "In case you haven't noticed, our raging Montana blizzard has cut us off from civilization."

The three boys crowded around the window to see mounds of snow over the porch.

They turned to one another with matching grins.

"So." Ben sauntered to the table, and the other two followed. "Now what?"

Mac shrugged and filled a mug with coffee before sitting at the head of the table. "I plan on eating, then heading to the barn for morning chores. I'd like the three of you to lend a hand."

"You want us to freaking work in your barn?"

"That's what ranchers do. Even in the dead of winter, stalls need mucking. Animals need feeding."

The youngest, Finn, looked over. "What's mucking?"

"I'll show you." Mac tucked into his food. "Right after breakfast."

The barn door was shoved open. Two old men, wide-brimmed hats and winter parkas mounded with snow, stared in surprise at the sight that greeted them.

Their friend Mac was forking dung-filled straw from a

stall into a nearby honey wagon. Beside him stood a skinny boy who paused between every forkful to hold his nose. In the stall beside theirs two more boys attempted to use pitchforks to imitate Mac's example. For every load that landed in the wagon, two more fell to the ground, followed by a stream of swear words guaranteed to curl their whiskers.

"What the hell...?"

Hearing Roscoe's voice, Mac paused to glance toward the two figures standing at the entrance. "You're back. I didn't think you'd be able to get through the trail."

The two men led their weary horses inside and began unsaddling them, tossing the saddles over the rails of empty stalls.

Roscoe shook his head. "Snow's belly-high already up in the hills. We figured if we didn't get going now, we'd be stuck up there for another week. Which wouldn't be all that bad, except we were running out of chow." He nodded toward the boys. "Where'd these three mangy mutts blow in from?"

"Caught in the storm." Mac set aside his pitchfork. "This is Ben, Sam, and Finn. Boys, meet Roscoe Flute and Otis Green."

The oldest boy shot Mac a narrowed look. "I thought you said the law couldn't get through the storm."

"Roscoe and Otis live here."

Little Finn stepped out of the stall where he'd been working. "You live here?" He looked Otis up and down, and then Roscoe. "Are you brothers, too?"

The two old men threw back their heads and chuckled.

Otis winked at Roscoe. "I like to think we're all brothers."

Finn leaned on his pitchfork. "If you live here, why aren't you doing this stinky work?"

"We were up in the hills with the herd." Roscoe took off

his hat and shook it against his leg, sending a shower of snow flying. "Besides, we'd rather leave the stinky jobs to newcomers. Consider this your baptism, boys."

The two men were laughing as they began rubbing down their mounts before filling troughs with feed and water.

"Okay, boys." Mac picked up his pitchfork. "Break's over. Let's get this done so we can move on to other things."

As the three bent to their task, the middle boy let out a stream of oaths that had old Otis looking up with annoyance. "You going to let him talk like that, Mac?"

Mac gave a weary sigh. "I've told the three of them at least a dozen times I won't have that kind of language in my home."

"We're not in the house now," Sam said logically. "We're in your smelly barn."

"It's my property all the same. And from now on, every time one of you says something I consider inappropriate, I'll add one more task to your list of jobs. You understand?"

Ben's mouth opened, and it was obvious he was about to swear when he caught himself. His mouth clamped shut. With narrowed eyes he forked a load of dung-filled straw and tossed it into the wagon with all his strength.

Seeing it, Mac bit back a grin. It might not be real progress, but it was a baby step. And for now, he'd take any improvement he could get.

Maybe, if this storm lasted long enough, these three might learn to say an entire sentence without cussing. Then again, he'd better be careful what he wished for. He was bound to run out of patience long before they ran out of swear words.

The grandfather clock on the stair landing was striking midnight. After insisting the three boys shower and change into

Robbie's old pajamas before hitting the sack, Mac descended the stairs and headed toward the kitchen.

Inside, the three old men looked up from the table, where they'd been holding a muted conversation.

Retired lawyer Zachariah York, white hair streaming down his back like a lion's mane, was wearing his favorite fringed buckskin jacket, which had been his trademark apparel when he'd been Montana's most admired trial lawyer back in the day. He had, as always, appointed himself spokesman. "Mackenzie, old friend, we assume you have some kind of plan for your... very interesting young guests. Care to share?"

Mac filled a mug with steaming coffee before leaning a hip against the counter. "I wish I knew. I'm fresh out of plans. With those three, there's no telling if they'll even be around tomorrow. After the way I worked them today, they'll probably try to get as far away from here as they can."

"If you think that, you're fooling yourself, Mackenzie."

Mac looked over at Zachariah. "And you know this because...?"

"They may have resented the work. It's pretty obvious they've never handled ranch chores before. But I watched them in the kitchen. They know how to clean up for themselves. They've probably been expected to carry their share of the work for as long as they've been thrown into foster care. A lot of ranchers only take in these kids so they have free labor and get paid by the state, as well. It's how the system works."

"Speaking of which..." Mac took a seat. "You know the law, Zachariah. Will I be in trouble for harboring runaways?"

"I doubt it. Especially if you explain that they broke in during a blizzard, and you were forced to keep them until the proper authorities could be alerted."

"If I alert the authorities, will those three be punished?"

Zachariah nodded. "Juvenile detention, most likely."

"And then they'll be returned to the system." Mac stared into his cup. "Which means they'll be separated again, and probably treated even harsher than before. Unless..."

He looked up to see the three old men watching him warily.

He sighed. "I've been thinking about something all day. They risked everything just to be together. I know there was physical abuse, but the mental abuse of separation seems to have been the driving force behind this odyssey of theirs. Do you think there's a chance I could...keep them together? Here?"

Roscoe and Otis shared a look of astonishment.

Zachariah steepled his fingers. "As fosters? Or adoption?"

Mac shrugged. "Whatever it takes to keep them together."

The old man had that pensive look he always had when he was mulling the intricacies of the law. Finally he nodded. "As soon as we get phone service, I'll make some calls. I still have friends on the inside who might be able to pull a few strings." At Mac's look of surprise he quickly added, "Now don't get your hopes up. There will be a lot of hoops to jump through." For the first time he smiled. "But I'm thinking the folks in authority might be relieved to be done with those three foul-mouthed hooligans."

He gave his friend a sharp look. "But, Mackenzie Monroe, that raises an even bigger question. If it all goes your way, what in the world do you think you're going to do with those three?"

Mac got wearily to his feet and headed toward the stairs. "That's the other thing I've been thinking about all day. Am I a glutton for punishment, or just plain crazy?" He turned and held up a hand. "Don't answer that. I already know." He gave a careless shrug of his shoulders. "The trouble is, I've got a war going on in my head, with a million questions, and at the moment I'm fresh out of answers. But I know this. Despite the deep-seated anger in those three, there's a fierce loyalty as well. I haven't a doubt in my mind that each of them would stand up and fight for his brothers. Or die for them, if it ever came to that. It's a rare and amazing trait they share. And I can't help admiring them for it. Maybe, just maybe, they ended up here for a reason and that reason is starting to become clear to me."

CHAPTER ONE

Haller Creek, Montana—Present Day

Ben Monroe stepped out of Sheriff Virgil Kerr's tricked-out SUV, with all the bells and whistles, lights flashing, siren blasting. With a twist of the ignition, the sudden silence in the air seemed shocking.

Folks around these parts wouldn't be surprised to see Ben in the lawman's car. He and his brothers had always been the ones considered most likely to be the cause of any trouble in the county.

What would surprise them was the shiny badge the sheriff had pinned on Ben's parka when he'd deputized him earlier that morning. A badge that winked in the autumn sunlight. Instead of handcuffs, Ben was holding a police-issue pistol, also on loan from the sheriff. The pistol was now aimed at the lanky cowboy standing in the leaf-strewn driveway, cradling a rifle and spewing a stream of vicious oaths at the man and woman watching from the front porch.

The man glanced from the sheriff, still sitting in his vehicle, nursing an injured leg, to where Ben stood alone. "What're you up to, Monroe? Back off. I've got no beef with you."

Ben held up a hand to silence him. "Sheriff Kerr brought me along to lend a hand while he recovers from a gunshot to his thigh. He told me about your feud with your wife. I know how you feel, Leroy."

"How would you know what I'm feeling? You ever have a wife cheat on you with your best friend, and then tell you the kid you've loved for years isn't yours?"

The sheriff had given Ben the bare bones of the story before asking him to ride along and lend some muscle. If the rest of the details caught him by surprise, Ben managed to hide his feelings behind a stoic mask he'd perfected as a boy in the foster-care system. "You know I've never been married, Leroy. But I've been mad enough to kill, and I'm glad cooler heads prevailed. You can't settle the score like this."

"Like hell I can't."

In his younger days, Ben had been better known around town as a guy who let his fists do the talking. Now, after years of Mackenzie Monroe's example, he spoke in a low, reasonable tone. "Once you kill someone, you can't get a do-over. You don't want to do this."

"Yes, I do. I'm going to kill that lying..." Leroy Purcell glared at his wife and hurled a string of oaths while his finger actually trembled on the trigger.

Ben reached out in time to stop him acting on his impulse.

That added to Leroy's pent-up fury, and he took a wild swing at the man with the badge, managing to land his fist smack in Ben's eye. "I told you, I'm going to kill my lying wife and Chester Bowling for what they did."

With a grunt of pain, Ben reacted, shoving the enraged Leroy up against a tree. Despite the string of savage oaths that bubbled up in his mind, he managed to keep his voice low and steady. "There's a better way to get your revenge."

"Yeah?" The only thing that kept the furious rancher from acting on his threat was Ben's hand, strong as a steel vise, pressed firmly to his throat, making his voice little more than a raspy croak. "You want to tell me how?"

Ben was breathing hard as he lowered his hand and fixed Leroy with the fierce look he'd perfected over a lifetime of protecting his brothers. "Walk away. When you do that, you win. You condemn Chet Bowling to a lifetime with your lying, cheating ex-wife and his kid, while you get to start over. And maybe next time you'll get lucky enough to find a woman who not only deserves you, but also appreciates you."

"And if I don't walk away?"

"Unless you drop that rifle and agree to come with me peacefully, I'll have to shoot you, Leroy. And you know I never miss. That's why the sheriff asked me to handle this for him. The choice is yours. Shoot Chester and Minnie and go to prison for life, or drop your weapon, cool your heels in jail, and get a do-over."

As if to goad him into doing something foolish, the couple on the porch began taunting Leroy with jeers and laughter.

"Look at those two drunken fools." Leroy raised the rifle, arm shaking with tension as he took aim.

Ben did the same, his hand steady as he pointed his pistol at the cowboy. "You'll never get off a shot before I take you down. Your call, Leroy. Live free or die."

Ben's words, spoken barely above a whisper, and the knowledge that he wouldn't miss, had the rancher suddenly tossing aside his weapon and lifting his hands in the air. "You better be telling me straight, Monroe."

"You know I am, Leroy." Ben picked up the rifle and held open the back door of the SUV.

As Leroy settled inside, he muttered, "Those two deserve each other. I hope Chester and Minnie have a dozen kids, and all of them lazy, no-good rotten cheats just like the two of 'em."

Sheriff Virgil Kerr had to struggle to hold back the laughter that bubbled, laughter that was as much relief as humor. "Hold on to that thought, Leroy."

As the vehicle pulled away from the patch of dry, barren yard in front of the neglected ranch and headed to the town of Haller Creek, the old sheriff turned to Ben. "Your pa would feel real proud that you were able to talk a gunman down without having to resort to violence, son."

"Yeah. Thanks, Sheriff."

"No. Thank you, son. I knew you were the right one to trust while this bum leg mends. You handled that just right."

The tires sent a flurry of red and gold leaves square-dancing across the interstate as Ben drove, deep in thought.

How odd that, even while facing down a gunman bent on killing, the one thing uppermost in his mind wasn't his own safety, but making Mac proud. But then, Mackenzie Monroe wasn't just his adoptive father. He was the man who'd given him back his life. Had made a home for him and his brothers all these years. And had given them all a sense of purpose. Of pride. Of family.

There was nothing in the world Ben wanted more than to be half the man his father was.

"Hey, bro." Sam, the middle brother and family jokester, wore a silly grin. "That's quite a shiner."

Ben washed up at the mudroom sink before taking a seat

at the kitchen table, where the rest of the household had gathered for supper.

As always, Mac sat at the head, while Sam and Finn were seated on one side of the table, with Otis Green, Roscoe Flute, and Zachariah York at the other side. Though they'd all changed over the years, the three brothers had changed the most. They were men now. Tall, rugged, handsome, with dark shaggy hair, smoky gray eyes, muscles honed from years of ranch chores, and smiles where there had once been only scowls. Best of all, their childhood doubts and fears had now been replaced with a sense of honor and trust, thanks to the men seated around the table.

"The sheriff asked me to go with him to the Purcell ranch."

Otis shared a grin with Roscoe. "Those two scrapping again?"

"More than a scrap this time. Leroy was hell-bent on killing his wife and Chet Bowling. Millie claims their kid is Chet's."

"That'd be enough to make a man want to resort to murder." Roscoe paused, his fork halfway to his mouth. "You two get into a brawl?"

Ben shook his head. "I was trying to reason with him when he sucker-punched me."

Sam's head came up sharply. "I hope you didn't kill Leroy."

"It crossed my mind." With a sideways glance at Mac, Ben reached for the gravy and poured it over a slab of roast chicken and a mound of mashed potatoes. "But I heard a certain guy's voice in my head, warning me to cool off. So I managed to talk Leroy down off that cliff."

Mac gave a satisfied grin.

"And then you flattened him?" Sam asked.

"I..." Ben glanced around. "I reasoned with him. I told him the best revenge would be to walk away and leave the two lovers to deal with the mess they've made of their lives. If he's lucky, they'll have a dozen or so kids just like themselves."

There were hoots of laughter around the table.

"Good one, son." Mac reached over to clap a hand on Ben's shoulder.

"Yeah." Finn nudged Sam. "Any man who'd sleep with Minnie Purcell has to be desperate, or out of his mind."

"Or in love." Zachariah shot the younger men a narrowed look. "Not that you'd understand, Finnian, my boy, since you seem to avoid romantic entanglements like a plague, but my grandfather used to say there's no accounting for love."

Finn had let his hair grow to his shoulders and was sporting a fringed buckskin jacket as homage to his hero, Zachariah. Fresh from passing the bar, he was settling in to life as a lawyer and rancher, just as Zachariah had done for most of his career.

"Which is why I intend to remain single until Dad takes a wife."

His remark had everyone around the table grinning like fools.

"I'll remind you that miracles do happen." Zachariah helped himself to more chicken. "Even your dear old dad could be bitten by the love bug. When passion flares, love isn't just blind. It's so dazzling to the ones involved that they can't see the flaws that are obvious to the rest of the universe."

Finn shared a grin with his brothers. "But we're talking about Minnie Purcell. Nobody can be that blind."

Zachariah bent to his dinner. "I'll remind you of those words one day when you're bedazzled by your lady love."

"I'm never falling in love," Finn declared.

"Me neither." Sam gave a firm shake of his head for emphasis.

"I'll remind you one day as well, Samuel." Zachariah was smiling broadly.

Beside them, Ben held his silence. He'd been sweet on a girl for years. It had started when he first came to Haller Creek.

He wouldn't call it love. They'd barely exchanged more than a dozen words. He wasn't certain, even now, what he felt for her. He hadn't seen Rebecca Henderson in years. She'd left for college in Bozeman and never returned, but he couldn't get her out of his mind. The feeling was different from what he felt for any other female, with the exception of Mary Pat Healy, but that didn't count, since she was as old as Mac.

Mary Pat was the county social worker, public health nurse, and traveling teacher who stopped by every ranch in the district every couple of months to look in on her students. It was Mary Pat who had worked with Zachariah and the county and state authorities to allow Mac to legalize the adoption of three homeless boys. It was also Mary Pat who persuaded Mac to remove the boys from the Haller Creek school and recommended they be homeschooled after learning they'd been engaged in playground fights on a daily basis. Most of the fights were fueled by Ben and his famous temper, because he felt honor-bound to defend his two younger brothers whenever they got into a scuffle.

After convincing Mac to take them out of school, Mary Pat had become a regular visitor to their ranch.

Years ago Ben had decided that if his mother had lived, she'd have been like Mary Pat. Smart as a whip, fun to be around, and the gentlest woman he'd ever known. It didn't hurt that she had a smile that could melt the snow atop the Bitterroot Mountain peaks in the dead of winter.

As the four older men enjoyed slices of Zachariah's famous apple pie, Ben, Sam, and Finn gathered up the dishes and cleaned the kitchen. It had become such a ritual, they were barely even aware of it anymore. Whoever made the meal got to relax while the others assumed the clean-up detail. Most times, Zachariah took charge of cooking while the others handled the ranch chores or rode up to the range to join the wranglers tending the herds. Though the ranch had become an even more successful operation over the past years, it still took the efforts of all of them to maintain it.

Years earlier Zachariah had arranged to merge his ranchland with Mac's, adding to Mac's property and putting even more money in Zachariah's already hefty bank account. Not that it mattered. The old lawyer often said money was just paper. It was his generosity that had made it possible for Finn to go off to college and later a prestigious law school. The old lawyer actually turned his back on his own property so he could stay here and be part of Mac's family. Family, even if not blood-related, was the only real treasure in life, according to Zachariah. Now, as usual, with dinner over, the old lawyer retired to his room to catch up on the fascinating cases highlighted in the latest issue of his legal journal.

Otis eased himself up from his chair before turning to Roscoe. "You ready to finish that gin rummy game?"

"I am. As I recall, I'm winning."

"In your dreams."

"I'll be happy to show you the tally."

"I intend to take a close look at it and tally it again my-self."

The two old men were still chiding one another as they

called good night to the others and headed out to the bunkhouse.

Sam tossed a couple of kitchen towels in a laundry basket. "I'm heading in to Haller Creek. Anybody coming?"

Finn nodded. "I thought you'd never ask. I spent the entire day poring over bankruptcy law, corporate law, and criminal law, and now I just want to kick back."

The two turned to Mac and Ben.

Father and son shook their heads.

"You'll be sorry." Sam paused in the mudroom and plucked a Stetson from a hook by the door. "I'm in the mood to entertain the boys at the Hitching Post with my amazing skills on the pool table."

"Just remember how hard you've worked all week for your paycheck," Mac called.

"Don't you worry. I will."

When the back door slammed, Mac and Ben shared a grin. Mac pulled a longneck from the refrigerator. "Want one?"

Ben nodded. "Sure."

The two men carried their beers to the front room and settled themselves in a pair of overstuffed easy chairs set in front of the fireplace.

"How'd you like working as a deputy for Virgil today?"

Ben gave a nonchalant shrug of his shoulders. "It was ... interesting."

"Says the man with the shiner."

The two shared an easy laugh.

Ben touched a hand to his swollen eye, knowing by morning it would be purple and green and painful as hell. "I'm just glad Leroy took his temper out on me instead of shooting Minnie."

"There was a chance he might have used his gun on you instead of his fist."

"He knew better. I'd have dropped him before he had time to pull the trigger."

Mac nodded, aware that Ben wasn't bragging. It was a simple fact. "You're a crack shot. That's one of the reasons Virgil asked you to lend a hand. That, and the fact that you majored in criminal justice in those online classes in college."

"Thanks to Mary Pat and Zachariah. They both pushed me in that direction."

Mac chose his words carefully. "I heard rumors that Virgil's injury is pretty serious. Did he talk to you about taking on the job of deputy full-time?"

Ben kept his gaze on the burning log on the hearth while taking a long drink of beer. "He mentioned it."

"And?"

"I told him it isn't possible to keep up with the ranch chores if I'm going to be chasing people around the countryside cleaning up their messes."

"There's a lot more to being a lawman than cleaning up after people."

Ben smiled. "I'm aware of that. But you know what I mean. I can't do both without having one job suffer at the hands of the other. If I have to choose, I'm going to choose to be a rancher like you."

Mac had to swallow hard before he could find his voice. The rush of pride had his heart swelling until his chest felt too tight. "Ranching is in my blood, son. It purely warms my heart to see all you boys following in my footsteps. But you need to know that you have a right to your own dreams."

"I can never repay you for what you gave me and my brothers. When we came here…"

Before Ben could say more, Mac held up a hand to silence him. "When I fought in court to make you and your brothers legally my sons, I wasn't looking for payback. And I didn't do it so I'd have a few extra hands around the ranch to help with the chores. I wanted you to be free. Free of the system. Free to follow whatever path each of you chooses."

"I know that. And I'm grateful as hell. But I'm happy here."

"And that makes me happy. But there's no law says you can't live here and still lend a hand with Virgil, at least until that leg of his heals."

Ben set aside his longneck and got to his feet, pacing to the fireplace and back. "I'd have to spend some nights in town. Sheriff Kerr mentioned taking the night shift sometimes, when the state troopers aren't available. With Finn starting his own practice, I'd be leaving a lot of the morning chores to you and Sam and Otis and Roscoe."

"We could all double up. We'll be bringing the herds down from the hills to the winter range in the next weeks. After that, we can manage until spring."

Ben slumped down in his chair and took a long pull on the bottle.

Seeing his mental struggle, Mac picked up his empty bottle and started toward the kitchen. "Why not give it a try, to see if the law fits. Then you can make a decision whether or not to make it permanent."

Minutes later, when Mac headed toward the stairs, Ben was still sitting in the chair, studying the fire as though it held all the answers to life's problems.

"Good night, Ben."

"'Night, Dad."

Dad.

Mac hugged the word to his heart. Though his three sons still struggled with that quick-triggered temper they all shared, the curses that bubbled up from time to time, and the occasional nightmare, they'd managed to put a lot of their demons to rest. They'd grown into fine men who made him proud.

And wasn't that enough for any man to achieve in one lifetime?

CHAPTER TWO

'Morning, boys." Otis turned from the stove and set a platter of crisp bacon on the kitchen table as soon as Ben, Sam, and Finn trooped in from the barn.

Mac stepped into the kitchen from the parlor, where he'd been going over some bills, while Roscoe hung his hat on a hook by the door. Both Mac and Roscoe were dressed for a long ride to the herd in the highlands.

Zachariah's door opened off the kitchen, and he yawned loudly as he joined the others at the big, scarred table.

Without a word Otis placed a cup of steaming coffee in front of him, and the old lawyer shot him a grateful nod before taking a long drink. Refreshed, he looked over at Sam. "Figured you might be playing catchup after last night in town, Samuel."

"Not when it doubled my paycheck." Sam gave a cat-that-swallowed-the-canary grin.

"That good, huh?" Roscoe winked at Mac across the table.

Sam nodded. "A fresh batch of suckers just down from Calgary. Signed on to the Fisher ranch, and it was their first night in town."

Finn helped himself to several eggs, bacon, and fried potatoes. "It was a beautiful thing to watch my talented brother teach those yokels the basics of nine ball."

Mac raised an eyebrow. "I hope you left them with enough cash to last until their next paycheck."

"Barely." Sam ate with gusto. After a late night of pool and an early-morning round of mucking stalls and hauling food and water for the horses, he barely took time to taste what he put in his mouth.

Ben nudged him in the ribs. "You know they'll come gunning for you next week."

"I'm sure they will, bro. But next time, they'll be a lot more careful with their money."

Roscoe shot a grin at Otis, who was circling the table, topping off mugs of coffee. "I guess we'd better remember to head to town next week for the show."

Otis chuckled. "Wouldn't miss it."

Mac drained his coffee before looking around the table. "Anybody heading to Haller Creek today? I phoned in a list to Henderson, and told him somebody'd be over to pick it up."

Ben pushed away and got to his feet. "I promised Virgil I'd stop by his office today. I can pick up the order."

Sam nudged Finn and the two shared a conspiratorial grin. "You're in for a surprise."

Ben shot his brothers a questioning look.

Sam, the joker, was obviously enjoying the fact that he'd snagged their attention. "Last night's news at the Hitching Post is that Rebecca Henderson came home to work in her father's hardware store."

Ben kept his gaze on the floor, hoping nobody noticed his jaw dropping.

"And there's more. Willy Theisen's back in town, too." On a roll now, Sam grinned at Finn. "Only now he's called Reverend Will Theisen. A couple of years at divinity school, and he's practically a saint."

"Yeah. A living saint." Finn chuckled. "At least according to Hank Henderson. I overheard a group of wranglers saying he'd bragged his daughter couldn't do better than a man of the church who doesn't drink, smoke, or swear. I guess that would leave the three of us out in the cold." As an afterthought, he added, "I don't know about you, but I just can't picture Rebecca Henderson spending a lifetime with Saint Willy Theisen. Except, why else would the two of them come home at the same time?"

Sam joined in the laughter. "Even so, I can't think of any female I dislike enough to condemn to a life with boring Willy."

"Now, boys." Zachariah struggled not to let his laughter bubble up. "What father doesn't want to see his daughter marry a paragon of virtue?"

"A paragon?" Sam clapped a hand on the old man's shoulder. "I love it when you and Finn use those fancy lawyer words. That's Willy, all right. A paragon."

Throughout their jokes, Mac studied Ben. Seeing his smile fade and his eyes darken with feeling, Mac picked up his empty plate and carried it to the sink. "Great breakfast, Otis. Thanks. Roscoe and I will be late."

"I'll keep your supper warm tonight."

Mac turned to his oldest son. "Thanks for offering to pick up the order, Ben."

"Yeah. Anytime."

Within minutes the men had pulled on parkas and hats and were headed in several different directions. Mac and

Roscoe rode their horses across a meadow that meandered up and up until it bled into a dense woods. Sam climbed into the cab of a flatbed truck while Finn, with no clients to deal with, pulled himself onto a tractor. The family recognized it as his way of clearing his mind of the clutter of the many demands of the practice of law.

Ben looked over at Otis. "You need anything from town?"

The old man nodded and handed him a slip of paper. "Got my list right here, son."

"How about Zachariah?"

"His things are on the other side."

"Okay. I'll see you at supper time." Ben stepped outside and sauntered toward the barn, emerging minutes later in one of the ranch trucks. Seeing Otis on the back porch, he gave a wave of his hand and started along the curving gravel drive.

As he drove, his thoughts were a jumble of images.

Of Rebecca Henderson, the first time he'd ever seen her, looking so small and frozen in place as a boy on a revved-up ATV was heading straight toward her. Without a pause, Ben had raced across the school yard and scooped her up, carrying her to safety. She was ten and he was twelve. When he set her on her feet, she'd offered him a breathless thanks before racing toward her friends.

His thoughts shifted to the night of her senior prom, standing in the school yard wearing a pretty pink formal, with R.D. Mason's corsage at her wrist.

When Ben drew near, he realized she was crying, and the front of her gown was torn. When she blurted what R.D. had tried to do to her, Ben had hunted him down and threatened him with murder. Then he'd picked her up and carried her home. When her father saw them coming up the walk, and the tell-tale signs of a struggle, he'd thrown a fit and jumped to the wrong conclusion while phoning the sheriff. Hours later, when Virgil Kerr had time to sort out the facts, he'd phoned Ben's father, exonerating Ben from any wrongdoing and praising him for being a hero. It took some explaining for Virgil to cool Mac's temper when he learned his son had been forced to spend time at the jail while the sheriff waded through Hank Henderson's ranting and raving. Then the sheriff had driven to R.D.'s house to confront him with the charges. The family left town that very night, taking only what they could carry in their truck. Little Haller Creek was glad to be rid of the town bully.

Days later, seeing Rebecca in town, Ben had approached to ask how she was. Her face had turned a dozen different shades of red, and she'd stumbled over her words while offering her thanks. And then her father had come storming out of his hardware store, ordering her to get away from "that hell-raiser."

And now, after college in Bozeman, and several more years working there, she was back.

Just as Will Theisen had returned.

As much as Hank Henderson disliked Ben through the years, he'd made his approval of Will Theisen abundantly clear. Will had been a regular guest at the Henderson Sunday dinners for years until leaving for divinity school.

Maybe their return was just a coincidence. Or maybe Hank would finally get his wish and his daughter would snag a minister.

Ben drove the rest of the way under a dark cloud.

He was torn between seeing Rebecca Henderson again after all these years and wishing he could avoid his first glimpse of her at her father's store with Hank watching.

The town of Haller Creek sported a string of shops that answered the basic needs of its citizens. The Haller Creek

Bank building, with its glass front and shiny chrome drive-through, looked oddly out of place beside the faded diner, with its green-and-white awnings and the weathered sign that read DOLLY'S DINER. The Family Shop offered everything in the way of necessary clothing for men, women, and children. There was a new Haller Creek Medical Clinic that took up an entire block. In between, old buildings had been turned into a barbershop, a beauty shop, a florist. At the end of the street, on a hill, a church steeple rose above an old stone church ringed by a cemetery that dated back to the 1800s and the days of Calamity Jane, the town's most famous citizen.

Ben slowed the truck in front of a converted warehouse that was now Henderson Hardware. Seeing an empty slot in front of a loading dock, he backed his truck into position and stepped down.

"Hey, Ben." Eli Adams, who'd started working for Hank Henderson back in high school, stuck out his hand.

"Eli. How're things?"

"Great. Just great. I took the call from your dad. I'll get started on his order."

"Thanks, Eli."

"Have you heard? Rebecca's back."

"Yeah. I heard. See you, Eli." Ben made his way around to the front door and stepped inside the retail space.

He heard Rebecca's voice before he could see her. When he stepped around a display of kitchen cabinets, he simply stood there, enjoying the sight of her. Pale hair falling soft and loose around her slender shoulders. Blue eyes crinkled in an easy, relaxed smile. A plain white shirt, sleeves rolled to the elbows, and trim denims hugging her slim legs.

To Ben, she looked the same, yet not the same. She was

thinner. A woman instead of the teenager he'd once known. And despite the shirt and denims, there was a city shine to her instead of that small-town look. And she was still the prettiest girl he'd ever seen.

"You're welcome, Tony. Will there be anything else?"

"Not today. Nice to see you, Rebecca. You're a lot easier on the eyes than your old man." The rancher tipped his hat before moving away.

She was chuckling as she began turning toward the counter.

When she spotted Ben, the laughter died in her throat. Her mouth rounded in soundless surprise.

"Hi, Becca."

"Ben." She waited until he'd walked closer, her fingers nervously tapping a paper on the countertop. "How is your father? Your brothers?"

"All good."

"I'm glad. I haven't…"

"Monroe." Hank Henderson's angry voice sounded directly behind Ben.

Ben turned, not at all surprised that Hank would be keeping a close eye on his daughter. "Mr. Henderson."

Hank stood back, studying him with a look of annoyance. "Nice shiner." His tone hardened. "I heard about Sam's string of luck at the Hitching Post last night. Looks like somebody didn't like losing to him. I'm not surprised you jumped into a bar brawl alongside your little brother. Seems like you've been doing that for a lifetime." Hank looked beyond Ben to where his daughter was standing. "As I've told you, some things in this town never change."

When he walked away, Ben handed the slip of paper to Rebecca. "These are some of the things Roscoe and Zachariah need. I can get them now, or you can pack them up and send them out back to Eli. He's busy loading an order in my truck."

Rebecca's cheeks were bright red as she accepted the paper from his hand. That's when she spotted the badge pinned to his parka. "You, Ben? A deputy?"

"Just temporary." For a moment he beamed with pride before looking down with a frown, trying to tamp down the pride he felt. "I'm meeting Virgil at his office. He injured his leg and asked me to give him a hand."

"I heard he was thinking of retiring."

Ben shrugged. "He'll probably think about it for a couple of years before he actually does anything about it."

"I don't know. He's been a lawman for a long time. Rumor has it Annabelle is pressuring him to retire."

Ben shook his head. "That's just gossip. You know how that goes."

"Yes." For a brief second a cloud seemed to pass over her features before her smile softened. "I think you'd make a great lawman…"

"Here you are, Rebecca."

They both looked up at the deep, cultured voice.

Will Theisen was wearing a black jacket and shirt that perfectly showed off his brand-new, starched white minister's collar.

When Ben turned, Will's gaze darted from Rebecca to Ben. "Hello, Ben. I didn't know that was you. I've been away too long." He stuck out his hand. "It's good to see you."

"You too. Hi, Will." Ben accepted the handshake. "I hear you're Reverend Theisen now."

"That's right. It was a lot of hard work and study, but I made it."

"Congratulations."

"Thanks." He nodded toward the badge. "I just passed the sheriff's office. He was bragging about you. He told me how you were able to talk Leroy Purcell down from a raging temper and prevented a possible homicide. Sorry it cost you a black eye."

Ben shrugged. "A small price to pay for preventing a crime. At least he used his fist instead of his gun."

"Reverend William." Hank Henderson's voice carried across the cavernous length of the store. "I was hoping I'd get to see you today. Come over here, son. I want to talk to you about dinner tonight."

"Yes, sir." Will turned to Rebecca and Ben. "Excuse me. I hope I'll see you both later."

As he walked away, Rebecca watched him before turning to Ben. "Why didn't you correct my father when he jumped to the conclusion that you got that shiner in a bar fight?"

Ben glanced at the man wrapping his arm around the new minister's shoulders before answering. "Why bother? Your father made up his mind about me years ago. Nothing will ever change that."

"But you have the right to defend yourself, Ben. Especially when he's so wrong about you."

"There's no way to correct him without sounding like a jerk. Besides, like I said, it doesn't really matter. Let your father think what he wants."

"Why?"

"The truth?" He took his time removing a pair of aviator sunglasses from his pocket and putting them on, effectively covering the swollen eye and giving him the look of a sleek, fierce panther. "We're not kids anymore. I gave up caring what he thought about me a long time ago." He shot her an easy smile. "It's great seeing you, Becca. Why don't you just put this order out back with the rest of my family's stuff? That'll ease your workload and spare your father from seeing you talk to the town's hell-raiser any longer than necessary."

He turned away and strode purposefully from the store, tipping his hat to an elderly woman as he made his exit.

CHAPTER THREE

Lost in thought, Rebecca stood staring at the doorway as Ben walked away. Seeing her father and Will laughing easily together, she walked in the opposite direction to give herself time alone. She paused at a display shelf and began straightening boxes of light bulbs. While she worked, she touched a hand to her heart. It was pounding like an out-of-control racecar. Nobody but Ben Monroe had ever affected her this way.

Even with that swollen black eye, he was still a commanding presence, with that sexy smile and that bold swagger. From the time he'd first arrived in Haller Creek, ready to take on the world and eager to fight anyone who stood in his way, he'd always exuded a bad-boy image. A sense of disdain for the rules. Maybe that's why so many of the girls in town had whispered about him and secretly lusted after him. He wasn't like the other boys. Even at a tender age when others were just trying to figure life out, Ben seemed to have already come to terms with it. Despite the rules of society, he followed his own path.

It's what had always excited Rebecca.

It's what absolutely terrified her father.

"I'll see you tonight, Rebecca." Will paused beside her.

"Tonight?" Distracted, she looked up.

"Your folks invited me to dinner."

"Oh. All right." She managed a smile. "I'll see you then."

When Will was gone, her father hurried over. "Maybe you'd like to leave early."

"Why?"

"I thought Will told you. He's coming to dinner."

"Yes. He told me."

"Well then, you'll want to head home to do all those fussy things young women do before meeting their guy."

"Dad, Will isn't my guy. He's a friend."

"A very good friend. And a great catch. Especially now, with that fine education behind him. He said he's weighing his options for the future."

"He told me."

Her father nodded. "I figured he'd want you to be the first to share that news with."

"Because we're friends."

"Uh-huh." Hank took the box out of her hands and set it on a second shelf. "I always put the smaller ones here."

"Why?"

"Because that's the way I've always done it. And if you're going to work here, you need to know how I do things. Now get out of here and get ready for tonight." He sauntered away, whistling a little tune.

There had been a time when her father's smug, know-it-all attitude had her gritting her teeth in frustration. She'd spent her entire childhood being forced to dance to his tune, or suffer his obvious disappointment in her. As an only child, she felt a keen need to please. Now, after enough time and distance away, she'd come to terms with the fact that she could never completely please everyone, especially her father. It would have to be enough to weigh the issues to see if the choices she made were worth the pain those choices could cause those who loved her.

It had taken a string of psychology classes, a great deal of introspection, and a long, hard look at herself before she'd been able to be honest about her life. During her college years and then afterward, she'd tried her hand at working for others, always in retail, and always moving up until she felt she'd earned the respect she deserved. Though her work was satisfying, she couldn't quite silence the little voice inside that kept reminding her that she wanted more. And then one day, after a phone conversation with her tearful mother saying she missed her only child, Rebecca realized that what she really wanted was right here in Haller Creek. She not only wanted but also craved life in a small town. The close-knit feeling of family and friends. The chance to actually know her neighbors, to reconnect with old friends.

She knew the decision to come home would bring problems. Though her parents were ecstatic, she knew them well enough to realize they expected her to come back as the same dutiful daughter who had left. And so she'd gone to great lengths to find a little furnished rental house a few blocks from her childhood home. She had agreed to help out at her father's hardware store, while keeping open the option of having her own shop. Her decisions weren't playing well with her father. As expected, he made it clear he resented the fact that she chose to live apart from him and her mother.

It just doesn't look right. Some folks might think you're

*a rule-breaker. A party girl. In my day, young women lived
with their parents. That's just how it was done.*

Rebecca looked around at the old, familiar displays.
Some of them hadn't changed since she was a girl.

She could see the potential of this big, faded building.
She had so many dreams. So many hopes.

Her father had made it plain that she would be treated no
different than any of his other employees. He had no intention of simply handing over the reins of his "little empire,"
as he referred to his business, even to his daughter. The very
mention of retirement had him bristling, even though her
mother dreamed of the chance for her husband to retire so
they could travel.

Rebecca found herself hoping he continued to work, if
only to have something to micromanage besides her life. If
her father had his way, he would plan every step of her future. And now that she'd tasted life on her own terms, she
knew she could never go back to being what he so desperately wanted for his only child.

Ben walked past the familiar shops, nodding at folks as he
made his way to the sheriff's office. He struggled to keep his
mind on business, but his thoughts kept straying to Rebecca.

If anything, she was even prettier since her return home.
Her soft, blond hair and warm smile. Not to mention that
fabulous body.

She was such a good person. Despite her father's over-
bearing attitude, she managed to remain nonjudgmental. Not
an easy thing to accomplish, considering.

One more reason why she and Will Theisen would make
the perfect couple. Haller Creek's minister and his wife.
She'd be a role model for all the mothers and daughters of
the town.

The thought didn't give him any joy.

Not that he had any right to complain. He'd already been given his miracle the day he'd led his brothers to a remote ranch where they'd met their hero, Mackenzie Monroe.

That would have to be enough for one lifetime.

Still, it wasn't his father crowding his thoughts at the moment. It was Rebecca.

If Hank's boast was true, there would soon be a big announcement about Rebecca and Will. But that didn't stop Ben from indulging in some purely fanciful thoughts of his own. He couldn't help it. When it came to Becca Henderson, his mind and heart were all tangled up in her.

He stepped into the sheriff's office and removed his sunglasses.

Virgil, talking on the phone, lifted a hand in greeting and indicated the chair across from his desk.

Ben sat, stretching his long legs out in front of him, and waited until Virgil rang off.

"Hey, Ben." The sheriff reached across the desk and shook his hand. "I hope you come bearing good news."

Ben gave him a lazy smile. "I want you to know I appreciate the fact that you trust me enough to offer me the job of deputy."

"There's nobody I'd trust more, Ben."

"Thanks, Sheriff. That means a lot to me. I needed to talk your offer over with my dad. My first concern is the ranch chores. Dad assured me he and my brothers can handle things without me. He really wants me to follow my dream."

"If the way you dealt with Leroy yesterday is any indication, I'd say you have a real talent for being a lawman, son."

"Thanks for your vote of confidence. I have to admit, I like the way it turned out." He touched a hand to his eye. "Except for this, of course. Leroy was a lot quicker than I thought. But at least there was no gunfire. I guess, in the grand scheme of things, that's a win when it comes to being a good lawman."

"You got that right." Virgil leaned back in his swivel chair. "So? You come to a decision?"

"I'm willing to lend a hand. At least until spring. We'll have things buttoned up at the ranch until then." He nodded toward the back room. "Isn't there a cot back there?"

Virgil nodded. "And a bathroom. Old Marvin Storey, the lawman when I first came here, was a bachelor and lived back there. His stove and refrigerator are still there, and I've added a microwave, for when I do night duty. But those rooms are old and dusty and would need a lot of cleaning and sprucing up if you're thinking of sleeping there."

"Only when things get too busy to drive back to the ranch. As for the clutter, I think I can handle cleaning and sprucing up."

Virgil's smile came slowly. "So, that's a definite yes?"

"Yeah."

Ben got to his feet and the sheriff rounded his desk to clap a hand on his shoulder. "I'm grateful, Ben. Even if you just handle the night watch for a while, or take on some of the out-of-town runs to distant ranches, it'll greatly relieve my burden."

"When would you like me to start?"

"As of now, you're on the clock." Virgil looked over when his phone rang. "I'll email you with the week's schedule. Whenever there's an emergency, I'll call. Make sure your cell is always on."

"It's always on. But up in the hills, there's a good chance I won't have service. We'll be bringing down the herds in the next couple of weeks."

The sheriff picked up the phone, cradling it in his hand.

"I understand. We'll figure out a way to get the word to you. Thanks again, Ben."

As Virgil settled himself behind his desk, Ben walked to the door. Once outside, he touched a finger to the badge.

It was official. He was a lawman.

A temporary lawman, he mentally corrected. At least for now.

The timing was odd. Tonight, Rebecca was having dinner with Will, probably to celebrate that big announcement Hank was hoping for. If that happened, Ben knew his life would be forever changed, his precious, closely held secrets shattered. He wasn't ready to let go of them.

Still, change was inevitable. Look at him.

Here he was, wearing a lawman's badge, doing the work of a lawman.

Wasn't life strange?

As a kid, he could never see himself on the right side of the law. But now that it was a reality, he felt a fierce sense of pride.

None of this could have happened in his life without Mackenzie Monroe. Without him, Ben knew, his life would have been much different.

Mac and Becca. They were as much a part of him as the air he breathed.

He couldn't imagine his life without either of them.

CHAPTER FOUR

Mac spotted the maroon van parked alongside the barn and felt the little sense of quiet joy that always touched him whenever Mary Pat Healy paid a visit. Mary Pat had been a part of his family's life since he first took in the three troubled boys who had become his adopted sons. Every time he began floundering, and feared he might drown in his own helplessness, she was there, like an angel of mercy, with her sage advice.

Mary Pat had never married. No children of her own, and yet she enjoyed the love and respect of hundreds of kids in this part of Montana who through the years had needed help in homeschooling, medical assistance, or just a warm hug. She did the same for their parents, many of whom were so bogged down in the endless ranch chores, sickness, or everyday problems of survival, they felt overwhelmed.

Mac took his time at the big sink in the mudroom, rolling up the sleeves of his flannel shirt, washing the dirt of the trail from his hands, wrists, arms, elbows, before stepping into the kitchen.

The others were already standing around, longnecks in hand, discussing the day. In their midst was Mary Pat, copper curls threaded with gray, her face bare of makeup and pretty as any teen, wearing her trademark faded denims and plaid shirt.

"Hi, Mac." She saluted him with a beer.

"Hi, yourself." He accepted a longneck from Otis and ambled closer. "How're things?"

"Couldn't be better." She looked around at the smiling faces. "And your family looks hale and hearty."

"That they are." He took a long drink to wash away the trail dust. Spotting the deputy badge on Ben, his smile grew. "I see you didn't give it back. Does this mean you're a lawman now, son?"

"For now." Ben returned the smile. "I told Virgil I'd give him a hand at least until spring."

Sam gave an exaggerated sigh. "Who'd have thought my big brother would be on *that* side of the law?"

"Yeah. I hope you realize"—Finn nudged Sam—"you'll probably be the first one he interviews whenever there's trouble in Haller Creek."

Sam shot him a grin. "I hope you realize we'll both be stuck with double the chores through the winter."

"Don't count on me, bro. I've got a law practice now, remember?"

"Some practice. Mostly drawing up wills, helping ranchers make sense of old deeds, and representing the drunken cowboys that start fights at the Hitching Post."

"A guy's got to make a living."

"I've got a better way." Sam gave his famous grin. "Shooting pool is a lot more fun."

Finn shared a laugh with Zachariah, who muttered, "Careful, Samuel. Pride goeth before a fall."

Zachariah turned to Mary Pat. "Would you like the honor of carving that roast, since you were the one to cook it?"

"I'd be happy to." She turned to the stove and picked up a knife.

Mac stepped up beside her. "You were here all day?"

"Long enough to volunteer to cook." Over her shoulder she called, "There are biscuits in the oven if someone would like to get them."

The men pitched in, with Roscoe filling a basket with hot biscuits, while Otis set out a pitcher of ice water and glasses. Ben ladled gravy into a bowl. Sam set out a plate of steaming carrots.

By the time Mary Pat placed a platter of thick slices of roast beef in the center of the table, they were gathered around, looking ravenous.

Out of deference to her, they joined hands and waited for her to offer a blessing. It was something she'd insisted upon since she'd first paid a visit years earlier.

She stepped up beside Mac and took his hand. "Bless this food, this family, and the roads we all travel."

"Amen."

They took their places and passed around the food. For long minutes the only sounds were the sighs of pure pleasure as they enjoyed beef that melted in their mouths and mashed potatoes as smooth as whipped cream.

Mac looked over at the woman beside him. "I'd like to know what you do to make this so good."

"It's my secret ingredient," she said with a sly smile.

Mac broke open a warm roll. "And what would that be?"

"Love." Otis, chocolate eyes gleaming, lips split in a wide smile, winked at Mary Pat. "That's what my mama always said when folks would ask her why her food tasted so good."

Mary Pat couldn't help laughing. "I like that better than the answer I was going to give."

"Which is?"

At Mac's persistence, she put a hand over his. "Garlic."

That had everyone chuckling.

Mary Pat's eyes crinkled. "You see why I like Otis's answer better?"

The old man gave a nod of his head. "Feel free to use mine whenever you'd like."

"Oh, believe me, I will."

Zachariah helped himself to a mound of potatoes. "Where have your travels taken you lately, Mary Patricia?"

"Clear across this county and back. One night I found myself stuck in mud over the wheels of my van at the foot of the Bitterroot."

Roscoe nodded his head. "A lot of rain falling lately."

"And the runoff in the foothills was really high this year."

Mac turned to her. "How'd you get out?"

She shrugged. "I dumped a mound of cat litter around my wheels. I carry it in my van for just such emergencies. Then I decided to sleep in my van and hope the sun would be bright enough by morning to harden some of that soggy earth." Her smile said it all. "And obviously it worked, because here I am."

"And we're glad of it. I've missed such fine cooking." Otis circled the table with a pot of coffee. "Mary Pat baked a cake."

Mac looked over. "Is it somebody's birthday?"

Mary Pat was chuckling as she crossed the room and began cutting the cake. "I can see that you men are in need of a woman's touch. Cakes aren't just for birthdays."

"They aren't?" Finn was grinning as she set a slice of gooey chocolate cake frosted with marshmallow crème in front of him. "You mean we don't need an excuse to eat cake?"

"Not in my world." Mary Pat continued passing around their dessert until everyone had a piece.

There was another moment of silence as they began to taste. And then the room was filled with the sound of murmured *ahhh*s, as they simply enjoyed.

"You'll stay the night." Mac stated it as a simple fact. No question.

Mary Pat nodded and watched as the three brothers tidied up the kitchen.

Otis and Roscoe had already taken themselves off to the bunkhouse for their nightly round of gin rummy. Zachariah excused himself and went to his bedroom with the monthly legal digest. Though he was retired, he managed to keep up with all the latest cases handled in the local jurisdiction.

"I always look forward to sleeping in a real bed." Mary Pat smiled. "Not that I mind crisscrossing the county. I love my job. But after a few weeks, I need an anchor. Your ranch has always been that for me, Mac."

"I'm glad. Because you've certainly been my anchor through the years." He gave a shake of his head. "I don't know how I would have made it through all the ins and outs of the system, even with Zachariah's help."

"Don't kid yourself. He was your best resource. Zachariah has one of the sharpest minds in the law."

Finn turned to add, "Don't I know it. My professors all knew his name."

Mary Pat nodded for emphasis. "In his day, Zachariah York was held in the highest esteem by the court and the judges. They knew if he represented a client, they'd better be at the top of their game."

Finn's smile widened. "I've always loved listening to him talk."

"Me too." Mary Pat turned to Mac. "As for me, I was happy to do whatever I could to cut through some of the red tape. The system is mired in rules and regulations that are supposed to be there for the safety of the children. But often they end up hurting more than they help."

"All I know is, without you and Zachariah, we'd have lost the battle."

Ben dropped a batch of towels in a basket and turned. "Okay. Kitchen duty is over. Anybody for a longneck?"

At the nod of heads, he reached into the refrigerator and handed them around. After twisting off the tops, they moved from the kitchen to the parlor, where a fire burned in the hearth.

Mac pulled an easy chair close to the fire for Mary Pat. Then he and the boys settled themselves around her.

"I'm glad you're not still stuck up in the Bitterroot." Sam was shaking his head. "I don't know too many females who would find themselves in that situation and just go to sleep, hoping it would all work out in the morning."

Mary Pat gave him a gentle smile. "When you've been doing this as long as I have, you learn it's best to not sweat the small stuff."

"Small? Stuck in the mud in the middle of the wilderness?"

She gave a laugh. "Well, when you put it like that, I should have been terrified."

The others joined in the laughter.

Ben took a chug of beer. "How did you happen to be in this work?"

Mary Pat shrugged. "That's a good question. Sometimes

I ask myself the same thing. I started out as a public health nurse, visiting some of the isolated ranches here in Montana."

"How could you reach them?"

"In the early years, I hauled a horse trailer, and rode in to some of the more isolated ranches on horseback."

Finn looked impressed. "So, you're like those pioneer women of the Old West."

Mary Pat gave a warm laugh. "I guess you could say that. On my visits, I realized that there was a lot more needed than just a quick look at someone's sore throat or a recommendation to head to the nearest clinic. During a visit, I would notice things like anger, depression, loneliness. So I went back to school and got certified as a social worker, as well. Then, when I saw how many children weren't able to attend school because they were too far from civilization, I got another degree in teaching, so I could help them with at least the rudiments of education whenever I paid a call."

"You're the medic, the shrink, and the teacher." Ben arched a brow. "Pretty impressive."

"Talk about impressive." Mary Pat gave a toss of her head. "Think of the changes brought about by the Internet. Now it's all high-tech and high-speed. Thanks to the Internet, I can coordinate homeschool lessons, email them to everyone, and even put these homeschool families in touch with other isolated families, so they can plan an occasional field trip together, or just get together socially."

Mac was watching her as she spoke, eyes glowing, smile bright. "You love your work."

"I do."

"That's good. Because I know the state doesn't pay you nearly what you're worth."

She chuckled. "Maybe you'd like to contact your congressman and put in a good word for me."

He returned her smile. "Like that would do any good. But I'm just saying, most people wouldn't be willing to do all you do, for any amount of money."

"There are times when I think I'm crazy for doing this. Other times I think I should consider retiring. Especially on days when all I see ahead of me is work that never gets done. But then I run into someone who was at the end of their rope, and now they can't wait to show me how they've turned their life around." Her smile bloomed. "And I think maybe I'll give it another day, or another week. Or maybe another year or so."

A faded photograph on the mantel caught her eye and she eased out of her chair to study it. "This is new."

Mac nodded. "Finn found it in a cupboard behind some things and wanted to know who the people were."

Mary Pat smiled. "There's no denying that dimple. The little boy is you. The teenaged girl must be the sister you spoke of."

"My sister, Ellen."

"The one who ran off with a cowboy your folks had hired. Other than that, I don't know much about her. You rarely talk about her."

He colored, feeling uncomfortable talking about deeply held family secrets. "Not much to tell. I was six when she left in the night with Shepherd Strump. We never heard from her again. My father went from worry to anger to outright rage and disowned her. From then on, there was a...distance between my parents. After my father died, my mother changed their will, decreeing that after her death the southern half of the land would be set aside for Ellen and any family she might have. Not long after, an official document arrived from the county seat, pronouncing five hundred acres adjoining this ranch would now be owned by Shepherd Strump, declared the legal husband of the late Ellen."

"I'm sorry to hear of her death. What do you think of her widower?"

Mac shrugged. "Never met him. He's never returned to work the land."

"How do you know if he's still alive?"

Another shrug. "I guess the county would notify me. Until then, that piece of land is declared off-limits to me and mine."

"How sad. Whenever I travel across it, I think how perfect it would be, with all that lush grass."

He nodded. "That southern parcel was always considered prime grazing land. But my mother's will ended any hope I had of claiming it."

Finn drained his beer and got to his feet, wrapping an arm around his father's shoulders. "I don't know about you guys, but after doing double duty this morning so Ben could play lawman, and then meeting with a couple of clients, I'm draggin' my wagon. I'm heading up to bed."

"Me too." Sam handed his empty bottle to his brother.

Ben walked to the kitchen to deposit the empties, then stuck his head in the door. "I just got a text from Virgil. He wants me in town tonight."

"I figured it wouldn't be long before he'd take advantage of having a deputy."

At Mac's words, Ben nodded. "He warned me that I was on the clock the minute I agreed to be his deputy. I'll see you in the morning."

When they were alone, Mary Pat sat back, staring at the fire. "This is nice."

"Yeah. I was thinking the same thing."

"You did something really good here, Mac. I don't mean just because you took in Otis and Roscoe and Zachariah and three homeless boys. What you did here is so much more."

He took a pull of his beer. "Yeah? And what's that?"

"You've made a family," she said with a smile and then got to her feet. "Okay, I'm heading up to bed now."

He stood. "I'll get you some sheets and blankets for that spare room."

"I know where they are." She gave him a quick hug. "You stay here and finish your beer."

"All right. Good night, Mary Pat. Thanks for that grand dinner."

"Any time. Good night, Mac."

As she climbed the stairs, he remained where he was, listening to the sound of her footfall on the steps. He heard the click of the linen closet door being opened and shut, the sound of the door at the opposite end of the hallway being closed.

And then the silence of the house closed in around him. He sank back down in his chair and stared at the dying embers of the fire.

A glance at the old photo had him trying to remember the sister who had left when he was so young. All he could really recall was the tension in the house after she'd left so abruptly. There had been a chasm between his parents that never really healed.

Maybe that was why the unconditional love of his wife, Rachel, and their son, Robbie, had filled him with such joy. And after their untimely death, such deep despair.

And now, with the house brimming with life and love, with curses and laughter, he felt again that quiet peace that came whenever he had time to reflect on his life. It seemed more complete somehow whenever Mary Pat came to call.

Odd. He could smell her here, at the open neck of his shirt, where her lips had briefly touched. That distinct scent of vanilla and some faint fragrance that reminded him of wildflowers in the spring after just bursting forth in the snow. So fresh and clean he wanted to breathe deeply and fill his lungs with it.

That was the essence of the woman. Mary Pat Healy was a breath of air on a hot summer day. A whisper of a soft voice in a world of harsh and often coarse chatter. A trill of laughter that purely lifted the soul.

She completed the circle of their odd little band.

He leaned his head back, content to just sit here, knowing that everyone who mattered to him was, for the moment, safe.

And really, what more could a man want?

CHAPTER FIVE

Rebecca lifted a pan of biscuits from the oven and placed them in a napkin-lined basket.

Across the room her mother was removing sizzling steaks from beneath the broiler.

"I brought a bottle of wine. Should I open it?"

Susan Henderson shot her a withering look. "For a minister?"

"It's Will, Mom. He drank beer and wine before he left for Atlanta. I doubt the years in divinity school have changed him that much."

Her mother gave a reluctant nod. "All right. I guess it won't hurt to ask him."

They both looked up at the knock on the door and heard Hank's voice calling a greeting.

Before Rebecca could use the corkscrew, her mother gave her a push toward the doorway. "We can take care of this in a few minutes. Let's go greet our guest."

Guest. There was a time when her parents had referred to Will Theisen as her classmate.

Rebecca was shaking her head as she trailed her mother toward the great room, where she could hear the men's voices talking in low tones.

As she passed a hall mirror, she caught a glimpse of her reflection.

If her father wanted something fussy, he would be disappointed. She was dressed in a simple charcoal sweater and matching slacks. She'd slipped her feet into black flats before walking the two blocks from her rental to her parents' house.

"Hi, Will."

"Rebecca. Mrs. Henderson." Will was on his feet, watching as they crossed the room.

Again he was dressed all in black, except that he'd added a suit jacket to his black pants and shirt. As before, the starched white minister's collar was in sharp contrast to the dark clothing.

"Oh, my." Susan touched a hand to her throat. "Doesn't our reverend look smart, Rebecca?"

Rebecca smiled. "Very sharp, Will. You must feel a sense of pride at having achieved your goal."

He touched a hand to his collar. "I confess I'm partial to this symbol of the ministry." He handed her mother a bouquet of roses. "For you, Mrs. Henderson."

"Oh, Will. That's so thoughtful." She dipped her face, breathing in the perfume of the flowers. "Isn't he thoughtful, Rebecca?"

"Yes, he is." Rebecca kept her smile in place. "That was sweet of you, Will."

"I'm just grateful to be invited for dinner. Now I feel as if I've really come home."

Hank Henderson was smiling broadly. "I hope you'll always consider our place your second home."

"I was just about to open a bottle of wine, Will." Rebecca caught the slight frown on her father's face. "Would you care for some?"

"Not yet. But maybe with dinner."

"All right. I'll just be a minute. Mom? Dad?"

Hank gave a quick shake of his head. "I'll wait for dinner, too."

Susan smiled. "Whatever your father says, dear."

Rebecca hurried to the kitchen and opened the wine, pouring herself a glass before returning to the great room.

"So." Hank shot a hopeful glance at his wife. "Have you been assigned a church, Will?"

Will shook his head. "Not yet."

Rebecca arched a brow. "I would have thought the school would offer its graduates a list of churches that were in need of ministers."

Will turned to her. "They do. With an aging ministry, there's a real need around the country for dedicated young church leaders. The school offers to place all its graduates."

Rebecca's smile was quick. "And yet, you came back to little Haller Creek. I hope you aren't thinking of replacing Reverend Grayson."

Even her mother had to chuckle at that. Though Haller Creek's widowed minister was growing frail, he had resisted all offers of an assistant. "I agree with my daughter, Will. I doubt Reverend Grayson would take kindly to an offer to replace him."

Hank's frown deepened. His tone was a bit sharper than before. "Did it ever occur to the two of you that Will may have come back to town for some other reason?"

Susan's smile disappeared as quickly as it had appeared.

Rebecca, however, refused to allow her father to steal her humor. "Have you paid Reverend Grayson a call, Will?"

He colored slightly. "That's on my to-do list for the coming week."

"I wouldn't wait too long. I'm sure by now he's heard that you're in town. He's probably wondering why he hasn't seen you yet."

Hearing the sound of the kitchen timer, Susan turned away. "Dinner will be ready in a few minutes."

"I'll help, Mom." Before her father had time to react, Rebecca followed her mother from the room.

A short time later they called the men to the dining room, where Susan Henderson had laid out a splendid feast, using her finest china and silver.

As they took their places around the table, Hank asked Will to lead them in a blessing.

Afterward, Rebecca filled their wineglasses.

Hank lifted his glass. "To Reverend Will Theisen. We're so happy you're here. May your years in service to the church be many, and may you find the perfect soul mate to work by your side."

Banking the temper that flared inside her, Rebecca averted her gaze as she touched her glass to the others and sipped.

As they passed around steak and twice-baked potatoes, the last of the green beans from Susan's garden, and soft, buttery rolls, Hank continued pressing Will.

"I'm sure your years in the big city opened your eyes to a different life than the one you lived here in Montana."

Will nodded. "Very true, sir."

Rebecca picked up on that. "Were you ever tempted to stay in Atlanta, Will?"

He blinked and busied himself buttering a roll. Seeing the others watching, he shrugged. "I've given it some thought."

"I'm sure some of those big-city churches are more like cathedrals, with really big congregations. Wouldn't it be fun to preach to a huge gathering?"

"I did it, along with the other students. That was part of our training."

"And was it a rush?"

He chewed, swallowed, as though assessing his words before speaking. "There's something to be said for having hundreds of people hanging on one's every word. I suppose you could say it gave me a thrill. But there's a danger in liking it too much. That could lead to false pride."

"So serious." An impish grin curved Rebecca's lips. "We wouldn't want you to be too proud, now, would we?"

Hank spoke quickly. "How's that steak, Reverend?" Without even waiting for a response, he glowered at his daughter.

"It's really good. You've always been a fine cook, Mrs. Henderson."

"Oh now, Will." Susan placed her hand over his. "I think it's time you started calling us Hank and Susan."

Will smiled. "Thank you. I'll try."

Rebecca sat back, sipping her wine, wondering when this interminable dinner would end.

"Another slice of cake, Will?" Susan hovered beside his chair. "Another dollop of ice cream?"

Will shook his head and took a long drink of tea. "Dinner was excellent. And your chocolate cake was the perfect ending. But I can't manage another bite."

Hank pushed back from the table. "Why don't we let the women clear the dishes while we head to the other room?"

"At school we were all expected to clean up after ourselves. As Reverend Palmer, our dean, always said, there are no servants or masters here. We're all here to serve one another."

"That's fine at divinity school, Will." Hank put a hand on his arm and steered him toward the doorway. "But in my house, the women do the cooking and cleaning. You and I can catch up on local news while Susan and Rebecca tidy up here."

Will had no choice but to walk away.

"Some things never change." Rebecca loaded the dishwasher, still fuming at her father's attitude.

"That's harsh, Rebecca. I know you're offended, honey. Your father doesn't mean anything by it. It's just his way."

"His way? Mom, hasn't he noticed that the world has changed while he's stuck in the last century?"

"Now, honey…"

"And you never disagree with him."

"You know I don't approve of airing differences in public."

"Then maybe, when the two of you are alone tonight, you can let him know how offensive his words were. Not just his 'let the little women clean up' words, but earlier, when he was practically offering me to Will as his soul mate. I was mortified."

Susan wrapped her arms around her daughter and kissed her temple. "In case I haven't told you, I'm so happy you're finally home for good. When you graduated and decided to work in Bozeman, I felt as if I'd lost you. And now you're back, and I just want you to know your father and I love you so much."

"I love you and Dad, too, Mom. And I love being back in Haller Creek. But…"

"Not now, honey. It's been such a special evening having both you and Will to supper. Don't spoil it."

When the two women entered the great room arm in arm, Will looked up with a smile. "I was just telling your father about my visit with Sheriff Kerr. He was bragging about Ben Monroe and how he handled himself taking Leroy Purcell into custody. Even though Leroy was drunk and waving a rifle like a crazy man, Ben managed to arrest him without a shot being fired."

Rebecca stared pointedly at her father. "And you accused Ben of a bar brawl."

Her mother gasped and put a hand to her mouth. "Hank, you didn't."

"It was a natural enough mistake. That hell—" He glanced over at Will and swallowed down the words he usually used to describe Ben and his brothers. "That hooligan has been in fights since the day he and those two brothers of his arrived in Haller Creek."

Will sat back with a grin. "And I'm grateful for him."

When the others simply stared, he explained. "I remember the time I was walking home from school. I was ten. Skinny. Glasses. A shiny new backpack. Reggie Mason shoved me into a fence so hard my nose was bloody and my glasses fell off."

At the mention of that name, Hank pounded a fist into his palm. "R.D. Mason. That monster."

"Yeah. R.D. He was every kid in school's worst nightmare. He said he was going to keep on punching me until I handed over my backpack. I was so scared, I was trying to get my arms out of the straps to do as he said, but he kept punching me. Then all of a sudden Reggie went down like a rock, and there was Ben." Will gave a shake of his head, remembering the moment. "He was new at school, and I didn't even know his name, but he hauled me to my feet and told me to go on home. I told him I was afraid to come back to school. R.D. had stolen lunch money from half the kids in my class. Ben said R.D. would never bother me again." Will's frown turned into a smile, remembering. "The next day I was quaking in my shoes, but when I passed R.D., he looked away. And just as Ben promised, R.D. never bothered me again."

A frown creased Hank Henderson's forehead as he fell silent.

Rebecca exchanged a glance with her mother and could see that she'd been deeply touched by what Will had just revealed.

Will looked over at Rebecca. "I didn't realize you moved out of your parents' place. Your father said you're living over on Maple. If it's okay with you, I'll walk you home. It'll give me a chance to burn some of the calories from that excellent meal." Before she could say a word, he added, "I already asked your father, and he approved."

"Of course he did." She darted a look at her father before turning toward the front closet. "I'll get my jacket."

Susan lay a hand on Will's arm. "Are you staying at your old family home?"

He nodded. "It's one of the reasons I came back. I decided it's time to go through their things before getting it ready to go on the market. I would have done it in the spring, after ordination, but I was still doing my final work with my mentor at a local church there, and things got complicated." He offered a handshake. "Susan, thank you again for the invitation to dinner."

"Anytime, Will. You're one of the family." She exchanged a bright smile with her husband, who was staring into space, before turning to her daughter. "You two enjoy the evening."

Will held the door as Rebecca preceded him down the steps and into the gathering shadows.

They walked slowly, enjoying the crunch of brittle leaves

beneath their shoes. A brisk autumn breeze sent more leaves dancing in a little whirlwind.

"I'm glad you told us about how Ben came to your rescue. I'd never heard that story before."

Will shrugged. "I know Ben and his brothers had a lot of rough edges. My folks thought Mackenzie Monroe was crazy to adopt them. But Ben's a good guy. He's always been fair with me. And that day, he really saved my hide. There are plenty of other classmates with similar stories."

They walked in silence until Will lifted his head. "I love this season. But with this chill in the air, we know what always follows. I don't like thinking about what's just around the corner."

"How can you live in Montana and not love winter?"

He shrugged. "I prefer sunshine."

"Doesn't everyone?" She hugged her arms about herself. "But there's something about that first snowfall. I'm like a kid at Christmas."

"Would you ever consider living anywhere else?"

"I did. I stayed in Bozeman after college."

He gave a dry laugh. "I meant anywhere besides Montana."

"Oh." She thought a moment. "I'm not sure I could. I love the sweep of mountains. Meadows alive with wildflowers. Cattle grazing in the distance. Those things are home to me." She paused to turn to him. "Are you thinking about settling somewhere else?"

"I—"

A sound shattered the silence. Rebecca stood perfectly still, trying to identify what she'd heard.

Then, as a second sound exploded and a bullet whizzed directly over their heads, Will pushed her to the ground before dropping beside her.

"What...?"

"Shhh." He put a hand over her mouth to silence her.

She shook off his hand and the two of them sat up at the sound of hurried footsteps retreating.

A car door slammed. Tires screeched as a vehicle roared into the darkness.

Rebecca got to her feet, peering into the distance, but the night was too dark, and the car was gone.

As Will scrambled to stand, she was already racing ahead toward her house, fighting desperately to hold back the terror that had her in its grip.

He caught her arm. "Wait. Where are you going? Shouldn't we run to your parents' place?"

"I left my cell phone at home. We need to call the sheriff."

Will had to struggle to keep up with her as she raced headlong toward the darkened outline of her home.

CHAPTER SIX

Will barely made it to Rebecca's living room before sinking down in a chair, his head in his hands.

After phoning a report of trouble, she looked at him with alarm. "What's wrong, Will?"

"I feel a migraine coming on. I don't have anything with me for pain."

"I'm sorry. It's probably triggered by that terrifying incident. I'm sure I have something for headaches somewhere." She left him and headed into the bedroom to rummage through some of the boxes she hadn't yet unpacked.

The doorbell sounded.

When it rang a second time, Rebecca realized Will hadn't answered it and she hurried to peer out the door before opening it.

Seeing Ben standing on the porch, she felt a wild sense of relief. It took all her willpower to keep from throwing herself into his arms.

"Ben."

"Becca."

For long moments, the two simply stared at one another.

It was Ben who broke the silence. "Dispatch said you called for help. A gunshot?"

"Yes." She was staring at his badge before looking up at him, as though unsure what to do or say.

He made it easy for her by taking control.

"Were you hit?" He was studying her closely, as if looking for telltale blood.

"No." She breathed a sigh of relief. "Please, Ben. Come in." She stood aside and he brushed past her.

As he did, she absorbed the keen tingle of awareness as their bodies brushed.

Seeing Will seated in the living room, his head in his hands, Ben looked from Will to Rebecca. "Was he hit?"

"No. A migraine." Rebecca handed Will a couple of over-the-counter headache pills. "I found these, Will. I hope they help."

"Probably not. But they won't hurt. I'll need some water."

Rebecca pointed to the other room.

Will got to his feet and made his way to the kitchen.

While he did, Ben took a moment to look around. The house was small and tidy, and sparsely furnished, with un-opened boxes in every corner, but the colorful pillows and mohair afghan over the arm of the sofa gave a feeling of warmth and style and comfort.

As soon as Will returned to the room, Ben studied the faces of both Rebecca and Will as he began his official interrogation.

"You specifically reported gunshots. Multiple. How many?"

"Two," Rebecca answered for both of them. "I didn't

know what I'd heard the first time. I guess maybe a car back-firing or fireworks. But when the second gunshot went off, I actually felt the rush of air, or maybe it was the sound of a bullet flying overhead. That's when Will pushed me to the ground and stifled my cry."

"So you recognized it as a gunshot and realized you were in danger." Ben fixed Will with a look. "Have you been shot at before?"

"Ben, Will is a…"

At Rebecca's words, he lifted a hand and continued studying Will. "I know you're an ordained minister. Have you ever been—"

Will didn't give him time to finish. "Of course not." His frown became more pronounced. "But, like Rebecca said, the bullet was too close to mistake it for anything else. Besides, I've been serving a parish in an impoverished inner city. Occasional gunshots come with the territory."

"Can either of you come up with the name of anyone who might want to do this?"

Rebecca went pale, her eyes wide, as though suddenly beginning to realize what had just transpired. "You're saying this was deliberate."

Ben chose his words carefully. "One gunshot could be a mistake. A pistol with the safety off, fired by accident. Two gunshots change everything. Two gunshots mean business."

With a gasp, Rebecca's hand shot out, clutching Ben's sleeve.

He moved quickly, his arm around her waist, guiding her toward a straight-backed chair where he helped her to sit.

Seeing her pallor, he asked, "Do you have any whiskey in the house?"

She nodded. "In one of those boxes next to the refrigerator."

He walked away, then returned with a tumbler of whiskey, which he held to her lips. "Drink."

She did, then sat stiffly, waiting for the weakness to pass.

"I hope you don't mind." Will started toward the door. His voice was barely a whisper. "I need to get my medication, before this migraine becomes full-blown."

"Hold on, Will." Ben gave a firm shake of his head. "You'd be foolish to walk the streets with a gunman loose out there."

"We heard an engine and the screech of tires. And I'm sure whoever did this wouldn't stick around once he spotted a police vehicle. Besides"—Will's voice sounded thin and strained—"if I don't get my medication soon, I could be bedridden for days. These migraines take on a life of their own."

"I understand. But, Will..." Seeing him pause, Ben added, "Be sure you stop by the sheriff's office whenever you're up to it and make a full report."

"I will. Thanks, Ben." He nodded toward Rebecca. "Sorry. I hate leaving you like this..."

"It's all right, Will. Take care of that migraine. Good night."

When the door closed behind him, she looked up at Ben. "I could make some coffee."

He shook his head. "This isn't a social call, Becca. But I'd feel better if you'd finish that whiskey. You're still too pale."

She managed a dry laugh. "You'd be pale, too, if someone nearly shot you." The minute the words were out of her mouth, she realized the irony. "Sorry. I forgot for a minute that you're here in your job as a lawman." She shook her head. "Do you ever get used to something like this?"

He gave a shrug of his shoulders. "I'll let you know. I'm new to this job."

"Oh, Ben." She downed the whiskey and set the empty tumbler on a side table before clutching her hands together in her lap. "Do you really think someone wanted to shoot Will and me?"

He tried to keep his tone bland. "If not the two of you, then maybe one of you. But which one?"

Seeing her wary look, he cleared his throat. "So, I need to ask. Do you have any enemies? Could there be a disgruntled lover in your past?"

Her face flamed, and she lifted her head a fraction, revealing the offended look that came into her eyes. Her tone was equally offended. "That's beneath you, Ben."

"I'm sorry, Becca. I'm asking as a man of the law."

"Of course you are." Her tone sharpened. "And you're enjoying yourself in the bargain."

Temper had the color returning to her cheeks, which only moments earlier had been too pale.

He gave her that sexy smile. "Can't blame a guy for getting his information any way he can."

"There was…a boyfriend while I was living in Bozeman."

"Was? Did it end badly?" Seeing the protest that sprang to her lips, he added, "Badly enough that he might come here seeking revenge?"

Her tone was pure ice. "I don't make it a point to date guys who want to shoot guns."

"I'll remember that for future reference."

"I wasn't talking about…you, Ben." She got to her feet. "Maybe I should drop by the sheriff's office tomorrow and file my report with him. That will give me time to gather my thoughts."

"I understand. I'm not handling this very well myself." He turned toward the door. "Do you have a security system in this house?"

"I...never thought I'd need one."

"I'd be happy to drive you to your parents' house."

"No." The word was spoken sharply. "That's not an option."

"You shouldn't be alone. At least for tonight, Becca."

"Then you believe the shooter will return?" She began wringing her hands. "You think he'll try again?"

He put a hand on her shoulder, hoping to soothe. "I don't know what to think. I don't even know who the intended victim is yet. But you're vulnerable here. No alarm." He studied the simple key lock. "Not even a dead bolt." His tone revealed his frustration. "Let me take you home."

"This is my home. I'm staying here. I'll..." She looked around frantically. "I'll jam a kitchen chair against the knob like they do in the movies."

"This isn't pretend. This is real life. You shouldn't be here alone."

She sank back down in her chair and looked like she might break down at any minute and cry. "You're scaring me, Ben."

"I'm sorry. I don't want to. What I want is for you to be safe. Let me drive you..."

"As terrified as I feel, I won't go running home to Daddy and Mommy. I've been on my own since college and I'm never going back. I...can't."

"I get that." He knelt down in front of her and took her hands in his. Despite the warmth of the room, they were cold. "I understand your need to be independent. But you've just had a terrible shock. You're feeling afraid and vulnerable. You need some time to process what happened tonight. And you need to feel safe. Since your current boyfriend didn't stick around to protect you, the sensible thing is to go back to your parents' house, at least for tonight."

Her head came up sharply. "Why did you say that? Will isn't my boyfriend. He's just a friend."

"I thought..." He paused. "Sorry. Since you and Will both returned to Haller Creek at the same time, I just assumed..."

"We didn't come together. We just happened to arrive a few days apart."

"And the dinner tonight? It wasn't arranged for any big announcement?"

"The only announcement was the one by my father, suggesting that renting this place was just wrong. I'm still his little girl, and I belong there, with him." She shook her head. "That's why I can't go back, Ben. If I do, my father will see it as an admission that he was right. I won't keep fighting all the old battles over and over."

"All right. I get it." He stared at their joined hands, then up at her mouth and felt his throat go dry at the thought of tasting those lips. Just being this close, holding her hands, had heat rushing through him. "Tell me what you want to do."

"I just want to feel safe." Seeing the way he was studying her, she took in a deep breath. "I'll lock the door and keep the lights on all night. If I have to, I'll sleep in this chair, with my cell phone in my lap. That way, if anyone rattles the doorknob, I'll hear it and dial nine-one-one."

Needing to put some distance between them, Ben stood and crossed to the window, drawing the drapes. Then he walked to the kitchen, and from there to the laundry room and back door. After some time he made his way to her bedroom and bathroom, before returning to the living room.

He struggled for an official tone. "All right. The back door and windows are secure. When I leave here, lock the front door. Leave all the lights on, including the porch light, so you can see anybody approaching. If there's trouble, you call immediately."

She nodded.

Ben held up a hand. "I agreed to take the midnight shift for Virgil. Since I'm on duty anyway, I'll try to make a pass through this neighborhood every hour or two. But I could be called away for emergencies. If I'm off on another call, the state police will cover me. So don't count on me, you hear? If anything at all bothers you, if you hear a noise outside, a sound you can't identify, dial that phone."

"Yes, sir." At his stern look she managed a smile.

He touched a finger to the curve of her mouth. "I'm glad to see your sense of humor returned. Are you feeling a little stronger?"

"Yes. Maybe your strength is contagious."

He started toward the door, with Rebecca trailing him.

Just as she reached for the handle, he turned. "Lock this when I…"

Their faces were nearly brushing. He breathed her in, and the scent of her filled his lungs. His heart. His very soul.

He leaned close just as she leaned forward. That was nearly his undoing. For one breathless moment he simply stared at her, fighting an almost overpowering need to hold her. To kiss her.

The sudden blaze of heat had him by the throat before he could compose himself. Without realizing it, he lifted a hand to her cheek. "I want to keep you safe, Becca."

She put a hand over his. "I know. That means a lot to me, Ben."

"I'm…" His voice was little more than a whisper. "I'm trying really hard to be professional."

Very deliberately he took a step back, and then another.

She smiled, and his heart did a slow, lazy dip.

"Despite the danger, I'm glad I came home, Ben."

"Me too." He managed a sexy grin, though he was feeling none too steady. "It's a little late but...welcome home, Becca."

He opened the door and stepped out onto the porch. "Remember. Lock this."

"I won't forget."

He stood perfectly still, staring at the closed door, listening to the sound of the lock being thrown.

As he settled into the sheriff's vehicle, he sat a moment before turning on the ignition.

His mind wasn't on the shots fired. There was only one thing that mattered.

She wasn't engaged to Will Theisen. He felt like he'd just climbed to the top of the highest peak of the Bitterroot Mountains.

His chest was heaving.

His hands were shaking.

His world was rocking.

And he wanted, more than anything, to go back right now and kiss her until they were both breathless.

CHAPTER SEVEN

Sam looked up from passing a platter of pancakes to Finn. "Well, look who's here. Our new lawman. Just in time for breakfast."

Ben gave a wicked smile. "I planned it that way." He hung his hat on a hook by the back door and washed up at the sink in the mudroom before taking his place at the table. "Where's Mary Pat?"

Mac frowned. "She had an early call. She was up and gone by dawn. I worry that she's taking on too much." He handed Ben a mug of steaming coffee. "How was your first night on the job?"

"Interesting." Ben poured syrup over the pancakes and helped himself to scrambled eggs, ham, and fried potatoes.

While the others paused, he dug into his meal.

Sam punched his arm. "Hey. You can't leave us hanging like that. What was interesting about your first night?"

Ben took a forkful of sweet pancakes and several swallows of coffee, enjoying the way the others merely watched.

"Well, let's see. There was an accident on the interstate. A cattle hauler was sideswiped by a logging truck. Nobody injured, but there were logs and cows all over the place. I had to call for wranglers from the Fisher ranch to come round up their cattle. As for the logs, it'll be another hour before they get them all loaded up and out of there."

"That doesn't sound too interesting to me." Finn shared a look with his brother. "So what else happened?"

"The usual. Minnie Purcell and Chet Bowling got drunk and disorderly at the Hitching Post. They're sobering up in jail. Two more clients for you, bro." He finished his eggs. "And then there were the gunshots in town."

At that, everyone at the table stopped what they were doing to stare at him.

"Gunshots in Haller Creek?" Mac set aside his fork. "Was it some drunken cowboy?"

"I don't know. The shooter was long gone by the time I got there."

"And the victim? Dead or alive?"

"Alive." He thought about the way he'd felt when he put his arm around Rebecca's waist and helped her to a chair. Oh yeah. Very much alive. "I don't know who the intended victim was. Rebecca Henderson and Will Theisen were walking to her place when somebody fired two shots. They weren't hit, but pretty shaken up."

Roscoe snorted. "I would be, too, if somebody shot at me in the dark. Or even in daylight."

Ben managed a smile at the old man's humor. "The call came from the house Rebecca is renting on Maple Drive. Will left with a migraine. Rebecca refused to let me drive her to her folks' place."

Mac set down his coffee cup with a clatter. "She stayed alone?"

Ben shrugged. "Her call. As she reminded me, she's been living on her own in Bozeman for years now. I managed to drive down Maple a couple of times during the night, but I got a little busy. I phoned her on the drive home this morning, and she said she was on her way to the sheriff's office to file an official report."

Finn nudged Sam before looking over at their older brother. "So Rebecca and Will were walking to her place together. Does this mean they made the"—he held up his fingers to mimic quotation marks—"big announcement?"

Ben's smile grew. "According to Rebecca, they're just friends. So she insisted there won't be any"—he imitated Finn—"big announcement."

"Whew." Finn wiped his brow. "I guess Rebecca dodged a bullet."

Sam chuckled. "In more ways than one." He turned to his brother. "And now you're going to be searching for a mysterious gunman while trying to keep Rebecca safe." He exchanged a grin with Finn. "Bet you weren't expecting this when you agreed to wear that badge, bro."

Finn nodded. "Pretty intense, if you ask me."

Mac looked around the table, seeing the look of concentration on Ben's face. "Well. Crisis averted. Now it's time to get to work." He shoved back his chair. "Great breakfast, Zachariah. Thanks."

"You're welcome." The old lion sat back, sipping his coffee as the others followed Mac's lead and stacked their dishes in the sink before heading outside.

When they were gone, he looked down the table at Ben, spooning orange marmalade onto a piece of toast. Despite the fact that Ben had been up around the clock, he didn't appear at all tired.

"Your first night on the job proved…interesting."

"Yeah." Feeling the old man studying him, he looked over. "Okay. You're leading up to something."

"I am?"

"Out with it."

Zachariah merely smiled. "You gave us the facts, Benedict. But I have a feeling you left out the most interesting highlights of the night."

Ben's smile came slowly. "You got that right."

Zachariah eased himself out of his chair and walked to the kitchen sink. A short time later, when he'd dried the last dish, he turned to see Ben still at the table, drinking his third cup of coffee, and still staring into space.

The old man knew better than to press for details. These three troubled boys had learned early in life to play their cards close to the vest.

Now men, the three never talked about their painful childhood, though they probably had plenty of stories to tell.

Like so many who had come through fire, part of their survival mode was to keep that part of their lives locked away in a secret place in their minds.

If he was a betting man, he'd put money on the fact that Rebecca Henderson was the reason for Benedict's look of extreme concentration this morning. The new deputy would now be responsible for the safety of Rebecca.

The mere mention of her name had always put a spark in that young man's eyes that seemed to light up his very soul.

Despite her father's reputation for micromanaging everyone and everything around him, especially his pretty daughter, Rebecca Henderson had always seemed friendly and untouched by Hank's chronic complaining.

And though she and Benedict had been apart for years now, there seemed to be something still there between them. Something undefined that had this young man dancing lightly around the mere mention of her name, as though afraid to sample the wine in case it went straight to his head.

To Zachariah's way of thinking, a taste of wine might be good for Benedict. He'd had to be the strong, unbending leader of his pack for too long now.

Maybe it was time for him to let go the straight and narrow and walk on the wild side.

"What do you make of that shooting, Ben?" Virgil Kerr sat behind his desk facing his new deputy.

"I don't know enough about it to have an opinion. Have there been other shootings I don't know about?"

Virgil leaned back, tapping a finger on the arm of his chair. "None. This is a first for Haller Creek. We've had the occasional cowboy getting drunk and firing off a round or two, but this has the feeling of a big-city crime. Two innocent people walking home. Two shots fired, barely missing them."

"Maybe that's the way the shooter wanted it."

The sheriff sat up straighter. "What's that supposed to mean?"

Ben shrugged. "He had two chances to hit a slow-moving target. According to Rebecca, they didn't drop to the ground until the second shot sent a bullet flying over their heads. Our gunman didn't have a very good aim."

Virgil gave that some thought. "Supposing your theory is correct, who was he warning? Reverend Will Theisen or Rebecca Henderson?"

"That's the million-dollar question." Ben leaned forward. "Have they both filed an official report?"

"They have."

"Anything in there that raises a flag?"

"Nothing. Just a normal evening stroll, and then, *bam, bam.* Two gunshots."

"Are you looking into their backgrounds?"

The sheriff nodded. "I sent the information to the state boys. They've got the manpower and special training to get on it. Since both Will and Rebecca have been gone for some years, there's no telling what they might have got themselves into. Maybe an old debt. Maybe an old grudge." He steepled his fingers on the desktop. "You notice anything peculiar about either of them last night?"

"Will went home with a migraine, and Rebecca refused to go to her parents' place." Ben gave a dry laugh. "Neither of which seems particularly weird considering what they'd just been through."

Virgil frowned. "Did Will say if his migraine is typical, or the result of what happened last night?"

"He didn't say, and I didn't think to ask."

"Did Rebecca say why she didn't want to stay with her folks?"

"She said she's been on her own too long to go running home to mom and dad."

Virgil gave that some thought before sighing. "Can't say I blame her. Hank Henderson can be a self-righteous, over-bearing fool at times."

Ben merely grinned. "You think?"

"I guess you'd know about that." Virgil gave a grunt. "Hank's never been shy about saying what he thinks about you and your brothers."

"The hell-raisers." With a sigh, Ben got to his feet.

Virgil glanced at the clock. "Your shift doesn't start for another hour."

"Thought I'd start cleaning out that back room. Maybe, if I'm lucky, I'll get a night without any drunks, accidents on the interstate, or unexplained shootings, and I can grab some shut-eye."

"Don't count on it, son." The sheriff picked up his hat and headed for the door. "Life has a way of spoiling the best-laid plans of mice and men."

He paused before striding through the open doorway and into the growing darkness. "I'll make a last turn around the town; then I'm going home."

"Sleep tight, Sheriff."

"Good night, Ben. Stay safe."

Ben made a slow turn around the town, grateful for the quiet evening. He'd had plenty of time to clean out the accumulated clutter from the back room. Another couple of hours in there and he'd be able to use it as a retreat, if he managed to find some downtime.

Jeanette Moak, on night shift at the dispatch desk in a small office across the street shared by both the sheriff and the volunteer fire department, had relayed the gossip being spread about the previous night's shooting.

"Who'd believe crime right here in Haller Creek? And especially involving Rebecca Henderson and Reverend Will Theisen? My Charley says you can't tell about a person. He has me wondering if one of them has a dark secret in their past that's come back to haunt them."

Charley was her rancher husband, who was laid up with a bad back.

Ben chuckled. "Maybe Charley's been reading too many mystery novels, Jeanette."

"I don't know, Ben. They say life imitates art." There was a spate of static over the line before she added, "Or is it art imitates life? Anyway, it's the most exciting thing that's happened around here in ages."

"Except for the two who got shot at. They're probably more scared than excited."

"Yes. There's that, of course."

"I'm heading out, Jeanette. Think I'll take a cruise around town."

"Okay. I'll relay any calls I get."

Ben turned the sheriff's squad car onto Maple, driving slowly toward Rebecca's house. As he drew closer, he recognized Rebecca on the front porch, head bent in conversation with Will.

The two looked up and waved.

Ben returned the salute and continued driving.

An hour later he made another tour of the town and again drove past Rebecca's house. He could make out her silhouette against the drawn shade in the living room. His first inclination was to stop. He really wanted to see her. To see how she was feeling, now that there'd been time to process what had happened.

Though he slowed down, the thought of coming up with an excuse for stopping by had him feeling like a fool. Besides, once there, he might be tempted to do what he'd wanted to do last night. No sense putting himself in that position again.

He drove on by and returned to the office before checking in. "Hey, Jeanette."

"Ben. Quiet night."

"Yeah. Think I'll just go in the back room and..."

He was just stepping through the doorway when Jeanette's voice came through the intercom. "Emergency call from 313 Maple. Rebecca Henderson says somebody is at the back of her house."

"Thanks, Jeanette." He was in the squad car and at Rebecca's house in record time.

As he rounded the house, he heard a crash and squeals that were almost human.

The strong, steady beam of his flashlight picked up the crime scene. An overturned trash can and a pair of masked critters waddling away.

With a laugh he righted the can and scooped up the litter scattered on the ground.

A few minutes later he knocked on the front door.

Rebecca's face, pinched and worried, peered out before the door was opened.

"Ben." His name came out in a whoosh of air.

"Everything's fine. Two masked bandits were attacking your garbage."

"My garbage? Oh. Raccoons?" She gave a weak laugh and laid a hand on his arm. "You'll never know the damage they just did to my heart."

At her simple touch, his own heart took a quick, hard bounce.

She stood aside. "Can you come in?"

"Sure." He removed his hat and stepped past her.

Again, he absorbed the quick tingle as their bodies brushed.

"I have coffee. Would you like some?"

"Thanks." He held up his hands. "I'd better wash up first. I cleaned the mess your critters left behind."

"You didn't have to do that. It's enough that you investigated and put my mind at ease." She led the way to the kitchen and pointed to the soap dispenser alongside the sink. "You can wash there."

When he was finished, she handed him a towel. As their fingers brushed, he absorbed a rush of heat.

She turned away and filled two mugs with coffee.

He took a seat at the small table and glanced at the plate of cookies. "You bake?"

She flushed. "I picked them up at the store after work."

He nibbled one. "You have good taste."

She laughed and put a hand over his. "Thank you for coming so quickly. I feel like such a fool."

He struggled not to react, though her touch had him sweating. "What you did was smart. People could avoid a lot of tragedies if they would only call the authorities the minute they feel threatened."

"You'll never know all the horrible things I imagined."

He closed his other hand over hers. Squeezed. "I'm glad I could ease your fears."

"That seems to be what you do best." At his questioning look, she related Will's childhood story. "And now my parents know the truth. Not only about how you got that shiner, but also about other heroic things you did when we were kids."

"They weren't heroic."

"What would you call the things you did?"

He shrugged. "Stepping in when I'm needed. I just have a problem with bullies."

When she withdrew her hands, he finished his coffee before looking around and quickly changing the subject. "I like your house, Becca. It suits you."

A softness came into her eyes. "Thanks. I'm really enjoying having my very own place."

He stood and carried his cup to the sink. "Thanks for the coffee."

When he turned, she was directly behind him. "You're welcome. I hope..." She drew in a quick breath. "I hope you'll come by another time, not out of any sense of duty, but just to visit."

He lifted a hand to lightly touch her shoulder. "I'd like that, Becca."

Her smile bloomed. A smile that aimed a dart straight to his heart.

Seeing it, he felt again that itch to just gather her close and kiss her breathless. Maybe it was a moment of weakness, or madness, but instead of turning away as he'd planned, he drew her close.

Seeing the smoldering look in his eyes, she leaned in, offering her lips.

"Becca..." The words he'd been about to say were forgotten. All his thoughts scrambled and fled the instant his mouth was on hers.

With a little moan of pleasure, she returned his kiss as her hands tangled in the front of his shirt.

The sound of the doorbell ringing had two heads coming up sharply.

Rebecca looked slightly disoriented before she stepped to the front door. Peering out, she hurriedly unlocked the door and threw it open. "Dad. I—"

Seeing Ben, he pushed past her and stood scowling. "More trouble?"

"No. Well, yes. I heard something and called nine-one-one, but it turned out to be raccoons in my trash."

"And you didn't think to call me?"

"Dad, I called—"

"I know who you called." He looked Ben up and down before glaring at his daughter. "Just like last night. You called him. And you didn't even bother to tell me. I had to hear it just now from a customer. When I get home and tell your mother, she's going to be so hurt to learn that you wouldn't even come home to be with us at such a terrible, horrible time. Are we such monsters that you can't even come to us with your troubles? You have to hide away in this..." He looked around with a visible shudder. "You need to move back home. To be with your parents. To let us keep you safe."

"Oh, Dad." She took in a deep breath, fighting to control the denial that sprang to her lips. "This is exactly why I didn't confide in you. I knew this was how you'd react to the news."

"And if the shooter hadn't missed? How would I have reacted to the news that my only child was dead? Would this...hothead be the one to tell me? Would that satisfy you?"

Ben stepped between father and daughter, hoping to give them both a moment to cool down.

Turning his back on Hank, he took Rebecca's hand in his. "I'm glad this was nothing more than a false alarm tonight."

He turned to Hank Henderson. "I'm sorry you had to hear the news of the shooting from a customer. Since both your daughter and Will are of legal age, the sheriff isn't permitted by law to share the details unless both of them agree in writing."

He stepped out the door.

As he started down the steps, he could hear Hank's voice, angry, accusing. "No doubt Reverend Will would be more than happy to confide in me. But my own daughter..."

He slid into the squad car and closed the door, shutting out the words.

For the longest time he merely sat in the silence, struggling with the wide range of emotions playing through his mind.

Elation at the fact that Becca had returned his kiss with one of her own. He was trying not to read too much into it, since she'd just been through another scare. But still, she hadn't pulled away. He couldn't help wondering what might have happened if they hadn't been interrupted by her father.

Her father.

It was, Ben thought, just one more reason to be grateful

for Mac Monroe in his life. Here he was, doing his best to repay Mac for all he'd done for Ben and his brothers, and Mac's only concern was to cut him loose to chase his dreams.

As for Rebecca, though she was doing her best to break free, her father was smothering her with his own version of love.

Poor, sweet Rebecca. Damned if she did; damned if she didn't.

And poor Hank. The tighter he held on, the more she was bound to push back, in order to be free to live her life.

CHAPTER EIGHT

Sheriff Kerr looked up when Ben walked into the office. "According to Jeanette's report, you had a quiet night."

Ben nodded and removed his hat, shaking it against his leg before setting it aside. "Nothing I couldn't handle. A drunken cowboy over at the Hitching Post who thought he was Superman."

Virgil grinned. "I hear you took him down without a scratch."

Ben touched a finger to his eye. The swelling had gone down, and there was just a hint of a bruise. "Lesson learned."

The sheriff laughed out loud. "Hell of a way to learn, son." He looked down at the documents atop his desk. "The state boys sent me a preliminary report on Reverend Will and Rebecca. In the coming days they'll do a lot more digging."

"That sounds like they have more questions than answers."

"You might say that."

Ben settled into a chair across from the sheriff's desk. "Are these questions about Will or about Rebecca?"

"Both." The sheriff handed over a sheaf of papers. "Take a look."

Ben read quickly, then took his time rereading certain pages before looking up. "According to this, the investigators have found some troubling things in Will's immediate past." Ben gave a shake of his head. "Will's immediate past was spent in divinity school. What could be troubling about that?"

"I can't imagine. But I have faith in the dedication of our state police detectives. If Will had a problem, even one he tried to bury, I have no doubt they'll uncover it."

Ben held out a second page. "And this. They claim that Rebecca had a serious relationship with a medical student, then abruptly broke it off. That's no crime. And the guy, Daryl Hollender, seemed angry and bitter." He arched a brow. "A bruised ego isn't a crime either."

"Unless he shows up in Haller Creek with a gun."

The sheriff pointed to the document in Ben's hands. "Rebecca's been gone for years now, Ben. Some young people can't handle the freedom that comes with college life, and then a career far from home. We know a lot of them get caught up in sex, drugs, and rock and roll."

Ben's smile was quick. "I think that was your generation, Sheriff."

Virgil chuckled. "You're right. But what I'm trying to say is, people change. Maybe Rebecca's choice of boyfriend wasn't a good one. Let's allow the state detectives to do their job."

"In the meantime, how do we keep Becca and Will safe?"

At Ben's question, Virgil shook his head. "We do the best

we can, but we have to allow them to live their lives." He pushed away from his desk. "I looked in the back room. If I didn't know better, I'd have thought you brought in an army of cleaning women. It's looking good, son."

"I'm glad you approve. Not that I'll be using it any time soon. I never got so much as an hour to myself last night. And it was what I'd call a quiet night."

"Jeanette also said you got a call from Rebecca about a disturbance at her place."

"Just a couple of pesky raccoons overturning her garbage cans and having a feast."

"That so?"

Ben nodded. "It just shows she's a lot more scared than she's letting on."

"Could be." He ambled toward the door before turning. "Or maybe she needed an excuse to have my good-looking new deputy pay a call." He shot Ben a look. "You might want to read that report again, son. You wouldn't want to be the next boyfriend to get dumped without a good reason."

"Sorry about the damage to your car, Fred." Ben finished writing up the fender bender on Main Street, and sent the unhappy rancher and his neighbor home to deal with their insurance agencies.

He thought about heading back to the office. He could chat up Jeanette on his police radio before taking a breather in his newly cleaned back room. Or he could stop in Dolly's Diner and catch up on all the latest gossip with the owner. Dolly Pruitt knew everyone in the town of Haller Creek by their first name, and could tell them more about themselves than their own mothers could. She was the town's historian and knew the latest gossip long before it hit the local newspaper. She was also happy to share it with anyone who walked through her door. Some said that was what brought in more customers than her famous meat loaf.

As tempting as it was to hear what she had to say about the shooting, he decided to swing past Rebecca's place first.

As he started along Maple, he slowed, admiring the tidy houses, the neatly trimmed yards, the small-town look of the neighborhood. Though he much preferred the sprawl of his family ranch, he could see why some folks were attracted to the area. They could visit with neighbors. They were within walking distance of church and school and all the nice shops in town. There was a sense of order and safety.

Ben frowned. Except now that sense of safety had been violated.

Rebecca's house was in darkness, except for the porch light. While he watched, two figures separated on a nearby front porch. Rebecca turned and said something to her neighbor, before hurrying toward her own house.

He waited until she'd gone inside, flicking on a switch and flooding the interior with light. He wanted to stop by, to see for himself that she was recovered from the shock of the shooting. But Virgil's words played through his mind.

It was true that he didn't really know that much about her anymore. In the time she'd been away, they hadn't once communicated.

A serious relationship with a medical student.

He frowned in the darkness and continued driving.

A coffee at Dolly's Diner sounded good right about now.

Horton Duke, owner of the Hitching Post, had a standing request for someone from the sheriff's office to take a turn through the parking area of his saloon every Saturday night, any time after midnight. That's when thirsty wranglers often decided to settle their differences outside, especially if two or more had their eye on the same pretty girl. Horton liked to say most of the ladies got better-looking after midnight, or after half a dozen shots and beers. Whichever came first.

Ben drove slowly past the line of trucks, many bearing the logos of nearby ranches. Seeing nothing out of the ordinary, he drove along Main Street, peering at the darkened shops.

Satisfied that everything looked safe and buttoned up, he turned toward the nearby neighborhoods. Eventually, he ended up on Maple. He tried to tell himself it was by accident, but his sense of honor wouldn't accept that.

He was here because of Rebecca.

He wanted to know she was safe. Secure. Unafraid.

At least that's all he'd admit to.

He stopped the car.

Her lights were on, the shades drawn. He watched her silhouette pacing back and forth, back and forth.

After debating the wisdom of what he was about to do, he stepped out, walked to her porch, and knocked.

The porch light came on. He saw Rebecca's face peering through the window.

When she opened the door, the relief on her face was obvious.

"Ben. Oh, it's so good to see you. Do you have time to come in?"

"I'll make time." He stepped past her, glancing around while she closed the door. "Something wrong?"

She shook her head. "Not really."

He noted the way her hands twisted together at her waist.

"Something's happened to have you pacing at this time of night. Want to talk about it?"

She sighed. "Do you have time for coffee?"

He shrugged. "I don't want you to go to any trouble…"

"I made a fresh pot." She started toward the kitchen, and he trailed behind.

He stood in the middle of the room and watched as she filled two cups and carried them to the table.

He took a seat across from her and lifted the cup to his mouth, giving her time to gather her thoughts.

"My parents called tonight. My dad put my mother on the phone, and she burst into tears, saying neither of them could sleep, they were so worried about what happened."

"I'm sorry."

She looked over, meeting his gaze. "I know this sounds cold, but I can't help questioning my father's timing. I have the feeling he called when he knew my mother's emotions were getting the best of her."

Ben put a hand over hers. "Rebecca, she wouldn't be much of a mother if she wasn't worried about you. It's not every day her daughter is caught up in a mysterious shooting."

"I know that. And I'm not finding fault with her. I understand exactly how she feels. I'm afraid, too. But now both my parents are putting pressure on me to move home."

"That's not the worst thing in the world. They love you. They want you safe."

She winced. "But for me, it would be an admission that all my hard-earned independence was just a joke. That when things get tough, I run home."

"What do you want to do?"

She gave a weary shake of her head. "Honestly? I'd like to crawl into my old bed and hide under the covers, and let my parents fuss over me until this nightmare is resolved. But I can't." She pulled her hand free of his touch, but not before he felt the quick, jittery pulse.

She started to pace, arms folded over her chest. "I've always been a coward, Ben. Afraid of everything. Breaking any of my father's rules. Getting less than perfect grades. Dating guys he didn't approve of." She paused. Looked over at him. "Don't you see? I stayed away until I thought I could come home on my own terms. And now, weeks into my noble decision, it's all falling apart." She took in a deep, shuddering breath. "You can't imagine how tempted I am to move home and hide. But I know if I do, I'll never find the courage to be my own person. And this means so much to me."

Ben got to his feet and crossed to her, laying a hand on her shoulder. "First of all, look at how you reacted when you were shot at, in the dark, by an unknown assailant. You didn't cry, or run to your parents' house. You phoned the dispatcher, reported the incident, and stood your ground even after Will left. That's not the behavior of a coward."

When she opened her mouth to protest, he touched a finger to her lips. Feeling the rush of heat, he quickly removed his hand and lowered it to his side, clenching it into a fist. "And another thing. Most people crave the comfort of family when things spiral out of control. It's the most natural thing in the world to want your parents to be there for you in times of trouble."

"But most parents wouldn't try to take over their child's life."

"You're an adult now, Becca. You have the right to set boundaries. Even where your folks are concerned."

He could see her considering all he'd said.

"Thank you, Ben. It's what I've been telling myself. I'm so glad you stopped by." She looked close to tears.

He didn't know what he'd do if she cried.

Yes, he did. If she broke down crying, he'd have to comfort her. And if he did, he might never stop until...

Very deliberately he started toward the front door. "I'm

glad, too. I hope you know you can call me any time you need a friend."

She moved past him and opened the door. "I may take you up on that."

"Good. Good night, Becca."

He almost made it out the door. Would have, if he hadn't looked down to see her struggling to smile, despite the glint of tears on her lashes.

He reached out a hand to her. "Rebecca, don't cry…"

Ashamed, she turned her head to hide her anguish.

He swore softly before gathering her into his arms. "Hey, now. It's going to be all right."

"Oh, Ben…"

His entire body was engulfed in heat.

It seemed the most natural thing in the world to frame her face with his hands and run soft butterfly kisses from her temple to her cheek and lower, to her mouth, while murmuring words of comfort. "You're safe now. You'll get through this."

"I know." With a soft sigh she returned his kiss with a sort of desperation that had him forgetting all his promises to himself.

The rush of heat became a raging inferno. His hands were in her hair, though he couldn't recall how they got there. His mouth moved over hers, taking the kiss deep.

She moaned softly.

Her hungry response had him throwing all caution to the wind. How could he resist when the need was so great?

She stood clinging fiercely, returning his kisses with a hunger that caught him off guard.

Her body fit perfectly against his, like the missing piece of a puzzle.

The smell of her perfume, faintly floral, went straight to his head.

With each kiss, she tasted like sin.

He took all she offered, devouring them both until alarm bells went off in his brain.

With a fierce oath, he lifted his head, breaking contact.

God in heaven. His heartbeat was thundering. His breathing ragged. He was surprised at how difficult it was to speak. "I can't…do this. I'm supposed to be professional…" He tried again. "I…have a job to do."

"I know." She stepped back, refusing to look at him. Instead she stared at the floor, color flooding her cheeks. "I have no right"—she spread her hands, still studying a spot on the floor—"to bother you with my personal problems, Ben."

He put a hand under her chin, forcing her to meet his eyes. The mere touch of her sent another series of tremors through his overcharged system.

Almost reverently he framed her face with his big hands. His tone was low with passion. "You know you can tell me anything."

He was rewarded by the slightest nod of her head. "I guess that's why I do it. You're so easy to talk to, Ben." She stood on tiptoe to brush a kiss over his cheek.

His hands were shaking, and he had to lower them to his side to keep from dragging her close. "I'll check on you whenever I can. Call me if you need me."

"I will, Ben. Good night."

He strode out the door, refusing to look back. If he did, he'd never make it to his car.

Once inside he turned the key in the ignition and noted idly that his hands were still trembling.

Right now, more than ever, he wanted to run back and lock himself inside with Rebecca. The only trouble was, she'd be in even more danger than she was now.

He wanted her. Dear God, he wanted her. And always had. In the years they'd been apart, nothing had changed.

Yet, in a way, everything had.

She'd come back to Haller Creek determined to make her own way, despite her father's efforts to take charge.

Rebecca may be winning the conflict with her father, but if she got to really know the darker side of Ben, with all its rough edges, she'd be shocked to her core.

Ben swore. And wasn't he the biggest fool in the world right now? Even knowing how right her father was...even knowing how wrong they were for one another, he wanted her. And would until the day he died. Probably while engaging in a bone-breaking, head-jarring, knock-down, drag-out brawl.

CHAPTER NINE

Hank Henderson set down the phone and walked over to the display of building materials. He stood to one side, watching and listening as his daughter finished writing up an order for a rancher.

Her smile was bright as she tore off a copy of the order and handed it over. "I'll get this to Eli right away. Do you have any other business in town, Roy?"

The rancher nodded. "Planned my day around this trip to town."

"Good. If you'll park your truck at one of the loading docks, Eli should have this ready for you within the hour."

"Thanks, Rebecca." He tipped his hat. Then, seeing Hank standing to one side, nodded a greeting. "You've got yourself one heck of an employee, Hank. She knows her stuff."

"Thanks, Roy. I appreciate that seal of approval."

When the rancher left, Rebecca turned. "Do you have a minute to talk, Dad?"

"What about?"

"About that little plot of fenced land by the side entrance to the store."

"Where I dump those wooden pallets and junk?"

She nodded. "I'd like to rent it."

"Now what foolishness is this?" He looked at her as though she'd grown two heads.

Rebecca thought about the way she'd rehearsed this request. She would be calm, cool, and collected. And no matter what her father said, or how he said it, she would stick to her request. "I'd like to clean it up and use it to display some things."

"What things?"

She shrugged. "I'm not sure yet. Things that might complement what you sell inside, without being in competition with your business."

"You mean like fancy, girly things?"

The sarcastic tone had her biting back a comment. If she were to let her father know how she really felt, he would shoot down her plans before she even had a chance to try them.

She turned toward the rear of the store. "I have to get this order to Eli."

"In a minute." Hank caught her arm. "Your mother and I invited Will to supper and want you to join us."

"Sorry. I can't. I'm working the late shift today. Remember?"

He smiled. "And I just changed the schedule." Before she could say a word, he held up a hand. "That's my right. Not only as owner, but also as your father. As of now, your shift ends at four. That will give you plenty of time to go home and change before you join us for supper."

"What about my plans?"

"Change them." His smile grew. "That is, if you actually have any."

"And what do I get in return?"

At her question, he paused before saying, "A promise that I'll give your request some thought."

"Fair enough." Rebecca walked away clutching the order. As she made her way to the back room, she had to admit that, though she found her father's tactics heavy-handed, he did promise to consider her request. It was a start. And for a man like her controlling dad, a big concession.

Her smile came slowly. In truth, she wouldn't mind a home-cooked meal. At least she wouldn't have another night of takeout in front of the television. Of course, as payment, she would have to tolerate once again being offered as the perfect soul mate to the brand-new minister.

She found herself wishing Will Theisen had returned to Haller Creek with a wife. Life would have been so much simpler.

"So, Will." After a meal of Susan Henderson's tasty pot roast and candied yams, Hank was feeling expansive as they gathered in the living room. "I hear you had a visit with Reverend Grayson."

"Yes, sir." Will settled more comfortably into the high-backed chair arranged to one side of the fireplace. "He said he's being urged by the women's committee to host a fundraiser, to cover the cost of a new roof."

"That won't sit well with the congregation." Hank frowned. "A lot of the ranchers are having hard times." He nodded toward his wife. "Susan knows I've had to arrange for monthly payments from a lot of them who are being eaten alive by debt. A lot of families with hundreds of acres can't keep up with taxes, insurance, and maintenance on their holdings."

Will shrugged. "Maybe they should sell."

Rebecca turned to him. "And then what will they do?"

The young minister looked surprised by her question. "I don't know. Get a job on someone else's ranch, I guess."

"And one day we'll wake up and realize there aren't any ranches left."

Will arched a brow. "I don't see how that would affect you. You have a comfortable life here in town."

"A life that depends on the success of the people around us. Without ranchers to buy our goods, the businesspeople in this town would have to shutter their doors and move."

Hank nodded. "Rebecca's right. Our success is directly tied to the success of everyone else, especially the ranchers."

Will looked properly impressed. "I guess I never gave it much thought until now. But I can see the wisdom of everybody working together for the common good."

Hank gave the young man a knowing smile. "I'm sure at your college it was nothing more than a concept. Out in the real world, it's an economic fact."

Rebecca turned to her mother. "That was the perfect comfort food. Thanks, Mom. But now I need to get home."

As she got to her feet, Will stood. "I'll walk you."

"I'd appreciate the company. Thanks, Will."

As she turned to fetch her jacket from the front hall closet, she saw the smile on her father's lips. She could almost see him rubbing his hands in glee as his scheme to throw them together was working as planned.

Will opened the door before turning toward his hosts.

"Thank you again, Susan." He bent to kiss her cheek.

"You're welcome, Will. Come again soon."

"Good night, Hank." The two men shook hands.

"'Night, Mom. Dad. Can we talk tomorrow about my plan?"

Seeing her mother glance at her father, Rebecca's smile remained. "I'm sure Dad will tell you all about it later." Rebecca brushed a kiss over both their cheeks and stepped out ahead of Will.

The older couple stood in the open doorway, watching.

"Getting a bit chilly," Hank called.

"Winter's coming." Rebecca turned to smile at her parents. "I can't wait for the first snow—"

The sound of a gunshot echoed across the night sky. For a moment nobody moved. Then, as realization dawned, Hank and Susan were reaching for their daughter at the same instant Rebecca rushed into their arms and was hauled inside.

Nearby a car door slammed, and tires screeched as a darkened vehicle drove away.

As soon as Will cleared the doorway, Hank slammed the front door and set the lock.

While the others gathered around in a frenzied need to comfort one another, Rebecca fished her cell phone from her pocket and dialed 911 to breathlessly report what had happened.

She listened to Jeanette Moak's calm reaction. "As long as there are no injuries, don't move. Sit tight. We're on it."

Rebecca had to swallow down the hard knot of fear clogging her throat. "Don't worry. We're not going anywhere."

Ben handed the ticket to the driver of the flashy little sports car. Her girlfriend in the passenger seat leaned over her friend to flirt shamelessly.

"How fast did you have to go to catch us, Officer?"

"Over a hundred, ma'am." He managed a smile. "You're both lucky there was no alcohol involved, or you'd both cool your heels overnight in Haller Creek's jail. As it is, you know that kind of speed could be called reckless. What you did, passing that line of vehicles, was downright dangerous."

"Fortunately, nobody got hurt."

"Except your wallet, ma'am."

The blond driver flashed him a toothy smile. "We were just having a little fun. Thank you, Officer."

"Ma'am. You may not be so thankful when you pay this fine." He tipped his hat and walked back to his squad car.

"Ben." Jeanette's voice sounded flustered. "Where've you been?"

"Writing out a ticket for a couple of tourists."

"There's been another shot fired. Over at the Henderson house."

"Anybody hurt?" For the space of several seconds, his heart stopped.

"No."

He took a quick breath. "Thanks. I'm on it."

"I called Sheriff Kerr at home when you didn't respond right away."

"Good. I'll meet him there."

Ben pushed his vehicle to the limit. Within minutes he pulled up in front of the Henderson house. In quick moves he exited his car and strode to the front door.

When it opened, he could see the disappointment laced with annoyance on Hank's face. "I called for the sheriff."

"He's on his way." When Hank hesitated, Ben pushed the door wider and went inside.

Rebecca stepped away from her mother and Will and hurried over. "Oh, Ben. Thank heavens you're here."

Knowing the others were watching, he resisted the urge to gather her close and kept his tone professional. "Tell me exactly what happened."

In a few words she described the scene.

"One shot?"

"Just one."

"None of you saw anyone?"

They shook their heads.

"You all heard a car door slam?"

Several nods.

"And the driver left in a rush," Hank added for emphasis. "I'm certain you'll find burned rubber on the street."

"I'll be sure to check it out." Ben looked over at Will Theisen, whose face was as pale as his new collar. "Do you have anything to add, Will?"

He shook his head and was comforted by Susan Henderson, who kept patting his hand.

Ben spoke to Rebecca. "Did you walk here from your place?"

She nodded. "I left my house around six."

"Did you notice anyone following you? Did you have an uneasy feeling about anything?"

"Nothing."

He turned to Will. "Did you walk or drive?"

"I walked."

"Then I ask you the same. Anyone following you? Any sense that you were being watched?"

Will hesitated for a fraction before shaking his head.

The sheriff's vehicle pulled up in front of the house, and Virgil Kerr limped up the walkway. Seeing Ben, he relaxed a bit. "Glad you got here so fast. Jeanette was worried."

"A ticket on the interstate. I came right over."

"Thanks, son." Virgil turned to the others. "Have you all given your statements to my deputy?"

Hank frowned. "I'd have rather spoken with you, Virgil."

"I don't know why." The sheriff's gruff tone revealed his annoyance. "When I chose Ben here to be my deputy, I did it because he's the most competent man for the job. If you've talked to him, you've talked to me."

Ben suppressed the little smile that teased the corners of his mouth.

Virgil turned to Rebecca. "You planning on staying here tonight? Or are you heading home?"

"She's staying here," Hank said firmly.

"Of course she is." Susan was equally firm.

Seeing Rebecca start to shake her head, both her parents started to speak at once.

She held up a hand. After taking a deep breath she stood a little taller. "I have a home on Maple, Sheriff. That's where I'm going."

He gave a curt nod of his head. "My deputy will take you and check your place completely before he leaves." Virgil turned to Will. "I'll drive you to your place, Reverend, and do the same there."

When Susan started to sniffle, he patted her shoulder. "I know you're worried about your little girl. It's only natural. But she's in good hands, Susan. You and Hank need to keep the faith. And as always, if any of you think of something you may have forgotten, you be sure to let me or my deputy know."

He stood aside, allowing Rebecca and Ben to leave first.

As they walked down the steps, Hank called, "Don't come into work tomorrow, Rebecca. I want you to stay home and rest."

"I'm not..."

"That's an order."

She gritted her teeth and followed Ben to his car.

When they were settled inside, Sheriff Kerr put a hand on Will's shoulder and steered him toward his vehicle.

Hank and Susan stood in the doorway, watching with matching frowns of concern as the two vehicles pulled away from the curb.

CHAPTER TEN

Ben watched Rebecca out of the corner of his eye as he drove in silence to her house.

When they arrived, he put a hand on her arm. "Wait here. I need to check a few things before you go inside."

She offered no protest.

He checked the front door and windows before walking around to the rear of the house and doing the same. Using his flashlight, he checked for footprints or indentations in the piles of leaves that had blown up against the house.

Satisfied, he returned to the car and held out his hand for the key. "I'd like you to wait while I check inside."

At his words, she clutched her arms about herself as he walked inside and moved through the house, turning on all the lights.

At last he came back. "All clear."

He took her hand and walked with her up the steps and into the house.

She rubbed warmth into her arms. "Would you like some coffee?"

"No. But if you'd like some, I'll make it."

She nodded and followed him to the kitchen.

He moved easily about, comfortable with the simple routine, and soon the kitchen was filled with the soothing fragrance of coffee.

He poured two cups and handed one to her.

"Thank you. And thank you for coming so soon."

"It's my job."

"As Sheriff Kerr said, you're good at it."

"I'm learning." He drank. "You going to make it through the night?"

She took her time sipping the hot coffee before giving a nod. "I'm determined to."

"One night with your folks wouldn't be an admission of weakness."

She merely looked over at him.

"Okay." He grinned. "I saw the way your mother was falling apart."

"Not to mention my dad."

"They have a right to."

"I understand their fears. I'm terrified, too." She hugged her arms to her chest. "Who's doing this, Ben? What's this about?"

"I wish I knew. It's all I think of, first thing in the morning, last thing at night. I can't stand the thought of you being a target for a madman. You sure you can't think of anyone holding a grudge against you?"

She looked away. "I suppose we all make a few enemies in life."

"Enemies mad enough to fire off gunshots?"

She set aside her coffee with a clatter. "No. I can't think of anybody who would want to hurt me."

"How about someone who'd like to scare you?"

She frowned. "I don't understand..."

"So far, three gunshots, and three misses. Someone has lousy aim. Or they're trying to send a message."

Her eyes went wide before she sank down on a kitchen chair.

Ben pulled his chair close beside hers. "Can you think of someone who's mad enough to go to all this trouble just to frighten you, Rebecca?"

"No." Her voice was barely a whisper.

"You might want to think long and hard about it." He picked up his cup. Drank. "I'm sure Virgil is having this same conversation with Will."

"So you both think this is a...scare tactic?"

"It's just one of many theories. Right now, we don't even know which of you is the target. So far, both incidents have occurred when you and Will are together."

She clutched her hands in her lap. The fear in her eyes had him yearning to comfort her. "I wish I could stay here all night and keep watch. But I'm on duty until morning."

"I wish you could, too. But I understand that you have a job to do, Ben."

"I heard your father tell you to stay home tomorrow."

She didn't reply.

"Tomorrow's my day off. Why don't I pick you up and take you home with me."

"I don't think..."

"It'll be a nice change of pace. You can be lazy if you want, or we could ride up to one of the herds. How long has it been since you've been on a horse?"

She managed a laugh. "Years. I never rode in college."

"There you go." He could see her mulling.

He stood. "I'm off work at seven. I'll pick you up and we can be at my place in time for breakfast."

Her smile was slow in coming, but when it did, it softened all her features. "I'd love it."

"Good. So would I." He picked up his hat. "See you in the morning. In the meantime, I'll be driving by every chance I get." He stared pointedly at her cell phone. "Call at the least sound."

"Don't worry. I'll take you up on that."

He strode quickly out the door, calling, "Lock this behind me."

Once in the car he relaxed.

He'd managed almost an hour alone with her and hadn't once given in to the temptation to haul her into his arms and kiss her breathless.

Ben left work at seven o'clock and was at Rebecca's place by 7:10.

He wasn't doing this just to get her out of town and keep her safe, he told himself. He was convinced a day away from all this turmoil would be good for her.

She opened the door and invited him inside.

She was wearing skinny jeans and a T-shirt the same blue as her eyes. Ben tried not to stare.

"There's coffee if you'd like, Ben. I'm sure, after a night of work, you'll want caffeine."

"Do you have a travel cup?"

She nodded and filled two cups before picking up a denim jacket and stuffing her cell phone, wallet, and keys into one of the zippered pockets.

Once they settled into Ben's truck, she sat back, sipping her coffee, enjoying the sunny morning.

When her cell phone rang, she studied the caller ID before answering. "'Morning, Dad." She smiled. "I slept well. How about you and Mom?" She listened, then said, "Of course I was serious about paying rent. I want this to be a business deal. My business." She fell silent before saying, "Really? That's perfect. Yes, I can manage that much. Thanks, Dad. I'll start cleaning up that spot first thing tomorrow." Another silence before she said, "I'm afraid not. I'm with Ben Monroe. We're driving out to his place for the day."

Ben could hear her father's voice lifted in protest.

Minutes later she hung up.

Ben lowered the window and leaned an elbow in the breeze.

She looked over. "You're not going to ask, are you?"

"Ask what?"

She gave a quick laugh. "Aren't you the cool one? I approached my father yesterday with a request to lease a little plot of land next to the building. You know. That little fenced area he currently uses as a dump."

Ben nodded. "I know the spot. What will you use it for?"

"I haven't quite figured it out yet. But I'll know when I see just the right thing."

"Sounds mysterious."

Her smile grew. "That's the problem. It's still a mystery to me, too. But in a good way."

He closed a hand over hers. "If you're excited about it, then I'm happy for you."

"Oh, Ben." She glanced at their joined hands. "After all the drama, it feels so good to just leave it all behind and think about spending a day away. I'm so happy you invited me along. Thank you."

"You're welcome. I did it as much for myself as for you. It's been too long, Becca." He kept hold of her hand as he drove the interstate until he came to the gravel road leading to his family ranch.

If this was any indication of the day ahead of them, he'd say it couldn't get much better.

"Whoa." Sam strode into the kitchen, fresh from washing up after mucking stalls.

Behind him, Finn lifted his face and breathed in the wonderful aroma of ham, eggs, and French toast. He looked around with interest. "Is this a holiday and nobody bothered to tell us?"

Otis chuckled. "Ben called to say he's bringing a guest for breakfast."

"A guest?" Sam nudged his brother. "With all this fancy food, let me guess. Is it the queen of England?"

Finn chimed in. "If I get a choice, I choose someone hot. Emma Stone. Carrie Underwood." He folded his hands in a prayerful pose. "Please, God. Let it be."

Zachariah exchanged a look with Roscoe and Otis. "In my day, I'd have probably prayed for Kim Novak. Now, that was one gorgeous woman."

Sam shook his head. "Never heard of her."

"Maybe you should look her up on the Internet to see what you've missed, Samuel."

Mac picked up a mug of coffee and merely grinned at the silly banter.

When Ben's truck drove up, his two brothers watched out the window as their bold, brash brother took Rebecca's hand and helped her from the passenger side.

"What do you know? Rebecca Henderson," Sam muttered before turning to Finn. "You owe me ten, bro."

Otis looked over from the stove. "What was the bet?"

"That big brother Ben would make a move on her as soon as he heard she wasn't engaged to Willy Theisen." He shook his head. "Let's face it. They haven't got a chance for a future. Not with her old man and the way he feels about us. But I swear Ben's been stuck on her since the first time he saw her in town."

Everyone was grinning as Ben and Rebecca stepped into the kitchen.

"Good timing, bro." Sam slapped Ben on the back. "You made it just in time for breakfast, and too late to help with morning chores."

"I timed it that way." Ben handled the introductions. "Rebecca, you know my dad and brothers."

There were smiles and greetings.

"This is the rest of my family. Zachariah York, Roscoe Flute, and"—Ben turned toward the stove—"this morning's cook, Otis Green."

Otis greeted her with a wide smile. "Morning, Miss Rebecca."

When they'd finished their greetings, they gathered around the table.

Ben led her to a seat next to his. "Something smells good."

"A special breakfast for a special guest." Otis began passing thick slices of Texas toast that had been soaked in a milk-and-egg mixture, fried until golden brown, sprinkled with cinnamon, and swimming in maple syrup.

"And we're grateful Otis considers you special." Sam grinned at Rebecca. "We don't usually get a breakfast like this."

"You don't consider my scrambled eggs and bacon special enough?" Otis set the skillet in the sink.

"Yeah. But this..." Sam spread his hands to indicate the meal. "Now this is a feast."

"You keep talking instead of eating," Finn said over a mouthful of French toast, "you'll be eating leftovers."

Everyone looked up at the sound of an engine.

Peering out the window, Finn announced, "It's Mary Pat. And something's smoking under the hood of her van."

Mac was out the door before the others could react. After lifting the hood of her van and waiting for the smoke to drift away, they spoke quietly before he led her inside, where she was introduced to Rebecca.

She hugged the young woman. "Hello, Rebecca. I remember you from school in Haller Creek."

Rebecca nodded. "You were our public health nurse. We always looked forward to having you come to talk to us about...things."

Sam and Finn picked up on her slight hesitation immediately.

"Would that be secret girl things?" Sam grinned at his brother.

Rebecca blushed. "Mostly girl things. And a few other things we couldn't talk to our parents about." She squeezed Mary Pat's hand. "But we knew we could always talk to Miss Healy."

Roscoe indicated the van parked outside. "What was that noise we heard?"

Mary Pat gave a shake of her head. "I haven't a clue. I started out this morning as I always do, and suddenly I heard a clunk, and then the smell of burning rubber. I kept hoping I'd make it here before everything shut down."

"Or burned up." Concern was written on Mac's face. "Did you take time to eat this morning?"

She shook her head. "No time."

Mac took her hand and led her to a seat at the table. "First we'll eat. Then we'll have a look at the car."

Mary Pat let out a sigh. "Oh, this all looks heavenly."

"Exactly what Finn and I were saying." Sam helped himself to ham, eggs, and French toast. "Or should I say praying for?"

"I believe you two were praying for some lovely ladies to grace our home." Zachariah shared a smile with Mac. "Thank heaven for answered prayers."

After the platters had been passed, they joined hands and waited for Mary Pat to lead a prayer.

Ben took Rebecca's hand in his and glanced over to wink.

Her cheeks were beet red as Mary Pat said, "Bless this lovely food and those of us assembled here, as we travel our many roads."

"And," Sam added, "bless that heap of metal parked outside, that it can last another hundred thousand miles or so."

Everyone laughed as they dug into their breakfast.

Mary Pat turned to Rebecca. "I heard about the shooting."

Rebecca stared hard at the table.

"That was days ago," Sam said.

"I'm talking about last night's shooting."

At Mary Pat's words, the others fell silent.

Seeing Rebecca's high color, Ben quickly explained. "There was another shot fired last night. At the Henderson house, just as Rebecca and Will were leaving. No damage done, and the shooter got away under cover of darkness. Since she has the day off work, I suggested Rebecca spend the day here, away from all those wagging tongues in town."

"Good thinking, son." Mac turned to Mary Pat, who artfully steered the conversation toward safer subjects, like her latest journeys.

"I was heading over to visit with Lamar and Lloyd Platt when my engine started acting up. I always try to stop by whenever I'm nearby."

Zachariah nodded. "I know them. Father and son. Lamar must be close to ninety by now."

"Eighty-eight," Mary Pat said. "And his son, Lloyd, is sixty-eight. Never married. Has lived with his father all his life."

"Sounds like us," Sam said with a grin.

Ben gave a mock shudder. "You, maybe. I can't see any female putting up with you—"

"When she could have me instead," Finn put in quickly, adding to their laughter.

The family took their time eating, while catching up on Mary Pat's travels.

Aware of the high color that touched Rebecca's cheeks whenever she found herself the center of attention, Ben carefully avoided any more mention of the mysterious shootings in town.

Even Sam and Finn, who loved to tease, backed off when they saw how protective their brother was.

Roscoe was the first to push away from the table. "Well, let's see if you're going to make that visit today to Lloyd Platt's ranch."

Otis joined him as the two trudged out to inspect Mary Pat's engine.

"I know you're eager to hear the verdict." Mac caught Mary Pat's hand and led her to follow.

When the three brothers began clearing the table, Rebecca started to help.

Ben put a hand on her shoulder. "We can handle this. It's our job. The others cook, and we clean up. We've been doing it since we were kids."

"Then I'll clean with you, since I didn't cook breakfast. Fair's fair."

Zachariah sat sipping his coffee. The mysteries of a car's engine held no fascination for him. The interaction of these four, however, intrigued him. He couldn't wait to see how Rebecca Henderson would fit in with this cast of characters.

Sam, always ready with a wisecrack, started things off by pushing Ben out of the way. "Move it, bro. I know you have a weakness for pretty girls, but you're crowding me."

Ben chuckled. "Careful, Becca. You might not want to get too close to Sam. He just spent the last couple of hours shoveling manure."

She turned to Sam. "I'll bet your father told you it builds character."

"Yeah. That's what all adults tell us when they want to get us to do the really stinky jobs."

She lightly touched his upper arm. "But it definitely builds muscle."

"Hear that?" Sam couldn't help preening and flexing his biceps.

"Don't let it go to your head, bro." Finn pushed Sam aside. "Rebecca, I shoveled manure, too."

"And it shows. You're as buff as your brothers."

With a side glance at the other two, he picked up a dishtowel while pretending to pump iron.

Rebecca filled the sink with hot water and liquid soap and began washing the dishes. "Congratulations, Finn. I heard you passed the bar on your first attempt. I have a friend in Bozeman who had to take it four times before passing."

Sam clapped a hand on his brother's shoulder. "Finn's brilliant. And he had the best teacher in the world."

"Really? Who would that be?" Rebecca paused.

"Zachariah."

Rebecca turned to the old man, seated alone at the table. "So you're Finn's secret weapon."

He gave a slight bow of his head, sending the mane of silver hair dancing at his shoulders.

"Lucky you, Finn." Rebecca held up the coffeepot. "Zachariah, I'm not sure how much is left, but you're welcome to it before we wash it."

"Thank you." The old man held out his cup. "Don't mind if I do."

She topped off his coffee before returning to the sink to wash out the coffeepot.

Ben gathered the damp towels from Sam and Finn and tossed them in a basket before catching Rebecca's hand. "Let's go see what Roscoe and Otis have decided about that old engine."

As they walked out, Sam and Finn followed.

Zachariah drained his cup before trailing slowly behind.

Sam and Finn kept up a running commentary about life on a ranch, the smelly chores they endured, and their need to head to town on a regular basis, in their quest for pretty women. And through it all, though Rebecca's cheeks bloomed with color, she good-naturedly joined in the laughter, and even added a joke or two of her own.

It occurred to Zachariah that this little female was a lot more than she'd first appeared.

He couldn't wait to see how all this would play out. As Finn had pointed out, these two, brash Benedict and Hank Henderson's only daughter, seemed totally unsuited, at least to her father.

Unsuited or not, there was definitely something going on.

For now, Zachariah decided to sit back and enjoy the show.

CHAPTER ELEVEN

So my old van will be out of commission for at least a day?" Mary Pat's expression betrayed her feelings. "I really wanted to see Lamar and Lloyd, but I understand these things take time."

Mac squeezed her hand. "I wish I could take you. But if Roscoe and Otis are going to spend the day tinkering with that engine, I'll be needed up in the hills with the herd."

"I could take you, Mary Pat." Ben nodded toward his truck. "Rebecca and I don't have any real plans. We just thought we'd spend the day away from town. What time would you like to go?"

"Are you sure?" Mary Pat turned to Rebecca.

Rebecca nodded. "I'd love to see some of the countryside. I've been away from Haller Creek too long."

Mary Pat took in a breath. "All right, then. We can go any time it's convenient."

Ben looked from Rebecca to Mary Pat. "How about now?"

The two women shared a smile.

They left the two old men, heads bent close under the hood, removing an array of hoses, caps, and filters.

Mac drew Mary Pat off to one side. "I think you should plan on staying the night. You never know what Otis and Roscoe will find once they start tearing that old engine apart."

She lay a hand on his arm. "All right. Let's see how it goes. And if I'm back from Lamar's in time, maybe I'll bake something special for tonight's dessert."

His handsome face was transformed from concern to joy as a wide smile crinkled the fine lines around his eyes. "Now that'll be worth a day in the hills alone with the cattle."

The day was a perfect Montana autumn day, with a sky filled with puffy clouds, the leaves of the cottonwoods drifting on the slight breeze. The hills were dark with cattle. There wasn't a soul around for miles.

As they followed the path of a narrow dirt trail, Mary Pat carried on an easy conversation with Rebecca.

"Are you happy to be back in Haller Creek, Rebecca?"

"I am. When I first left for college, I swore I'd never come back."

"Why is that?"

Rebecca gave a soft laugh. "I was feeling..." She paused, gathering her thoughts. "I guess I was feeling crowded. I'm an only child. Both my parents tend to push me toward the goals they've set for me, without asking me what I want."

"And what goals are you chasing?"

Rebecca sighed. "I'm not really sure. I just know I want to try some things. Like having my own place. I arranged to rent a small house a few blocks from my parents."

"How is that working out?"

"There are days when I love the freedom. At other times it's lonely." She looked over at the older woman. "I've always admired your independence, Miss Healy. I know you travel all around the county. Are you ever lonely?"

"First, call me Mary Pat. You're out of school now, Rebecca. And the answer is yes. Being lonely comes with the territory. There are days when I question everything about my life. Both my parents are gone now. No husband. No children. And then there are days when I think about the hundreds of children and their families who've touched my life, and I feel lucky to do what I do."

"Are there things you hoped to do but didn't?"

Mary Pat gave her a gentle smile. "I'm sure everyone looks back on their life and sees things they didn't accomplish. But it's important to concentrate on the things that matter."

Ben looked over. "I hope you know how grateful my brothers and I are for you every day, Mary Pat." To Rebecca he added, "Without her help, we might not have become the family we are today."

Mary Pat reached across Rebecca to squeeze his arm. "One of my most cherished accomplishments. You and Sam and Finn are like my own."

Hearing the obvious affection between these two, Rebecca found herself comparing their conversation to ones she'd had with her father. If he weren't so difficult and demanding, she would love to be able to tell him how much he meant to her. Instead, she seemed to spend all her time having to defend herself against all the little jabs he lobbed her way. Jabs he probably wasn't even aware came across as insults.

Mary Pat looked up. "There's the Platt ranch."

The two-story farmhouse sat in a high meadow. Directly

behind it was a barn, its once-red paint now faded and peeling. If it weren't for the cattle off to one side and a rusty truck parked beside the barn, it would appear deserted.

They pulled up behind the truck and stepped out.

Hearing men's voices, they walked into the barn.

Mary Pat cupped her hands to her mouth. "Hello. It's Mary Pat Healy."

"Well now." A gray-haired man in overalls and a plaid shirt stepped out of a back room. "Pa was just saying the other day that we haven't seen you in quite a while." He waved a hand. "Come on back here. We're in Pa's workroom."

Mary Pat led the way, with Ben and Rebecca trailing behind.

They stepped through an open doorway into a big room filled with overhead lights. An old man, dressed like the younger version of himself in overalls and a plaid shirt, his hair white as Montana snow, was busy brushing liquid on a swing made entirely of logs. The room smelled of varnish and turpentine and the wonderful fragrance of freshly hewn logs.

"Mary Pat." The older man set aside his brush and wiped his hands with a rag before hurrying over to give her a warm embrace.

"Lamar. Oh, don't you look good."

"I was just about to say the same. You're a sight for these old eyes."

"Lamar, this is Ben Monroe, Mackenzie Monroe's oldest son, and his friend Rebecca Henderson."

Sharp blackbird eyes studied the young couple as he offered a handshake. "I know your daddy. A good man. Welcome to you, and you, Rebecca." He turned. "This is my son, Lloyd."

The strength in both men's handshakes was impressive. A lifetime of ranching had kept them strong and active.

Mary Pat turned toward the log swing. "I see you're still spending your time staying busy."

Lamar nodded. "Been doing this for so many seasons, it's second nature to me now."

Rebecca looked around at the half dozen swings, as well as the log tables that lined one wall and the log chairs that lined another. All bore the bright shine of clear varnish, allowing the grain of the wood to show through.

"Oh, these are so solid and sturdy." She turned to the men. "Do you mind if I sit on one?"

"Just pick one of those over there." Lamar chuckled. "If you sit on this one I just finished varnishing, you'll be stuck there until next spring."

They joined in the laughter as she crossed to a swing and tentatively sat on it, setting it into motion. Minutes later Ben joined her and the two of them leaned back, enjoying the gentle motion.

Lamar and Mary Pat sat in a second swing, while Lloyd took his time cleaning brushes before setting them aside.

Too restless to sit for long, Rebecca moved around the room, studying the picnic tables, the big, solid chairs, the number of swings. "I can see these in a backyard, or on a big, sunny porch. How much do you sell them for?"

The old man grinned. "I couldn't say."

She looked over. "What do you mean? Don't you sell them?"

He shrugged. "Give 'em to friends who want 'em, mostly. The rest just sit here gathering dust."

"You don't make them to sell?"

He thought about that for a moment, before looking over at his son. "I started making them because we had too much timber on the property. It was a way to thin the woods, and it gave me a way to fill the hours through the long winters."

"Mr. Platt—" she began, but he lifted a hand.

"Just Lamar."

She walked closer. "Lamar, would you let me buy one of each of these? A table, a chair, and a swing?"

He lifted his shoulders. "I wouldn't know what to charge you."

"How about fifty dollars for each?"

He mentally calculated. "You're going to give me a hundred and fifty dollars for a table, a chair, and a swing I made for nothing?"

"The logs may have been free, but it took hours of your labor."

He gave a deep roar of laughter. "I'm more than happy to oblige you. But I swear I'm getting the best of this deal. How're you planning on taking them with you?"

Rebecca turned to Ben. "Will they fit in the back of your truck?"

He nodded. "We can try."

Lamar smiled. "You want Lloyd to give you a hand, Ben?"

"Thanks."

Ben backed the truck into the barn and as close to the doorway of the workroom as he could go. The two men loaded the back of the truck, while Lamar and the women watched.

Afterward, the old man heaved himself from the swing. "Come on inside. I'll make us some coffee and you can sample Lloyd's biscuits."

They sat around a scarred wooden table, in a kitchen that probably looked the same as it had when the house was built by Lamar's father more than a hundred years earlier.

As Rebecca sipped her coffee, she thought father and son could be out of a photo of Montana's early settlers. They wore matching smiles, matching dark, piercing eyes, and a look of complete, utter contentment.

She withdrew a folded blank check from her wallet and made it out for the amount promised. As she handed it to Lamar, she said, "I hope you don't mind a check. I know it isn't convenient having to take it to the bank."

"Don't you worry." The old man accepted it with a look of wonder. "Lloyd and I usually go into Haller Creek once a month or so. I never expected to be putting money in the bank. For my hobby."

Rebecca's voice was filled with a sense of contained excitement. "If I'm right, Lamar, this could be the start of many more checks."

He tucked it away in his shirt pocket and broke open a flaky biscuit. "What do you think of Lloyd's baking?"

Mary Pat helped herself to a second one. "These would certainly win a blue ribbon at the county fair, Lloyd."

Father and son shared a smile.

Mary Pat took a small notebook from her pocket. "I should be heading back this way in about a month. Is there anything you can't buy in Haller Creek that I could bring you?"

Both men spoke in unison.

"I know Lloyd would enjoy—"

"I know Pa would like—"

The two men stopped and grinned.

Lloyd bowed his head to his father. "You first, Pa."

The older man chuckled. "We're probably going to ask for the same thing. I know my son was really fond of those chocolate chip cookies you brought us on your last visit."

Lloyd nodded. "I was about to say the same about you, Pa. You always did have a sweet tooth."

Smiling, Mary Pat made a notation in her book. "I baked them especially for the two of you. And next time I head this way, you can be sure I'll have plenty of them."

Lamar polished off his biscuit and drained his coffee. "We'd be obliged."

"What sweet men." Rebecca turned for a final wave before fastening her seat belt.

"I always look forward to our visits." Mary Pat put on her sunglasses. "Years ago, when I first paid a call, I thought they might be lonely, living way out here, so far from civilization. But through the years I've come to realize they're perfectly suited to this life. They have their land, their cattle, and each other. They continue working the way they did in their younger days, tending the land, the cattle, and in autumn and winter, they stay busy with their hobby. Speaking of which..." She glanced at the rear of Ben's truck, crammed with log furniture. "Did you buy all that for your rental house?"

Rebecca gave a shake of her head. "Actually, seeing them gave me an idea." She looked over at Ben. "I asked my father if I could rent a small plot of fenced property that sits alongside his hardware store. Right now, he's using it to store trash. I'm still not sure whether or not I can make it work, but now I'm thinking I'd like to make it into a little garden area."

Ben muttered, "With winter coming, I'm not sure folks are thinking about garden stuff."

"I agree. But I can see these things on a front porch, or under a big, spreading tree, as comfortable in snow as in summer sunshine. They're sturdy and durable and natural. Not like the stuff that's made of plastic and blows away in a good wind, or made of metal that rusts in the rain and snow.

But there's something even better than all that. They're made locally, by a neighbor. I think that will appeal to folks in Haller Creek."

Ben could hear the thread of excitement in her voice. He turned to study her, aware that she'd just volunteered something deeply personal. "You know what?"

She looked over.

He winked. "I think you're on to something. Most folks like the idea of helping a neighbor. But if they can do it by buying something really well made, practical, and something that will last for years, they're twice as happy." He paused and reached for her hand. "What are you going to call your little garden area?"

She shook her head, looking down at their joined hands. "I don't know. This is all so new. I wasn't even sure what I'd do until I saw Lamar's log furniture. Now I guess I'll just take it a step at a time until something sounds right."

Mary Pat smiled and nodded. "A journey of a thousand miles begins with but a single step."

Her voice trailed off when she realized the two weren't listening to a word she said. She turned to stare out the window to hide her knowing smile.

CHAPTER TWELVE

When Ben pulled up to the ranch a little while later, both Otis and Roscoe were standing by Mary Pat's van. Alongside them in the late afternoon sun was a long worktable holding an assortment of tools and engine parts.

Ben, Rebecca, and Mary Pat hurried over.

Ben peered over the old men's shoulders. "How's it going?"

"Good." Roscoe wiped his hands on a rag before stuffing it in his back pocket. "It's slow going, but when we're through here, this little baby will be purring."

Otis lifted his head long enough to ask Mary Pat, "You mind staying the night?"

Mary Pat shook her head. "When my old van is getting star treatment at the hands of two skilled mechanics, I'm more than happy to stick around until the job is finished. I just wish I could repay the two of you."

Roscoe smiled. "You may want to pay us by lending a

hand in the kitchen. Zachariah knows his beef, but nobody can bake desserts like you."

"Flattery will get you everywhere." She kissed each of their cheeks before heading toward the ranch house.

A short time later Mary Pat walked out carrying a tray of thick roast beef sandwiches and frosty glasses filled with lemonade.

"If you two have been working since we left this morning, you need a break." She passed around the food and drinks.

Ben caught Rebecca's hand and indicated the horses in a nearby corral. "There's plenty of time to ride. Want me to saddle up a couple? We could ride up to the herd in the high country."

Rebecca turned to Mary Pat. "Or I could lend a hand in the kitchen."

The older woman gave a firm shake of her head. "Zachariah and I have it covered. You two enjoy the sunshine while you can."

While Mary Pat stood talking and laughing with Otis and Roscoe, Ben and Rebecca cut two horses from the herd and led them to the barn. A short time later they could be seen riding across a high, grassy meadow.

Their laughter drifted on the breeze.

"Oh, Ben. It's been too long." Rebecca gave her mare her head and they sailed across the field, with Ben's gelding keeping pace.

They rode side by side until they came to a stream. The horses stepped into the water, dipping their heads to drink. When they crossed the stream, Ben slid from the saddle, and Rebecca did the same.

They held the reins lightly as they paused.

Rebecca looked out across the rolling meadows. "Is all this yours?"

A smile touched his mouth, softening all his features. "Yeah."

"I didn't realize how big the ranch is."

"It was once even bigger." He pointed to the lush range-land in the distance. "The southern range was deeded to my father's sister. She left home at sixteen and nobody has seen her since, but the land is still being held in her name and the names of any heirs she may have."

"Sounds very mysterious."

He nodded. "I suppose so. It's just part of the family lore. I know the story, but just barely. It's not something my dad likes to talk about. He'd rather just mind his own business and tend his land."

"It's all so beautiful." She studied the way his gaze moved over the rolling hills. "And you love it."

When he turned to her in surprise, she laughed. "It's writ-ten all over your face." She lifted a hand to his cheek. "You have a very expressive face, Ben."

He caught her hand, holding it against his flesh. "Thanks for that warning. I'll try to hide some of my more...wicked thoughts."

"Wicked? You?" She gave a shake of her head. "You're one of the best men I know, Ben Monroe."

Seeing the way his eyes darkened with feeling, she turned to indicate the lovely rolling hills. "It's so peaceful out here. Living in town, I forget how different it is up here in the hills, away from stores, cars, people."

"When I'm up here, I think how lucky I am to be living in paradise. My life could have been so different."

"Why?"

He seemed surprised. "You don't know? My brothers

and I weren't born here. Thanks to the efforts of Mary Pat and Zachariah, we were able to be adopted by Mackenzie Monroe."

"I knew you and your brothers were adopted. But I never knew any more than that. How did your father find you?"

Ben gave a wry laugh. "We found him."

As they walked through waist-high grass, he told her how he and his brothers, desperate and ready to fight for their freedom, had broken into Mac's house during a blizzard, and the amazing turn of events that had forever changed all their lives.

When he'd finished, she put a hand on his arm. "What a story. You could write a book."

"Not my style." He closed a hand over hers. "Maybe Finn will write it one day. He's the brain of the family."

"And you're so proud of him."

"I'm proud of both my brothers. Don't let Sam's zany sense of humor fool you. He has more fun than anybody I know, but when it comes to ranching, he takes it seriously. In a lot of ways, he's the most like our dad."

"You call Mackenzie Monroe Dad?"

He grinned. "It took me a while. I wasn't sure just what I was getting into. But I knew one thing. I was never going back to the life I had before I met him."

"Was it bad?"

His smile faded. "I'd rather hear you talk about your dream for that little plot of land."

She could feel the sudden darkness that came over him.

Sensing his need to change the subject, she sighed. "I wish I knew more. Right now, I can see Lamar Platt's log furniture luring shoppers in. But I'll need a whole lot more than a swing, a chair, and a table."

"You'll figure it out. But at least you're beginning to see the possibilities."

"Oh, Ben." She squeezed his hand. "I can't wait to get started."

Ben lifted her hand to his lips and was about to draw her close when he heard a voice.

"Hey, you two."

"Hey, Dad." Ben waved before he and Rebecca led their horses toward the horse and rider in the middle of a herd of cattle.

Mac dismounted, whipping off his hat and wiping his brow with the back of his hand. "Did you two enjoy your time with Lamar and Lloyd Platt?"

Rebecca and Ben both nodded.

Rebecca's smile said more than words. "I told Ben and Mary Pat they're two of the sweetest men I've ever met."

"That's them." Mac chuckled. "My Rachel used to send them a huge tin of peanut butter fudge every Christmas Eve. Lamar told her it was always gone by Christmas night."

"He did admit to having a sweet tooth. In fact," Rebecca added with a laugh, "the only thing he asked Mary Pat to bring him on her next visit was her chocolate chip cookies."

"Some things never change." Mac nodded toward the distant barns far below. "Let's head home. I'm sure Zachariah will have supper ready by the time we get there."

Ben held the reins of Rebecca's horse as she pulled herself into the saddle. "Mary Pat is lending a hand. I think I heard Roscoe hinting for pie."

"That man does love pie." Mac turned his mount toward home. "And so do I. As long as it's baked by Mary Pat."

As they rode up to the ranch house, Ben turned to Mac. "I'll rub down your horse, Dad. You go ahead inside and clean up."

"Thanks, son." Mac slid from the saddle.

"I can take yours, too." Ben turned to Rebecca, but her

attention was fixed on a faded garden standing in a small, fenced-in area to one side of the barn.

"Who's the gardener?"

"That's all Otis. He's been fascinated with growing vegetables and fruits and berries for years."

She dismounted and followed Ben to the barn, where they proceeded to rub down their horses before turning them into a corral.

Inside, they washed up at the sink before stepping into the kitchen, where the others had gathered for their daily ritual.

Mary Pat was handing around frosty longnecks. Both Ben and Rebecca took long swallows.

"Nothing better after a long, hot ride," Ben said.

Rebecca nodded, enjoying how casual and comfortable this all felt. "I was just thinking the same." She looked around. "What's that amazing smell?"

"Lemon meringue pie." Roscoe spoke the words almost reverently, causing everyone to burst into laughter.

"It's the least I could do for my mechanic." Mary Pat put a hand on Otis's shoulder. "You realize I still owe you."

"Yes, ma'am." His lips split in a wide grin. "But I'm not sure you know how to make ham and collard greens the way my mama used to."

That had everyone grinning.

"I could probably make it, but I'm sure it wouldn't taste as good as your mama's," Mary Pat said.

"Nobody's could ever taste that good. Probably 'cause it's one of my happiest memories. And real life can never hold a candle to our memories."

"Well, my man, I did my best with roast beef," Zachariah announced.

"I know you did." Otis breathed in the perfumed steam as Zachariah opened the oven door.

Soon, after Mary Pat intoned a blessing, they gathered around the table, feasting on roast beef so tender it melted in the mouth, along with oven-roasted potatoes, the last of the garden tomatoes cut into thick slices, and sourdough rolls.

"More potatoes, Roscoe?"

When Ben offered him the platter, the old man shook his head and patted his middle. "I'm leaving plenty of room for Mary Pat's lemon meringue pie."

And he did, helping himself to a second slice only slightly smaller than the first.

"That," Mac said with a sigh, "was amazing."

"The best ever," Roscoe added.

When the meal was finished, and Sam and Finn stood up to start the dishes, both Ben and Rebecca shoved them away.

"You guys did the barn chores this morning," Ben said.

"That's right." Rebecca put a hand on Finn's arm to steer him back to the table. "All we did was play the whole day. Now it's our turn to do something useful."

Sam circled the table, topping off cups of coffee while Finn helped himself to a beer.

He leaned close to Rebecca. "Careful. I could get used to watching a pretty woman do my work."

Ben gave him a friendly punch to the shoulder. "Find your own pretty woman, bro."

The others laughed as they sat back, feeling relaxed and replete.

Zachariah noted that Rebecca's cheeks weren't nearly as red as they'd been earlier. Could it be she was already getting accustomed to Ben's rowdy brothers?

Rebecca hung a damp kitchen towel on a hook to dry. "We should be getting back."

"Okay." Ben looked around at the empty kitchen. "Where did everyone go?"

"I think they're outside, looking at Mary Pat's van."

"Okay. Let's join them before we say good-bye."

She nodded.

Ben took her hand as they walked out the back door and down the steps.

The entire family was gathered around the van, with Otis and Roscoe explaining what had gone wrong with the engine.

"The main question is," Sam said with a straight face, "will it be good for another hundred thousand miles?"

The two old men shared a laugh. "The truth?" Roscoe chuckled. "This old engine should have been given a funeral years ago. But we've just given it a new life. I think it's safe to say you won't be grounded any time soon, Mary Pat."

"My heroes." She patted the hood. "So, can I leave in the morning?"

"More like noon," Roscoe said. "I'd like to do a full evaluation and take it for a test drive first."

"All right. That sounds fair." Mary Pat turned to Otis. "That will give me time to fix those collard greens just like your mama's."

He pointed to a box. "I was hoping you'd say that. I'm going to see what's left to pick in my garden right now."

Rebecca walked up beside him. "Can I help?"

He gave her a wide smile. "I'd be happy to have your help, Miss Rebecca."

When they circled the barn, she pointed to the field of pumpkins. "Did you plant all these?"

He gave a huff of laughter. "I tossed some seeds, and I swear, every one of those vines produced a dozen or more of those blasted pumpkins."

"You don't like them?"

He shrugged. "What're they good for except pies? We've already baked half a dozen. Even Roscoe is sick and tired of pumpkin pie. And that man does love his pie."

"Could I buy some from you?"

"Buy them? Why would you buy pumpkins?"

"I was thinking they'd look festive in a space I'm planning."

"Miss Rebecca, you can have all the pumpkins you can carry home. I'm more than happy to get rid of them."

"Do you mean it?" She walked over and began to pick up a pumpkin.

"Not that one." Otis stepped up beside her and thumped it with his fist. "Hear that?"

She shrugged. "What am I listening for?"

"A heavy sound. Like it's full of pulp. This one's hollow. No good for pies."

"But probably really good for carving."

"Oh." His smile grew. "Yes, ma'am. I'd say it would be very good for carving, if that's what you're after." He turned. "I'll be right back."

Minutes later he returned.

Ben trailed behind him, hauling a wagon. "Otis says you've found something else to take home."

"I hope you don't mind."

He was grinning. "Otis is happy to get rid of these. They're just food for the deer once the snows come."

In no time, with all three of them working, they'd filled the wagon with dozens of bright orange pumpkins. That didn't even make a dent in the number still left behind in the garden.

Ben started away. "I'll load these in the back of my truck."

"Thanks, Ben." Rebecca turned to help Otis pick greens. As they worked, she said, "You really have a green thumb, Otis. How did you get so good at this?"

He huffed out a breath and sat back, looking up at the sky. "I'm just one of those people who had to learn everything the hard way. Gardening wasn't something I could do, growing up on the streets of Chicago."

"How did you get from a big city like Chicago to a tiny town like Haller Creek, Montana?"

"It was quite a journey. I grew up in the projects, and was still living there years later, with my wife and two little boys."

"You have a wife and sons?"

He went still for a moment. "Had. They were the light of my life. They all died in a fire, and I wanted to die with them. I was a lost soul."

"Oh, Otis." She touched a hand to his arm. "I'm so sorry."

He seemed to go somewhere in his mind. "I couldn't handle the loss. I wandered around for weeks in a daze. Then one night I got so drunk, I decided to sleep in a boxcar parked along the railroad tracks. I woke up in that same boxcar, except that it was somewhere in Iowa." He shook his head, remembering. "I'd never been outside Chicago. But here I was, alone, no money, no place to sleep. I had to survive, so I took a job in a diner, washing dishes, and sleeping in the back room. Then I hitchhiked across Nebraska and..." He shook his head. "I just kept going, working whenever I could. And one day I looked up and all I could see were miles and miles of rolling green hills and more cattle than people. I should have been scared, but in truth it felt like I'd died and gone to heaven. I walked most of the day. Then I walked up to this door and said I'd do whatever they needed done if I could have a meal and sleep in their barn.

And this beautiful lady with a smile that could rival the sun and eyes that danced whenever she smiled took me in, fed me, then introduced me to her husband and said to do whatever he asked. I expected to be gone in a day, but they told me I could sleep in the bunkhouse, and I could work there as long as I wanted. And here I am. Still living and working here all these years later."

"You met Mackenzie Monroe's wife?"

He nodded. "Rachel. And their son, Robbie. Such good people. I don't think they even noticed that my skin wasn't the color of theirs, or that I was a city dude who'd never been up close to a horse or cow before."

She said in awe, "Rachel and Robbie."

"When they were killed in an accident up on the interstate, I knew exactly what Mac was going through, because I'd been there myself."

Rebecca knelt in the dirt beside Otis. "I can't imagine your incredible journey. Especially after the pain of losing your wife and sons."

"I thought at the time I'd never get past it." He shook his head. "Funny, how time has a way of healing even the deepest wounds."

"Would you ever go back to Chicago?"

He looked over at her. "There's nothing there for me. This is my world now. My life. And it's a good one." He looked up at the fading sunset trailing ribbons of pink and gold across the sky. "I do believe there are no accidents in life. It's all part of a grand plan. That boxcar started what you called my incredible journey. And I'm still on it. Riding through a life I never could have dreamed."

Seeing Ben starting toward them, Rebecca put a hand on the old man's sleeve. "Thank you for sharing your story with me, Otis. And thank you for the pumpkins."

When Ben reached her side, she stood. "Enjoy your collard greens tomorrow."

"Oh, you know I will. Good night, Ben. And, Miss Rebecca..."

She paused.

"You're easy to talk to. I've never talked about that part of my life before. I guess it's because you're such a good listener."

When she turned away, Ben took her hand and led her back to the others. After saying good night to everyone, he helped her into his truck.

As he put the truck in gear, he turned to her. "What did Otis talk to you about?"

"About what brought him here to Montana."

As they started away, she turned to wave and felt her eyes fill.

Ben looked over. "Tears?"

"Just dust in my eye." She blinked furiously. "I really like your family, Ben. All of them."

"Yeah." Seeing that she was embarrassed by her tears, he decided not to ask anything more. "They're something, aren't they?"

She nodded, unwilling to trust her voice.

On the long drive home she thought about what Otis had told her.

There were no accidents in life. It was all part of a grand plan.

Everyone, it seemed, had to deal with life in their own way. Now if only she could find the courage needed to deal with hers, and to continue on the course she'd set for herself before coming back to Haller Creek.

CHAPTER THIRTEEN

The lights were on in the houses and shops as Ben drove through the streets of Haller Creek.

When he pulled up to Rebecca's house, he walked her to the door.

She glanced toward his truck. "What about all my things?"

"Since the hardware store is closed now, why don't I unload them tomorrow morning, before I head back to the ranch after work?"

Her eyes widened. "You're working tonight?"

He nodded.

"Oh, Ben. I thought you had the night off. You're not wearing your uniform."

"Virgil ordered new ones for me. He said they'd be coming today and that he'd hang them in the back room."

"But you didn't get any sleep today."

"Don't worry. This isn't the first time I've had to work around the clock. Ranchers don't get the luxury of sleeping if there's a snowstorm, or a flood, or the hundred and one things that can go wrong on a ranch the size of ours. Besides, this day was better than sleep."

"It was the best. Thank you, Ben."

"Good night, Becca." He kept his eyes steady on hers as he lowered his mouth to hers. Just a butterfly brush of lips to lips, tasting, testing. When she didn't resist, he drew her fractionally closer and moved his mouth over hers again, absorbing a rush of heat that had him thinking about devouring her in one quick bite. Instead he cautioned himself to move with care.

He saw the way her lashes fluttered, before her eyes closed. He could feel the way her breath came out in a sigh, filling his mouth with the sweet taste of her.

She reacted to his touch like a deer being offered a carrot. Too hungry to flee, but watching warily with each delicate taste.

And so he fed her.

He brushed soft kisses to her temple, her cheek, the corner of her mouth. Against her lips he murmured, "Remember to lock your door."

He ran his hands across her shoulders, down her back.

"Yes. I...will." Though she stood perfectly still, the little tremors that shot through her were a sign that she wasn't immune to his touches, his kisses.

"I'll see you in the morning."

"All right."

He turned away.

"Ben..."

He turned back.

She looked as surprised by her outburst as he was. "I just...wanted to say..." Her smile bloomed. "I had the best time today. Thank you for...everything."

"My pleasure, ma'am." He pulled her up against his chest and indulged in a hot, hungry kiss before releasing her.

With a delighted grin he strode to his truck and climbed inside.

Still grinning, he waited until the lights went on inside her house before driving away.

Ben printed out his last report and set it on the sheriff's desk. "I didn't realize there would be so much paperwork involved in being your deputy."

"You complaining, Ben?" Virgil chuckled. "Hell, son. At least you don't have to do this in pencil and paper like I once did. Computers cut the time in half."

"If you say so."

"What's all that junk in your truck parked out back?"

"Some things Rebecca Henderson bought. I told her I'd bring them by after work. She's thinking of setting up a little garden area beside the hardware store."

"A garden area? How did she ever talk Hank into that?"

"I'm not sure. I think she caught him in a weak moment after that shooting, when he'd have promised her the moon."

Virgil's smile faded. "I don't like knowing the state boys still have nothing to go on. None of this makes sense. Why would anybody want to shoot at a minister and a sweet young lady like Rebecca?"

Ben shook his head. "I wish I had the answer."

"You heading over there now?"

He nodded.

"Don't forget—you're off tonight and tomorrow night."

"You working?"

"No, but the state police will be. We have an agreement. They cover me certain days of each month. So you and I will both get the next two nights off."

"Thanks, Chief." Ben was already thinking about all the chores he'd been neglecting out at the ranch. "See you on Thursday."

It was a clear, cloudless day. The sun had already burned off the last of the morning mist, and a fresh breeze blowing down from the Bitterroot Mountains carried the hint of cooler weather on the way.

People were out walking their dogs, picking up a coffee and their morning newspaper at Dolly's Diner. Shopkeepers were open for business. A big yellow school bus drove past, filled with laughing children.

When Ben drove up to the side of the hardware store, he was surprised to find Rebecca hard at work, the wooden pallets stacked neatly against the far side of the building, a trash barrel filled to the brim with debris.

She was dressed in work boots, faded denims, and a gray hoodie. Her hair was in a ponytail, her face free of makeup.

Seeing him drive up, she slipped off her work gloves as she hurried over.

When he stepped out of the truck, she put a hand to her throat in a gesture of surprise. "Oh. Don't you look . . ." She gave him a bright smile. "Positively handsome, in a military sort of way."

It took him a moment. "Oh. The uniform."

"This is the first time I've seen you in it. Now your position as deputy feels official."

"I don't want to get too used to it. This is only temporary, until Virgil is fully recovered." He looked around at the freshly raked earth. "You got a lot done already. Did you start at dawn?"

"Just about." She laughed. "I couldn't sleep. I'm so excited about this."

"Tell me where you want the furniture and pumpkins."

She had already marked off various areas with a can of spray paint. "The swing there. The table over there. The chair…"

He lowered the tailgate and hopped up into the back of the truck, moving the furniture to the edge before climbing down.

Rebecca called Eli over to lend a hand, and the two men managed to set the pieces exactly where she'd indicated.

While they hauled the log furniture, Rebecca was busy setting out clusters of pumpkins. She made a display in the center of the table, and another alongside a stack of corn stalks she'd borrowed from her neighbor's garden.

Eli hurried back to the loading dock, while Ben stood to one side, watching as Rebecca fussed over her arrangements.

Finally, satisfied with what she'd done, she joined him. "What do you think?"

"It's certainly colorful. You're going to have a lot of folks in town smiling whenever they walk past."

"That's the idea. And if a few of them stop in and buy, that's even better."

He nodded toward the overflowing trash barrel. "Want me to haul that away?"

"You don't mind?"

"Of course not." He lifted it easily and stored it in the back of his truck, securing it with a bungee cord.

He pointed to the wooden pallets. "How about those?"

She stood a moment, considering. "I think I'll hold on to them for a while."

"They take up a lot of space."

"I know. But there's so much wood there. It seems a shame to just toss them in the trash. I wonder if Lamar and Lloyd could think of some use for them."

He looked at her with new respect. "It's worth asking them."

"For now, I'll just leave them over there and give it some thought."

"Okay." He closed the tailgate. "I wish I could stick around and watch your customers' reactions, but I'd better head home."

"Thank you for all this." She spread her hands to indicate the clever displays. "I hope you get some sleep today."

"I will." He thought about kissing her good-bye, but when he caught sight of her father heading toward them with a frown, he merely waved to her before climbing behind the wheel.

Putting his truck in gear he leaned out the window to say, "Bye, Becca. Good luck with your new venture."

"What was that hell..." Seeing Rebecca's smile fade, Hank Henderson stopped and started over. "What did Monroe want?"

"He was delivering these." She indicated the display.

"Isn't it a little late in the season for outdoor furniture? That stuff could all be covered with snow in a few weeks."

"Snow won't hurt it. In case you haven't noticed, the furniture is made of logs."

"What catalog did you order it from?"

"I bought it from Lamar and Lloyd Platt."

"Those two old reclusive ranchers up in the hills?" Her father walked closer to run a hand over the table, before nudging the swing into motion.

Just then Dolly Pruitt, carrying a sack of groceries for her diner, paused and stepped into the enclosure. "Well, now, what've you done here?"

Hank turned. "Not me. This is all Rebecca's doing." He

gave a snort of derision. "She's hoping to sell outdoor furniture in the snow, I guess."

"You'll notice it doesn't squeak." Rebecca felt the need to play up her purchases. "That's because each piece is made by hand, by Lamar and Lloyd Platt."

"You don't say?" Dolly set her sack on the log table and dropped down onto the swing, using her foot to set it into motion.

"Unlike plastic outdoor furniture, this will never blow over in a high wind. And it'll never rust like those metal swings."

"I was just thinking the same thing." Dolly looked around with a smile. "I can't tell you how many of those cheap things I've bought through the years. But they never last." She continued swinging, while her gaze moved over the table and the big sturdy chair. Finally she stood up. "I wish you had a pair of those chairs. I'd like to put one of them on either side of my front door at the diner."

"I could get a second one later in the week. Lamar has more up at his ranch. That is, if you're really interested."

Dolly nodded. "I may be. How much?"

Rebecca took a deep breath. "How about two hundred for a pair of chairs?"

The older woman didn't even hesitate. "Sold."

Rebecca couldn't help herself. Without thinking she hugged the woman. "Oh, thank you, Dolly. You're my very first customer."

Surprised and more than a little pleased by Rebecca's reaction, Dolly returned the hug. "Well, I guarantee you, honey, I won't be the last."

"Come inside and I'll write up the sale."

Dolly shook her head. "No time. I have to get to the diner. I left Loretta alone, and the breakfast crowd is still there."

She picked up her sack of supplies. "I'll pay you whenever you stop by." She turned away, then suddenly turned back. "Oh, and add a couple of those pumpkins. I like the way they look. They'll add some color at the diner."

Before Rebecca could say a word she hurried on her way.

Hank stood a moment, looking as startled as Rebecca felt, before a slow smile creased his face. "If I hadn't seen this with my own eyes, I'd have never believed it." He shook his head slowly. "You may be on to something."

As he walked back inside the hardware store, Rebecca stood perfectly still before suddenly breaking into a happy dance.

Then she pulled her cell phone from her pocket and dialed Ben's number. She couldn't wait to share her good news.

CHAPTER FOURTEEN

It was barely dawn when Sam and Finn strolled into the barn. Both blinked in surprise to find Ben just finishing up mucking the last stall.

"Two mornings in a row?" Sam grinned at Finn. "Is the world about to end?"

"There must be something cataclysmic about to happen." Finn slapped his oldest brother on the arm. "Okay, bro. What's going on?"

Ben merely grinned at them as he hung his pitchfork on a hook along one wall. "Just trying to make up for all the chores I've been missing since signing on to help out Virgil."

"Yeah. Speaking of which...How's that going?" Sam easily lifted the handles of the honey wagon and hauled the dung and wet straw out the side door of the barn.

Ben waited until he'd returned before bothering to answer. "Some nights it's slow and dull. Other nights it gets... interesting."

"Like the mysterious shooter." Sam sat on a bale of straw. "You ready to commit to signing on for good?"

Ben stripped off his work gloves and tucked them in his back pocket. "That decision will be up to Virgil. I'll let him be the judge if I'm cut out to be a lawman."

"You had lots of practice over the years. Not as a lawman, but we all had our share of dealing with the law." Finn unlatched a bin of oats and scooped some into a trough. "Is Virgil pressing for an answer?"

Ben shook his head. "Not really. There are rumors that he's thinking of retiring, but those have been passed around town for years. I'm not sure he's ready to hang it up yet. He said, 'I'll know when I know.'"

"Huh." Sam was grinning. "Is that supposed to be brilliant? That's like saying you'll know you're in love when you know it. But how the hell could a guy ever know, when there are so many pretty women out there turning his head?"

Ben laughed. "Maybe that's when he knows."

At Sam's quizzical look he added, "When all those pretty women don't matter anymore."

"That's not love, bro. That's when you'll know I'm dead."

The three brothers were still laughing as they made their way to the house for breakfast.

Ben drove through town and parked outside the hardware store, noting idly that the once fenced-in area was bare except for a layer of fresh straw on the ground.

Rebecca stepped out the door carrying her purse and looking as pretty as a flower in her denims and rose-colored corduroy jacket. "Thank you for coming, Ben. I was hoping to borrow one of my dad's trucks, but he said no."

For a minute Ben simply stared, wishing he could scoop

her up and kiss her. Instead he settled for tugging on the collar of her jacket. "What's going on there? What happened to all the stuff?"

"I sold it." Her breathless tone said more than words.

"Everything?"

She nodded and caught his arm. "Come on. Let's load those pallets in the back, and then I'll tell you all about it on the ride up to the Platt ranch."

"No need for you to get dirty. I can load them."

She shook her head. "This is my business. I'm going to help."

Before he could argue she had already crossed the yard to pick up the first of a dozen wooden pallets lying in a pile.

Ben carried three at a time, and in minutes they'd loaded them in the back of his truck and secured them with bungee cords.

He helped her into the passenger side before circling around to climb in the driver's side.

As they pulled away, she turned to him with a radiant smile. "Dolly bought the chair. Actually, she wants a pair of them. And the next day I sold the table and the swing."

"And the pumpkins?"

"The school principal bought all I had on hand to use in each of the classrooms. I have an order for fifty for the town's Autumn Festival. And the mayor said they may need more, depending on how many sign up for the pumpkin-carving contest."

Ben turned to her with a grin. "What did your dad have to say about this?"

She laughed. "He doesn't know what to make of it."

"I'm betting he's proud of you."

"He hasn't said it in so many words, but he's stopped reminding me the weather is all wrong for outdoor furniture and that nobody would buy pumpkins when practically everyone in town has a pumpkin or two growing in their own backyards."

"That's a start." As they turned onto the interstate, he glanced over. "Are we heading to the Platt ranch?"

"Yes, please. And then, if you don't mind, I'd like to go to your place and see Otis about some pumpkins."

He sent her a grin that had her blushing. "My day is yours."

"I'm sure you're neglecting a lot of chores."

"The chores will be there tomorrow, and the next day, and the next. But spending time with you..." He shot her a dangerous smile. "Becca, I can't think of anything I'd rather do."

And, he thought, getting her as far away from town as possible was just frosting on the cake. A day spent in the glow of Becca's smile, while keeping her safe, meant the world to him.

They found Lamar and Lloyd in their workroom in the barn. The two men looked up with matching smiles.

Lamar set aside his brush and wiped his hands on a rag before walking over. "Two visits in a week. What's the world coming to?"

"If my first sale is any indication, the world will soon be coming to your doorstep." Rebecca removed an envelope from her pocket and handed it to him.

He tore it open and merely stared at the money inside. "What's all this?"

"The profit from the sale of your table, chair, and swing."

"You already paid me." He counted out the bills. "There's three hundred dollars here."

Rebecca nodded. "Dolly Pruitt was my first customer, and I wasn't sure just how much to charge her when she asked for two of your chairs. So I asked for two hundred dollars, and she didn't seem to think that was too much."

Lamar turned to his son. "Imagine that. Two hundred dollars for two of our chairs."

"Actually, I went online, and found similar furniture that's mass-produced selling for hundreds more. So I'm thinking of setting the prices a bit higher from now on."

"From now on? Are you thinking you can sell more?"

Her smile widened. "I already have several orders. Dolly paid me for a second chair, and Phil and Kathy Ritter want a swing for the front of their hair salon. Three families have requested your table for their backyards."

The old man sank down on the edge of a tool bench. "Who would have believed it?"

Rebecca sat beside him. "I wasn't certain other people would love your furniture the way I do. But now, I'm convinced I can sell all you have here."

When Lloyd finished wiping his hands, he walked over to join them. Noting the round cookie tin in her hand, his eyes widened. "Is that what I hope it is?"

"Oh." She looked down. "I almost forgot. They're chocolate chip cookies."

"You baked them?" The two old men shared a look.

"No. Sorry. I'm not very good in the kitchen. I asked my mom to bake some. I think you'll like them."

Lamar got to his feet. "Let's go inside. Lloyd will make coffee, and we'll give them a taste test."

The four trudged up to the house. A short time later they were seated around the kitchen table, sipping strong hot coffee and nibbling Susan Henderson's chocolate chip cookies.

"Mmm-hmm." Lamar kept smiling and nodding as he ate one, then a second, and finally a third. "Now these are the real McCoy. Homemade and perfect. You be sure to thank your mama for us."

"I will."

Lloyd peered out the window at Ben's truck. "What's that in the back?"

"Wooden pallets," Ben said. He turned to Rebecca to explain.

"My father gets a lot of these, loaded with items for his hardware. He's been tossing them in the little fenced area I'm now using for my garden center. I thought, instead of throwing them away, I'd see if they were something you could use."

"Well now." Lamar stood. "Let's have a look."

Once outside, Ben backed his truck to the barn before hauling one of the pallets from the back of his truck.

The two men carried it to the workroom and began turning it this way and that.

Finally Lamar looked over at Rebecca. "You thinking of making something out of this to sell in your garden area?"

"If you think it's worth selling."

Lamar ran a hand over it. "This is nice, rough, unfinished wood. It's better suited to outdoors than indoors. How about turning them into shelving? You think there's a call for that?"

Rebecca was already smiling. "Oh, yes. Shelving for a garage, a potting shed, or to hold tools for a backyard barbecue. You would have to make them a bit stronger, and add some more shelves."

"Easy enough," the old man said with a grin.

"Would you paint them, or leave them natural?"

Lamar turned to his son before asking, "Why not a little

of both? We'll leave some as they are, and paint or stain a few others. The next time you come, you can let us know which ones you prefer."

"Do you want all of them?"

He nodded, and while Ben and Lloyd removed the pallets from the back of the truck, Lamar showed them where he wanted them stored in the workroom.

While the men were busy with the pallets, Rebecca moved slowly around the room, counting the number of chairs, tables, and swings.

"All right," Ben called. "The back of the truck is ready for new stock."

While Rebecca and Lamar pointed out the furniture to be hauled, Ben and Lloyd carefully loaded as much as they could.

When all was in readiness, Ben opened the passenger door.

Rebecca was about to climb inside when she suddenly turned and flew across the barn to hug Lamar, and then his son. "Thank you for giving me the inspiration for my new business."

Though they both looked surprised, slow smiles spread across their faces.

"I think we should be thanking you, Rebecca," Lamar said. "It never occurred to us that our simple hobby could bring us money."

"I hope you get to see five times that amount in the weeks to come." She accepted Ben's hand and climbed up to the passenger seat.

As they rolled along the driveway, she turned and waved to the two men, who returned her wave.

When she finally sat back, Ben caught her hand in his. "You realize you've made those two very happy."

"Not nearly as happy as they've made me. Oh, Ben." She looped her arm through his. "It's my very first solo venture."

"And just look at you." When she tilted her face to him, he winked. "In case you haven't noticed, little bird, you're flying."

CHAPTER FIFTEEN

Look." As they pulled up to the ranch, Ben pointed to two horsemen moving across a high meadow.

At Rebecca's arched brow, he said, "Otis and Roscoe."

"How can you tell from this distance?"

He grinned. "I recognize that orange bandana Roscoe always wears around his neck. We keep threatening to buy him a new one, but he swears it's his good-luck charm."

"Why?"

Ben shrugged. "According to him, he was wearing it the day he first arrived, out of money, out of a job, and out of luck. And then Dad's wife, Rachel, asked him to stay on and keep all the equipment in good repair in exchange for free room and board."

Rebecca smiled. "I can see why he'd hate to part with his good-luck charm."

They stepped from the truck and walked inside to find Zachariah busy at the sink.

"You pull kitchen duty again?" Ben crossed the room to peer over the older man's shoulder.

"No choice. Everyone else is busy." Spying Rebecca, he called out a greeting. "How is your new business venture going?"

"I sold out."

"That sounds promising."

She managed a laugh. "Well, I didn't begin with much. Just a few pieces of furniture and some pumpkins. But I'm here to restock."

"I'd say that's reason to celebrate. Congratulations."

"Thank you." She nodded toward the hunk of meat marinating in a plastic bag. "Do you need help?"

"Can you cook?"

She flushed. "Not really. But I'm willing to slice, dice, or chop if you need a pair of hands."

"I may take you up on that. For now, we'll let that beef soak up my spicy marinade. Or maybe I should say Mary Pat's recipe for marinade. Last time she made it, I asked her to write it down."

"It smells wonderful."

"And tastes even better. At least I hope mine will come close to tasting as good as hers." He motioned toward the living room. "Finn's in there, preparing for his first court case."

"Court? Really?" Ben led the way to the other room, where Finn had every inch of Mac's desk covered with legal tomes as thick as dictionaries. Finn scribbled in a notebook before looking up.

"Hey, bro." Ben looked around with a grin. "Looks like someone's doing his homework."

"Yeah. I figured I'd be done with all this once I passed the bar. Now I realize the real bookwork is just beginning."

"Lucky for you, you've got your own private tutor in the kitchen."

"And I intend to put him to good use." He turned to Rebecca. "How's your new business going?"

"So far, folks in town seem interested."

"Good for you. So why are you taking the day off?"

"So I can stock up on supplies. I sold what I had and I'm back for more."

"Speaking of which..." Ben pointed. "Roscoe and Otis are out in the barn."

As the two started away, Rebecca turned. "I hope we didn't disturb you, Finn."

"If all my distractions were as pretty as you, you'd never hear me complain."

Ben turned. "Very smooth, bro."

Finn shot him a wicked grin. "Hey, I do my best."

As they started out the door, Rebecca was laughing. "He's sweet."

"You mean all that cheap, overrated flattery works?" Ben caught her hand and gave her a steady look that had her blushing. "I'll have to remember to give it a try."

"You don't need to try, Ben." Her cheeks grew bright red. "When you look at me like this, I feel special."

He brushed a quick kiss over her lips. Against her mouth he whispered, "You are special. Don't you forget it."

With a warm glow they strolled into the barn, where Roscoe and Otis were busy unsaddling their horses before turning them into a corral.

The two men looked up with matching smiles as they whipped off their wide-brimmed hats in a courtly gesture.

"Miss Rebecca." Otis tossed his saddle over the railing of a stall. "How're those pumpkins working out for you?"

"I sold them all." She reached into her pocket and handed him an envelope.

"What's this?"

"Open it."

He did, and stared at the money inside. "Where did this come from?"

"The sale of all those pumpkins."

"This is yours." He tried to hand it back, and Rebecca jerked her hand away.

"Otis, we both made a profit. This is your share."

"And there's more where that came from," Ben said. "Becca's here to pick more pumpkins."

"You want more? How many more? They're all yours for the asking."

"I'll take as many as Ben's truck will hold. The town is planning its annual Autumn Festival, and the mayor wants a pumpkin-carving contest for the kids, and another for the teens. He said he'll buy all we can supply."

Otis turned to grin at Roscoe. "Do you believe this?"

Roscoe was chuckling as they headed toward the garden. "I know one thing. Next time we head to the Hitching Post, you're buying."

Ben's truck was brimming with pumpkins. The overflow had been put in crates and stashed in the backseat.

They looked up at the sound of a tractor's engine as Mac drove toward the barn.

He climbed down and pressed a hand to the small of his back.

That had Ben frowning. "I knew he was taking on too many chores. And all because I accepted Virgil's request to be his deputy."

"Now don't go blaming yourself, son." Otis put a hand on Ben's shoulder. "Ranching is an equal-opportunity employer. Even the youngest and healthiest among us suffer aches and pains at the end of a long day of ranch chores."

"But I could ease his burden."

"This ranch and its chores aren't a burden to your pa. It's the love of his life," Roscoe said softly as Mac made his way toward where the others were standing.

Mac looked at the loaded truck. "What's all this?"

Ben couldn't stop the proud smile that spread across his face. "Becca's garden business is really taking off."

"You don't say? You mean people want those?" Mac turned to smile at Otis. "I guess this resolves your pumpkin problem. Now you don't have to haul them all the way to the pasture and scatter them to the four winds just to get rid of them."

"Not only that, but Rebecca paid me." The old man held up the envelope of money.

"And there's more coming." Rebecca told Mac about the Autumn Festival and the pumpkin-carving contests.

"This calls for a celebration. I hope Zachariah has something special for supper."

Ben nodded. "It's special if you like Mary Pat's spicy marinade."

Mac's smile grew. "You just said the magic words, son. Let's start with some frosty longnecks."

They were all in high spirits as Mac led the way toward the house.

The kitchen was filled with the most amazing fragrance as they all gathered around the table, tipping beer, catching up on the day.

Under Zachariah's direction Rebecca filled a big bowl with greens from the garden, adding little green onions, tomatoes, and some sliced peppers for color and flavor.

Ben lifted a pan of biscuits from the oven, while Zachariah mashed potatoes and stirred gravy atop the stove.

When everything was ready, they took their places.

Mac surprised them by saying, "In honor of Mary Pat and her marinade, I think somebody should offer a blessing."

They joined hands and Otis said, "Bless those of us here, and those we wish were here. And," he added with a grin, "bless those crazy folks in town who are willing to pay for pumpkins."

With a laugh they began passing platters.

Ben held a big plate of roast beef while Rebecca helped herself. She, in turn, held it while he did the same. They looked at one another with matching smiles that weren't lost on the others around the table.

When they thought no one would notice, they joined hands under the table, casting sidelong glances and smiling. Always smiling at the lightness around their hearts.

After tasting the beef, Sam looked up. "Who's going to give Mary Pat the sad news?"

Mac's head came up sharply. "What sad news?"

"That she's been replaced by Zachariah."

Everyone grinned.

Mac shot a glance at the old man across the table. "I'll admit you did a fine job duplicating her spicy recipe. But somehow I don't see you replacing her completely."

"Nor would I even attempt such a thing." Zachariah used his best orator's voice. "Some people are irreplaceable. That woman is one of them."

"I agree." Finn shot a sideways look at his dad. "Nobody gives hugs like Mary Pat."

"Now that's the truth." Mac chuckled.

"I don't know." Ben stared pointedly at Rebecca. "I saw two old guys up at the Platt ranch enjoying bear hugs from a certain new businesswoman."

"I haven't had much experience. My family doesn't hug."

Rebecca's face flamed as Ben related to the others her un-characteristic behavior.

Zachariah studied her with a knowing look. "It would seem after just a day in our company, we're beginning to rub off on you."

Before she could say a word, Sam had them all laughing by catching her hand in his. "Any time you feel the need to practice those hugs, I'm more than happy to be your guinea pig."

She burst into laughter along with the others. "Why, Sam, how noble of you."

He gave a slight bow of his head. "Anything for a pretty lady."

Later, when the meal was ending, Rebecca clapped a hand to her mouth. "Oh. I almost forgot." She turned to Ben. "I need to get something from your truck."

She excused herself and hurried out the back door. Minutes later she returned carrying a cookie tin.

"I asked my mother to bake chocolate chip cookies for Lamar and Lloyd, and she made enough for all of you, too."

"Homemade cookies?" Roscoe and Otis shared matching grins as she slid the cookies onto a plate.

Minutes later, as the plate was passed around, the men tasted, murmured words of approval, and gave a thumbs-up.

"Rebecca," Finn said around a mouthful, "any time your mother feels the urge to play in the kitchen, we'll be more than happy to take whatever she bakes. Especially if she's baking chocolate chip cookies."

"I'll be sure to let her know."

They spent another pleasurable hour around the table, relating the news of the day and drinking endless cups of coffee.

Finn was the first to stand. "Sorry to leave you, but I have hours of preparation ahead of tomorrow's trial." He nodded a head to Zachariah. "My compliments to the chef."

The old man was grinning. "Now I'm a chef. An hour from now I'll turn into a retired lawyer who is expected to dredge up every vestige of memory about similar trials and how they were won."

"And both sides of you"—Finn looked around at the others—"chef and lawyer, are proving to be essential to my survival."

When he sauntered back to the living room, the others pushed away from the table.

Ben and Rebecca insisted on doing the cleanup, leaving the others to spend their evening as they pleased. Zachariah retired to his room, vowing to find any papers pertinent to Finn's coming trial. Otis and Roscoe, still arguing about the latest gin rummy score, headed toward the bunkhouse. Sam and Mac ambled away.

A short time later Ben and Rebecca called good night to Finn and Zachariah before making their way out the back door.

Sam and Mac were sitting on the porch steps, their backs to the railing, sipping frosty longnecks.

Mac pointed with his bottle. "Your truck's really loaded."

Ben grinned. "If Becca sells all this, next time we may have to haul along a trailer."

Rebecca put a hand to her heart. "Oh, wouldn't that be sweet success?" She called good night to Sam and Mac before following Ben to his truck.

He put a hand beneath her elbow and helped her inside before circling around to the driver's side.

As they pulled away, they both waved.

Rebecca turned to Ben. "Your family is such fun to be around. You're all so relaxed and easy."

His gaze narrowed on the road ahead. "When my brothers and I first came here, I didn't believe what I was seeing. The goodness. The decency. The shared chores. The easy camaraderie. I kept waiting for that awful other shoe to drop."

"Why?"

He looked over. "You've heard your father. He's just expressing what most people thought about us when we first came to Haller Creek. My brothers and I were considered delinquents. Incorrigible. Headed straight for jail."

"And now you're a lawman. Why were you and your brothers so rough at such a young age?"

"Survival." He surprised her by shifting topics. "Will we unload all this tonight?"

Understanding his need to avoid talking about something so painful, she simply nodded. "If we catch Eli at the store before he leaves for the night, I'd like to ask him to help us get everything set up before morning."

He gave her a knowing smile. "So you can surprise your father?"

"There's that." She laughed. "And also so everyone who passed by my empty yard all day will have to pause and see what's been added as they pass by on their way to work in the morning."

He joined in the laughter. "I hope your father realizes what an astute businesswoman his daughter has become."

CHAPTER SIXTEEN

As Ben parked his now-empty truck in front of Rebecca's house, she gave a sigh. "Thank heaven we caught Eli before he left for the night."

Ben nodded. "I couldn't have done it without him." He stepped out of his truck and circled around to help her down.

She looped her arm through his as they walked to her front door. "And I couldn't have done any of this without you, Ben." She unlocked the door before turning to him. "Thank you for another amazing day."

"What's amazing is how you managed to turn a yard filled with furniture and pumpkins into such an inviting display. It's going to turn heads in town, Becca."

"Do you know, you're the only one who has ever called me that?"

"Called you amazing?"

"No. Becca. I love it when you call me Becca." Her tone softened. "My parents never believed in nicknames."

"That's easy enough to understand. I'm sure when they named you, it was because they loved the name Rebecca, and didn't want to see it changed in any way."

"I was named for my grandmother. She was a very formal lady." She gave a soft laugh. "I guess that explains why my father is the way he is. He's like his mother. But when you call me Becca, it feels special." She put a hand on his arm. "Why don't you come in, Ben?"

Though he was surprised by the invitation in her eyes and in her voice, he needed no coaxing. He was more than ready to accept.

He stepped inside and pulled the door shut behind him. Except for the porch light, the room was in darkness.

Her voice was hushed as she looked up at him. "I could make some coffee."

"Don't bother. I'd rather…" He leaned close and brushed a soft, tentative kiss over her mouth, as though testing her reaction. When she didn't back away, he put a big arm around her waist, drawing her even closer. "This is all I want, Becca."

He whispered soft kisses over her face. "I've been thinking about this all day."

His words had her wrapping herself around him as his lips covered hers in a hot, hungry kiss. "Oh, Ben." She sighed and lifted her arms to encircle his neck. "And I've been thinking…"

The sound of his cell phone shattered the stillness.

"Who…?" She started to pull away, but he drew her closer. "It doesn't matter. I just want…"

The ringing continued. And though he struggled to ignore it, the mood had already shifted.

He swore under his breath as he plucked the phone from his shirt pocket and studied the caller ID.

He took a step back as he answered it. "Yes, Jeanette." He paused. "The sheriff…?" He listened, then said, "I'll be right there."

He touched a big palm to Rebecca's cheek. "I'm sorry. An emergency. I'm not on duty, but Virgil needs me. I have to go."

She gave a reluctant nod. "I understand."

"I could come back later…"

She was already shaking her head. "It's late. I have to be at the store early. We both need our sleep."

His grin was quick and dangerous. The words tumbled out before he could stop them. "I could always sleep here. It's a lot closer than the ranch."

"Nice try, Ben." She softened her words with a smile.

"Can't blame a guy for trying." He turned away and opened the door. "Good luck tomorrow."

"Thanks." She put a hand on the door. "Good night, Ben. And, Ben?"

He paused.

"Thanks for today. It was really special to me."

"Yeah. Me too. Night, Becca."

He was whistling as he made his way to his truck and drove away.

Mac ambled in from the barn and washed up at the big sink before stepping into the kitchen. Spotting Ben standing with the others, his smile grew. "It's good to see you, son. You've been putting in some long hours. Does this have anything to do with Virgil's leg?"

"It's not healing properly." Ben set aside his longneck. "Dr. Huddleston ordered him to do physical therapy three times a week for the next month. When Virgil said he couldn't take the time from work, Doc warned him he'd be taking early retirement if he didn't follow orders. So it looks like I'll be doing double-duty until his doctor is satisfied with the results."

Mac slapped Ben's arm. "It's a good thing he has you."

"I guess that's so." Ben frowned. "But it also means that you and the others have to pick up the slack here on the ranch."

"Don't get on a guilt trip, boy." Zachariah stood at the stove, carving up a slab of ribs into manageable portions before setting them on a platter. "You knew there'd be some rough patches along the way."

Otis grinned. "Sort of like life."

That had them all relaxing and grinning.

As they gathered around the table, Ben turned to his youngest brother. "I've been too busy to ask how that trial's going."

"Long and slow." Finn shot a look at Zachariah across the table. "My mentor here says that's good news. It means the jury is paying attention. All I know is, I'm trying not to let them see me sweat."

Sam poked an elbow in Finn's ribs. "I think you're loving every minute of it, bro."

"The truth?" Finn's smile came slowly. "Every day it gets easier. And every day I find myself thinking this is the best part of being a lawyer. I love listening to that hotshot attorney for the state spouting off about his theory that my client pulled off the crime of the century, while dodging the facts. I can hardly wait for the summation."

Zachariah sat back with a look of supreme pride. "And that, gentlemen, is the mark of a true litigator. It's not just about winning freedom for your client. It's that cat-and-mouse game of drawing the opposition into a box of his own making, from which he cannot escape."

Sam turned to Ben. "Don't you just love it when they start talking all that formal lawyerese?"

"Yeah." Ben joined in the teasing. "All those fancy words, but in the end, it's what we've been doing for a lifetime." He shot a grin at his brothers. "Instead of fists, our lawyer here uses big words to beat up his opponent."

"Forget court." Sam shook his head. "Give me a good knock-down, drag-out fistfight any time."

The others rolled their eyes and groaned as they continued their lighthearted banter over dinner.

Hank Henderson reluctantly handed Rebecca the keys to the hardware store's fancy new truck with the hydraulic lift on the back. "I'm surprised and pleased that you keep selling out as fast as you stock up. But I don't understand why you can't ask Lamar and Lloyd Platt to deliver their own furniture."

"Because," she said patiently, for at least the fourth time, "Lamar is nearly ninety, and his son is years older than you, Dad. If I asked them, I know they would make the attempt. But it just isn't right. Their only truck looks as old as they are."

As she climbed into the cab of the truck, her father pointed to the two men walking toward him.

"I asked Eli and our new stock boy, Rodney, to go along and do the heavy lifting."

The two climbed into the truck and fastened their seat belts.

Her smile bloomed. "That's sweet, Dad. Thanks."

"I'm not doing it to be nice. You've never driven a rig this size before. I just want to make sure you've got some muscles with you, in case of trouble with my pricey equipment."

"I should have known. Some things never change." Her smile faded. "We'll be back before closing."

"See that you are. I'm not going home until you get this truck safely back to the store."

As she pulled away, Hank stood watching with a look of concern.

When Rebecca had first asked about using the truck, he'd been determined to refuse. But then he considered the alternative. On both earlier excursions into the hills, she'd enjoyed the company of that hell-raiser. If giving her the use of the truck meant eliminating Ben Monroe, he figured it was worth it.

To his way of thinking, the new deputy was good for one thing only: keeping Rebecca safe until this mysterious gunman was arrested.

As for her future, as long as Will Theisen was still in town, there was hope.

"Oh, just look at these." Rebecca clapped her hands together when she had her first look at the once-rickety pallets, now made sturdy with log reinforcements and transformed into colorful shelving.

Some were natural, others had been painted brown, black, or white, and all would be perfect in a potting shed or in a backyard. And then there was the neon yellow pallet that would look perfect in a garage or on a back patio, holding children's outdoor toys.

She turned to the two old men, beaming their pleasure at her reaction. "These are amazing. I thought you'd be able to do something with them, but I never dreamed they could look this good."

Lamar Platt put a hand on his son's shoulder. "You can thank Lloyd for that bright one. He thought he'd give it a try, but I wasn't so sure you'd like it."

"I don't just like it. I love it. I love all of them. And

I really believe my customers will love them, too." She
turned to Eli and Rodney. "You can go ahead and start
loading up."

Lamar stood beside Rebecca while Lloyd pointed out to
Rebecca's assistants which pieces of furniture to load.

While they worked, Rebecca handed the old man a tin
of cookies and an envelope. The first thing he opened
was the cookie tin, helping himself to one of Susan's
homemade chocolate chip cookies. He gave a purr of
pleasure before opening the envelope and counting out
the money.

He shot her a look of astonishment. "Didn't you take any
for yourself?"

"I did. This is for you and Lloyd. Your share of the prof-
its." She looked at the bare walls of his workroom. "Maybe
it's a good thing winter is around the corner. From the look
of things, we're just about to clean you out."

He gave a slow shake of his head. "If anybody had
told me, just a month ago, I'd be making money off
my hobby, I'd have said they were crazy as a loon." He
watched as Eli and Rodney loaded yet another swing
onto the hydraulic lift. His gaze swept the nearly empty
workroom. "I haven't seen the walls of this side of the
barn in years."

"Think you'll have it filled up by spring?"

He shrugged before tucking the money carefully in a
pocket of his overalls. "Looks like Lloyd and I won't have
time to just sit around and watch the snow fall." His smile
came easily. "And that's a good thing. I don't like idle time
on my hands."

"Neither do I." Rebecca watched as Eli closed and locked
the back of the truck. "Now it's time for me to get to work
selling all this."

Again she hugged both Lamar and Lloyd before pulling herself up to the driver's side and starting the engine.

With a wave of her hand she was gone.

Eli peered out the truck window. "This isn't the way to town."

"I know." Rebecca had been smiling for the past half hour, lost in thought.

She'd been seeing in her mind Ben's father and brother, Sam, sitting on the steps of their back porch, casually sipping their beer and talking in low tones about their day.

The porch ran the width of the Monroe ranch house and was, like so many working ranches, devoid of anything except a few utilitarian things. A rough wooden bench that held a bucket or two. An antique milk jug. Sacks and pots holding a multitude of necessary items.

Her smile grew as she turned onto the long gravel drive leading to the Monroe ranch. There were no trucks parked alongside the house or barn, which meant that the men of the house were already up in the hills or busy with chores.

She drove directly to the porch before stopping. After knocking on the back door and hearing no answering call, she returned to the truck.

Eli lowered the window. "What're we doing here?"

"Delivering some much-needed merchandise." She beckoned both the men to follow her.

After unlocking the back of the truck, she climbed up inside and said, "We'll need this, and that, and those."

Half an hour later, under Rebecca's direction, the back porch had been transformed with the help of a log swing, four log chairs, a pallet shelf in natural, and in the yard, beneath a giant ponderosa pine, one of the biggest log tables Lamar and Lloyd had made.

Satisfied, she gave a nod. "Okay. We're done here. Let's head to town."

On the long drive back, Rebecca could hardly contain her excitement. What she wouldn't give to see the expressions on Ben's family's faces when they returned home and found her gifts. Especially when they found the little note she'd tucked on the center shelf, anchored beneath a tin of her mother's cookies.

CHAPTER SEVENTEEN

Took you long enough." Hank Henderson was pacing outside his hardware store.

As Rebecca stepped down from the truck, he extended his hand for the keys. "I was getting ready to phone the sheriff to ask if there were any accidents on the interstate."

"Dad, we all have phones. If there'd been any trouble, one of us would have called you." She turned to thank Eli and Rodney for their help. "We'll unload in the morning."

Relieved that they didn't have to stay, the two employees waved good night and began heading home.

Hank pocketed the keys and took her arm. "Come on. It's getting dark. I'll walk with you."

"Okay." Feeling mellow, Rebecca moved along beside him, looking up at the moon, just beginning to peek through the clouds. "I love this time of year."

Hank nodded. "You always did."

"Maybe it's the brisk air. And the color all across the

hills. The end-of-summer rodeos, and the feeling of endings and beginnings." She turned to her father. "Do you feel it, too?"

"All I feel is…annoyed."

She turned her head to look at him. "Are you annoyed at me?"

He shrugged, clearly uncomfortable talking about his feelings. "I'm not sure. Maybe it's my age. I probably felt the way you do, but that was when I was young and foolish."

"Somehow it's hard for me to see you as young or foolish."

"And just how do you see me?"

Now it was her turn to feel uncomfortable. "For as long as I can remember, you were always all business and no time for fun."

"Fun is overrated. Your mother keeps talking about what we could be doing if we weren't tied to the hardware store. She doesn't understand that I can't think of anything I'd rather be doing than working."

"What would Mom do if you took some time off?"

Another shrug. "I think she has her sights set on a cruise."

"Where to?"

"Knowing your mother, it'll be someplace warm. Hawaii. The Bahamas."

"What about you, Dad? If you didn't have the business to run, what would you like to do?"

He gave a snort of disgust. "I thought I just told you. I like working. I like being the boss. I don't have time for foolishness. I'm a husband and father. Like my mother always said, once you marry, you put foolish dreams aside and take responsibility like a man."

"Dad, you've always been responsible. But you and Mom deserve to follow your dreams."

"Now you're beginning to sound like Susan. I don't have big, fancy dreams. I just want to do what I've always—" His words abruptly ended as a figure loomed up in the darkness.

"Will." Rebecca was the first to recognize him. "You startled us."

"Sorry. I was just leaving Reverend Grayson's, and thought the voices I heard were yours."

Hank took in a deep, relieved breath. "You in a hurry, Will?"

"Not at all, sir. If you don't mind, I'll just walk along with the two of you."

Hank glanced at the porch lights just coming on. "We're at my street. As long as Rebecca isn't alone, I'll head on home, knowing she's in good hands." He pressed a kiss to his daughter's cheek.

"Very smooth, Dad." Though her voice was barely a whisper, she didn't bother to hide the sarcasm.

"I thought so." He turned away, calling over his shoulder, "Good night, Will. Take care of my girl."

"I will. Good night, sir."

Will and Rebecca continued along the sidewalk.

At first they walked in silence, hands tucked in pockets, listening to the sound of back doors slamming and children's voices raised in laughter. Nearby, a dog barked and continued barking until a door was opened and the dog's owner shouted a command. Minutes later the door closed, and the dog's barking, now muted, continued indoors.

"How was your visit with Reverend Grayson?"

Will turned to her. "It was good. I've asked him to counsel me about how to choose my ministry going forward."

"I thought you'd already chosen a ministry. Are you asking him about specific churches in certain locations?"

"Not really. I'm determined to be somewhere warm." He

drew his jacket up around his neck as a stiff breeze ruffled his hair.

"Well, that narrows your search. What about the church in Atlanta where you did your internship?"

Will ducked his head. "I don't know if that position is still available."

"Really?" Rebecca looked over. "Have you asked them?"

"I…haven't been in contact with them since I came home."

"Oh, Will." She touched a hand to his sleeve. "It isn't like you to back away from commitment. Call the pastor there and see if the position is still open."

"It isn't that simple."

"Well, it should be. If they don't yet have a new pastor, and they approve your credentials, what would stop them from inviting you to at least give them a try?"

"There could be dozens of newly ordained ministers hoping for the job."

"But they aren't you." As they climbed the steps to her porch, she pulled the house key from her pocket before turning to him. "Will, I've never known you to be shy about your talents. You could outshine a hundred opponents, if you wanted to."

He was smiling and shaking his head. "Rebecca, I wish I had your—"

The silence of the evening was shattered by the now-familiar sound of a gunshot. It rang through the air as a bullet whistled past their heads and embedded itself in the wood molding above the door. Though her first instinct was to freeze, Rebecca grabbed Will's sleeve, nearly dragging him with her as she leapt off the porch and fled to the rear of the house. Once there she unlocked the back door, pulling Will inside before retrieving her phone. Her hands shook as she frantically dialed 911.

Jeanette Moak's voice was as calm as if she were discussing the weather. "Stay inside and wait for law enforcement, Rebecca."

"Thank you. Tell them to please hurry." Rebecca's voice was a sob catching in her throat.

When the police van arrived, both Virgil Kerr and his deputy stepped out. Ben sprinted up the steps while the sheriff limped along more slowly.

The front door was opened before Ben had time to ring the bell.

"Becca." He stepped inside, noting Will seated at the kitchen table, sipping from a glass of water. "Will."

The young minister stood and hurried over. "That was fast."

"The sheriff and I were close by." He turned to Rebecca, wishing with all his heart he could drag her close. Instead he said softly, "Are you hurt?"

"No. But the bullet flew right over our heads, Ben. I heard it hit the wood of my house."

"Show me." He followed her to the front door, where Virgil was just about to enter.

"Sheriff." Rebecca paused. "Are you all right?"

"Just a little stiff from therapy."

Ben withdrew a flashlight from his belt. "Becca said the bullet hit the house."

The two lawmen studied the bullet hole in the circle of light.

"I'll want that sent to the state police lab, Ben."

"Right."

Virgil turned to Rebecca and Will. "Why don't we sit over here and you two can tell us exactly what happened tonight." He settled himself in a straight-backed chair, extending his leg stiffly before facing Rebecca. "You can begin. And, Will, if you think of anything Rebecca has forgotten, fill us in."

. While the two described the uneventful evening walk home, and the sudden, shocking shooting, Ben stood as still as a statue, watching and listening.

"You didn't hear a car approaching?"

Rebecca shook her head.

Will did the same.

"How about after the gun was fired? A car door slamming? A screech of tires like before?"

Rebecca thoughtfully mulled that over before responding. "I was so scared, all I could think of was getting away. I don't recall any other sounds." She turned to Will. "Did you hear a car?"

"Not that I can recall." He looked at the sheriff. "Could the shooter be still out there, hiding in the darkness?"

Virgil looked over at Ben, who was out the door in an instant.

While he was gone, the sheriff asked both Will and Rebecca dozens of pointed questions, sometimes making notes, at other times merely nodding his head as they answered. Whenever they paused, he waited patiently, giving them as much time as they needed to formulate a response.

When Ben returned, he met their questioning looks. "The back lawn is damp. Anyone out there would have left prints. Except for those leading to the back door, there are none. The same with the front yard. It appears our shooter followed his targets along the sidewalk, and took the shot while they were distracted on the porch." He spoke to Rebecca. "Were you digging out a key?"

"I may have been." She thought a moment before shaking her head. "Wait. The key was in my hand. We were talking..." She closed her eyes a moment. "I remember. We were talking about that fact that Will needed to contact his mentor about serving as pastor at the church where he interned before ordination."

Will was nodding in agreement. "That's right."

"Were you face-to-face? Or were you both facing the door?"

At Ben's question, Will answered for both of them. "Face-to-face. I remember thinking that Rebecca was challenging me, and I wasn't exactly happy about it."

That had the sheriff raising an eyebrow. "Challenging you?"

Will shrugged but said nothing.

Ben was looking at the two of them. "On your walk home, did you hear anything out of the ordinary?"

The two were shaking their heads when Rebecca suddenly remembered. "There was a barking dog."

Virgil frowned. "You'd hear that in any neighborhood."

"Well, yes, of course." She nodded. "But even after its owner brought it inside, it kept on barking."

"Maybe it spotted the two of you."

She considered. "We were well past the house by then. But if someone was following us..."

Ben exchanged a look with the sheriff before asking for the exact location of the house. "I'll find the dog's owner and talk to him."

Virgil rubbed his knee. "If you don't mind, I'll just stay here."

As Ben walked outside, Virgil turned to Rebecca. "This could turn into a long night."

She crossed to the kitchen counter, idly noting that her hands were still shaking. "I'll make coffee."

At a knock on her door, Rebecca hurried over to peer through the window. Seeing Ben, she quickly unlocked the door and opened it to admit him.

He paused to touch a hand to her cheek. "You okay?"

She nodded, but he could see the strain in her eyes.

"Hold on," he whispered as he strode to the kitchen, where the sheriff and Will were seated at the table sipping coffee and nibbling some of Susan's chocolate chip cookies.

Virgil looked up. "What did you find out, Ben?"

"The dog's owner is Adlai Iverson."

Virgil thought a minute. "I know him. Works for the fairgrounds, outside of town."

Ben nodded. "Adlai relaxed once I assured him no neighbors had complained about his barking dog. He said the dog was clearly agitated and kept standing at the front window, barking its head off, even after being called inside. When he started to pull the dog away, he noticed a stranger standing behind a tree, watching something up ahead. The dog's owner couldn't see past the ring of streetlights, and after a while, his dog gave up and retreated to the laundry room, where his dish of kibble is stored."

Ben turned to Rebecca. "So your instinct about the barking dog was right on."

"Good work, Rebecca." Virgil drained his coffee before getting stiffly to his feet. "We'll head on back to my office now. Before we go, I'll have Ben retrieve that bullet from your door frame. The state lab will be able to tell us more after they run some tests."

Ben yanked open the door and reached up with a Swiss army knife he'd retrieved from his pocket. After removing the bullet, he bagged it and handed it over to the sheriff.

When Will started out the door, Ben paused and turned. "You're not sticking around?"

"It's late. I need to get home."

Ben looked beyond Will to where Rebecca stood, her hands twisting nervously at her waist. "You don't want to be alone tonight."

"I'll...be all right."

"No." He thought a moment before saying, "I know you don't want to ask for help, but maybe just for tonight..."

She was already shaking her head, anticipating his suggestion.

He turned to the sheriff. "You need me tonight, Virgil?"

The older man smiled. "I'm grateful for your help, Ben, but the state boys will take over as soon as I get back to my office."

Ben nodded. "Okay then." To Rebecca he said, "As soon as I drive Virgil back to the station, I'll come back for you. Pack what you need for the morning."

"Where...?"

"To my family's ranch. Just for the night."

If he expected her to argue, he was pleasantly surprised when she merely nodded. "Thanks, Ben. If you're sure they won't mind, I'll be ready."

CHAPTER EIGHTEEN

That didn't take long." Rebecca stepped out her door the minute Ben knocked.

"The state police fill in whenever Virgil needs them. They take pride in being on time." He took the overnight bag from her hand and led her toward his truck, helping her into the passenger side before circling around.

She fastened her seat belt. "I hope you called ahead to alert your family that I'm barging in."

"You're not barging in. You're my guest. Zachariah took my call and said I could expect a surprise when I got home. He made it sound like something good. I wonder what that's about."

Rebecca smiled in the darkness. "Yeah. I wonder."

"We'll find out soon enough." He reached over to put a big hand on hers. "You feeling all right?"

"I'm fine now. But I have to admit, I was really scared."

"Not according to Virgil." He gave her a steady look.

"The sheriff said that Will admitted to freezing the minute he heard the gunshot, until you caught his arm and nearly dragged him around the house to the back door. You were the one who locked the door. You were the one who called Jeanette. Virgil said you did all the right things." His voice warmed in the darkness. "You sure you're not a secret agent?"

She laughed, and it felt so good to have something to laugh about. "More like a secret coward."

"You just don't get it, do you?"

At his question, she turned to him.

"Anybody would be afraid when they hear a gunshot. Especially if it's directed at them. But cowards don't react the way you did. Whatever you may think about yourself, Becca, you're no coward."

"Thanks. Now if only my inner child can remember that."

"Your inner child is doing just fine. And your outer child is, too." He fought to keep his tone bland. "Where were you and Will coming from?"

"Hmm?" She glanced up. "Oh. I was walking home from the store with Dad, and Will was heading home from a visit with Reverend Grayson."

Ben felt a wave of unexpected relief. Though he didn't want to read too much into his reaction, he had to admit the truth. He'd experienced a wave of jealousy at the thought of Will spending time with Becca.

Rebecca's voice lowered. "When we got to Dad's street, he asked Will to walk me the rest of the way." She took in a deep breath. "At the time, I was annoyed with Dad for trying to play Cupid again. But now I'm so grateful I wasn't alone. There's no telling what might have happened if Will hadn't been there with me."

"Unless..." Ben paused, wishing he could call back the

word. It had slipped out before he'd had time to compose himself.

"Unless?"

He sighed. "Unless Will is the target, and you just happened to be with him."

"Will?" She pulled her hand away and turned toward Ben. "Why would anybody want to harm a minister?"

"Why would anybody want to hurt you?"

"I don't have an answer. I can't imagine anyone wanting to cause me harm." She fell silent as she turned to stare out the side window.

Even though Ben was relieved that she hadn't been on a date with Will, he couldn't take any comfort in that fact. There were just too many questions swirling around in his mind.

So far, nobody had been harmed. But this bullet came closer than the others. And even under the best of circumstances, a stray bullet could prove to be deadly.

Someone wanted to create a sense of fear. But was the target Will? Or Rebecca?

Almost at once his mind rejected that. Not Rebecca. Please not Rebecca.

He could keep her safe for tonight. But what about all the tomorrows?

Ben drove along the familiar gravel driveway that stretched for nearly a mile before the lights of the ranch house came into view. It was a sight that never failed to stir his soul. Each time he approached his home, he found himself wondering what his life would have been like without this place, and these good men offering him and his brothers a haven.

Folks around here referred to that historic blizzard as the storm of the century. He would always think of that fateful night as a gift from heaven.

As he parked behind a row of trucks, his first thought was that every light in the house was on.

He stepped down and circled around to take Rebecca's hand. When they turned, the entire family had gathered on the back porch.

Ben looked up at the gathering. "Somebody having a party without letting me in on it?"

"We're having a celebration of sorts." Mac walked down the steps and greeted Rebecca with a hug. "But now that you two are here, the party's complete."

"I don't get it."

At Ben's words, the sea of men parted, and Roscoe threw on the porch lights to illuminate Rebecca's handiwork.

"What the...?" Ben bit back the oath before studying the array of furniture. He turned to her. "How did you...? When did you...?"

"How do you know I had anything to do with this?"

He grinned. "Because it looks just like that display in town. All pretty and perfect. But when did you do this?"

She was flushed with pleasure. "Earlier today. After I drove to the Platt ranch to pick up more stock. I realized just how perfect these would be here." She climbed the steps and smiled as Zachariah, Otis, and Roscoe settled comfortably in the log chairs, while Sam and Finn staked out the swing.

Ben was shaking his head in disbelief. "Wait a minute. You drove to the Platt ranch?"

She nodded. "I had to do some fancy persuading to get my father to trust me with his new truck." She glanced around. "The one with the hydraulic lift."

"A little thing like you drove that monster piece of equipment?"

She blushed.

"But how could you load all this?"

"Oh." She laughed. "My father insisted on sending Eli and our stock boy, Rodney, along. Dad did it because he didn't think a female could handle his precious equipment. But those two were a blessing in disguise. They easily handled all the heavy lifting."

"Heavy indeed." Zachariah patted the arm of the chair. "These logs are good and solid."

"Lamar says they'll last a lifetime in sun and rain, snow and sleet."

Mac was smiling broadly. "We'll be happy to take Lamar at his word. This old porch has never been so comfortable. When Ben called to say he was bringing you here, we decided to surprise him the same way you surprised all of us." He shook his head. "I can't remember the last time we could all gather around this old porch at one time. Thanks to you, Rebecca."

"You're welcome." She was beaming with pride as she glanced at Ben.

He caught her hand. "I'm going to take your things upstairs to the guest room. If you'd like, you can sit here with the family."

Zachariah's words stopped him. "Have you two eaten?"

Ben shook his head at the same time that Rebecca did.

The old lawyer got to his feet. "Then come inside. There are enough leftovers from supper for a couple of hot roast beef sandwiches."

Both Ben and Rebecca were salivating as they followed him to the kitchen.

A short time later, as the others gathered around the kitchen, talking and laughing, Ben and Rebecca devoured everything Zachariah set in front of them. Slabs of tender beef on sourdough bread and covered with rich, brown gravy. A plate of oven-roasted potatoes. Corn from the garden. And for dessert, Susan's chocolate chip cookies and mugs of steaming coffee.

Ben sat back, replete, content. "That was almost as good as the surprise out on the porch."

Rebecca merely smiled, feeling a warm glow. "I'm so glad I followed my instincts. Afterward, I worried that I might have offended your family. After all, I never asked anybody's permission to leave all that furniture."

Ben looked around at the others. "Apparently you've never heard the Monroe code."

At her arch look he grinned, and every man there sing-songed in unison: "Remember this. It's always easier to ask forgiveness than to seek permission."

There was a round of raucous laughter, and it was obvious they'd shared those words many times before.

They took their coffee out on the back porch, and once again the entire family gathered around, enjoying the comfort of the new furniture.

Rebecca and Ben took to either end of the swing, until Sam and Finn crowded in, forcing them to sit close together.

Mac and Zachariah settled into the log chairs, while Otis and Roscoe drained their coffee before excusing themselves to retire to the bunkhouse for their nightly game of gin rummy.

Rebecca sat listening to the rumble of masculine voices as Finn talked about his day in court, and Mac made plans for bringing the herds down from the hills.

The gentle motion of the swing and the rumble of easy laughter had her letting go of the tension that had earlier held her in its grip.

Why did she feel such a sense of peace here, so far from town?

Why did she feel safe here, with Ben and this strange assortment of men?

The answer came instantly. Here in this place, she didn't feel she was being judged. She didn't have to live up to her father's strict code of behavior. She didn't have to prove anything.

She was, quite simply, accepted for who she was.

Ever since Ben had told her about how he and his brothers had come here, she was fascinated by the goodness of Mackenzie Monroe. What a gift he had. A gift of being able to accept people and love them as they were, not as the world wished them to be.

She was so caught up in her thoughts, it took a moment for Ben's words to break through.

"...know you're tired. Come on. I'll show you the guest room."

"Thanks, Ben." Rebecca turned to the others. "Good night all."

A chorus of deep voices called their good nights as she and Ben walked inside and climbed the stairs.

He led her along the upstairs hallway before opening a door. "Since Mary Pat isn't here, you can have this room tonight." He set her bag on the bed. "It's bigger than the second guest room down the hall."

"I don't need a big room, Ben."

He smiled. "This one has its own bathroom. That way you won't have to share with a bunch of big hairy guys in the morning."

That had her laughing. "Then I'm grateful. Being an only child, I'm not very good at sharing."

"Oh, I have to disagree with that." He was standing very still, watching her in that quiet way he had. "You shared something special with my family today, and look how happy you made them."

"They are happy, aren't they?" Her smile was radiant. "I'm so glad now I followed my first instinct, before I could talk myself out of it."

"Why would you talk yourself out of something so generous?"

She shrugged, obviously uncomfortable talking about herself. "I've never been spontaneous. I was raised to think things through before acting on my impulses."

"That's too bad." His smile faded.

"Why?"

"I'm about to do something impulsive, and I don't want you running like a rabbit."

She lifted her chin, though it quivered slightly. "I'm not a scared little rabbit, Ben."

"I know." His big hands were at her shoulders, drawing her ever so slowly toward him. His eyes remained steady on hers. "You're a woman, Becca. A beautiful, tempting woman who makes me want things I have no right to."

He dipped his head, his mouth on hers. The kiss was slow and easy, but the underlying tension was a palpable thing, shimmering like a wall of fire between them.

The heat, the need, came sneaking up, catching them both by surprise.

Ben lifted his head, staring at her with a look she couldn't fathom. For a moment it seemed he would step back, but then with a savage oath he dragged her firmly against him and kissed her until they were both breathless.

The sound of men's voices downstairs alerted them that the family was preparing to head to their beds.

With her hands against his shoulders she began to push away. "Ben, we shouldn't..."

"The hell we shouldn't." His hands were in her hair as he kissed her with a thoroughness that had them both trembling.

The protest she'd been about to utter was forgotten. Everything was forgotten except Ben and this moment. She was so aware of him. Of the strong arms that held her against him. Of his thighs pressed to hers. Of his heartbeat as out of control as hers.

She twined her arms around his neck and gave herself up to the pleasure as his mouth moved on hers, drawing out the exquisite taste like a man starved for her.

"Becca." He whispered her name like a prayer.

The voices grew closer as his family climbed the stairs to their rooms.

Ben lowered his hands to his sides and took a step back, and then another, until he felt the edge of the open door.

"Good night, Becca."

"Good…" She drew in a shallow breath. "Good night, Ben."

He turned and was gone, pulling the door closed behind him.

Ben stepped into the living room and found Mac seated alone in front of the fire.

"You're still awake?"

"The others are off to bed."

"Want a beer?"

When Mac nodded, Ben walked to the kitchen and re-turned with two longnecks. After handing one to his father, he took the seat beside him, and the two men tipped up their bottles and drank.

As the fire burned low, Ben remained in the living room, seated by the fire, talking quietly with Mac about his day, his work, and finally about the latest incident with the shooter and Will and Rebecca.

"What do you make of it, son?"

Ben shook his head, staring into the fire. "I don't know what to think. I'm glad the state boys are on it. They've had experience with this kind of thing. And I'm...too close to the case to think clearly."

Nearly an hour later, when Ben finally called good night and made his way up the stairs to his room, Mac sat listening to the silence that settled over the old house.

He thought of Ben's words. *"I'm...too close to the case to think clearly."*

It was obvious in so many ways that Ben had fallen hard for the young woman upstairs. Yet after showing her to the guest room, he'd returned here, killing time, when he could be upstairs sharing a few stolen kisses and a lover's conversation.

So why hadn't he seized the opportunity?

Had he deliberately been waiting, hoping she would be asleep before climbing the stairs?

A slow smile spread across all Mac's features.

Of course. Avoiding temptation.

And maybe that was a good thing.

Mac had a feeling that when this big, rough bear of a son finally gave in to the building passion, it would be earth-shattering. Not just for Ben, struggling to be noble, but for the woman he loved.

Love.

He'd know a thing or two about it. Even now, the thought of Rachel and Robbie could bring a glow of exquisite joy or a feeling of deepest sorrow.

It was true he'd moved on with his life. Having so many good people around him helped. But there were moments when he found himself wondering what his life would have been like if his wife and son had lived.

He worked overtime to keep from torturing himself with

such thoughts. When they came creeping into his mind, as they did now, he refused to indulge himself in fantasies. He'd learned that the best solution for sorrow was taking joy in the little things that life provided each day.

His smile came slowly.

Like that brand-new furniture on that old back porch, a gift from a young woman who was beginning to mean a great deal to all of them. Without realizing just what she'd given them, it provided another place for his family to gather.

Family.

How odd that this strange assortment of men the world would consider misfits had bonded so tightly. They worked together, relaxed together, and shared a common goal.

And wasn't that another form of family?

His family.

He loved each and every one of them as fiercely as he cherished the memories of his Rachel and Robbie.

CHAPTER NINETEEN

Morning sunlight filled the upstairs hallway with light and shadows.

Ben knocked on the guest room door. "You awake, Becca?"

She surprised him by pulling the door open immediately. "Yes. Good morning."

He couldn't stop staring. She was wearing a simple denim shirt and jeans. Her hair was crackly and shiny, as though she'd been brushing it for an hour. Her smile would rival the sun outside her window.

"I hope you were able to sleep."

"I slept like a baby. Probably because I was so far from town and the shooter." She flushed. "But I'm sure part of the reason was knowing there were so many big, strong men around."

He grinned. "I guess that seems strange when you're an only child."

"I guess so. But in a good way." She touched a hand to his arm. "I really like your family."

"They like you, too. And after your... surprise, I'm sure you've earned a place at the top of their list." He took her hand. "Come on. Zachariah said breakfast is ready."

"Are you just getting up?"

Her question had him laughing. "I've been up since dawn. Sam and I took barn duty, to free Finn up for his trial."

"You've already done your chores?" She sounded contrite. "I wanted to join you."

He paused halfway down the stairs. "Why?"

She shrugged and looked embarrassed. "Partly to see all the things you do on a ranch. And partly to pay your family back for putting me up for the night."

He touched a hand to her arm. "Becca, you don't owe any debt here. But if you really want to see ranch chores, I'm happy to set you up on one of our tractors after breakfast. Sam and I are planning on moving a mound of earth in the north pasture."

She shared his smile. "Why not? Now that I've driven my father's truck, I think a tractor would be a piece of cake."

He tried, and failed, to imagine this fresh-as-a-daisy little woman driving a tractor.

They were both laughing as they entered the kitchen and joined the others for breakfast.

Zachariah passed around a platter of scrambled eggs, while Roscoe filled a second plate with thick slabs of ham.

Finn walked in carrying an attaché case and wearing his trademark buckskin jacket and Stetson.

Zachariah beamed his pleasure, since the jacket and hat had once been his. Finn considered them his good-luck charms. "Ready for another day in court?"

"You bet."

Mac set down his mug of coffee. "You got time to eat, son?"

Finn shook his head. "I want to meet with my client before court."

"All right." Mac put a hand on his shoulder. "Go get 'em, tiger."

"You know I will."

When Finn was gone, the others passed around the platters and filled their plates.

Sam settled himself next to Rebecca. "I missed seeing you in the barn this morning."

She stared pointedly at Ben. "Somebody forgot to let me know chores start at dawn."

"To make up for it, Becca wants to drive one of the tractors." Ben winked at his brother.

"Give her old Betsy. I've got dibs on the new one."

"Okay." Rebecca looked from Sam to Ben. "What's the joke?"

"Old Betsy was Dad's first tractor. Old as the hills, and likes to quit and take frequent naps." Ben was grinning.

"Naps?" Sam shook his head. "More like complete breakdowns. At least once every hour. And when that old machine quits, there's no getting her started until we tinker, twist, and apply tourniquets to various hoses. Old Betsy's on her last leg. Or I should say piston."

Around the table, the others were chuckling.

Mac indicated the two men across the table. "Otis and Roscoe have resuscitated that old tractor so many times, we've decided she's like a cat with nine lives."

"Only she's already passed ninety lives," Roscoe added. "And we're ready to give up on her."

Mac shrugged. "We'll keep her around for parts."

Otis winked at Rebecca. "Mac isn't ready to accept that there's no call for sixty-year-old parts."

"My sixty-year-old parts still work." The minute the words were out of Mac's mouth, the room exploded with laughter.

Ben lifted his mug toward his dad. "And may they continue for sixty more."

This brought another round of laughter and much teasing.

Rebecca and Ben stood on the porch. The others had scattered to attend to ranch chores.

"Are you still up to driving a tractor?"

At Ben's question, Rebecca shook her head. "Old Betsy certainly sounds...challenging. But I need to get back to town. I'm sure by now my parents have a million questions about what happened last night."

"You didn't call them?"

She looked away. "I just wasn't ready to talk about it. But after a good night's sleep, and a healthy dose of your family, I'm feeling up to the reaction I expect will be...stormy."

He nodded. "If you get your things, I'll bring the truck around."

"I hate taking you away from your chores. I hope you don't mind."

He touched a hand to her cheek, then abruptly drew it away. "I don't mind."

When he walked toward the barn, Rebecca stood still, her body still tingling from his touch.

She felt confused.

Did he feel this same sexual awareness? Or was a man like Ben Monroe immune to such things? There were times when she could feel his passion. Like last night. That kiss had been electrifying. She'd wanted more. And then, when he realized the family was near, he'd just walked away.

He had more self-discipline than any man she'd ever met.

And maybe that was part of the attraction. When he touched her, kissed her, he poured himself fully into it. And then, just as fully, when necessary, he was able to step away.

She strode resolutely into the house and up the stairs. Minutes later she returned carrying her overnight bag.

Ben halted the truck and climbed out to take the bag from her hands before helping her into the passenger side.

As they headed to town, he slipped on his sunglasses before pointing. "Look at that."

She swiveled her head.

His voice was low with feeling. "I can't imagine not seeing this every day of my life. The cattle. The hills. All this glorious sunshine."

She nodded. "I know what you mean. I love the four seasons. Spring, with these hills bursting into flower. The hot sticky summers. And now, fall, with its cool breezes and the trees changing color. I even love winter, and the first snowfall."

He turned with a grin. "How about the last snowfall, just when you're ready for spring flowers?"

She laughed. "I know. It's a real let-down. But even then, I just love all of it." She turned to him. "Will told me he can't abide winters here. He's hoping for an assignment in a warmer place."

"Good for Will. People should be free to go where they want. But as for me, this place owns my heart."

Owns my heart.

He'd said it with such passion.

She felt her pulse quicken. It was the same passion he'd let her glimpse last night. A passion that had left her trembling with need, her poor heart yearning for more.

"You sure you want to be dropped at your father's store? I could take you home first."

"I need to face the music, Ben. By now, I'm sure he's heard about the latest trouble."

He came to a halt in front of the hardware store. "Want me to go in with you?"

She managed a weak smile. "Thanks. I know you're trying to give me moral support, and I'm grateful. But I need to do this alone." She stepped down from the truck and clutched the overnight bag to her chest.

As Ben watched her figure recede in the rearview mirror, he was reminded of that terrified teen he'd carried home after her prom. So wounded, yet so stoic.

Was that when he'd fallen in love with her?

Love? Where had that word come from?

Love. He huffed out a breath as he headed back to the ranch. What would he know about such things? He knew he and his brothers were loved unconditionally. But he'd been denied the love of his parents. The men who surrounded him were all single. Maybe at some time in their lives they'd been married, or had loved someone, but for the better part of a lifetime they'd lived without a woman. He'd never had the chance to see how they acted around a woman they loved.

He looked out across the rolling hills, black with cattle. He loved this place. He loved his brothers. He loved Mackenzie Monroe fiercely. He loved Zachariah and Otis and Roscoe. Hell, that ought to be enough love for any man.

And he loved Rebecca Henderson, too.

The thought slammed through him with such force that he applied the brakes and was grateful there were no vehicles on the interstate.

He sat a moment, breathing deeply.

He loved Becca. And though he'd fought hard to deny it, he'd loved her for years.

It didn't matter if she returned his feelings. A woman like

Becca deserved someone refined. Educated. A teacher, or a banker, or a...minister.

He shook his head, trying to think this through. She'd made it clear that she didn't think of Will Theisen as anything other than a friend. He wasn't a rival for her affection. Still, he was the kind of man Becca deserved.

Or was he?

Ben thought back to the few times they'd kissed. She'd been an eager participant.

He was sweating as he put the truck in gear and continued along the interstate until he came to the turnoff for the ranch.

What he needed was a full day of hard, mind-numbing ranch chores. Work had always been the best way to clear his head.

CHAPTER TWENTY

"Close the door, Rebecca."

Hank Henderson strode briskly into his tiny, cramped office, the desktop littered with flyers, empty boxes, pamphlets, and shipping orders.

He circled around the desk before turning to his daughter. "I'd rather the employees not overhear what I have to say."

Rebecca closed the door and stood, ignoring the chair facing his desk.

"Not that it matters," he added tiredly. "I'm sure they know more than I do." He picked up a pen, clicking it several times in rapid succession before tossing it aside. "I tried calling your house last night, after I heard about the latest shooting. There was no answer, so I drove over. You weren't there."

"I spent the night at the Monroe ranch."

"You did what? With a houseful of crazy old men living there?"

"You make it sound dirty, Dad."

"That's not what I..." He sighed and tried again. "Why would you prefer spending the night with a bunch of misfits instead of staying with your parents?"

"Those misfits, as you call them, are all gentle people. They're good and decent and treat me with respect."

"And your mother and I don't?"

"I didn't say that."

"You implied as much. Why do you avoid us?"

"I don't..."

He held up a hand. "And don't deny it. It's obvious you don't want to spend any more time than necessary with your mother and me."

She took in a deep breath and fought to keep her tone reasonable. "Ever since I returned to Haller Creek, I've had the impression that I'm a disappointment to you and Mom."

"We would never say such a thing."

"I know that, Dad. You're both too kind to say so. But your feelings are obvious. I don't do things at work the way they've always been done. I don't have feelings for Will, even though you've already decided that he would make the perfect husband. And now I'm bringing notoriety to the family by being the victim of some crazy guy with a gun."

"You certainly can't help that."

She managed a weak smile. "I'm glad we can agree on at least that one thing."

"Rebecca, in time you'll learn to do things around the store the way I've always done them."

"You're assuming that I agree with the way things have always been done."

He chose to ignore the sarcasm in her tone. "And you can definitely avoid gossip by not seeing that hell...Ben Monroe."

She sank down into the chair and met his stern look. "And you're assuming that I can just avoid Ben and find someone else to love."

"Love?" His head came up sharply. "When did I ever mention love?"

"You haven't, Dad. That's the problem. You think I should find someone who suits you, and marry him. Love never enters the equation."

"It's overrated."

"Would you care to say that in front of Mom?"

He flushed. "Your mother knows I love her. I don't need to say it. But I happen to love her a lot more now than I did when we were first married. We were practically strangers, living with our parents until the day we married. Now we've had years to build a good, solid relationship."

"I think it's a shame to admit you didn't love Mom when you married. But at least now you love her, and that's a good thing. As for me, I don't plan on marrying anyone unless I love him with all my heart and can't bear the thought of living without him."

"So much passion. Is Monroe the reason for all this? Is that hell—" He huffed out a breath and started over. "Is Monroe part of your plan?"

She got to her feet and started toward the door. With her hand on the knob she turned. "I'll let you know when I've figured that out."

Rebecca spent the day working harder than she'd ever worked before. Not only did she handle orders and returns with careful attention to every detail, but she also managed to straighten dozens of shelves, and whenever there was time, she went out to the loading dock to lend a hand helping Eli load supplies onto ranchers' trucks.

She'd once again sold almost everything in her fenced area, including at least a hundred extra pumpkins that hadn't been promised to the town for the Autumn Festival.

By early evening all she wanted was a long, hot bath and some quiet time. But her hopes were quickly dashed when her mother called to insist she come to dinner.

"Your father assured me you'll be leaving work with him. I'm going to have your favorite fried chicken and mashed potatoes."

"I don't want you to go to any trouble, Mom."

"Too late, honey. I've already shopped and baked. Now I expect you and your father to humor me and eat every bite."

"Thanks, Mom. I'll be there."

She hung up and glanced to where her father stood across the room. His smile told her he was well aware of Susan's plans. And approved of them. In fact, he'd probably been the one to arrange all this. There was nothing to do now but go along with the plan.

She slipped into a jacket and bid good night to the few remaining employees before stepping outside and walking beside her father.

Hank looked up at the sky. "It's getting dark a little earlier each week. Pretty soon it'll be dark before we leave work."

Rebecca knew he was trying to avoid saying anything personal. Grateful, she played along. "I like watching the lights coming on in houses as I walk past them."

He turned to her. "Why?"

She shrugged. "I'm not sure. Maybe I like wondering about the people living there. Are they gathering for a meal? Is it a widow, eating alone and trying to hold back the darkness? Are there little kids fighting over the last cupcake?"

He shook his head. "I never knew you were..." He struggled for the words. "Such a dreamer."

"I guess I've always been. I used to wonder what it would be like to have a big brother who would fight anyone who offended me. Or a little sister I could dress up like a doll. Or a pet I could sneak into my bed after you and Mom fell asleep."

He chuckled. "Much more than a dreamer. You were given to wild flights of fancy. I guess that would explain your attraction to the hell-raiser."

"Why do you do that, Dad?"

"Do what?"

"Spoil things by calling Ben by that name, knowing how much I dislike the word."

"It suits him. Oh, he may be wearing a badge now, but that doesn't change the fact that he is, was, and always will be a hell-raiser, and all wrong for you."

The mood shattered, Rebecca dug her hands in her pockets and walked the rest of the way in silence.

Why, she wondered, did she even bother to keep trying to find some connection with her father? Since returning to Haller Creek, she'd been forced to watch as the chasm between them grew wider with each day. No matter how hard she tried to communicate her feelings, he refused to listen.

It hurt. Oh, how it hurt to have her own father treat her feelings with such disdain.

"Rebecca." The minute the front door opened, Susan rushed forward to wrap her daughter in a hard hug. "Oh, your father and I were so worried last night when we heard about another gunshot."

"I'm sorry I didn't call you. I was hoping you wouldn't hear about it until today, so it wouldn't ruin your sleep."

"Sleep? What's that?" Susan gave a dry laugh. "When Hank told me you weren't home, we were both convinced you'd gone home with Will. But when we phoned him and he couldn't say where you were, we were frantic. We were up all night, pacing the floor."

"She spent the night at the Monroe ranch with that bunch of…" Hank's words fell off when he spotted the sparks shooting out of his daughter's eyes.

"Yes. Well…" Susan patted Rebecca's arm. "You're here now, and that's what matters." She turned away, calling over her shoulder, "Go ahead and hang your jacket while I get our supper."

Rebecca shed her jacket and hurried to the kitchen to lend a hand.

A short time later they sat in the dining room, talking about anything except the thing uppermost in their minds.

Susan's smile was forced. "How is your little business going, Rebecca?"

Rebecca decided not to make an issue of the term *little business*. "It's showing a small profit."

"Enough to pay the rent?" Hank broke open a biscuit.

"Are you worried about your payment, Dad?"

"Of course not. Just pointing out that you can't really consider your profit until you pay off your debt. There's not only rent, but also the price of buying the products from the manufacturer, shipping cost, which includes maintaining the equipment needed to transport your product, and paying the wages of the employees who lend a hand in the sale or transportation."

"I'll pay Eli and Rodney for the day they spent with me. And I filled your truck with gas before returning it to the hardware store."

Hank gave a hiss of annoyance. "I'm not asking you to pay all that. I'm just saying, after years in the business, it's important that I give you my expert opinion so you remember to weigh all the costs before counting your profit."

"More chicken, Hank?" Susan held the platter in front of him and gave him a pointed stare.

"Thank you." He took the platter and helped himself before passing it to Rebecca.

She set it aside.

Susan pouted. "You've hardly eaten a thing, Rebecca."

"It's really good, Mom. But I'm just not hungry tonight."

Susan brightened. "That's all right. I'm glad you're saving room for my special dessert."

A little while later Susan left the room and returned with a chocolate layer cake.

As she cut it and began passing around the slices, topped with vanilla ice cream, she babbled about the book she was reading, the silly thing her neighbor Lorie Reardon said, and a medical tip she'd gleaned from a television show.

Taking pity on her mother, Rebecca paid careful attention, asked pointed questions, and laughed at all the right places.

Susan relaxed and sipped her tea.

By the time the table had been cleared and the dishes stacked in the dishwasher, Susan felt mellow enough to ask her daughter if she'd be willing to spend the night.

"Just so you don't have to be alone, honey."

"Thanks, Mom. I really appreciate the offer. But I need to face my fears and learn to deal with the reality of my life."

Hank looked up from the evening news on TV. "And just what is the reality of your life?"

Rebecca took her time slipping her arms into the sleeves of her jacket and zipping it before answering.

"I'm young and healthy. I have a house that I intend to turn into a comfortable home, parents who love me, and a job I'm enjoying, along with"—she stared pointedly at her mother—"a little business that seems to have caught the eye of some people in this town. For now, I'll concentrate on these things."

"You do that." Hank's voice was low with a combination of anger and fear. "Meanwhile, there's the little matter of a monster shooting at you."

"I can't control that, Dad. But what I can do is trust the sheriff and the state police to resolve the issue."

"You forgot to mention your precious deputy, Ben Monroe."

Susan's mouth opened, but before she could say a word, Rebecca put in, "I know how much you resent him, Dad. You've made that perfectly clear. But know this. Ben is a good man. Nothing you say will change that. But each time you say something against him, you'll only make me want to defend him more."

She bent and kissed his cheek, then walked with her mother to the door before enveloping her in a warm embrace. "Thank you for that lovely dinner, Mom. I never get tired of your cooking. I just wish you'd taught me all your cooking and baking tips when I was growing up so I could come close to duplicating your skill. Good night."

As she stepped out the door, she called, "I love you both."

"We love you more." Susan's words carried on the breeze as Rebecca walked down the porch steps and into the night.

When the door closed, Susan remained, peering through the narrow side window as Rebecca's figure blended into the darkness.

"You should have offered to walk her home, Hank. She shouldn't be walking out there alone."

"You heard her. She doesn't want our help."

"That isn't what she said."

"It's what I heard."

Susan crossed the room and sat on the arm of her husband's chair before taking his hand. "All my friends used to say how hard it was to watch their children grow up and leave the nest. So many of that generation rejected all the fine ideals their parents held in such high regard."

"And now our own daughter is doing that very thing. Rejecting out of hand all we taught her. Defending that hellraiser. Spending the night with his crazy family of misfits."

Susan squeezed his hand. "No, Hank. She's testing her wings. Seeing if she can fly. And as painful as that is to watch, we have to stand by and let her try."

He swore. "While you're spouting all those warm fuzzies, what if this madman kills our daughter? Are we supposed to just shrug it off and say she was trying to fly?"

Tears pooled in his wife's eyes, but she managed to say, "I'm so proud of Rebecca for trying to function normally while her world has turned upside down. I'm not sure I'd have her courage. But for now, I'm going to trust that we've raised a fine young woman who will do the right thing."

At his hiss of anger she leaned close and pressed a kiss to his temple before going off to their bedroom alone.

CHAPTER TWENTY-ONE

Take a seat, Ben." Virgil was at his desk, sorting through a stack of official documents. "Did you enjoy your weekend?"

"The time flew while I tried to catch up on all the ranch chores." He looked away. And the nights dragged on for hours, while he thought about Becca in town. In the line of fire.

The sheriff held out a clutch of papers. "The state boys concluded their in-depth reports after interviewing a list of students who knew Rebecca Henderson in college."

Ben's head came up sharply. "You really think that was necessary?"

"It's not for me to say. The state boys are the professionals. They wouldn't do it if they didn't think it was necessary." Virgil pointed to the papers in Ben's hand. "When you read those, you'll see why they're concerned about one student in particular."

Ben didn't bother to look at them. Instead he glowered

at the sheriff. "Are they suggesting that she's responsible for bringing a shooter to our town?"

"Not at all. In fact, until the state detectives conclude their interviews with the people who worked with Will Theisen for the past couple of years, they don't want to speculate on which of them is the intended victim of this shooter's rage. But since Rebecca and Will were together whenever these incidents occurred, the state police have to do all they can to look into the backgrounds of both Rebecca and Will."

Ben held up the fistful of papers. "What do you want me to do with these?"

"You'll need to familiarize yourself with the details. Take them with you."

"With me? Where?"

"That's what I was getting at. A detective with the state police is on his way to talk to Rebecca, to corroborate what information they have so far, and to conclude their investigation into her activities over the past couple of years. Since I'm busy here, I want you to meet him at her place and act as my liaison."

Ben was shaking his head. "There's no way. I don't want to have any part in this interview. Do you know how humiliating this will be for her, to be forced to talk about her personal life in Bozeman in front of..." He stopped, then continued lamely, "Somebody like me from town who knows her?"

"Go on now, Ben. You don't want that sweet young lady dealing with some hard-ass detective alone, do you? She needs to know there's somebody in the room that's on her side. You need to be there for her."

Ben clenched his teeth. "When you put it that way..." He got to his feet and strode to the door.

"And, Ben…"

He turned.

"After the interview, feel free to go home. The state boys will be covering us the rest of the week. They're hoping to set a trap for this shooter. And frankly, with this leg keeping me out of commission, I'm happy to step aside. You should be glad, too. I've been putting way too much on your shoulders."

"You know I don't mind, Sheriff."

"I know. And I'm grateful. But I'm sure you and your family will welcome the break as much as I will. You've been doing double-duty for way too long."

"That's my choice, Virgil." He paused at the door. "I'll take my own vehicle and leave your official car here."

"Right."

Outside, Ben climbed into his truck, dreading what was to come. He knew one thing. As soon as the embarrassing interview between the detective and Rebecca ended, he'd head home and bury himself in ranch chores.

He had studiously avoided seeing Becca for the last two days. It had taken a good deal of mental persuasion, but it seemed the wisest course of action. They were getting into some dangerous territory, and he was losing his objectivity.

Tonight, he would sit through the brutal, tedious interview and do everything in his power to remain neutral. But if he saw the detective crossing a line with Becca, he'd intervene. Until and unless that happened, he would just keep his mouth shut and get through it.

Yeah.

Right.

He swore, loudly. Fiercely. That was his story, and he was sticking to it. But, in truth, no matter how painful this was for Rebecca, it would be twice as painful for him.

He just wanted this business concluded as quickly as possible. At least then he could slink away and hide up at the ranch. Poor Rebecca would have to remain here in town, holding her head up high while the rumor mill went into overdrive.

"So, this medical student." The state police detective glanced down at his notes. "Daryl Hollender. He swears he didn't do anything that could be construed as controlling or aggressive, and yet, after a long and to his way of thinking very satisfying relationship, you broke up with him without any warning."

They were seated in Rebecca's living room. She had chosen an upholstered, straight-backed chair, where she perched on the edge of the cushion looking as though at any minute she'd bolt from the room.

Detective Russ Godfrey, well over six feet of muscle, his state police uniform crisp, his demeanor professional, was sitting on the comfortable sofa, a sheaf of documents spread out around him on a coffee table. Through years of training, he kept his tone low and impersonal, with almost no inflection that could be construed as casting judgment.

Ben sat in a chair by the front window, as far away from Rebecca and the detective as he could get. With every probing question, he'd had to clench his hands into fists at his sides, fighting a raging desire to tell Russ Godfrey to stop this intrusion into the victim's privacy and shove his ugly questions where the sun wouldn't shine. But because he knew it would do no good, he held his silence while inwardly fuming. Every rich, ripe curse he'd ever spoken hovered temptingly on his tongue.

Detective Godfrey had already gone through the names of every student with whom Rebecca had a friendship during her years in Bozeman. Young women who boasted of her kindness and ambition. Young men who admitted they'd tried to have a relationship with her but had always been held at arm's length.

Though her face flamed and her eyes were often downcast, to her credit she'd answered every question the detective asked.

"Daryl was known to be intense." Her voice was barely above a whisper. "In his academic studies and in his personal life. It was only natural that he wanted our relationship to be as intense as everything else in his life. But I...just couldn't give him what he wanted."

"And so, without any warning, you abruptly broke off the relationship."

She nodded.

"Did he seem angry and threatening to you?"

"Angry." Becca nodded. "I'm sure his feelings were hurt. He was considered a big man on campus. Handsome. Driven. The guy most likely to succeed. There were plenty of women who would jump at the chance to date him. I'm sure his ego was bruised when I was the one to break off our relationship." She chewed her lip. "But he certainly wasn't threatening. Not at all threatening or dangerous. As far as I could determine, after our breakup he threw himself into his medical studies with a renewed passion."

"You know he owns a gun."

"So do dozens of students. This is Montana."

The detective nodded. "He swears he's never been to Haller Creek. As far as you know, is that a true statement?"

She shrugged. "I've never seen him here. Why wouldn't I believe him?"

Russ Godfrey glanced at his watch. He'd been questioning the young lady for nearly two hours. He stood and offered a handshake. "I think that will do for now, Miss Henderson. If I have to do any follow-up interviews, I'll let you know."

After his handshake, Rebecca gripped her hands tightly at her waist. "I guess this means you know for certain I'm the target of that gunman, and you're going to look at every facet of my life through a magnifying glass."

"I'm sure it seems that way to you, ma'am. And I'm really sorry about this. But my job is to figure out why the little town of Haller Creek has been visited by a shooter, and who the target may be. Once we complete our examination of Reverend Will Theisen's past years at divinity school, we hope to have a clearer picture."

"But in the meantime, I'm to be viewed as some sort of magnet for a crazed gunman."

"I never said..."

"No. You were too polite. But the fact that you interviewed everyone I knew in Bozeman seems to imply that you believe that I deserve to be followed and shot at."

The detective's voice remained deadly calm. "I'm really sorry if I've given you that impression, Miss Henderson. I've just been doing my job, while working diligently to remain nonjudgmental. You should understand that each interview offers us another piece of a puzzle. When all the pieces are in place, we'll be able to solve not only the puzzle, but also the reasons behind it. I'll say good night now."

Detective Godfrey turned toward the door, opened it, and stepped into the darkness, pulling the door closed behind him.

Rebecca turned to Ben, who had remained absolutely silent throughout the entire interview.

"I could feel you staring at me. I'm sure you found this...enlightening."

He shook his head, struggling to find the words of comfort she needed to hear. "I told Virgil I didn't want to be here. That it would be awkward and painful for you to have such intimate details laid bare and calmly discussed like the weather. But the sheriff insisted that I act as his liaison in case you felt overwhelmed by the detective."

Her hands on her hips, she turned the full force of her embarrassment and anger on him. "And you always do the right thing, don't you, Ben."

He got to his feet. "You know I haven't always. But I'm trying."

"Do you believe that I'm responsible for bringing a gunman to Haller Creek?"

He put a hand on her arm. "Of course I don't, Becca. But..."

Her eyes blazed. "But what?"

He looked away. Swallowed.

She finished for him. "You're still thinking about the detective's profile that suggests I have a problem. A problem with commitment." She flung the words at him. "Do you have any idea how this hurts? Do you even care why I could never commit to Daryl?"

Her voice broke. Her eyes filled and she turned away to hide the evidence of tears. She'd been so determined to remain calm and steady, and now she was about to blubber like a baby.

"You don't owe me any explanation, Becca. I just want you to know how sorry I am. I'm sorry that I was forced to be here, listening to intimate details of a relationship that was none of my business. I'm sorry for all you've had to go through. The shots fired. The disruption of your entire life. And none of it your fault. I hope you understand that. None of this is your fault. You didn't cause it. You don't deserve it."

He lay a big hand on her shoulder, but when he felt the tremors rippling through her, he turned away and beat a hasty retreat toward the front door, hoping to spare her any more humiliation.

As he opened it, she cried, "Don't you want to know why my relationship with Daryl failed? Why in the world I dumped him the minute he began to talk about a future with me?"

He was shaking his head, his hand on the doorknob, when her words just came spilling out in a torrent of passion.

"I tried. I really did. I thought I could put this town, this life, behind me and have a better future as far away from here as I could get. I was torn between trying to please my father and trying to be a strong, smart, independent woman. But as hard as I tried, it all fell apart because"—the words were torn from her lips before she could stop herself—"because all I really wanted was here in Haller Creek. All I wanted was a life with you, Ben!"

CHAPTER TWENTY-TWO

He was halfway out the door when her plaintive cry rained over him, striking his heart like shrapnel.

For several long moments there was a sudden, shocking silence as her words played through his mind.

"...all I wanted was a life with you, Ben."

At first, they made no sense. And then, stunned as their meaning washed over him, he looked over to see she'd turned away from him to hide her tears. Her shoulders were shaking as great, gulping sobs broke from her lips.

He was across the room in quick strides, standing as still as a statue for the space of several moments. Finally, tentatively, he touched a hand to her hair. His voice was little more than a whisper. "Are you saying...?"

She shrank from him before looking up, eyes too wide, face tearstained, looking absolutely horrified at what she'd revealed. "I tried to block you from my mind and pretend that I could have a relationship with someone. Anyone. But all I wanted, all I've ever wanted, is you, Ben. And now I've ruined everything…"

There would be time for words later. But now, in this moment, there was no need.

"Shhh." His eyes were hot and fierce, his arms almost bruising as he dragged her against him. For long moments he simply held her as she wept. Then, without even realizing it, mouth was on hers, and her sobs turned to moans.

For every press of his mouth she responded with a hunger that matched his, returning his kisses with a ferocity that staggered him.

With all barriers now shattered, they were practically crawling inside one another's skin, hands and mouths eager, bodies straining.

"I never knew." His hands were in her hair as he rained kisses over her upturned face, seeking to calm, to soothe.

To devour.

Every touch, every kiss enflamed them more.

"I thought you knew and just didn't care. Why should you? You were the guy every girl in town wanted. And I was just…the daughter of a man who was openly hostile to you, no matter how hard you tried." She swallowed hard. "Despite my father, it's always been you, Ben."

He sucked in a breath, wondering that his poor heart could still beat. For a lifetime he'd wished for this. Only this. And now, his greatest hope, his fondest desire, which only minutes ago had seemed impossible, was being offered to him.

"You never said." He whispered soft, feathery kisses over her upturned face.

"I didn't know how to." She framed his face with her hands and pressed wet, eager kisses to his mouth.

Tasting the salt of her tears, he stared down into her eyes

and felt his heart contract with such overwhelming passion that she could want him. Only him.

And he wanted her. He knew in his heart he'd been wanting her for a lifetime.

"Sweet heaven, Becca. Do you know how long I've dreamed of this?"

"You, Ben? Really? Truly?"

He saw her eyes go wide and could read in them her utter, complete joy.

"Really. Truly." He lingered over her lips, loving the sweet, fresh taste of her. He had to call on every bit of willpower to keep from taking her like a brute. "It's always been you, Becca."

"Oh, Ben." She wrapped her arms around his neck and offered her lips for more.

He could feel his control slipping. There was a storm building inside him. A monstrous storm that, once released, would devour them both.

He lowered his head, kissing her with an urgency that had her lifting herself on tiptoe to offer more. His mouth left hers to roam her throat and the tender flesh between her neck and shoulder, before moving lower to the soft swell of her breast.

She moaned and arched her neck, giving him easier access. It was all the invitation he needed to feast.

Greedy, his mouth closed around one erect nipple, and despite the barrier of her clothes, it hardened, shooting hot, burning sparks through them both.

His blood turned to molten lava, raging through his veins.

His big fingers fumbled as he tore her shirt from her, popping buttons as he did. Beneath it she wore a bit of lace that revealed more than it covered. With one quick tug it fell at their feet.

For the space of a heartbeat he simply stared. "You're so beautiful, Becca."

"So are you." She'd unbuttoned his shirt and had to stand on tiptoe to slide it from his shoulders.

He managed a soft chuckle. "Now there's something I've never been called before."

"It's true, Ben." She ran her lips across his hair-roughened chest and felt his trembling response. "You're the most beautiful man I've ever seen."

Frantic, they tore away the rest of their clothes, before his gaze moved slowly over her. "Do you know how long I've waited, Becca?"

She gave a little laugh. "No more than I."

His mouth moved slowly over her upturned face, while his big, clever hands moved over her with exquisite care. In turn she sighed and moved in his arms, her fingers digging into the back of his head as she clung and offered him more.

With each touch, each kiss, their breathing grew more shallow as the passion rose, taking them higher, deeper.

Needs so carefully banked now blazed out of control and without warning had them by the throat.

He struggled to slow down the tide that was carrying them along. "I don't think I can hold back. Tell me you want this, Becca."

"I do, Ben. I do."

"Thank heaven." Half crazed with desire he drove her back against the wall. His fingers found her and he watched her eyes widen before glazing over as he took her on a wild ride.

He loved watching her, those big expressive eyes devouring him as he gave her no time to recover before taking her again.

"Ben. Wait. I..."

"Don't tell me to stop." His heart missed several beats. "I'd rather die than stop now."

"No. Please don't stop. But..."

He rested his forehead against hers as his poor heart began pumping furiously. "It's too late to think. Not a minute longer. I've waited so long. Wanted you forever. If I don't soon end this, I'll explode. My body is on fire. I'm about to lose all control."

"You're not the only one. Yes, Ben. Now. Please." She indicated her room. "My bed..."

"Too far...I'm not sure we can make it to the sofa."

"I don't need it. I just need you, Ben."

On a grateful sigh he lifted her, wrapping her legs around him.

Her hands were in his hair, her fingers digging into his head.

He framed her face, staring into her eyes. "Look at me, Becca. I want to see you as I make love to you."

"Love. Do you, Ben? Love me?"

"With all my heart." His words were torn from a throat too clogged with needs to manage more, before driving himself into her.

At her soft cry he tried to ease back. "You're such a little thing. I'm so big and clumsy. I'm hurting you."

"No. Oh, no." Frantic, she clutched him to her. "You're... just right, Ben."

"You're sure?"

"I'm sure. You're not hurting me. You could never hurt me." Even as she said the words, she knew them to be a lie. She was opening herself to him. Giving him the perfect opportunity to hurt her if he chose to reject her.

"Just love me, Ben. Love me."

And then were no words as they began to climb high, then higher, until, hearts pumping, breath hitching, bodies slick with sheen, they moved together, climbed together, to the very pinnacle of a mountain before they stepped free.

And soared.

Through a blinding mist of passion they reached a shuddering climax before their world slowly began to settle.

It was the most amazing journey of their lives.

Ben stood, holding her in his arms, her body still wrapped around him in the most intimate way.

His lips brushed her cheek. "You all right?"

She sighed and managed to lift a hand to his face. "Better than."

He smiled then. "Yeah. Me too. That was…"

"Awesome."

"Mmmm." He brushed soft kisses over her temple to the corner of her eye, where he again tasted the salt of her tears.

Tears?

"Oh, baby. Don't cry."

"I'm not." She gave a huff of breath. "Well, maybe I am, but these are happy tears."

"You're sure?" He carried her across the room to the sofa and lowered her to the cushions before lying beside her and gathering her close.

"I'm sure." She looked up at him and smiled. "This evening was so unbearably painful and humiliating. It may have been the worst moments of my life. And now…" She touched a finger to his lips. "I can't believe you were able to turn it into this incredible joy."

His lips curved into his trademark rebel smile. "My pleasure, ma'am. I have to say, you made my evening pretty amazing, too. I never saw this coming."

"You've been my secret love since I was a little girl."

"You sure do know how to keep a secret. I didn't have a clue."

"How could I admit something so impossible? There you

were, this tall, dark, mysterious stranger who walked into school and put all the other boys to shame, with that chip on your shoulder and that fearless swagger."

His smile grew. "That's how you saw me?"

"That's how everybody saw you, Ben. You've always been larger than life."

"I don't know about that. But I've always been grateful I was big enough to lift you out of the way of that runaway ATV. I figured you were a goner."

"And you kept asking me over and over if I was all right. And I was absolutely speechless, wondering what I could possibly say to bad boy Ben Monroe. I was tongue-tied and trembling."

"I was so afraid you'd been injured, my hands were shaking."

"And I was so in awe of you, I couldn't think of a thing to say."

"You stuck your nose up in the air and backed away. And all the time I thought you hated me."

"How could I ever hate you, Ben? You just purely owned my heart."

"Dear God, Becca." He lowered his head and kissed her with a kind of reverence that had her sighing with pleasure.

She wrapped her arms around his neck and returned his kisses with a hunger that matched his.

And then there were no words as they took each other again, ever so slowly, as if to make up for the explosion of their first time. Gently, as if they had all the time in the world, they showed each other in the only way they knew how, all the things they'd kept locked in their hearts for all these long, lonely years.

"Where are you going?" Rebecca felt the mattress sag as Ben moved away from her.

Sometime during the night he'd carried her to her bedroom, where they had snuggled and whispered and loved until they were sated.

"I thought I'd see what's in your refrigerator."

"You're hungry?" She started to scramble up. "I'll fix..."

"You stay here." Gently he lay a hand on her shoulder, pressing her back against the pillows. "I can find my way around a kitchen. I'll fix something for both of us."

"Okay." She lay back, watching as he pulled on his jeans, leaving them unsnapped at the waist before sauntering from the room.

This felt like a dream. A wonderful, joyous dream that she hoped would never end.

Ben Monroe here. In her house. In her bed. Loving her.

She tucked her hands behind her head and smiled. Her dreams had never been as wonderful as this. Last evening, with its humiliating visit from the police detective, had felt like her worst nightmare. And then suddenly Ben was beside her, turning it all upside down.

What sort of magic did he possess that he could turn her worst day into her best night ever?

During their lovemaking he'd whispered love words that had her, even now, blushing like a schoolgirl.

She sat up, letting the bed linens slip away, unconcerned about her nakedness. Ben Monroe loved her. It had been her heart's secret yearning since she was a girl. And now, he was here with her.

Ben walked into the room carrying a tray.

Seeing her, his smile grew. "I thought I was hungry, but seeing what I'm seeing, I realize it isn't food I'm craving."

She glanced down at herself before bursting into laughter and pulling the covers up to her chin. "Sorry, cowboy. First you have to feed me. Then we'll deal with what you're craving."

"You've got a mean streak in you, Becca Henderson." He set the tray on a night table before shucking his jeans and climbing into bed beside her.

He broke open a banana-nut muffin and offered her a bite. "These look home-baked."

"They are." She swallowed. "My mother is the baker in the family."

"Tell me about her."

Rebecca smiled. "She's a really private person. She and Dad are the perfect team. Fussy, almost to a fault. They don't like anything that disrupts their quiet lifestyle. I learned early in life to go along or face their disappointment."

"Did they punish you?"

She shook her head. "Not the way you'd think. They never raised a hand against me. But I could always tell, by the looks on their faces, that they weren't happy with something I'd done. And having them disappointed was the worst sort of punishment." She leaned back, remembering. "I was hardly ever defiant the way my friends were. I didn't like breaking the rules. But there were things I yearned for, and I didn't feel free to confide in my parents, because I knew instinctively they wouldn't understand."

"Like what?"

She laughed. "A puppy. I was fixated on getting a pet, and my parents were just as adamant that they were never allowing an animal into their well-ordered life. Mom said they mess on the rugs. Dad said they have to be walked, even in bad weather. I remember begging, pleading, saying I'd do all the work, but in the end, they won."

"Not having a pet isn't the worst thing in the world."

Rebecca nodded. "I know. That's what I told myself. But they always won. Maybe because I just wasn't willing to fight hard enough for what I wanted."

"How about now?"

She shrugged. "After my years in Bozeman, I thought I'd developed a little backbone. I learned a lot about myself while I was away."

"Like what?"

She pursed her lips, thinking. "I learned that I was stronger than I thought. I could step away from the protection my parents always gave me, along with their strict control, and not only survive but also thrive. I studied hard and worked. I discovered that I like retail, not because of my father, but for myself. When I came home, I decided that my own business would be my first step toward independence. And so far, my parents are going along with it, though to be honest, I think they're just humoring me. I suspect they hope I'll lose interest and they can get back to the way things were."

"You know what I think?"

She glanced over.

"I think they're good people who love their only child, and they're probably as eager as you are to make things right between you."

"You're such a forgiving man, Ben."

"I learned from the master. My father, Mackenzie Monroe, is the kindest man I know." He set aside the rest of the muffin and gathered her close. Against her temple he murmured, "I kept my word. I fed you, a lot more than one bite. Now I want to feed something else."

"Not fair. I bet you take a whole lot more than one..."

Her words were swallowed by his kiss. And then everything she'd been about to say was forgotten as he took her on the most delicious ride to paradise.

CHAPTER TWENTY-THREE

"What are you doing?" Rebecca awoke to find Ben leaning up on one elbow, watching her.

"Thinking of words while I watched you sleep."

"Words?" She ran her hands across his shoulders, loving the feel of all those corded muscles. His body, honed by years of ranch chores, was perfectly sculpted. He could be a poster boy for the State of Montana. Cowboy. Rebel. Hell-raiser. Her father's favorite description slipped unbidden into her mind. It suited Ben, until her father made it sound like something evil.

"Words like *beautiful. Sweet. Surprising. Soul mate.* You're all those things I never thought could be mine. For the past half hour I've been looking at the most beautiful woman in the world, and wondering how I managed to sweet-talk myself into her bed."

"Is that what you did?" She gave a soft laugh. "And I thought I was the one who'd dragged you here."

"I don't care who did the sweet-talking and who did the dragging. All I know is, I'm where I never thought I could be, even though it's been my heart's desire."

"Heart's desire." She gave him a dreamy smile. "I love hearing you say that. And you're mine, Ben. My lifelong secret heart's desire."

He nodded toward the soft, dawn light just beginning to filter through her bedroom window. "It'll be morning soon. Want to start the day with breakfast, or something else?"

"That depends. What 'something else' are you suggesting?"

"Pretty much the same things we've been doing all night. I don't know about you, but I just can't get enough."

She made a purring sound in the back of her throat. "I like the way you think. Why don't we hold off breakfast for a while, and think about...something else?"

"A woman after my own heart." He rolled her over, until she was lying on top of him. At her look of surprise he said with a grin, "You have five whole minutes to do with me what you please."

"Five whole minutes? How generous, Deputy."

His smile grew. "I figure that's just about the limit of my self-control. After that, I just might have to let loose and join in the activity."

She ran nibbling kisses down his throat, then lower, across his hair-roughened chest before making little murmuring sounds of approval as she continued a downward trail of kisses.

His hands fisted in the sheets and he struggled to remain as still as a statue. Finally his arms came around her and he dragged her up the length of his body until her mouth was on his.

"You promised five minutes..."

"Sorry. I lied." His voice was a growl of pleasure as they

came together in a storm of passion that caught them both by surprise.

"What's this?" Rebecca opened her eyes as the wonderful aroma of freshly ground coffee filled the bedroom.

"I made breakfast."

"And here I am, sleeping like a lazy slug."

"A beautiful, beguiling slug, I might add." He leaned down to kiss the tip of her nose.

She sat up and reached for his shirt. He paused, a steaming cup of coffee in his hand, watching her through narrowed eyes.

Seeing the intensity in his gaze, she looked up. "What's wrong?"

He gave a slight shake of his head. "Nothing's wrong. Everything is so right. Even the way you look in my shirt." He grinned. "I like it better on you than on me."

She ran a hand up his arm. "Me too. I like you shirtless."

He affected a drawl. "I could say the same for you, little lady."

He held out the cup. "High-octane coffee and toast with scrambled eggs and bacon."

"All this food." She took a bite before setting aside the plate. "I never eat breakfast."

"This isn't just breakfast. This is fuel for our next round."

She arched a brow.

He gave her a devilish grin. "Did I happen to mention that I don't have to work?"

"How did you manage that?"

"The sheriff has my shift covered by the state police. So I can be as lazy as I please. And I'm hoping you'll agree to be lazy with me. Think of all the things two lazy slugs could do in an entire day."

She gave a dreamy smile before shaking her head. "I wish I could. But I have to show up for work. There's nobody to cover my shift."

"Could you be late?"

She sighed, considering.

Ben leaned in, nibbling a trail of kisses across her shoulder to her neck.

She shivered. "You know what that does to me."

"Yes, I do. You think you might consider being a little late today?"

"Oh, Ben." She set aside her coffee and wrapped her arms around his neck, drawing him in. "How could I possibly resist such an invitation?"

They were both laughing as they rolled around the bed. And then their laughter turned to soft sighs and whispered words as they lost themselves once more in passion.

"I really need to get to work, Ben." Rebecca stretched before sitting up beside him. "I wish we could just lock the doors and keep the world away while we play, but I have a business to attend to."

"No need to apologize. From what I've seen, your business is really taking off."

His words warmed her heart as nothing else could have. "Oh, Ben. It means so much to me to hear you say that. Maybe because it's all mine. Or maybe because even my own parents don't believe it will amount to anything. They're simply humoring me."

"But so far, they're going along with your plans. And that's a start."

"I don't want them to just go along. I want them to cheer me on."

"Give them a chance, Becca."

She leaned over to press a kiss to his mouth. "You're a good man, Ben Monroe."

"I only care if I'm good enough for you."

She took his face between her hands and stared down into his eyes before leaning close to kiss him again. "You're the only one for me."

He gathered her close and took the kiss deeper.

On a sigh she pushed free of his arms and sat up, her breathing shallow, her skin flushed. "One of us needs to be sensible. I'm getting out of this bed and going to work. Now."

"Yes, ma'am." He lay grinning as she hurried into the shower.

Minutes later she felt strong arms slide around her and turned to find him standing under the spray.

"Ben. What are you doing?"

"Helping you get ready for work."

"Helping? Or hindering?"

"Your choice, ma'am. What's your pleasure?"

With a laugh she poured herself into a kiss, and as the warm water played over them, they gave themselves up to yet another pleasure.

"What are you doing, Ben?"

He was standing at the front door, hat in hand. "I'm driving you to work."

"When will I see you again?"

He touched a finger to the little frown line between her brows. "I was thinking I'd pick you up after work and we'd head to the Hitching Post for supper."

Her smile was radiant. "I'd love it. And then we can come back here for...dessert."

Her hesitation wasn't lost on him. He gave a warm

chuckle. "Whatever you say, ma'am. We can have...dessert here. Or anything your little heart desires."

"Oh, Ben." She raced up to him and threw her arms around his neck, hugging him fiercely. "I hope you don't mind. I'm not used to any of this yet, and seeing you at the door, I was afraid you'd had enough of me and wanted to escape."

He lifted her off her feet, so her eyes were level with his. "Get this straight, Becca. I'm not interested in hot, mindless sex." A look came into his eyes, and he couldn't stop the laughter that broke free. "Wait. Let me start over. I love hot, mindless sex. But only with you. And I'm not going anywhere, unless it's with you. I'm here for the long haul. Got it?"

She felt absolutely weightless, held so easily in his arms. But it was his words that touched her heart so deeply, he made her feel light as air.

She wrapped her arms around his neck and kissed him full on the mouth. "Okay. I get it."

"Good." He returned her kiss. "And if you don't stop doing what you're doing right this minute, you're going to be late for work."

"Oh." She pushed a little away and he set her on her feet before pulling open the front door.

As she started down the front walk, he caught her hand.

"The neighbors will see us."

"Good." He winked, melting her heart. "Let's give them something to talk about." He paused at the passenger side of his truck and bent to kiss her before holding open the door.

He circled around to the driver's side and climbed in. Then, for good measure, he leaned across the seat and kissed her again. Finally he sat back and turned the key in the ignition. "I guess that'll have to hold me until tonight."

She touched a finger to her lips. "You pack quite a kiss, cowboy."

"Just trying to take care of business, ma'am."

They shared a smile as the truck rolled down the street.

When they stopped in front of the hardware store, Rebecca caught sight of her father just walking in the door. Hearing the truck, he paused and turned.

"I guess another kiss is out of the question." Ben shot her a grin.

"I think it might be too much of a shock for my poor father. I'm sure, seeing you this early in the morning, his mind is already going into overdrive."

"You know I'll want to talk to him."

She put a hand on Ben's sleeve. "Not yet, Ben. Please."

"Just so you know. I have no intention of doing anything behind his back."

She sighed. "I know. I wouldn't expect anything less of you. But give me a day or two to get him used to the idea of the two of us."

He nodded.

"I'll see you tonight." She opened the door and hurried to catch up with her father, who stood frowning.

As Ben drove away, he could see father and daughter in his rearview mirror, facing one another. Though he couldn't hear their words, their body language told him more than enough.

It was just one more hurdle, he told himself.

He'd spent a lifetime climbing mountains. What was one more, when the prize awaiting him was worth more than gold?

Spotting one of his ranch trucks approaching, he came to a halt and watched as the vehicle pulled up beside the hardware store. Otis and Roscoe stepped out, causing Rebecca and her father to hurry toward them.

Puzzled, Ben backed up and stepped from his truck.

The two old men circled to the rear of their vehicle and began muscling out an ornate piece of wrought iron.

"Need some help?" Ben offered a hand, which the two men gratefully accepted.

Under Roscoe's direction, Ben hauled it toward a break in the fenced area.

"Right here will be perfect." Roscoe stood back, pointing as Ben set the heavy arch in place.

When he stepped back, Rebecca studied the arch before clapping a hand to her mouth in surprise.

"I figured, since Otis was supplying you with his specialty, I'd offer something of my own. I hope you like it, Miss Becca."

Rebecca stared up at the beautifully sculpted wrought-iron leaves and flowers adorning a heavy gate, and a sign at the very top of the arch that read, in ornate letters, BECCA'S GARDEN.

Tears flooded her eyes and she couldn't stop them spilling down her cheeks as she turned to the old man and hugged him fiercely. "Oh, Roscoe, I love it. I had no idea you had such a talent."

He blushed clear to his toes at her display of affection. "Well, I haven't tried anything this fancy before, but you're such a special lady, I purely wanted to make something special for you."

"You did." She stepped back, wiping at her eyes as her father and several of his employees walked over to admire his work. "Roscoe, this is absolutely perfect. And I don't have to wonder what I'll call my business. You've given it the perfect name. Becca's Garden." She squeezed his hand before turning to Ben, who stood quietly beside her. "Did you know about Roscoe's talent?"

Ben was grinning from ear to ear. "I've seen him work wonders with the machinery around our ranch, but this is something way different." He reached out a handshake with the old man. "You do good work."

"Thanks, son." Roscoe stood a little taller as the others congratulated him on the quality of his gate.

A short time later he and Otis said their good-byes and drove away, leaving Rebecca shaking her head in wonder.

Who would have believed that unassuming old cowboy hid such an amazing talent?

Becca's Garden.

As she waved good-bye to Ben, she felt as if she were floating, her feet barely touching the ground.

She couldn't imagine a day this wonderful getting any better.

CHAPTER TWENTY-FOUR

Rebecca stood in the little fenced area beside her father's hardware store and began tallying the sales for the day. When a representative from the mayor's office had arrived with a check for the last hundred pumpkins needed for the Autumn Festival, she'd far exceeded her anticipated total.

Her heart did a funny little dip as Ben's truck pulled up and came to a halt outside the fence. He stepped from his vehicle and hurried over.

"How was your day?"

"Even better than expected. And yours?"

A smile tugged at the corners of his mouth. "How could my day be anything but sweet after the night we shared?"

"Did your family wonder where you were last night?"

He shot her a quick grin. "If they did, they're too polite to ask. In case you haven't noticed, I haven't had to report in for years. I'm a grown man, Becca."

She touched a hand to his arm, feeling the corded muscles beneath the plaid shirt. "Oh, I've noticed."

They shared a laugh.

"Ready to head over to the Hitching Post, or would you rather eat at Dolly's Diner?"

Rebecca's eyes danced. "Dolly makes the best meat loaf."

"Dolly's it is."

She nodded. "Just let me close out my register."

After running the tape and emptying the till, she put everything into a heavy bank bag and zipped it shut before turning. "I'll just be a minute. I want to put this in the safe."

Minutes later she danced out the door and hurried over to Ben's truck.

He helped her into the passenger side before climbing into the driver's side.

He drove through the streets of Haller Creek until they came to the little diner, where half the town managed to eat at least once a week.

After finding a parking space around the corner, Ben caught Rebecca's hand as she stepped from his truck. Keeping her hand tucked in his, he led her inside, where they were greeted by a chorus of voices mingled with trills of laughter from the tables of ranchers and their families. Above it all was the sweet, tearful voice of Patsy Cline singing about being crazy for someone.

The words went straight to Ben's heart. The old familiar song had a brand-new meaning for him now.

"Hey, Ben. Rebecca." Dolly, in a spotless white dress and apron, with a pretty brooch at the high neckline, hurried over to greet them. "I've got a booth in the corner."

"Great." They trailed the owner and were forced to stop at nearly every table to speak to someone they knew.

"Hey, Ben. Got yourself a pretty lady tonight."

"You got that right, Van." Ben winked at the owner of the cleaners before moving on.

"Evening, Rebecca. How'd you lasso our new deputy?"

Rebecca shared a laugh with the circle of church ladies. "I guess I caught him in a weak moment."

"He's a keeper," one of the women called as they continued trailing Dolly.

When they were finally seated at their booth, Dolly handed them menus. "The special tonight is meat loaf."

Ben looked at Rebecca before saying, "Two."

"You get a choice of coleslaw or broccoli with your mashed potatoes."

At Rebecca's grin, Ben said, "One of each."

Dolly nodded. "I know you're having coffee, Ben. Rebecca, you having your usual tea?"

"Yes, please."

"Lemon and honey?"

"Fine."

"You got it."

As Dolly walked away, Ben was chuckling. "Why does she bother with menus? She knows what everybody in this town likes."

"And that's why she's so successful. She anticipates what we want before we know we want it."

He reached over to take her hand in his. "I've known what I wanted for a long time now. I'm just happy that the object of my affection finally figured it out."

Her cheeks turned a becoming shade of pink.

He loved the fact that she could still blush like a schoolgirl, but taking pity on her, he changed the subject. "How did your morning go?"

She shrugged, knowing he was asking about her father's reaction to seeing him. Ben was too kind to put her on the spot by mentioning it aloud.

She stared hard at the tabletop. "Now that I'm here with

you, I can't remember a thing about the morning, except Roscoe's beautiful arch and gate."

"That was a special surprise. So now, let's just enjoy our supper. And then there's always"—he wiggled his brows like a movie villain—"dessert at your place."

Her smile was brighter than ever. "It's all I could think about all day."

"Me too. And believe me, when I'm mucking stalls and riding into the high country to babysit a herd of ornery cattle, I'm grateful for any happy thoughts that come my way."

"You work so hard, Ben."

"No harder than any other rancher around here."

Their conversation came to an abrupt halt when Dolly set down glasses of ice water and their coffee and tea. Minutes later she returned with their dinner, and they both dug in.

Ben moved a little dish in the center of the table. "I'll let you taste my coleslaw if you give me one piece of your broccoli."

"You like veggies?"

"I had no choice growing up. All those men sat around the table monitoring everything my brothers and I ate." Ben laughed, remembering. "They were determined to teach us to eat healthy, after a childhood of being forced to hoard whatever food we could steal."

Rebecca looked absolutely horrified. "Your foster families didn't feed you?"

"Some did. After years apart, we started sharing stories of those times, and we discovered that we had similar experiences. Some of the families really tried, but after years of abuse, my brothers and I had turned into pretty nasty rebels. Fighting became a way of life, and most good people just can't be bothered with that much disruption in their lives."

"Oh, Ben." Rebecca laid a hand over his, her eyes moist.

"Hey now." He reached across the table to brush a tear from her cheek. "Let's not rehash the past. Let's just celebrate what we've found."

She closed her fingers over his wrist and met his steady gaze. "Right now, what we've found is so much better than anything I could have hoped for."

"Yeah. I agree. Our future's looking a lot better than the past."

"Hey, you two." Horton Duke, owner of the Hitching Post, paused beside their table. "Get a room."

Ben threw back his head and roared. "What are you doing here, Horton?"

"Checking out the competition. Besides..." He leaned down to add in a whisper, "Dolly's meat loaf is my weakness. Every time she makes it, I just have to stop by and sample it. But if you're hoping for a cool longneck before heading home, stop by my place."

"Thanks, Horton. We'll keep that in mind."

"Or, if you're planning on a long, romantic night, I could always sell you a six-pack to go."

While Rebecca's cheeks bloomed, Ben merely shared a laugh with the old man.

When he was gone, Ben kept his voice low. "Judging by Horton's remarks and from the looks we're getting from the folks around us, I don't think we can keep our feelings secret very long." He paused a beat before asking, "Is that going to be a problem?"

She couldn't help the smile that put a light in her eyes. "It isn't a problem for me if it isn't a problem for you."

He released a slow breath. "Becca, if it were up to me, I'd be shouting the news from the rooftops."

They shared a laugh as they finished their meal.

Dolly hurried over to take away their dishes. "In honor of the town's Autumn Festival, I made pumpkin pies."

They nodded in unison.

She gave a throaty laugh. "I figured that would get to you. Ice cream or whipped cream?"

Ben winked at Rebecca. "Can we have both?"

"You sure can."

Dolly hurried away and returned with two big slices of pumpkin pie frosted with a side of vanilla ice cream and topped with a mound of freshly whipped cream.

Later, Ben caught Rebecca's hand, and the two strolled out of the diner, calling good night to friends and neighbors.

As they stepped out into the night air, Ben was aware of the way many of the patrons of the diner watched their progress with interest.

"You realize that someone in your neighborhood will spot my truck in your driveway tonight. By morning, even more tongues will be wagging."

Rebecca settled herself into the passenger side and watched as he drove through the darkened streets. "Right now, I don't mind if the whole world knows."

While Ben hung their jackets on a coat tree by the front door, Rebecca hurried to the kitchen. Minutes later she returned with two Champagne flutes.

Ben gave her a slow, appraising smile. "Champagne?"

"I've been saving this for a special occasion. I think this qualifies."

"Oh, yeah. This qualifies." He touched his glass to hers. "What will we drink to?"

"To…" Her cheeks were flushed as she paused before saying, "Dreams coming true."

They sipped.

She looked over. "You're doing it again."

"Doing what?"

"Just staring at me."

"I can't help it. Becca, every time I look at you, you take my breath away."

She dimpled. Uncomfortable beneath his steady look, she turned. "Is there anything you'd like?"

"You know what I want." He set aside the half-filled glass and put a hand on her arm. Just a touch, but it was enough to have her bobbling her glass and spilling the liquid over the rim.

"Oh, dear."

"No harm." He set her glass aside before taking a crisp handkerchief from his pocket and wiping her hand dry.

Without a word he led her toward the bedroom. Standing beside the bed, he reached for the buttons of her shirt. His voice was low. Solemn. "I've been thinking about this all day."

He unbuttoned her blouse and slid it from her shoulders before reaching behind her to unfasten her lace bra. He unsnapped her jeans and slid them down over her hips before easing her to the edge of the bed. He knelt to remove her shoes, and then her jeans.

He ran a hand along her calf to her thigh, then higher, until she gave a gasp of surprise.

"Ben..."

"Shh. Indulge me my fantasies. Let me pleasure you, Becca."

His touch was so gentle, all she could do was sigh as, with lips and tongue and fingertips, he took her high, then higher still, until all she could do was hold on as he took her up and over, until her entire body seemed to shatter into splinters of fire.

When she thought there was nothing more she could possibly feel, he shed his clothes and joined her on the bed. Holding her as tenderly as a fragile flower, he entered her.

Her eyes went wide as even more pleasure shot through her.

"Oh, Ben." She wrapped herself around him, moving with him, loving the feel of him, flesh to flesh, his heartbeat as out of control as hers.

Suddenly, everything changed. One minute their movements were slow and measured. The next they felt a wildfire raging through their overheated systems, electrifying them as they raced into the heart of the blaze. By the time they'd come out the other side, their bodies were slick with sheen.

They lay, breathing labored, heartbeats thundering.

And as their world slowly settled, they clung together, feeling like the only survivors left in the universe.

"What was your father's reaction yesterday morning?"

It was nearly dawn, and the two lovers had spent the most amazing night together, discovering the many secrets they had never shared with another.

"I'm not sure what bothered him the most. Seeing you driving me to work, or realizing your truck was parked in my driveway overnight. I think he was more concerned about what the neighbors would say than the fact that you and I spent the night together."

"Maybe that's a good thing."

She shot him a look of surprise.

"If he's willing to accept the fact that we're together, maybe he can take the next logical step and consider letting go of his prejudices about me and my family."

"Ben, we're talking about my father. He's not the easiest man in the world to accept change."

"It'll happen whether he's ready or not." Ben took her hand, measuring its size against his own. "I'd like your permission to talk to him."

She was already shaking her head. "I don't know..."

"I do. I owe him enough respect to tell him how I feel about his daughter."

She laughed and touched a finger to his lips. "Maybe you ought to let me in on how you feel."

He shot her a wicked smile. "If you haven't figured it out by now, we're in trouble. I've been in love with you from the first time I saw you. But when I carried you home after your prom—"

She put a finger to his lips to halt his words. "That night is burned into my memory. First, the horror of what almost happened, and then you coming to my rescue. And then my father having you arrested, even though I kept telling him you were my hero, not the villain. And..." She looked away, ashamed even now. "I never had a chance to thank you."

"Becca, you were in shock. None of it was your fault."

"But my father..."

"Went a little crazy when he realized what almost happened to his little girl. It's old news now." Ben gathered her close to whisper against her temple, "Right now, that's all just a dim memory. All I can think about is loving you. And that's why I need to talk to your father. This can't wait."

"Oh, Ben." She wrapped herself around him, loving the feel of all those muscles making her feel safe. Making her feel special. "I hope you're prepared for fireworks."

He pressed a kiss to her throat. "I wouldn't back down even if your father was holding a bazooka."

She absorbed a series of tremors along her spine. All he had to do was touch her, kiss her like this, and she was lost.

"All right." She sighed. "But for now, how about a little more...dessert."

And then there were no words as they slipped into that special place where only lovers can go.

CHAPTER TWENTY-FIVE

Ben."

At the sound of Virgil's voice on his cell phone, Ben set aside the coffee he'd been enjoying at Rebecca's kitchen table. "Yes, Sheriff."

"The state boys have concluded their investigation into Will Theisen's years at divinity school and have set up a meeting with Will for nine o'clock this morning at his place. I'd like you at that meeting."

Ben glanced at the kitchen clock, noting that he had less than half an hour. "I'll be there."

"Good. Remember to wear your uniform, since you're representing me. Afterward, I'd like you to stop by my office and we'll talk."

"Depending on how long it lasts, I should be there before noon."

"Good." The sheriff hung up.

Ben glanced at Rebecca seated across the table. "Good thing I washed my uniform last night."

Rebecca laughed. "I believe I boasted that having you here was like having my very own housekeeper, since you did my laundry with yours."

"That's what comes of living with a houseful of men. Whenever one of us does a load of laundry, we do everybody's laundry." He looked down at his shirt and pants, and the badge winking at his breast pocket. "A state police detective is meeting with Will in half an hour. Virgil wants me there as his liaison."

Her smile faded slightly. "I hope Will's interview goes more smoothly than mine."

"You realize I won't be able to fill you in on the details. Whatever I hear will remain part of the police file."

She nodded.

On a sigh she said, "I may as well head over to work."

"I'll drop you on the way to Will's."

Minutes later, as they walked outside to Ben's truck, their moods had gone from lighthearted to somber. Though neither of them spoke of the shots that had been fired, they were both keenly aware that nothing had changed. Somewhere in town someone wishing them harm was in hiding, and waiting for another opportunity to stalk Rebecca or Will for some reason known only to the stalker.

Ben brought his truck to a smooth stop outside the hardware store. "How late do you work tonight?"

Rebecca paused before climbing from Ben's truck. "We're planning on closing early, since the town is filling up with ranchers for the start of the Autumn Festival. The high school plans a kickoff relay race at noon."

"Why don't I pick you up whenever I can get away? If it's early enough, we could grab something at the Hitching Post and still find a spot along Main Street to watch the race."

"All right." She reached over to squeeze his hand. "Last night was . . . amazing."

He shot her a devilish grin. "This morning wasn't bad, either, ma'am."

They were both laughing as she stepped down from his truck and stood watching as he pulled away.

"Ben." Will Theisen seemed surprised to see him when he opened the front door.

"Will. Sheriff Kerr asked me to sit in on the interview as his representative. I'll be meeting with him at his office afterward."

"I see."

"Whatever is disclosed here will remain confidential, except for law enforcement."

"Thanks. I appreciate that." Will stood aside and indicated the parlor, where Detective Russ Godfrey was seated.

After Ben and the detective shook hands, Ben chose a seat some distance from Will, giving the young minister some space.

Ben glanced around the old-fashioned parlor of Will's family home. Will's parents had passed away several years earlier, and the house had been through a succession of tenants, none of whom had made any improvements. Now the walls showed faded imprints where old photos had once hung. Most of the furniture had been arranged in clusters awaiting pickup by a local charity before the house was put on the market. The rooms looked old and faded.

Detective Russ Godfrey began by mentioning Will's mentor, Reverend Palmer, the dean of the divinity school.

"Reverend Palmer told me about a . . . situation between you and a woman named Mercy Martino."

Will blanched. "I'd hoped to move on from that."

Detective Godfrey continued smoothly. "I understand you were counseling the lady, who was a member of the inner-city church you'd been assigned to."

Will nodded.

His hands, Ben noted, were clasped tightly in his lap, as though holding himself together by sheer force of will.

"Tell me about Mercy Martino."

Will swallowed. "She's young. Barely eighteen, and already the mother of a two-year-old and another on the way."

"The father of her child?"

"Ranaldo Rider. Also eighteen. He runs with an unsavory bunch. He boasted to her that his friends don't marry their women."

"How did you feel when she told you that?"

Will frowned. "I told her that's not love. If he loved her, he would make a commitment to be her husband and a loving, caring father to their children."

"How did that sit with the young woman?"

Will's tone lowered with undisguised disgust. "She said that's just the way things are. She would have to accept it because she loved him but could never change him."

"And you were okay with that?"

"How could I be?" Agitated, Will stood and began to pace. "That goes against everything I believe as a minister. I told Mercy that if she wanted respect from Ranaldo, she would first have to respect herself."

"And how should she do that?"

"By laying down the law to him. When she told me how much Ranaldo loved their two-year-old son, Hunter, I told her to use that as leverage to get what she needed. If she should refuse to allow Ranaldo to see his son and let him know that he would never get to see the baby girl she was carrying, Ranaldo would come around and realize that he needed to do the right thing, if not out of consideration for her, then at least so he could have what he wanted from their relationship."

"Did you discuss this with Reverend Palmer before counseling Mercy?"

Will stopped his pacing. "No."

"Why not?"

Will sighed. "I knew what his advice would be."

"And that is?"

"He would have told me to step away. The rule of counseling is to never get too emotionally involved with the people you're trying to help. But that rule makes no sense. If I'm going to help someone, I need to get close enough to learn the whole truth of their situation."

"Even if it means violating a rule?"

Will sat down heavily in the chair. "She was so young. And she looked tired and beat. She lives with her widowed mother, who works two jobs just to keep ahead of their bills. A two-year-old, another on the way, and little or no help from the father of those children. It isn't right."

"It may not be right, but that was her choice."

"I know that. But don't you see? I was showing her a life she could have if she made better choices."

"And if your advice backfired? Were you going to be there for her if Ranaldo left her? Would you be there to rush her to the hospital, or to comfort her if Ranaldo and his friends decided to 'teach her a lesson'?"

Sweating now, Will pressed the back of his hand to his brow. "Obviously I can't be there physically for her. But I firmly believe it's my duty to show her the right way."

"While she's left alone to pay the piper."

Will lowered his head. "I didn't think about that." He looked over. "Is she...all right?"

"As far as I know."

Will audibly exhaled.

"But that raises a question. Could our mysterious shooter be this Ranaldo Rider? And if so, isn't it safe to assume you could be the target?"

Will's eyes went wide. "Do you know that for a fact?"

"What I know is this. Ranaldo went to Mercy's place. She told him you'd been counseling her, and because of that he couldn't come in and wouldn't be allowed to see Hunter or be there for the birth of their daughter unless he agreed to show his respect by marrying her and supporting all of them. He went off the deep end and threatened her and her mother. When her mother phoned the local police, Ranaldo ran and hasn't been seen since."

Detective Godfrey waited a beat before lowering his voice. "I need to know. Was this a romantic involvement on your part or on the young woman's part?"

"No." Will gave an emphatic shake of his head. "I would never…" He paused before trying to explain. "If anything, I thought of Mercy as a little sister. I just wanted to do what was right, not only for her but also for her children."

"All right. I'm willing to believe you. Reverend Palmer believes that, as well. So, there was no romantic relationship between you. But you know you messed up. You should have confided in your mentor. That's his job, to counsel the counselor, and he takes it very seriously."

Will bowed his head. "I know."

"Reverend Palmer feels he failed you. Because of your inexperience, you have put the lives of innocent people in danger. Mercy and her son, her unborn baby, and even Ranaldo."

"Ranaldo?" Will's head came up sharply.

"He's young. Angry. Scared. And probably being taunted

by his friends for letting his woman push him around. That can cause a young man with a gun and a hair-trigger temper to do foolish, dangerous things. Right now, he isn't wanted for any serious criminal activity. But all that could change. For all we know, he could be here in Haller Creek right now, seeking revenge against the man who started this downhill slide in his life."

Will lowered his head to his hands. "I never thought it would go this far."

"Nobody ever does." Detective Godfrey stood. "I suggest you stay close to home. Don't walk the streets. And stay away from the crowds at the Autumn Festival until this is concluded. We have a photo and description of Ranaldo Rider circulating among law enforcement agencies. We intend to keep a close eye for any sighting of him. At this point, because of the previous shootings, we have to believe he's armed and dangerous. That means that the police have the right to treat him as a dangerous criminal and use deadly force if necessary."

The detective glanced at Ben, who had remained silent throughout the entire interview. "I believe we now know the intended target of those shootings. I'll be contacting Ms. Henderson with the news that she is no longer considered a target."

"Thanks, Detective."

Ben shook hands with Will and put a hand on his shoulder. "Stay indoors, Will. I'll drive past your house as often as I can, just to make sure nothing seems out of place. Call if you see anything suspicious."

"Thanks, Ben. I will. And, Ben..." He swallowed. "I appreciate all you've done."

Ben followed the state police detective down the steps to his truck. Once there he turned toward the sheriff's office.

As he drove, he breathed a sigh of relief. Even though this shooter hadn't been found yet, it was enough to know the name of the suspect and to be assured that Rebecca was no longer the target.

Now to get this young punk off the streets before he did something he would live to regret.

Regret. Poor Will was learning a thing or two about that.

Ben tapped a finger on the steering wheel. His dad often said hell is paved with good intentions. A single deed, like a stone tossed into a pond, can create ripples that go on and on, changing calm waters to raging tides.

"So, our new minister was counseling a pretty young thing." Virgil was seated at his desk, listening as Ben filled him in on the interview.

"He urged her to assert herself. When you think about it, that's what most of us would want for her. But Will's mentor, Reverend Palmer, claims it's a mistake too many amateurs make. They forget about the consequences of such actions. In this case, the father of her kids is young and running with a bad crowd. Now he's between a rock and a hard place. He loves the girl and their son but has to save face with his buddies."

"And he decided to punish the one who got into his business."

Ben nodded. "Detective Godfrey ordered Will to stay off the streets until this is resolved. I promised Will I'd drive past his place several times today and every day, just to see that he's safe until the shooter is apprehended."

"Good idea. The state police told me they'll be patrolling the highways around Haller Creek and will have some undercover agents standing in the crowds at the festival. Hopefully, if that hoodlum comes within miles of our town, they'll soon have him off the streets and in custody." Virgil steepled his hands on the desktop. "You've got to be plenty happy to know Rebecca's in the clear."

"Yeah. Though I can't tell her the details of the interview between the detective and Will, I thought I'd drive over to the hardware store and buy her lunch. Detective Godfrey was planning on giving her the good news that she's no longer a target."

"That should make the Autumn Festival a lot more fun for both of you."

"Yeah. This is a huge relief." Ben was smiling as he got to his feet and started toward the door. "But I'll feel even better when the threat to Will is ended."

Though he would be driving past Will's place several times and was wearing his uniform and police-issue gun, he decided to drive his own truck, since he was officially off-duty while the state police filled in.

He couldn't wait to see Rebecca's face when he told her the good news.

CHAPTER TWENTY-SIX

It was almost noon, and Rebecca was getting ready to close her business for the day. Her smile was as bright as the afternoon sun. The detective's news that she was no longer considered the target of that shooter had given her an amazing sense of freedom. She hadn't realized just how tense and fearful she'd been, and how much of a dark cloud had been hanging over her, until the fear and tension were suddenly lifted from her shoulders.

When she'd asked the detective about Will, he'd said only that she didn't need to be concerned. She hoped and prayed that meant that they had both been cleared of any threat.

Rebecca closed out the cash register and began counting the money. Out of the corner of her eye she spotted sudden movement and glanced over her shoulder.

"Hi. Sorry. I didn't see you there. I'm afraid we're closed now." She nodded toward the throngs of people walking along the street. "Autumn Festival is just about to start. But if there's something I can help you with, just say the word."

When the stranger didn't respond, she turned to him.

The young man was good-looking in a rough sort of way. His jeans were worn so far beneath his waist they appeared to be falling off. His muscle shirt looked out of place in the cool autumn breeze, especially in a town where most of the young men wore denims and plaid shirts. Long black hair was blowing across his dark eyes. He lifted a hand to brush it aside.

That's when she spotted the shiny object in his hand.

Rebecca froze, her gaze riveted on the pistol.

She held out a fistful of money. "Here. Take it. Just take it and leave."

She turned away, hoping to run to the safety of the hardware store.

The sharp sting of metal against her temple had her seeing stars as the money slipped from her nerveless fingers and dropped to the ground, where it began blowing across the yard.

She stumbled, then righted herself and gained her footing, desperate to escape.

He lashed out a second time, hitting her harder.

His voice was a low rasp of barely controlled fury. "I didn't come for the money, bitch. I came for you. You make a sound, you're dead."

Those were the last words she heard as her legs failed her and she felt herself slipping down, down into a long tunnel of darkness.

Ben was forced to leave his truck parked on a side street, since the main street along the downtown area had been turned into a pedestrian walkway for the race.

He started along Main Street on foot, enjoying the festive air.

The Hitching Post had wisely parked a food truck along the route, and a long line had formed to buy chili dogs and beer.

Dolly's Diner was offering wrapped sandwiches and soda at a curbside tent. Families were lining up, eager to get ahead of the crowd before the race began.

The crowds had already begun forming on Main Street. The runners, each with a number across their chest, were milling about, stretching and trying to stay limber.

As Ben walked past the throng, he was forced to stop and chat with dozens of neighbors.

The mayor and the town council were gathering around a makeshift stage and viewing stand, where a microphone had been set up, along with a row of chairs for the officials to watch the race.

After his usual speech, the mayor planned to fire off a shot to signal the start of the race.

Everyone's attention was focused on the mayor holding up the pretty gilt statue of a runner that would be awarded to the winner.

After passing the reviewing stand, and saluting the mayor and council members, Ben turned toward the hardware store, hoping he could find Rebecca in this crowd. Maybe, if he was lucky, she was still at work, and he wouldn't have to hunt for her.

He was smiling as he ambled toward the fence marking her business alongside the hardware store. The sight of Roscoe's fancy wrought-iron gate had his smile widening.

As he drew nearer, he saw Hank Henderson on his cell phone, gesturing wildly. Beside him, his wife, Susan, was crying.

Crying? That didn't make any sense.

A crowd of people had gathered outside the fence, staring in grim silence.

As Ben shoved past them, his cell phone rang. He plucked it from his shirt pocket, noting the sheriff's number.

"Yeah?" As he spoke, he saw Rebecca lying in the dirt in the center of her garden area and a young man crouched over her.

In that same instant his heart stopped when he heard someone in the crowd cry, "Gun! He has a gun!"

Ben's family finished their ranch chores early and headed to town in a festive mood. Sam was at the wheel of the truck, with Mac seated between him and Finn. In the backseat, Roscoe, Otis, and Zachariah were carrying on a lively discussion of where they should end the day. Zachariah was singing the praises of Dolly's meat loaf, while the two old cowboys voted for the Hitching Post's half-pound burger and cold longnecks.

By the time they'd arrived at Haller Creek and located a parking place, they'd come to an agreement. They would have dinner at the Hitching Post and top off the evening with pie and coffee at Dolly's diner.

Mac looked around at the nearly empty viewing stand. "Did we miss the race?"

Roscoe was shaking his head. "I thought we left in plenty of time..."

Sam pointed. "There's something going on over at Henderson Hardware. Look at the crowd."

The six men started over at a quick pace. Halfway there Finn spotted Horton Duke.

"Hey, Horton. What's up with that crowd?"

The old man gave a quick shake of his head. "Some

wild-eyed gunman is holding Hank's daughter hostage." He looked over at Mac. "With the sheriff out of commission, your boy's alone, staring down the barrel of a gun. If you ask me…"

He found himself talking to air as the six men began running flat out toward the scene.

For the space of a heartbeat, Ben's blood seemed to freeze in his veins.

Instinctively his hand went to his holster, and he removed his pistol before striding forward.

The sheriff's voice was high with emotion. "Ben. I just got a report from Hank Henderson that Rebecca is being held hostage by a crazy gunman."

"I'm here. I see them both. I'm on it, Virgil." Ben automatically slid the phone into his shirt pocket before he stood, feet apart, facing Rebecca and the stranger.

Rebecca had been dragged to her feet, though she appeared dazed and wobbly. The man's arm around her waist was holding her upright. In his other hand was a gun, pressed to Rebecca's temple.

Ben knew, from the photo Detective Godfrey had shown him, that this stranger was the shooter they'd been hunting.

A shooter now holding Rebecca hostage.

At first, all he could focus on was the confused, terrified expression in her eyes and the blood dripping from an ugly cut to her temple.

Blood.

He'd hurt her. This madman had hurt sweet Becca.

Had she tried to resist? Or had he simply hurt her for the thrill of it?

Ben's finger actually trembled on the trigger. All his old survival instincts kicked in. He was thrust back into a brutal childhood, where a sadistic man who'd passed himself off as a father figure had beaten a helpless boy for the slightest infraction of his rules. A past where two little brothers had clung to him during a rare reunion, begging him to find a way for them to escape their endless hell. He'd risked his life, and theirs, to make it happen.

All the pain of those years, all the feelings of desperation, were nothing to the fury that rose up in him at the sight of his beloved Becca at the mercy of this madman.

His icy demeanor masked the white-hot fury boiling inside.

But this time, he wasn't a helpless kid.

His primal instinct took over his reasoning.

He knew, without a doubt, that he was the best marksman around. He was absolutely certain he could take this guy out with a single shot. But was he quick enough to keep this gunman from killing Becca in that same instant?

"Stop right there, Cop, or I blow her away."

Ben stood quietly, absolutely determined to do what he had to.

From somewhere nearby came Reverend Will Theisen's voice, trembling with emotion. "Let her go. I'm the one you want."

Ben whirled to see Will standing, pale and shaking, just about to step inside the fenced area.

He kept his voice low, controlled. "You were told to stay indoors."

"Rebecca's father called to tell me she's in trouble. This is all my fault, Ben. I brought this trouble to her doorstep. I want to help."

"You can help by staying as far away as possible." Ben moved, carefully positioning himself between Will and the gunman so there could be no clear shot to the unarmed minister.

The stranger shouted, "Yeah. You're the one I want,

Preacher. You're the self-righteous pompous ass who persuaded Mercy to turn away from me unless I married her. Because of you she won't even let me see my own kid. So now, Preacher, you're going to see how it feels to have somebody take over control of the ones you love. Oh, don't worry. I'm not going to kill you. That would be too easy. Instead, I'm going to take out this pretty lady while you're forced to watch. Then, just like me, you'll never again get to see your woman."

Ben kept his eyes steady on Rebecca's, willing her his strength. "You made a big mistake. She's not his woman. She's mine."

The stranger swore, loudly, fiercely, before shouting, "You're lying, Cop. That's what guys in power like you do to guys like me. You're trying to confuse me. But I'm not stupid. Every time I trailed that preacher, he was with this woman." He jammed his gun hard against Rebecca's bloody temple, causing her to cry out as fresh blood streamed down the front of her shirt.

There was an audible gasp from the crowd of onlookers, who were watching the scene unfolding with looks of horrified fascination. Like witnesses to a horrible train wreck, they couldn't tear their gazes from the gunman tormenting their neighbor and friend, even though it was heartbreaking to see.

"I saw how cozy the preacher and this female looked. So don't try to lie. I know she's his woman."

Ben's finger hovered on the trigger of his gun while his mind circled every angle. Will's arrival had caused this gunman to become even more agitated, and that made him all the more dangerous.

In Ben's misspent youth, he'd been fearless, engaging in bloody, knock-down, drag-out fights without regard to anyone but himself and his own survival. This time was different. Rebecca was counting on him to save her. Her safety, and hers alone, had to be his only concern.

His own death didn't even enter the equation. He would gladly die if he could save Becca from any more pain.

He'd never been forced to test his skill against such overwhelming odds. But he sensed, without a doubt, he could take out this gunman with a single shot, if only he could be certain Rebecca would be spared any more pain.

And then he caught a glimpse of his family. For the space of a single moment his gaze locked with his father's. He could hear, in his mind, Mackenzie Monroe's constant lectures about the Golden Rule. About doing to others what he wished for himself.

Mac called it karma. Getting back what was given.

Did it apply here? Now?

Why was he letting such thoughts crowd his mind? How could such rules matter at a time like this, when Becca's life was held in the balance?

The answer came in a sudden jolt of understanding.

Without dwelling on what he was about to do, Ben called, "Listen to me, Ranaldo."

The gunman showed a glimmer of surprise before glowering at him. "How do you know my name?"

"By now every police officer in the state of Montana knows your name and what you look like."

Ranaldo swore and yanked Rebecca's head back sharply, causing her to cry out again. "They'll really know me after I kill the preacher's woman."

"You don't want to do that, Ranaldo. I was telling you the truth. She isn't the preacher's woman. She's mine."

Will's voice rang out loud and clear. "Listen to him. She's the innocent party in all this."

"Innocent? Even if you're telling me the truth, and she's your woman, Cop, that makes her my enemy as much as you are. A cop's woman doesn't deserve to live any more than a cop does."

"Not all cops are bad."

"Oh yeah?" He pointed his gun at Ben's hand holding the pistol. "Look at you. Big man with a gun. If I kill your woman, I'm a scumbag. If you kill me, you're a hero. The only difference between us is that shiny tin badge. A badge that says you're allowed to kill without blame. You're all alike. You know if you kill someone like me, all the local yokels will be patting you on the back." His voice rose in fury as he waved his pistol in the air. "Look at them. They all want me dead."

Outside the fence, the murmur of the crowd grew to a roar.

"And what do you want, Ranaldo?"

The gunman was caught completely by surprise at the question. After a moment he shouted, "I want the preacher to pay for what he did to me. He took away my woman and my kids."

Ben turned to Will. "You're a distraction I can't afford. I want you to step away from the fence. Now."

"If I move, he'll kill me."

"He doesn't want you dead. He wants you to suffer by watching helplessly from the sidelines. You have to trust me on this, Will. Move away."

The fierce look in Ben's eyes had Will acquiescing without an argument. He stepped back and was instantly swallowed up by the crowd.

Ben kept his tone low and easy, with no hint of the range of emotions roiling through him as he turned back to the gunman. One wrong word, one wrong move, could mean the difference between life and death for the woman he loved. "I know you're angry because Mercy won't let you see your son."

"My son has a name. Hunter. His name is Hunter. And he's my kid. Mine. Not just hers. Now she's decided I won't ever see our baby girl after she's born, either."

"Have you thought of a name for your baby girl?"

This line of questioning was a sudden distraction, and the gunman could be seen struggling to mentally switch gears. "Angela. I wanted to name her Angela. It means little angel."

"That's pretty. I like it. What does Mercy think of the name Angela?"

The gunman's eyes narrowed. "You're just trying to keep me talking while you figure out how to get what you really want."

"And what do I want?"

"I know how you guys work. You want to keep me from doing what I came here to do while you get a bunch of sharp-shooters lined up to take me down."

"Then use me as your shield. Let the woman go and take me instead. They won't shoot at one of their own."

The gunman's eyes widened, then narrowed as he gave it more thought. "Another trick. You think if I let her go, you can overpower me. Look at you. Big, muscle-bound cop. You're just waiting for your chance to kill me."

Ben took a step closer, keeping his gaze steady on the gunman's. "If I wanted you dead, you'd already be lying on the ground."

"Not while I use your woman as a shield."

"Is that what you think?" Ben managed a grim smile. "I think you should know, I'm a crack shot. If I aim at something, or someone, I never miss. Right now, you're a head taller than the woman in your arms. If I'd wanted to, I could have put a bullet between your eyes before you had time to blink."

The last of the crowd that had gathered for the race and festivities had now heard about the drama and milled around the fence, doubling the size of onlookers. At Ben's words, some in the crowd gasped, while others began spoiling for a gunfight.

"Come on, Monroe. Do what a lawman's supposed to do."

"Yeah, Mr. Tough Guy. Let's see you take out this punk."

"Quit all your talking. I know what I'd do if someone threatened my girlfriend."

"The best way to treat a scumbag is to shoot first and ask questions later."

Hearing them, Ben realized that all this attention from the bystanders was adding to the gunman's already out-of-control temper. Ranaldo was twitching with nerves, like a puppet on a string. Ben knew if he didn't act quickly, it could cause this city thug, lost and far from his comfort zone, to do the unforgivable.

Out of the corner of his eye, Ben saw the sheriff motioning for the crowd to move away, while taking up a position to back up his deputy with a rifle.

Since Ranaldo Rider was considered armed and dangerous, his job was to take out the shooter whenever he had a clear sight to the target.

"Listen to me, Ranaldo." Ben kept his voice low, persuasive. "Let the woman go. If you do, I give you my word I'll drop my weapon."

"Liar! You're just like all the rest. Why should I believe you?"

"Because I don't want you to die. I want you to live."

"Why?"

"I know some things about you, Ranaldo. One shot and your son, Hunter, and your unborn baby, Angela, will be forever without their father. Is that how you grew up?"

The gunman blinked hard, and Ben knew he'd found his weakness. "One shot and Mercy will be forever denied the comfort of the man she loves."

"If she loves me, why is she listening to some fancy-talking, backwoods preacher?"

"She wants to do the right thing. Not only for herself and her children, but also for you. Because she loves you, Ranaldo."

"Love." He spat the word.

"Yes, love. The way you love Hunter. Think about this. Without a father, Hunter and his baby sister will be alone in a hard, cruel world."

Ben allowed himself to look at Rebecca, blood oozing from the cut at her temple. Her eyes were wide, the pupils dilated. Shock. She'd been dealt a severe blow and was suffering the effects of it.

His heart took a hard, heavy bounce. "Please let the woman go, Ranaldo."

"Please? Now you're asking pretty please?" The shooter's voice went up a notch, with a sudden sense of power. "Maybe I'll ask you to crawl on your belly like a snake and beg in front of the hometown crowd. Would you do that, Cop?"

Ben nodded. "I'll do whatever it takes to get you to release the woman."

"I'd love to see that, Cop. But why should I bother releasing her? She's my guarantee I walk out of here."

"You harm her, you won't live to walk again." Ben kept his tone low and even. "I know you don't want to trust a man wearing a badge. So, to prove to you that I'm not interested in using my badge to kill you..." So carefully that it seemed to be happening in slow motion, Ben set his pistol on the log table beside him.

There were moans and cries from the crowd, now herded to a safe distance away. The onlookers, eager for blood, were hoping for a fierce fight, either with guns or at least with fists. After all, Ben Monroe was the town's toughest citizen. A brawler. A known street fighter. If anybody could put on a hell of a show, it was Ben.

Ben struggled to drown out the distraction of the crowd.

His voice was firm, with no hint of the nerves bubbling just beneath the surface. "All right, Ranaldo. There's my weapon. It's proof that I trust you to do the right thing. Release the woman."

CHAPTER TWENTY-SEVEN

Sam and Finn needed no words between them to know what they had to do.

While Finn raced back to the ranch truck to retrieve their weapons, Finn made his way to the hardware store and began exploring rooms until he found what he was looking for.

Minutes later he texted Sam and the two climbed out an upper window and made their way across the roof until they had a clear view of the scene below.

They stood, side by side, rifles aimed and ready.

From the time they were boys, they'd always had one another's backs. This time was no different. Ben was in trouble. They had to be here for him.

When Ben set aside his pistol, a murmur of disbelief ran through the crowd. Their thirst for a gunfight had taken over their reasoning. The more agitated they became, the louder grew the words, until they were practically begging for the chance to witness a bloody shoot-out.

Hank Henderson spotted Sheriff Kerr taking aim with his rifle and grabbed him by the front of his shirt, his voice raised in absolute terror. "Tell that cowardly hell-raiser to pick up his gun and do what he's paid to do."

"In case you haven't noticed, Hank, that's what Ben is doing."

"He just set down his gun. While he plays some sort of Wild West poker game out there, he's risking Rebecca's life."

"Take another look. He's risking his own life, too." Virgil Kerr pried Hank's hands from his shirtfront and gave him a shove backward.

The sheriff turned to Susan Henderson with a stern look. "Keep your husband quiet, or I'll have him hauled to jail. Do you understand?"

She nodded before wrapping her arms around her husband, who looked for all the world like a man ready to suffer a complete breakdown.

Virgil had to shout to be heard above the chorus of angry voices. "The rest of you will stop the noise this minute, or I'll have the lot of you arrested. I want absolute quiet. Step back and be respectful of all that's happening here. This isn't a TV show. This is real life, and lives hang in the balance. Do you understand me?"

At the sheriff's threats, the crowd fell back to a safe distance, silent and watchful.

The sudden silence carried its own distraction, causing the gunman to glance uneasily at the audience he'd attracted. For long moments he continued holding Rebecca as a shield while he studied the distance between Ben and his gun.

"I don't trust you, Cop." He waved his gun. "Give me one reason why I should trust you."

Sensing that Renaldo could be wavering, Ben decided to

push harder. "When you say you love Mercy and Hunter and Angela, do you mean it?"

The gunman's voice was barely a whisper. "Don't you dare call me a liar, Cop. The only reason I'm here is because I love them."

"Then think what you're doing. Think what their lives will be like if you go through with your plans to kill a police officer or your hostage. You'll be dead, or doing hard time. Either way, Mercy will be forced to move on with her life, and your children will never know their father. Now think about those so-called friends of yours. Have you ever crossed any of them? Or made them mad enough to want revenge? Which of them will try to move in and make Mercy his woman?"

Seeing Ranaldo's stunned reaction to his words he pressed on. "Will he be tender to her? Or abusive? What kind of stepfather will he be to Hunter and Angela? Will he ignore them? Mistreat them? Worse, will he have them running with a gang by the time they're barely in their teens?"

"Shut up, Cop. Just shut up."

"You need to face the truth, Ranaldo. Or are you afraid of it?"

The gunman waved his pistol wildly. "I'm not scared of anything. Here's the truth. The preacher will still suffer, whether I kill the woman or you, Cop. He'll spend the rest of his life knowing he was the cause of someone dying."

"Nice try, Ranaldo. That may be your version of the truth, but here's the facts. We make choices in life, and then we have to live with them. Nobody made you do this. At least, if you're bound and determined to have your revenge on a well-meaning preacher, release the woman. She's done nothing to you. She's the innocent victim in all of this."

"I don't care who's innocent. And you're right. I'll make

the choice. And I've decided I want both of you." With a savage oath, the gunman pressed his gun to Rebecca's temple.

Rebecca's reaction was completely unexpected. Though she'd appeared helpless, she jammed both elbows into the gunman's midsection. Caught by surprise, he loosened his grip on her just enough that she managed to drop to the ground, giving Ben the opportunity to retrieve his pistol and fire off a shot, aiming for the gunman's leg.

With a string of oaths Ranaldo dropped to the ground, blood pouring from the bullet wound, costing him precious seconds before he could take aim. It was all the time Ben needed to fire off a second shot, hitting the gunman squarely in the shoulder. The sound of the gunfire reverberated in the air, causing many in the crowd to flinch and drop to the ground in terror.

At almost the same moment, the gunman's shot resonated, and though Ben tried to evade, blood spurted from his side. The force of the bullet had him stumbling to his knees before he was able to regain his footing and close the distance between them. Once there, he managed to kick the gun from Ranaldo's hand before the gunman could fire off another shot.

Weak as a kitten, Rebecca pushed herself to her knees.

Seeing her, bloody, disoriented, Ben allowed himself one brief moment to gather her close. He could feel the tremors rocketing through her slender body, and his heart ached for her. "Oh, baby, he hurt you. You okay?"

"Yes." Her lips were trembling.

"Run." He released her, turning her toward the gate. "Get away from here now while you can."

She shocked him by clutching his arm. "You've been shot."

He gave a surprised glance at the blood streaming from

his side. In the heat of the moment he'd been able to ignore the pain. Now he could see the extent of his wound.

"I'm not leaving without you, Ben."

His voice roughened with alarm. "Becca, this could all go wrong in an instant. It's important for me to know you're safe."

"And I want the same for you, Ben." She took in a deep breath. "I know I don't have your courage. But I'm not going anywhere unless you do." She gripped his arm tighter. "We're in this together."

Hearing her, Ranaldo began rummaging around in the dirt before his fingers closed around his gun.

He took aim. "That's real tender, Cop. Now what're you going to do?"

At Ranaldo's words, Ben stepped in front of Rebecca to shield her. "Just drop your weapon, and this can all end peacefully, Ranaldo."

"I know every trick a cop can try. I've got my gun; you've got yours. I guess we'll just have to see who's a better shot."

"This isn't a game. I give you my word, Ranaldo. You put down that gun, you'll live, and be able to see the birth of little Angela."

That had the gunman going very still. "Why are you doing this? You told me you were a crack shot. You could have killed me with your first shot."

"I told you the truth. I don't want you to die."

"Even after I hurt your woman? Why?"

Ben sighed. "Because I've been where you are. I've been mad at the world and willing to hurt anybody who got in my way. And I was where your kids will end up, if you don't surrender." Ben struggled to clear his vision. The pain was growing intense, threatening to take him down. "Let's just say I believe in second chances."

The gunman fell silent.

Ben studied Ranaldo's hand, still clutching the pistol. "Since you told me your son's name, you should know that the woman you held hostage is Rebecca. Her parents are over there, waiting to hold her, the way you want to hold Hunter."

At the mention of his son, the gunman ever so slowly lowered his gun a fraction.

Rebecca continued clinging fiercely to Ben.

Ben pressed a kiss to her temple. "Go now, while you have the chance."

She shook her head, while tears flowed down her cheeks, mingling with the dirt and blood. "I told you. I'm not leaving you. We leave here together. Or we don't leave at all."

Ben turned to the gunman. "See how our women listen to us?"

Seeing the slight curve of the gunman's lips in the faintest hint of a smile, he added, "Good women are like that. Loyal. Stubborn. They turn into fierce wounded bears when they see the ones they love heading down the wrong path. That's why your Mercy dug in her heels. It wasn't about punishing you. It was about wanting you to choose the right path."

He took in a slow breath, forcing himself to keep his tone low and even, so his words didn't come across as a stern command. If he didn't end this soon, he would probably fall on his face. "Now, Ranaldo, you need to hand over that weapon so your good woman can see you again."

"And if I don't?"

"You won't get a second chance to do it right." He nodded with his head and Ranaldo followed the direction of his gaze and caught a glimpse of the two armed men standing on the roof.

"Those two are my brothers. They'll shoot before you

can pull that trigger." Ben held out his hand. "Be smart, Ranaldo."

For long, strained moments the two men remained mere feet apart and the crowd went deathly silent, barely able to breathe as they watched the drama unfold.

Without a word the gunman tossed his weapon aside.

Ben moved closer and tucked the pistol in his waistband before kneeling in front of the gunman.

Ranaldo's attention was captured by the small cluster of men pushing their way inside the fence. "Who are those weirdoes?"

Ben followed the direction of his gaze. Despite the pain, his face creased into a smile. "They're my family." His gaze locked with Mac's, and he saw the look of pride in his father's eyes.

"Even that old toothless cowboy and the black dude?"

"Yeah. My family." Ben's voice softened with warmth.

The sheriff and Detective Godfrey walked up to stand on either side of Ranaldo.

The detective handcuffed Ranaldo and read him his rights before he was lifted onto a gurney and rolled toward a waiting ambulance.

As soon as they left, the crowd surged forward, then stepped back a pace as Rebecca's parents raced across the distance that separated them and caught her in a fierce embrace. All three of them were crying and clinging to one another.

Virgil Kerr put a hand on Ben's shoulder. "You almost stopped my heart, Ben."

"Mine, too, Sheriff."

And then Ben's family gathered around him, shutting out the voices in the crowd.

His two brothers hadn't bothered with stairs, lowering

themselves instead by hanging off the roof and dropping to the ground just feet away.

Sam slapped his brother on the back. "You had me scared, bro. But you knew what you were doing."

Ben whispered, "The truth? I didn't have a clue."

Finn hugged his oldest brother before giving him a fist bump. "You just put a whole new spin on police work, bro. That was either the dumbest thing ever, or absolutely brilliant."

"Not to mention very brave," Zachariah said. "You took a huge risk, Benedict."

"I thought his life was worth it. I hope he proves me right."

Roscoe and Otis pumped his hand, grinning from ear to ear.

Roscoe studied the flow of blood from the gunshot. "You need help standing, Ben?"

"I'm not sure how much longer I can do it."

At once, Otis and Roscoe took up positions on either side of him, their arms around his waist.

Mac clamped a hand on Ben's arm. His words were spoken quietly. "You made me proud, son."

"That's what gave me the courage to try it." Ben looked into his father's eyes. "I could hear your voice in my head, saying the easy way isn't always the best. It would have been easy to just fire off a shot and kill that young punk. Especially since he was threatening Rebecca, and that had my blood so hot I could hardly see. But then I thought about his kids and knew they deserved better. And so does he."

He looked over at Rebecca, being consoled by her weeping parents. He ached to go to her. To hold her. And though he wanted more than anything to carry her away to some secluded spot, he was forced to watch from a distance while the crowd surged around. From the look on Hank Henderson's face, he wasn't about to let go of his daughter any time soon.

A team of state police medics rushed over to place Ben on a gurney. Within minutes they had inserted an intravenous line and were heading toward a waiting ambulance, while his family raced to keep up.

As they passed Rebecca and her parents, he asked the medics to pause. Before he could say a word, Hank Henderson turned his back on him, shielding Rebecca from view.

After a moment's hesitation, Ben told them to move on. He caught the arm of one of the medics. "Miss Henderson needs medical help."

"Don't you worry, we'll see to it right away, if her parents don't handle it first."

As they began lifting Ben's gurney into the ambulance, Ben turned to Finn. "This may take some time. I intend to do whatever I can to see that I keep my word to Ranaldo. I'd like his future resolved by the time his baby is born. Maybe you could use your influence with the court..."

His family watched helplessly as the pain took him down. But even then, as the ambulance left for the clinic, sirens screaming, they could see Ben, still fighting, still trying to take charge as he slipped into blessed unconsciousness.

From the determined look on his face, his family had no doubt he would see his job through to the end. From the time he'd been that angry, wounded boy, he'd always finished what he'd started, no matter what it cost him.

CHAPTER TWENTY-EIGHT

Right this way." Dr. Clark and his pretty nurse, Jenny Turn-bull, met Rebecca and her parents at the door to the clinic and led them to an examining room, where Rebecca was asked to lie on an examining table.

Hank and Susan stood on either side, holding her hands while the doctor probed her bloody wound.

"You've become our town's celebrity," the doctor said.

Rebecca closed her eyes. "I don't want to be a celebrity. I'm just relieved this is over."

The doctor paused. "You can't stop people from talking. Especially when half the town saw your courage under fire."

The nurse nodded. "And just so you know, there's a re-porter waiting outside to interview you."

Rebecca's only reaction was to groan before lifting a hand to cover her eyes.

"This will sting." The nurse rubbed the skin with a disin-fectant before applying an injection to numb the area.

Within a short time the doctor had stitched the cut and covered the area with gauze. "You're going to have quite a headache. You're lucky, after that blow to the head with a gun, that the cut wasn't worse or that you didn't suffer a concussion, Rebecca."

Her father's command was stern. "I want you to give my daughter a strong sedative to help her through the night."

Rebecca's protest was ignored.

"You're right, Hank." The doctor looked over at Susan. "I hope Rebecca will be staying with you."

Susan nodded. "Hank and I wouldn't think of allowing her to be alone after such an ordeal."

Before Rebecca could say a word, the doctor nodded in agreement. "That's good to hear." He turned to Rebecca. "You've been through a difficult trauma. I want you to go straight home with your folks and let the drugs do their job. You need to rest in order to heal."

He directed his words to Hank and Susan. "If you think your daughter needs any help, there are counselors here who will work with her."

To Rebecca he added, "The sooner you can put this behind you, the better."

Hank lifted his cell phone and dialed the hardware store, ordering Eli to bring a truck to the clinic.

"I'm glad you're taking charge, Hank." The doctor seemed pleased. "Jenny will give you a list of instructions when you leave. See that your daughter follows them to the letter. I'll see you back here in a week."

"Thanks, Doc." Hank shook the doctor's hand and he and Susan helped Rebecca from the table before easing her into a wheelchair.

When they reached the entrance to the clinic, they could see the crowd gathered just outside the glass doors.

"Smile." Jenny handed Susan a printed sheet of instructions on how to care for her daughter's wound. "You're about to be on TV."

As Rebecca was wheeled outside, a pretty young local reporter who had been hastily recruited by a national news service rushed up to them.

She turned so the camera would catch her best side, along with her brilliant smile. "And this is the Haller Creek resident who was being held hostage by an armed gunman."

The fashionable reporter was in sharp contrast to pale Rebecca, her clothes smeared with dirt and blood, looking as frail as a wounded bird.

"Tell us what you were thinking while you were being held hostage at gunpoint."

Rebecca blinked against the glare of bright lights. "I don't remember. It all happened so fast, there was little time to think at all. But once Ben arrived on the scene, I knew everything would be all right."

The reporter attempted to clarify her statement. "Miss Henderson is referring to Ben Monroe, the town's deputy sheriff." She turned to Rebecca. "How would his presence bring comfort? After all, the deputy is new to the job. He hasn't really been tested until today. And there are some in town who are questioning the way he handled this situation."

Rebecca's voice softened. "Ben Monroe is the kind of man you instinctively trust to always do the right thing."

Her words had many women in the crowd sighing, while their men stood a little taller.

"Now, if you don't mind," Rebecca added, "I just want to go home."

The young reporter doggedly carried on. She thrust the microphone toward Hank. "You had a personal stake in all this, Mr. Henderson. What do you think about the deputy's actions today?"

Hank's eyes narrowed in fury. "What do I think? The same as any father whose daughter was in danger of being killed. I expected a man of the law to put my daughter's safety ahead of some two-bit, big-city punk holding a gun to her head. By setting aside his weapon and trusting that wild-eyed gunman, he risked my daughter's life. I intend to see that Ben Monroe never wears a badge again."

"Dad—" Rebecca's words were abruptly cut off as Hank turned her wheelchair away from the crowd and the cameras, the throngs parting as he made his way toward the hardware truck idling at the curb, with Eli behind the wheel.

With Hank and Susan on either side of her, Rebecca was eased into the backseat, and the truck left in a cloud of dust, while the curious crowd began to speculate on what would happen next in their once sleepy little town.

Virgil and a throng of state police officers were huddled in his office. When Ben arrived, his torso beneath his torn, bloody uniform swathed in dressings, a sudden silence descended.

Virgil cleared his throat. "Chief Archer and I were just discussing a few things, Ben."

The state police chief's eyes narrowed. "What you did, setting aside your weapon, goes against a lawman's training. Why would you even consider relinquishing your weapon while a criminal was holding an innocent woman hostage at gunpoint?"

Ben's words were measured. "I thought about taking him out with a single shot between his eyes. It would have been a risk. He could have reacted quickly enough to kill his hostage. Knowing what I did about him, and seeing that he was more scared than angry, I decided to go with my instincts and see if he couldn't be persuaded to end things peacefully, so he could get a second chance. I've been raised to believe in karma. The good you do in life comes back to you."

"Karma." The chief's face was blank, but his tone of voice revealed his skepticism.

"Well, now." Virgil managed a shaky smile. "Ben, your brother Finn was already here while you were being patched up, offering to represent Ranaldo Rider."

Ben shot him a grin. "Finn doesn't let any grass grow under his feet."

"Neither do you, son." Virgil was working overtime to smooth things, while the state police chief fumed. "You've been through a tough day. I'm sure that bullet wound is going to cause you a lot of pain. Until the official investigation is complete, it's standard operating procedure that you can't return to your duties, so you're on paid leave until you're certified. Why don't you head on home?"

Ben stood his ground. "And Ranaldo?"

"Chief Archer and his men will handle the details of jurisdiction of the prisoner and his transportation. He's in good hands."

"I gave him my word he'd be treated with respect."

The chief's voice was pure ice. "He'll be treated no better or worse than any other prisoner."

"Thank you, Chief." Ben turned to leave.

"Deputy." Chief Archer put a hand on his arm as he turned away. "What were you thinking out there?"

Ben looked from the state police chief to Sheriff Virgil Kerr. "I know what I did was unorthodox and not at all what I'd been taught. But I had to go with my gut feelings. I believe Ranaldo Rider was running scared, and what he really wanted was someone to save him from himself. Does that make any sense?"

While Virgil Kerr fell silent, the state police chief said what all of them were thinking. "You got lucky, Deputy. You took a big risk, with a hostage's life on the line. Of course, if it had all gone wrong, we wouldn't be having this conversation. You'd be stripped of your badge and branded as an incompetent rookie."

Virgil put a hand on Ben's arm. "I want you to know I was proud of you, Ben. What you did out there took real courage."

"Thank you, sir."

Ben was surprised when the other state officers stepped up to shake his hand or give him a fist bump while congratulating him on having the entire incident end without death.

Virgil was all smiles until dispatcher Jeanette Moak rushed in and pointed to the television on the wall.

Turning up the volume, they all watched in silence as Rebecca and her parents were being interviewed.

Ben's gaze was riveted on Rebecca, pale and silent, a patch of gauze covering the wound to her temple, the front of her shirt still bearing the bloodstains. The very sight of her had his heart aching.

And then the camera shifted to her father as he vented his anger.

"What do I think? The same as any father whose daughter was in danger of being killed. I expected a man of the law to put my daughter's safety ahead of some two-bit, big-city punk holding a gun to her head. By setting aside his weapon and trusting that wild-eyed gunman, he risked my daughter's life. I intend to see that Ben Monroe never wears a badge again."

The room filled with lawmen had gone eerily silent.

The sheriff was the first to speak. "You know Hank Henderson. Always spouting off about something. When he cools off, he'll regret his public statement."

The state police chief shook his head. "Never underestimate the fury of a father who feels his child was mistreated. This could end up being an ugly scar on your town, Sheriff."

"I know." Virgil laid a hand on Ben's arm. "This isn't the first time Hank has accused you of something he had to recant later."

Ben's mind returned to the time he'd rescued Becca from R.C. Mason's assault, only to have Hank Henderson accuse him of the very thing R.C. had done. Ben had been forced to cool his heels in jail for hours until the misunderstanding had been cleared up.

Virgil's eyes narrowed. "Apparently Hank hasn't learned anything from his mistakes. Here he is, flinging wild-eyed accusations again. And this time, in an even more public forum." Virgil squeezed Ben's arm. "Despite what Hank thinks or does, I'll stand with you, son."

"Thank you." Ben turned away and stepped out of the sheriff's office before making his way to his truck idling at the curb, his brothers inside.

While he settled himself in the backseat, he thought about Becca, so pale and wounded. He longed to go to her. To comfort her. To just hold her.

"Turn on Maple."

Sam did as he asked.

They drove past Rebecca's house. There were no lights on inside. No sign of life.

"Drive to Becca's parents' house."

They drove slowly.

The lights were on in her old bedroom.

Ben sighed. "I'm sure Hank and Susan will see to it she stays the night."

His brothers nodded.

"She'll need them to ease her pain, and to see to it that she's shielded from the public while she heals. I know she'll see it as an admission of weakness, but her parents are right to take their daughter home with them."

Sam muttered, "She didn't seem inclined to run to them when this was going down. Seems to me she'd rather be staying with you."

Ben's silence dragged on until he suddenly said, "Stop here."

At Ben's words, Sam and Finn exchanged knowing looks.

Sam studied Ben in the rearview mirror. "By now everybody in town knows what Hank Henderson thinks about the way you handled this. He won't be happy to see you, bro."

"I know. Open the door."

Ben stepped out, wishing he'd taken the bigger dose of the pain meds the medic had suggested. His entire body was throbbing, and he felt sick to his stomach. Despite the pain, he needed to see Becca, just for a moment, to assure himself that she was all right.

At his knock a porch light came on, and Susan peered out before opening the door.

"Mrs. Henderson." Ben held his hat in his hand. "How is Becca?"

"She's…"

Susan was forcibly moved aside and Hank stood scowling at Ben. "How dare you come here? You're not welcome in my home, Monroe."

"I won't stay long. I just want to see for myself that Becca is all right."

"Her welfare didn't matter to you earlier today." Hank barred his way. "Now I'll say this just one time. Get off my property, Monroe. Or I'll have you arrested for trespassing."

"I'd like to see Becca."

"What you'd like doesn't matter. What I'd like is to see you barred from ever wearing that badge again."

The door was slammed, the lock turned, the porch light extinguished.

The two brothers in the front seat kept an eye on Ben as they traveled the distance to their ranch.

Ben's emotions wavered between simmering anger at Hank Henderson and worry over Becca.

The music on the truck radio, lamenting long-lost love, mocked him until he ordered Finn to turn it off.

The sudden silence seemed even louder.

Ben was reminded of how much he'd come to love the sound of Becca's voice. Her throaty laughter. And all the little things about her. Her touch. The clean, fresh scent of her. The way her eyes lit with pleasure whenever she looked at him.

Their lovemaking.

And then the doubts began to creep into his mind.

Was Hank Henderson right?

Had he spent too much time worrying about the fate of Ranaldo Rider, at the expense of Becca's safety?

Had he actually risked her life in order to rescue a lost soul?

As he continued the long ride to the ranch, the litany of questions and accusations taunted him until he could feel his confidence sink to a low ebb.

His poor heart sank even lower with every mile.

He hadn't felt this low since he was that twelve-year-old kid determined to escape a life of despair no matter what it cost him, only to find himself leading his two trusting little brothers into a raging Montana blizzard.

What kind of fool was he to think he could be entrusted with the safety of anyone?

He'd almost cost the life of the only woman he would ever love.

And maybe now, after what he'd put her through, she would come to the same conclusion as her father. And who would blame her?

CHAPTER TWENTY-NINE

Ben had napped badly, his thoughts as dark as the sky outside his window. He took his time descending the stairs, to find his family and Mary Pat gathered around the fireplace in the parlor, talking in low tones. The minute they saw him they fell silent.

He could tell, by the looks on their faces, they'd been engaged in a serious conversation. "I guess the TV networks have been replaying Hank's television interview."

"Yeah." Sam's hand curled into a fist. "Same old Hank Henderson. Always shooting from the hip."

Zachariah started toward the kitchen. "I saved you some supper, Benedict."

Ben shook his head. "Thanks, Zachariah. I'm not hungry."

Mary Pat laid a hand on Ben's arm. "How is Rebecca holding up?"

"She's at her parents' place. I tried to see her. Hank barred my way."

"Yeah. That son of a..." Sam hissed out a breath, but catching the look in his father's eyes, held his silence.

"Hank will need some time." Mac kept his tone even. "I'm sure, after he's assured that his daughter is back to her old self, he'll come around."

"Come around?" Ben shot him a narrow look. "He won't be satisfied until he gets his pound of flesh. It's what he's wanted all these years. He's determined to prove to his daughter that I'm a good-for-nothing guy who should be locked up." Ben turned away. "Maybe he's right."

Finn put a hand on his brother's sleeve. "What's that supposed to mean?"

Ben shook off his touch. "What was I thinking? Was I a police officer or a school counselor? Maybe I was so intent on saving that misguided punk, I forgot the first rule of law. Instead of keeping Becca safe, I actually put her life in danger."

"Hey now..."

Seeing his father's slight shake of the head, Finn let his words die.

As Ben started toward the back door, Mac called, "Where are you going, son?"

Ben shrugged. "I'm going for a ride. Don't wait up. I need some time up in the hills to think."

The bleak look in his eyes was a warning to all of them to stand back and give him the room he needed, while he sorted out his troubling thoughts.

Mary Pat leaned her head back on the sturdy log swing, studying the stars. The gentle motion of the swing, along with the canopy of the night sky, had her sighing.

She glanced over at Mac, who had grown silent. Silent and stone-faced. Though she longed to comfort him, she knew he was a man who dealt with life on his own terms.

"What are you thinking?"

He kept his gaze fixed on the distant hills. "I hate to see Ben questioning his actions. But I hope, in time, he'll come to realize that what he did was not only right, but also heroic." He sighed. "I'm a lucky man."

She waited, knowing he was searching for the words. As the comfortable silence stretched between them, he turned to her. "Know what I like best about you?"

At the sudden shift of topics, she merely looked at him.

"You don't feel a need to always fill the silence with words."

"Why bother, unless I have something to say?"

"Yeah. Exactly. I like that."

They rocked together for a while longer.

Mac's voice was little more than a whisper. "When did that angry, confused boy I took into my home become the man Ben is today?"

He didn't wait for a reply. Instead he went on as if he hadn't asked that question. "There was a moment today when my heart stopped."

Mary Pat waited.

"I watched Ben put down his gun." Mac shook his head. "Even though I knew he was doing it for all the right reasons, I wanted to beg him not to risk it. Then I figured I'd keep an eye on the shooter, to warn Ben if he made a move to fire. But I couldn't do it. I couldn't take my eyes off Ben. I absolutely couldn't look away. There he was, no longer that cocky boy, always ready with his fists, but now he was this larger-than-life man of peace. Perfectly calm. In control. He never flinched when the crowd turned on him. I doubt he even heard them. He went with his instinct to win that nervous punk's trust. Today, I watched my son take a leap of faith." He inhaled deeply. "And land safely."

"Oh, Mac." Overcome, Mary Pat closed her hand over his and fought the sting of tears.

"And now, because he did what he thought was the right thing, he may have to pay a very steep price." Mac studied the stars. "Hank Henderson is a stubborn, controlling man who has backed himself into a corner by making a public statement he won't want to retract. That makes him a dangerous adversary."

"You said yourself Ben is a man."

Mac nodded. "A man in love with a woman who could very well become the bargaining chip in a contest of wills between two very tough opponents."

Mary Pat squeezed Mac's hand. "If it comes to that, my money is on Ben."

"From your lips..."

They remained there for an hour or more, comfortable in their shared silence, quietly hopeful that love could prevail.

"You wanted to talk to me, Sheriff?" Ben removed his hat and took the chair opposite Virgil's desk. The bulky dressings of the first few days had now been replaced with lighter dressings as the bullet wound began to heal. The doctor had reminded Ben how lucky he was that the bullet hadn't pierced any vital organs.

Virgil nodded toward the state police chief, seated beside his desk. "Chief Archer has some news."

"Hank Henderson spoke to an attorney." Chief Archer handed Ben a document. "He's been looking for a way to have you removed as a deputy."

Ben studied the document before handing it back. "That's his right."

"I'm afraid not." The chief cleared his throat. "If you recall, I was concerned that you'd violated police procedure by setting aside your weapon."

Ben nodded, preparing himself for the worst possible scenario. "It was my choice entirely. I take full responsibility. And if I have to…"

The chief held up a hand to stop him. "I had a meeting with my team of professional hostage negotiators. Some of them have been working in the field for years. They are all in agreement that in order to successfully end a scene such as the one you faced, they must first earn the complete trust of the one holding a hostage. By setting aside your weapon, you took that first all-important step. And you never actually put the hostage in danger. You had to be aware of your brothers on the roof of the hardware store. I'm told they're nearly as good with a rifle as you are, and would have taken out the shooter before the hostage could be harmed."

Ben nodded without saying a word.

"Would you like to know what my team is calling you?"

Ben shared a look with the sheriff.

"The coolest rookie ever." The chief smiled. "Quite a compliment for a deputy on his first real test, coming from a team that is known for its success in hostage negotiating."

"The coolest rookie ever." Virgil Kerr rubbed his hands together. "I like it, Ben. Suits you."

Ben sat back, letting the words of these two lawmen swirl around him while he reminded himself to breathe. When summoned here, he'd half expected to be stripped of his badge and possibly his freedom.

"So, there will be no lawsuit?"

Virgil swore. "Ben, you should know that Hank's just too stubborn to back down. The son of a—" He stopped himself. "Hank mouthed off in public, and now he's been trying to justify what he said. But the lawyer told him he doesn't have a legal leg to stand on." Virgil paused. "So, as far as any legal battle, this is the end of it. But if there's anything..." He took a long look at Ben's face. "Personal between you two, you'll have to deal with it on your own dime."

"Yeah." Ben shifted, thinking about his failed attempts to see Rebecca this past week.

Her house remained vacant. No one answered the door at her parents' house. And his phone calls went unanswered. Her father had had plenty of time to persuade his only child that her so-called hero was really an incompetent fool.

For all he knew, maybe he was. Maybe he'd actually let his concern for a misguided gunman color his judgment.

He pulled himself back from his troubling thoughts. "What about Ranaldo Rider?"

Virgil glanced at Chief Archer. "These state boys work fast." He handed Ben a series of documents. "This is a transcript of Rider's preliminary hearing. You'll notice your brother, Finn, was there to represent him."

"Yeah. Finn told me." Ben skimmed the document. "I see he managed to have the kidnapping charge reduced to assault."

Chief Archer gave a grim smile. "By the time Finn got finished, the punk's rap sheet read like that of a damned Boy Scout."

"Not quite." Ben chuckled. "I see Ranaldo admitted that the car he drove here was stolen. That's grand theft, though he claims he borrowed it from a friend."

"If he can prove he wasn't the one who stole it, he could have that charge dropped, as well," the chief said.

"The mother of his child...soon to be children," Virgil corrected, "testified on his behalf, and said he was a loving, attentive father. And her mother testified that he's promised to marry her daughter, get a job, and do his best to support his family." The sheriff gave a shake of his head. "That's a lot of promises for one street-tough delinquent to keep."

"But at least he's willing to try."

"If he ever gets out of jail."

Ben grinned. "Not 'if.' 'When.' With Finn representing him, Ranaldo may not do more than the minimum time. But he'll be so tied up with legalities, he'll walk the straight and narrow or find himself going back to jail."

Chief Archer added, "Best of all, the dean of divinity school offered to mentor Ranaldo, to see that he gets the emotional support he needs to stick to his promises."

Ben looked over at the sheriff. "And Will Theisen?"

Virgil shook his head. "I haven't heard a word. He's still living in his parents' house, and pretty much staying by himself, off the grid. Probably trying to decide what his future will be. If he even has a future as an ordained minister." The sheriff sat back, assuming a contemplative posture. "I have to admit I'm relieved things are moving so quickly. It eases my mind to know I won't be leaving any unfinished business."

"Leaving?" Ben sat up straighter. "What's this about?"

Virgil sighed. "Now that I've had a few more physical therapy sessions, I have some decisions to make, too."

Ben gave him a surprised look. "About what?"

"My future. The doctor said I can expect some long-term effects from this injury. One is arthritis. I can already feel it in the joint. Another is the challenge of passing a fitness test to remain in this job."

"You're as fit as anybody."

"I used to think so. Not anymore." The sheriff managed a grin. "I'm getting older. My wife wants me to step aside and enjoy life."

"You don't enjoy life now?"

Another grin. "I love being a police officer. It's been my whole life. But I've been thinking about what I could do if I walked away from this. Annabelle and I love to fish and camp and hike. We've talked for years about hiking the Grand Canyon. If I'm going to do it, I can't wait much longer." He rubbed his leg. "Especially if this continues to get worse." He looked over. "So, this is my long-winded way of saying, I know you told me you were only taking on the job of deputy until my leg healed, but if you're willing to take on the job full-time, I'd like to recommend you to replace me as sheriff of Haller Creek."

Ben went very still before slowly getting to his feet. "What you're offering is an honor, Virgil, but I'm still on leave."

"You've been cleared to return to duty."

"I'm not sure the town is ready to accept me in a position of authority."

"The town loves you, Ben. You've become their hero."

Ben actually flinched at the word. "There are probably plenty of people who agree with Hank Henderson's assessment that I shirked my duty to protect his daughter while coddling a criminal."

"Son, you'd be hard-pressed to find many folks in this town who agree with Hank about anything. They know he likes to flap his jaw. They also know you, and most of them would rather entrust their safety to you than to Hank." The sheriff shot him a long, steady look. "What do you say about the job offer?"

Ben shrugged. "I want you to know how honored I am, Virgil. I came here expecting bad news, and you're offering me my heart's desire. For a kid who knows the other side of the law, this is the offer of a lifetime. But I'd like to take some time to think long and hard about it."

"Don't take too long, son. My Annabelle is already making plans for our first trip. If you don't agree"—he turned to Chief

Archer—"I'll have to ask the state police to recommend a replacement from within their ranks. And speaking of the state boys, Chief Archer assures me they'll be filling in for me for the next couple of weeks. Consider this a well-earned vacation. So use this time to get your ducks in a row, Ben."

With a thoughtful look and a handshake, Ben strode from the office.

"You can't leave yet, Rebecca." Susan stood in the doorway of her daughter's old bedroom, watching as Rebecca began packing an overnight bag.

"Mom, I'm fine. In fact, I've been fine for days now. The only reason I agreed to stay on is because you and Dad were so adamant about my remaining here until I saw the doctor. Now that I have, and he's given me a clean bill of health, there's no reason for me to stay. I really need to get back to my own place."

"But your dad will be upset if you leave while he's at work."

Rebecca knew it was cowardly, but she'd planned it this way. With her father away, it would prove easier to persuade her mother. "I'm only two blocks away. You and Dad can come over any time you want, just to assure yourselves I'm all right."

Rebecca picked up her bag and descended the stairs, with her mother trailing behind. At the front door she turned and embraced Susan. "I love you, Mom. Thanks for all the chicken soup and chamomile tea. I feel really lucky to have you and Dad in my life." She glanced around. "Where did you put my cell phone?"

"It's...charging in the kitchen." Susan kept up the lie Hank had been using for the past days, to keep their daughter safe from any attempt by Ben Monroe to contact her. First he'd told Rebecca her phone had been lost during the incident with Ranaldo Rider. Then, when she'd attempted to order a new phone, Hank said her old phone had been found in the dirt and was being repaired.

Susan hurried to the kitchen and returned with her daughter's phone, knowing Hank had deleted all earlier calls.

"Thanks, Mom." Rebecca pocketed her phone before hugging her mother.

As she walked the two blocks to her place, she scrolled through her phone, noting that Ben's name was conspicuously absent.

Rebecca unpacked and moved listlessly from room to room.

She had no doubt Ben knew about her father's very public angry tirade. Everyone in town knew about his feelings toward Ben.

Ben was such a proud man. And a good one. But not even a saint could take public condemnation without feeling its effects.

Was that why Ben hadn't called or paid a visit?

She hoped, now that she was home, she could find a way to persuade him to give her another chance.

Or had her father's television interview ended their relationship? Ben would have surely seen that horrible interview and watched her father's hostile reaction. She had no doubt everyone in town had witnessed it by now. Did Ben think she agreed with her father? Had he started to believe that she shared her father's anger and had turned against him?

Just thinking about that horrid interview and the hateful things her father had said had her cringing. How could she ever face Ben's family after such a thing?

His silence since the incident with the shooter spoke volumes and had her questioning everything.

Why would a strong, capable man like Ben Monroe waste his time with a grown woman who still couldn't muster the courage to live her own life without worrying about what her parents would say?

No wonder he'd gone silent.

What other reason could there be for this unexpected distance between them?

She chewed on her lower lip, deep in thought. Maybe it was even worse. Had he grown tired of her? After all, they had, for a short time, been inseparable. Now, with a tragedy averted, instead of growing closer, they'd become two strangers.

Did they even have a relationship? A few short days and nights of bliss offered no guarantee of a lifetime of love, as she well knew. Still, she'd thought she and Ben had found something rare and wonderful.

Had he given up on her? Was Ben weary of the push-and-pull with her father, after a lifetime of love and acceptance within his own family? It would be so hard for a proud man like Ben Monroe to think of any kind of future with a woman whose father was so narrow-minded.

She felt a wave of annoyance. She was doing it again. Examining an issue from every angle, and then coming to the conclusion that the fault had to be with her.

What about Ben? He wasn't Mr. Perfect. Hadn't he admitted to having a temper? Hadn't he said he was rough and coarse and always waging a battle within himself to keep all the ugly words he'd learned as a boy from spilling out of his mouth? Hadn't he kept his distance from her throughout their younger days, even though he'd admitted to caring about her? Would he have ever made a move if she hadn't initiated it? Did that prove that his feelings weren't as strong as hers?

When she felt tears burning her eyes, she blinked them away, determined to clean her house until it sparkled. If this was to be her new reality, she would work until she dropped. It was the only way she would get through the first long, lonely night of the rest of her life.

CHAPTER THIRTY

Rebecca walked to the hardware store. Instead of going inside, she walked around to the fenced area, pausing to smile at the lovely wrought-iron leaves and flowers that spelled out BECCA'S GARDEN on the beautiful arch over the gate.

It was hard to believe this peaceful garden had held such terror for her just a week ago. She'd spent too many nights waking from the lingering nightmare. It was always the same. A sense of horror and revulsion, and then a shadowy figure stepping forward, easing all her fears with quiet confidence.

Though she always woke before she could see his face, she knew the man in her dreams.

"Hey, Rodney." She waved at the stock boy who had been pressed into service while she was out of commission.

She walked closer, seeing the bare spots in her displays. "Did you have many sales?"

"Did I ever." He hurried over. "Ever since the Autumn

Festival, folks have been stopping by and ordering the items
that are out of stock. And that"—he pointed to the arched
gate—"I think half the town wants to buy a fancy gate like
this, with their family name on it. I told them I'd have to
check with you to see if the artist is willing to take special
orders."

The artist.

The very words had Rebecca smiling. She couldn't wait
to pass along the exciting news to Roscoe.

Roscoe. The thought that Ben's family had gone silent
caused a terrible ache around her heart. It wasn't just Ben
who was missing from her life. She'd grown to love all his
family. City-born Otis, with a heart-wrenching tale of love
and loss. Roscoe, who despite his disheveled outward appearance had the soul of an artist. Prim, brilliant Zachariah,
so formal and yet so sweet. Mackenzie Monroe, who had so
generously opened his home and his heart to three difficult
boys. And Mary Pat, who had been a substitute mother and
teacher to every child in the town of Haller Creek.

She missed them all.

In fact, she realized with a lump in her throat, she loved
them all.

She swallowed. "Did Deputy Monroe stop by while I was
recovering?"

The young man shook his head. "Not while I was working. You might want to check with your dad, though, since
he came by every evening to tally the sales and empty the
register. He didn't want anybody but him handling the de-
posits."

Rebecca nodded. "Yeah. That's my dad. He has to be in
charge of everything."

When she'd asked about Ben, her father said he'd neither
called nor paid a visit. Her mother confirmed what Hank

said, but then, didn't her mother always agree with her father?

At the time of her recovery, the news that Ben was absent had been devastating. Of course, her mind had been clouded by the pain medication.

Now she was clearheaded, and her father's explanation had too many holes in it.

Where were the calls from her friends, who had resorted to dropping by without warning? Had they tried to phone her first? Had those calls somehow been deleted from her phone?

Of course. Her father would have convinced himself that he was doing the right thing for his daughter.

Without giving a thought to the consequences, she dialed Ben's number.

Instead of ringing, it went straight to voice mail.

Her voice was almost breathless. "Ben, it's Becca. I've seen the doctor and he's cleared me to return to my house and resume work. Call me as soon as you get this message."

To keep busy, she spent the next hour or so making a slow circle around the displays, rearranging the merchandise, noting the items that had sold out and needed to be replaced with fresh merchandise, and thinking about what else to add. Lamar and Lloyd Platt were going to have a very busy winter.

Ben had been up before dawn, riding with the others into the hills to bring down the herds. It was dirty work, eating trail dust behind a sea of cattle, but he and his family worked as a team until the herd was installed in the lowlands for the coming winter.

While the others drifted off to shower and catch a break from the never-ending chores, Ben worked alone in the barn, mucking the stalls.

Sam and Finn, freshly showered, went to call him for supper.

Seeing the overflowing honey wagon, Sam reached for the handles, but Ben shoved him aside. "I've got this."

While Sam and Finn stood watching, Ben wheeled the wagon, filled to the brim with wet straw and dung.

His muscles strained as he hauled it out of the barn and up the hill to where Otis was working in his garden, digging out roots and plants and dropping them into a pile for compost.

Without pausing, Ben dumped the wagon load and made his way back to the barn, where he set aside the wagon and climbed to the hayloft to fork fresh hay to the floor below.

Sam put his hand to his mouth to shout, "Come on, Ben. Zachariah called us in to supper."

Ben scowled. "You two go ahead. I'm not hungry."

Sam looked up. "That's what you said this morning. And yesterday."

"Just tell the family to eat without me."

"Yeah. Sure thing. But at least join us for a beer."

"In a few minutes."

Sam turned away. In the doorway of the barn he paused to look back. Ben was attacking the hay the same way he'd attacked the filthy stalls and, earlier, the ornery cattle, with a vengeance that had him muttering under his breath.

Sam nudged his brother. "And we worried we'd be doing double-duty."

"Yeah. Lately he's been doing more than the rest of us combined." Finn gave a mock shudder as they stepped into the kitchen. "I just hope he gets his smile back soon."

Beside him Finn muttered, "What's he got to smile about?"

Hearing them, Zachariah glanced at Mary Pat, who had

stopped by after a visit with Lamar and Lloyd Platt and was busy tossing a salad.

"We're all worried about Benedict. He's been in a foul mood for days now."

She turned to Mac, who was sipping a longneck and staring morosely out the window. "Any more talk about Hank Henderson's lawsuit against him?"

Mac shook his head. "According to the sheriff, that's a dead issue."

"Then his mood must involve…" She paused. "Has he talked with Rebecca since the…incident?"

"Not that I know of."

"I see." She fell silent. "Then I guess we all know what the trouble is."

Mac turned away from the window and drained his beer. "We know. And there isn't a thing we can do about it. They're two adults. They'll work this out, or they won't."

Hearing his father, Sam opened the refrigerator and handed Finn a longneck before helping himself to one. "If they don't figure things out soon, it's going to be a long, cold winter."

Rebecca closed up her business and checked her phone for messages. Finding none, she dialed Ben's number and listened as it went instantly to voice mail yet again.

"Ben." She tried to keep her voice calm, despite the sense of desperation she was experiencing. "I've left you half a dozen messages, and you haven't returned any of them. I hope everything's all right between us. I know we haven't talked since that…incident, but my phone wasn't available until now. Please call me when you get this."

As she slipped her cell phone into her pocket, she felt a deep shadow of fear worrying the edges of her mind. She didn't want to overthink this, but Ben's absence had to be deliberate.

He'd given up on her.

She wanted to be angry with him. It was true, he had some faults. But they would never keep her from wanting to be with him. How dare he turn away from her, without a word? Unless...Could her feelings for him be stronger than his feelings for her?

Maybe it wasn't so much that her feelings were stronger than his, but rather that his discipline, his inner strength, kept him from acting on his feelings out of a sense of respect or duty.

She stood perfectly still as a jumble of thoughts struck.

Respect. Duty.

Those were words that truly defined the man Ben had become.

But her father's hateful words spoken in such a public forum, plus his attempt to sue to keep Ben from ever wearing a badge again, may have been the final straw.

Determined to act before losing her nerve, she strode inside the hardware store and went in search of her father.

Hank was out back, at the loading dock, giving Eli a hand with an order. He looked up with a frown. "You shouldn't be here. I thought you were just going to stop by to check out your business, and then head home."

"I'd like to borrow one of the company trucks."

"This isn't the time for such things. You need to rest."

"I've spent a week resting. I need the truck, Dad."

"Why?"

"I..." She avoided his steady gaze. "Have a run to make."

"More merchandise for your garden shop?"

She shrugged, uncomfortable with even that small attempt at a lie. If her father knew how desperate she was to see Ben, to talk to him, he would find a way to deny her the use of a vehicle and probably try to lock her away as he had for the past week. And so she held her silence, fearing this may be her last chance to get things right.

Hank spared her any guilt by giving a grudging nod. "Take the smaller truck. That way I won't have to worry if you mess up. The keys are on my desk."

"Thanks, Dad." She hurried away, nerves frayed to the breaking point, her stomach in knots.

As the truck drew near the Monroe ranch, Rebecca spotted Roscoe and Otis just walking into the house.

Seeing her, the two men broke into wide grins.

Otis waved. "Now aren't you a sight for sore eyes. How are you, Miss Becca?"

"I'm fine, Otis. Roscoe."

As the old cowboy held the door, she stepped past him and struggled to keep her tone casual. "I realize it's supper time. I hope I'm not intruding."

"You're never an intrusion, Miss Becca."

Both men paused to wash up while she walked into the kitchen, where she greeted Zachariah, Mary Pat, Mac, and Ben's two brothers. Her smile faltered slightly when she realized Ben wasn't with them.

"What brings you here?" Sam winked before adding, "I bet you just happened to be in the neighborhood."

"Yes, I..." She knew her cheeks were red, but she gamely plowed ahead. "I borrowed my father's truck and thought..."

"I'll have that beer now." Ben's voice was a growl as the back door slammed. He rolled his sleeves and paused at the sink to wash.

Sam nudged Finn. "Coming right up, bro."

He stuck out his hand, holding up a longneck as Ben stalked into the kitchen.

The bottle was halfway to Ben's mouth before he caught sight of Rebecca standing there. For the space of a heartbeat he seemed frozen in place.

"Hello, Ben."

At the sound of her voice he struggled to compose himself. "Becca."

"Isn't this a lovely surprise?" Mary Pat set the salad in the middle of the table. "Rebecca, you'll stay for supper, won't you?"

"I don't know. I guess that depends." She stared pointedly at Ben. "Am I welcome here?"

"You're always welcome . . ." Sam's words faded when he realized the entire family was giving him the hairy eyeball.

He closed his mouth and joined the rest of them staring from Ben to Becca and back to Ben.

Ben took a swig of beer. "You heard Sam."

"I want to hear it from you, Ben."

He swallowed. "You know you're welcome to stay."

"Is that what you'd like? Or are you just being polite?"

His tone hardened as his hand snaked out, snaring her wrist. "Considering the mood I'm in, I'd rather not hash this out in public. Let's take this in the parlor."

"No. Stay—" Sam's words were abruptly cut off by Finn's hand over his mouth.

Ben practically dragged Rebecca through the doorway into the front room before slamming the door.

He lowered his hand, clenching it into a fist at his side to keep from dragging her against him. For long moments he merely stared at her like a starving man seeing a banquet. And then he caught the glint of fire in her eyes. "All right. What game are you playing, Becca?"

"This isn't a game, Ben. I'm sick and tired of playing games. Did you try calling me while I was at my parents' house?"

"I called. A few dozen times. You never once returned my calls."

At his words, her heart took a hard, joyous bounce.

"I stopped by to see for myself how you were feeling, but your father ordered me off his property and threatened to have me arrested for trespassing if I showed up again. At first I figured he was just being overprotective. But after a while, I started to wonder why I was fooling myself. The message that I wasn't welcome came through loud and clear."

"That was my father. That wasn't me."

Ben gave a negligent shrug of his shoulders. "If you say so."

Gathering her courage, Becca's eyes narrowed and she poked a finger in his chest. "I came here to say something. And I'd like you to give me the courtesy of listening."

The look in his eyes had her taking a step back. Then, before she could lose her nerve, she lifted her chin a fraction. "Remember that sweet girl you once knew?"

His nostrils flared, but he held his silence.

Rebecca thought about taking another step back, away from the hot, blazing flare of heat, but instead she stood her ground. "I didn't like her. Timid doesn't win wars. So she's gone for good."

"You're out to win wars now?"

She nodded. "This isn't exactly the kind of battle I wanted, but now that I'm stuck with it, I intend to see it through."

"Who are you fighting?"

"My father. Or I should say, his pigheaded attitude."

There was the slightest curve of Ben's lips, but his eyes remained hot with anger.

"And you, Ben. Or I should say, your damnable stoic acceptance of my father's narrow-minded prejudice."

His smile was instantly wiped away. "Stoic? What would you have me do? Engage your father in a knock-down, drag-out brawl in the middle of town?"

"I'm sure that would be satisfying for everybody to see. But there would be no winners." She shook her head. "I didn't come here to talk about getting even. I want to know why you've been avoiding my calls."

"You called?" He lifted his phone from his pocket. "I was up in the hills most of the day. There's no service up there." He paused, seeing what he'd missed earlier. "What about my calls to you?"

"When my phone was finally returned to me today, it was wiped clean. I believe my father erased all my phone messages. I know he was determined to keep me quiet so I could heal, but you know how controlling he can be. Even my mother refuses to cross him. He was furious with the way you handled that... situation, and I'm sure he believed he was doing the right thing by keeping us apart."

Ben's voice was weary. "Maybe your father is right."

She studied the way he looked, a stubble of beard darkening his cheeks and chin, his eyes red-rimmed from lack of sleep. "Why this change of heart, Ben? Why weren't you willing to keep on fighting for me?"

He took his time, choosing his words carefully. "Virgil is thinking about retiring. He asked me to consider becoming sheriff."

Rebecca was caught by surprise. "That's a wonderful compliment to you, Ben. Congratulations."

"There's nothing to celebrate."

"I don't understand. What did you tell him?"

"That I need some time."

"Time? Why? Ben, everyone in Haller Creek, with the exception of my father, thinks you're perfect for the job. You don't agree?"

He shrugged and looked away.

"Are you thinking, after that...incident in town, that your family would rather have you work on the ranch?"

"My family will back me up on whatever choice I make in life."

"Then why the hesitation?"

He set aside his beer and gave her a long, steady look. "There are risks involved. Not every conflict can be resolved without a gunfight."

"In all the years I've known you, Ben Monroe, you've never backed away from a fight, whether it's with your fists or your gun."

He shook his head. "You know me too well, Becca."

"Then why...?"

He put a hand over hers, and the look he gave her had her heart stopping. "Every peace officer wears a bull's-eye on his back. He's a target for anyone who runs from the law."

"After that incident, you're...afraid?"

"Not for myself. But if I want a future with..." He stopped and tried again. "Becca, a lawman makes a lousy partner in life. Not every woman can be married to such a man. Especially a woman with parents like yours. Every day, there are risks that could mean life or death."

"Wait. Are you considering..." As his words sank in, she had to swallow and try again. "Are you saying you'd walk away from me rather than ask me to worry over you?"

"Think about it, Becca. That would be your future. Wondering every time I left for work if this is the day I don't make it home."

"And here I thought..." She stopped.

"What did you think, Becca?"

"That you'd given up on us. That you just didn't want to see me anymore."

"How could you even think such a thing?"

"First, there's my father. He's made no secret of his feelings about you."

"We're two adults. Your father doesn't enter into this."

"All right." She gave a slow shake of her head, as though trying to take it all in. "I thought, after all my father put you through, that this was that karma you're so fond of talking about."

His smile was slow to come, but when it did, he allowed himself to touch her, framing her face with his big hands and staring down into her eyes. "Becca, this past week I've been trying to imagine my life without you in it. I've been miserable. I can't do it. That's why, if you aren't comfortable with marriage to a sheriff, I'll gladly step away from it."

"Oh, Ben. I came here thinking I'd have to fight to get you back. More than anything, I want to share my life with you. Whether you choose to be a lawman or a rancher, all I ask is that you never shut me out."

"You're sure?"

"I've never been so sure of anything in my life."

"Thank heaven." He lowered his face and poured himself into a kiss that left her no doubt of his feelings.

Breathing deeply, Rebecca touched a hand to his cheek. "I can't believe this is happening. All the way here I was beating myself up for being blind to what my father must have put you through. I've spent a lifetime trying to find the courage to stand up for myself."

He touched a finger to her lips to still her words. "Courage? When the chips were down, you were absolutely fearless. When you jammed your elbows into Ranaldo's ribs, catching him by surprise, you changed everything. And then, when you could have fled to safety, you chose instead to stand beside me and face down death. If that isn't true courage, then I don't know what is." He tipped up her face and brushed her lips with his. "You're my very own fierce defender. My brothers have always had my back, but I never thought any woman would stand and fight beside me. You're the only woman I've ever wanted. The only one I'll ever want. And right now, if you say you'll marry me, you'll make me the happiest man on earth."

"Oh, Ben. Yes. Yes. I love you so. That's why I'm here. I came to fight for you..."

"Now that's what we've been waiting to hear." Sam's voice, high with excitement, shattered the mood.

The door to the parlor was pushed open and Ben's family spilled into the room, gathering around the happy couple and embracing them.

Zachariah shook Ben's hand and hugged Rebecca. "Congratulations to both of you. Not that I ever had a doubt, of course."

While Sam and Finn took turns embracing Rebecca, Roscoe and Otis were pumping Ben's hand and slapping him on the shoulder.

Mary Pat caught Rebecca in a warm hug before turning to do the same with Ben.

Mac stood back, waiting until the others were finished congratulating the happy couple before he caught Ben in a fierce bear hug.

As always, his words were understated. But his emotions were front and center in his eyes, in the husky edge to his voice. "I'm happy for you, son."

"Thanks, Dad."

Mac turned to Rebecca. "This will be a real treat for us. Our first daughter."

"Your daughter?" Rebecca wrapped her arms around his neck. "I can't think of a nicer compliment. I can't wait to join your family."

As they stepped apart, Zachariah nodded toward the kitchen. "Dinner's getting cold. Why don't we celebrate over a meal?"

Ben was laughing. "I'm suddenly starving. But I don't want to eat here." He caught Rebecca's hand. "Think you could pack up some food for us, Zachariah? I have something special in mind."

Sam put his hands to his ears, while Finn covered his eyes.

"If you don't mind, bro, we'd rather not see or hear any of the details of your planned celebration."

"I was talking about showing her my special piece of land up in the hills."

"Oh."

The entire family burst into peals of laughter.

Mary Pat and Zachariah led the way to the kitchen, where they packed up fried chicken, potato salad, and corn bread.

A short time later Rebecca and Ben walked hand in hand toward his truck, carrying enough food for an army.

The family watched from the kitchen window as they drove across a field before the truck disappeared into high country.

With the tension lifted, the Monroe family gathered around the table to enjoy a leisurely supper. The voices, which for days had been muted, were now once again joyous and filled with laughter.

"See?" Sam's grin was infectious. "That wasn't so hard now, was it?"

Finn punched him on the arm. "You're acting like you had something to do with those two getting back together."

"I did. We all did." Sam began passing around a platter of fried chicken. "I'm just sayin'. No woman can resist the charm of the Monroe men."

Mackenzie Monroe sat back, letting the sound of all that joyful noise wash over him. He turned to Mary Pat, and without a word, she closed a hand over his.

They sat, holding hands under the table, letting the tensions of the past days slip away as the people who mattered the most to them formed a circle of love around them.

CHAPTER THIRTY-ONE

Rebecca awoke in Ben's sleeping bag and spotted him seated nearby on a boulder, his knees drawn up, his gaze on the distant horizon. His rugged profile reminded her of a Remington sculpture of an Old West cowboy. He was so solid. So rock-steady, the mere sight of him made her heart stutter.

Seeing her awake, he scrambled from the rock and hurried over to gather her close. "Good morning. You realize, in all the excitement last week, we missed the end of the Autumn Festival."

"I like our celebration better. Maybe we should call this our very own version of the Autumn Festival, and return to it every year."

They shared a laugh before he added, "And after our... celebration, you fell asleep."

"Mmm. In your arms. It was the best feeling in the world."

"Yeah. There was a moment a week ago, during that confrontation, when I wondered if I'd ever get to hold you again."

"Once I saw you standing there, I could feel my fears evaporating." She shook her head, remembering. "One minute I was terrified, and the next, there you were, and I just felt this amazing sense of calm come over me." She touched a finger to his mouth. "Now tell me what you were thinking while I was sleeping."

"I was thinking..." He smiled before gathering her close. "That I'm not sure I'll ever again be able to let go of you, Becca. Any regrets about spending the night up here in the hills instead of the comfort of your own bed?"

She rubbed her lips over his. "None. You're right about this place. I know it sounds silly, but sleeping here under the stars, knowing there's nobody around for miles, makes me feel gloriously free."

"Yeah. It's always had that effect on me. You can see the entire town from up here. And that way"—he pointed to the distant hills rising up, layered with brilliant fall colors— "there's nothing but wilderness. Wild horses and mountain goats, and the kind of peace you can't find anywhere else on God's green earth."

He waved a hand to indicate the sweeping landscape. "When my brothers and I became legal sons of Mackenzie Monroe, he brought us up to these hills and told each of us to choose our own special place, and he would make certain it was legally ours. A place where we could sink roots and know with certainty that nobody could ever take it from us."

"And you chose this."

He nodded. "You can't imagine how special it was, to a kid who'd never had a home, to hear that all this could be mine forever. That no government agency could come along and take it from me. That the only way I could ever lose it would be from my own careless actions."

"Oh, Ben. I can see why you love it."

"Can you? Really?" He paused. "I'd like to build a house up here. Away from the town. Away from the world. How would you feel about living up here so far from people?"

"As long as you're here with me, it will be our very own little slice of heaven. Oh, Ben." She wrapped her arms around his neck and snuggled close. "I've never been so happy."

"I know what you mean. It's like the last cloud has lifted, and all around is blinding sunlight." He brushed his thumbs over her mouth, staring deeply into her eyes. "You're my sunlight, Becca. You're my everything."

"And you're mine, Ben Monroe." As he began nuzzling her neck, she added, "So don't you even think about leaving me in the dark ever again. If you're troubled, share it with me. We'll work things out together. You hear me?"

He chuckled against her throat, sending heat spiraling through her veins. "Yes, ma'am."

She lifted her face to his. Against his mouth she whispered, "I love you, Ben Monroe."

"And I . . ." The rest of his words died as he nuzzled her cheek, her temple, her nose, before taking her mouth in a kiss that spun on and on until no words were needed to say what they were both feeling.

"Ben, you won't believe it." Rebecca threw open her front door as Ben walked up to the porch of her little rental house.

"I won't?" He gathered her close and gave her a long, slow, simmering kiss. "If that's the case, I'm guessing proof of life has been discovered on Mars. And somebody reported pigs flying."

Laughing, she poked a finger in his chest. "Oh, you." She led him inside. "My parents have agreed to come to dinner tonight, even knowing your entire family will be here."

"Is that all?"

"Ben. Do you know how amazing this is? My parents are about to mingle with your father and brothers, and Mary Pat and Otis and Roscoe and Zachariah, over dinner. These are people my parents once thought of as..."

He touched a finger to her lips to still her words. "That's all in the past. Give them some credit. They've come a long way, baby."

"Haven't they?" A smile split her lips as she shook her head in wonder. "Haven't we all? But we're talking about my parents."

"Don't do that, babe. They're good people. They love you."

"So much so, they've spent a lifetime smothering me with their love."

"At least you know they care. There are kids who never feel any love."

She gave a shake of her head. "How come you manage to see the good in everyone?"

"Because someone bothered to see the good in me."

He said it so simply, she merely stared. Then, with a soft sigh, she wrapped her arms around his neck and kissed him full on the mouth. "And I'm so glad of it."

He began unbuttoning his shirt. "How long do we have?"

"Hmm?" She glanced at the clock. "Oh, an hour or more."

"Good." He caught her hand and started toward the bedroom. "How would you like to...?"

Reading his thoughts, she drew him back and stood on tiptoe to kiss him. Against his mouth she murmured, "I thought you'd never ask."

"Sorry we're late." Hank Henderson greeted his daughter with an apology as he stepped through the front doorway.

"Reconsidering your agreement to come tonight?"

He flushed.

"It's all right, Dad. You're among friends." Rebecca brushed a kiss over her father's cheek.

"Welcome, Hank." Ben offered a handshake before leading her parents into Rebecca's small living room, where the others were gathered.

Ben handed Hank a longneck, before turning to Will Theisen. "Will was just telling us that he's been in contact with his old mentor at divinity school. He's been invited to join their staff as an assistant pastor."

Susan crossed the room to brush a kiss on Will's cheek. "That's wonderful news. I'm so happy for you, Will."

"Thanks." He shared a handshake with Hank.

"You should be proud, Will." Hank patted his shoulder. "I never got to tell you how amazed I was when you faced that gunman. That takes real courage."

"That wasn't courage. That was guilt. After all, I was the cause of all that trouble."

Hank Henderson shook his head. "Now, Will..."

Will held up a hand to stop him. "You don't know what I did." He lowered his head. "Instead of following directives on how to counsel a troubled young woman, I was convinced that I knew better than the experts, and all I did was make things worse for her and her family. I was the reason Ranaldo Rider came all this way for revenge. And all because I thought I knew the perfect solution to all his woman's problems."

Mary Pat put a hand on Will's arm. "Don't think you're alone, Will. Everyone who goes into the business of counseling troubled people has to learn how to keep personal feelings out of the mix."

"I doubt you ever let your personal feelings steer you wrong, Mary Pat."

She merely sighed. "I didn't learn overnight. Like you, I had to learn from my mistakes. The only difference between an amateur and a professional is time, Will. The more time you spend in the field, the more you'll be able to see people without judging them. My motto has always been this: Most people are doing the best they can with what they have."

"I'll remember that when I join my ministerial team in Atlanta."

"I know you're going to be successful, Will."

Susan turned to Rebecca. "Your father and I have been talking about the wedding plans. You'll want Reverend Grayson, of course. He officiated at our wedding. And since Hank and I held our reception in the church hall, we thought you'd probably want to do the same. I've been going over the list of your school friends. You'll want five or six brides-maids, don't you think?"

Rebecca and Ben shared a smile.

Rebecca kissed her mother's cheek to soften her words. "Thanks for offering to help, but Ben and I have already made our plans, Mom. We want to be married at our own special place in the hills."

Hank frowned. "How are all the guests supposed to get to some primitive place up in the hills?"

"We're hoping to hold the ceremony with just our families."

Susan was wringing her hands. "Poor Reverend Grayson wouldn't survive a trek to the wilderness, honey."

"That's true." Rebecca turned to Will. "Ben and I would like you to officiate before you leave, Will."

The young man's face creased into a wide smile. "Really? I'd be honored. This will be the first wedding for me."

When Hank opened his mouth, his wife patted his cheek. "Maybe you and I should give our daughter a hand in the kitchen."

Rebecca draped an arm around her mother's waist. "Why not let Dad visit with Ben and his family, and you and Mary Pat can help me."

"Of course, honey." Almost in a daze Susan turned away.

Mary Pat got to her feet and caught Becca's hand.

The three women made their way to the kitchen, leaving the men to finish their beer while their hunger sharpened considerably as they inhaled the most amazing fragrances wafting on the air.

"Your father and I were hoping to give you a memorable wedding, Rebecca." Susan kept her voice soft enough that the men in the other room wouldn't overhear.

Rebecca put a hand on her mother's arm. "I know you want to share our day with all your neighbors and friends. But Ben and I really want the day to reflect who we are and what matters to us. Maybe during the holidays you and Dad could host a party. Or better yet, next spring, you could have a barbecue in the backyard. It would be relaxed and easy, and you can show off your brand-new son-in-law."

Susan drew in a breath and managed a smile. "I guess I was thinking more about myself than about you and Ben. I do love the idea of showing the two of you off. Oh, honey." She gathered her daughter into her arms and kissed her temple. "I hope you'll be patient with us while your father and I muddle through."

"I'm really proud of you and Dad. I know it's a lot to take in." Rebecca exchanged a smile with Mary Pat before giving her mother a fierce hug. "A very wise woman told me that as long as mistakes are made in love, they're always forgiven. I know you and Dad love me. I hope you know I love you even more."

Mary Pat lifted a roasting pan from the oven. "And now, we've made those poor men suffer long enough. Let's overwhelm them with some love from the kitchen."

The three women were laughing together as they carried platters to the table and called the men to dinner.

Susan touched a napkin to her mouth. "I don't know when I've tasted pot roast that tender. Rebecca, darling, what did you do to make it so tender?"

"Beer." She enjoyed the look of surprise in her mother's eyes. "A trick Mary Pat taught me."

Mary Pat nodded. "Whenever I'm out of beef stock, I just pour a bottle of beer over my roast. It adds a lovely flavor, don't you think, Susan?"

"I do." She turned to her husband. "And I noticed you had three helpings of those mashed potatoes."

He nodded. "They're really tasty. I can't place the flavor that was added."

"Cream cheese." Rebecca and Mary Pat shared a laugh, while Mary Pat explained. "Through the years, living on the road so much, I've had to learn to improvise."

"Cream cheese." Susan smiled. "I'm filing that away in my mind, too. And I'm hoping we can repay this dinner by having all of you to our house for dinner very soon."

Across the table, Rebecca went silent.

Ben caught her hand under the table. "You feeling okay?"

She nodded. "Just...wondering who these strangers are and what they've done with my parents. I'm afraid I'll wake up and find out this is all a dream."

The two shared a knowing smile.

Susan turned to Otis. "Rebecca tells us she got all the pumpkins from you for her little business."

The old man winked at Rebecca. "Yes, ma'am. But I wouldn't call it a little business. Your daughter's got quite a head on her shoulders."

Hank's look sharpened. "In what way?"

"She turned a garden full of useless pumpkins into the centerpiece of the town's festival. And she took old Lamar Platt's hobby and has the whole town clamoring for all the garden furniture he and his son can make. I've heard they're thinking of hiring some folks around these parts to lend a hand. There are a lot of ranchers looking for ways to make some extra money. Now that's what I call a head for business."

"Thanks for that reminder. I guess I need to stop seeing Rebecca as my little girl and start seeing her the way all of you see her." Hank looked at his daughter with new interest.

She turned to Roscoe. "By the way, I have half a dozen orders from folks in town who want you to create a garden gate and arch like the one you made for me."

The old man couldn't hide his surprise. "You mean they want to pay me?"

"Of course. Just be sure to charge enough to show a profit."

Hank chuckled. "I see what you mean, Otis. My daughter has a head for business."

"I hope you all saved room for dessert." Her cheeks pink from all the praise, Rebecca began cutting slices of her homemade apple pie, topped with a dollop of vanilla ice cream.

"Mom, this is your recipe," she announced. "If I wasn't surrounded by so many good cooks, I'd still be reduced to ordering takeout."

While she passed around dessert, Ben circled the table with steaming cups of tea and coffee.

Later, while Susan and Mary Pat took second cups of tea to the living room to sit by the fire, the men passed around longnecks and joined them.

From the kitchen came the sound of raucous laughter as Ben, Sam, and Finn, along with Rebecca and Will, did the dishes and cleared the table.

Curious, Susan walked to the doorway to watch and listen.

Hank joined her, and the two of them were amazed at the transformation in their daughter. She was having the time of her life, giving as much teasing as she got, flicking a damp dishtowel at Sam's backside, ducking when he tried to return the insult. She was even seen flirting shamelessly with Ben, and hiding behind Will when Finn threatened to dump water on her head.

When they turned, they found Mac standing behind them.

"Are they always like this?" Hank asked.

"They are. Except sometimes, when they're even wilder and louder."

Susan shook her head. "Our house is so quiet. Always has been. They make even doing kitchen duty look like a game."

"It is. In fact, whenever this bunch gets together, everything they do is fun."

Susan put a hand on her husband's arm. "I don't think I've ever heard Rebecca laugh so much."

Hank nodded. "I was thinking the same thing." As an afterthought he added, "After all we've been through, it's pure music to my ears."

The family gathered on Rebecca's small front porch to say their good-byes as a brilliant red sun disappeared behind the peaks of the distant hills.

Will and Mary Pat were talking quietly together, and the words *faith* and *counseling* could be heard by the others before Will made ready to leave.

After complimenting her daughter once more on the lovely meal, Susan turned to Ben. Tears shimmered on her lashes. "I'll never be able to properly thank you for saving my daughter, Ben."

Ben shook his head. "There's no need..."

Hank cleared his throat, the only sign of his agitation. "At first, when you set aside your gun, I thought you were a damned fool. And I had no trouble telling everyone around me what I thought."

Ben held up a hand. "You had a right, Hank."

"No." Hank's voice lowered with feeling. "I wasn't thinking straight. All I could think about was punishing the crazy man who was threatening my baby girl. I wanted that thug dead. But now that Susan and I have had time to talk, I see the wisdom of what you did. Rebecca could have been caught in the crossfire. Any number of things could have gone wrong. Instead, with all that cool control, you managed to bring that whole ugly mess to a safe conclusion." He shook his head in wonder. "Rebecca's safe. That shooter gets a second chance to fix his life. And all thanks to you." He stuck out his hand. "Ben, I had it all wrong. And I had you all wrong. You and your family. I was judging you..." He turned to include the others. "All of you, without ever knowing you. I hope you'll accept my apology."

Ben shook his hand.

One by one the others followed suit.

Together Susan and Hank began their walk home, calling their good nights as they did.

Will paused to thank Rebecca and Ben for inviting him to officiate at their wedding. "I can't think of anything that will make me happier."

As he left, Ben's family piled into trucks for the long drive back to the ranch.

In the backseat, Finn gave a mock sigh and put an arm around Sam's shoulders. "You realize it's the end of an era. Our big brother is officially off the market."

"Yeah. You know what that means?" Sam's lips split into a wide grin. "More women for us, bro."

Mackenzie Monroe, at the wheel, squeezed Mary Pat's hand and laughed along with the others.

And as the truck ate up the miles to the ranch, he found himself wondering, as he did so often, what his fate would have been if three angry boys hadn't made a break for freedom and found a haven at his ranch in the middle of a raging blizzard. A blizzard that changed all their lives forever.

EPILOGUE

Autumn in Montana is a fickle woman. Mild, sunny weather one day, followed by frost glistening on the meadows and snow dusting the highlands the next.

On this day, autumn had decided to play the part of a fairy godmother, with a day balmy enough to make the entire wedding party think it was midsummer.

Mackenzie Monroe climbed the hill behind his ranch and stepped inside the little wrought-iron fence before pausing by the two headstones. His look was pensive as he ran a calloused hand over the names inscribed on the marble.

Minutes later he was joined by the rest of his family.

Zachariah carried a bottle of aged whiskey. Otis and Roscoe carried the crystal tumblers.

Ben in his shiny new uniform, and Sam and Finn, dressed in white shirts and string ties, their boots polished to a high shine, were laughing easily together as they joined the others.

As the glasses of whiskey were passed among them, Mac cleared his throat. "I thought it only right that we come here. Those who are no longer with us are never far from my thoughts. And on this day, I know they're celebrating along with me." He lifted his glass. His voice was tight with emotion. "To Rachel and Robbie, who will forever hold my heart."

The others drank.

"And to Ben." Mac's voice softened. "Who, along with these rascals he calls his brothers, fill my life."

"Here's to us rascals, bro." Sam, grinning from ear to ear, clinked his glass to Ben's and Finn's, before touching it to the others.

Ben said, "And here's to Becca. I still can't believe she would consent to be my wife."

"Love's blind, bro. That's the only explanation I can think of." At Sam's words, the others broke into laughter before tossing back the last of their drinks. With a wink at the others Sam added, "Now let's go get this done before Becca has time to change her mind and choose me instead."

A convoy of trucks moved across a high meadow, where the beginnings of a house had already been laid out.

The foundation was dug, blocks marking the outlines of a sprawling ranch house that would afford a spectacular view of the countryside below.

Hank and Susan stepped out of their truck and joined Will, looking proud in his black suit and starched round white collar.

Mackenzie helped Mary Pat from his truck, and the two of them waited for Zachariah, Otis, and Roscoe, who had been driven by Sam and Finn.

Ben and Becca arrived together, breaking with tradition.

When Ben helped Becca from his truck, Susan had to wipe away tears at the sight that greeted her.

Becca had asked permission to wear her mother's wedding gown. But this dress bore little resemblance to that old gown she'd worn in her own wedding. The many petticoats and the lace overlay had been stripped away, leaving a simple column of white silk that fell to Becca's ankles. The long lace sleeves had been removed, leaving cap sleeves that ruffled in the slight breeze. Instead of a veil, the bride wore a sprig of wildflowers fastened in her hair.

Ben in his uniform, the shiny badge winking in the sunlight, was tall and handsome, and looking more relaxed than his family could ever remember.

As the bride and groom approached, Sam gave his oldest brother a fist bump. "I've got to say. Marriage looks good on you, bro."

Ben gave him a jab to the shoulder. "Maybe you should give it a try."

"No thanks. I'll leave the love stuff to you."

Will opened his prayer book. "Are we ready?"

Ben nodded.

At the bride and groom's request, his two brothers stood on either side of Mary Pat as their witnesses.

Will began to read from his prepared text. "Benedict and Rebecca..." With an embarrassed grin he paused before saying to the assembled, "That's way too formal for this occasion. Ben and Becca, we are gathered here..."

He stumbled several more times, much to the amusement of the others, before finally saying, "By the power vested in me, I now pronounce you husband and wife."

He paused long enough that Sam prompted from the sidelines, "Um, what about the kiss?"

"Oh. Yes. You may kiss your bride, Ben."

"About time," Finn said in a stage whisper as Ben and Becca came together in a warm embrace.

They moved among their families, hugging and laughing, until Zachariah announced in his most official tones, "The wedding supper awaits us back at the ranch."

The convoy of vehicles moved in a slow line down the hill until at last they returned to the ranch, to enjoy slow-simmered roast beef, lobster on the grill, Mary Pat's oven-roasted potatoes, and Susan's amazing four-layer strawberry-and-crème wedding cake, as well as many Champagne toasts.

By the time evening shadows began sliding slowly over the land, Susan and Hank approached their daughter and new son-in-law, who had changed into denims and warm jackets.

Becca embraced each of them before turning to her mother. "Still sorry we didn't have a traditional wedding like yours?"

"Oh, honey, this day couldn't have been any better. It suited the two of you perfectly." She laid a hand on her husband's arm. "And isn't that what a wedding day should be?"

He nodded. "It was a good day, Rebecca. I'm proud of the two of you for doing things your way."

Ben extended his hand. "Thanks, Hank."

Hank accepted his handshake. "My daughter has good taste."

When they'd said their good-byes, Ben and Becca embraced all of Ben's family.

Zachariah was the first to say, "You haven't said where the honeymoon will be."

Ben shook his head. "That's right. We haven't. Nice try, Zachariah."

While the others laughed, Ben caught Becca's hand and led her toward his truck. "The state police will be handling things while we're away."

"When will you be back?"

"Next week."

They left in a cloud of dust.

Once out of sight of the ranch, Ben circled around and turned the truck toward the high meadow before winking at his bride. "You sure you want to camp out for a full week? The weather could turn at any time."

She merely smiled and closed a hand over his. "Not a doubt in my mind, Sheriff Monroe. I have a real weakness for the first snowfall of the season. I hope it happens while we're in the highlands. I'm sure a big strong lawman like you can find a way to keep me dry and warm."

"For the rest of our lives together." He paused to brush a kiss over her mouth, and enjoyed the wild rush of heat that flared.

Here was one more sure thing. He was the luckiest man in the world. His wife was smart, and brave, and beautiful. But none of that could compare with the fact that she loved him.

Love.

To a man who'd never known such a thing as a boy, this was the greatest gift of all, and he made a vow to treasure this woman, and her love, for a lifetime and beyond.

Mary Pat's Beer Pot Roast

When you're traveling the county as Mary Pat does for her clients, you need to use whatever is readily available when cooking. If you have no cooking wine, try beer. Ranchers and folks with hearty appetites love it, and you'll love the flavor.

- 3 pounds roast beef (rump roast, round roast, or sirloin tip roast)
- 1–2 tablespoons olive oil
- Salt and pepper, to taste
- 1–2 cloves garlic
- 1–2 onions
- Choice of vegetables: carrots, parsnips, potatoes, celery, mushrooms, peppers
- 1 bay leaf
- Salt and pepper
- Can of your favorite beer

Preheat the oven to 325°F.

Pat the roast dry before rubbing with olive oil and then sprinkling with salt and pepper.

Place the roast fat side up in a cast-iron pot or heavy roasting pan, to allow the fat to drip over the meat as it cooks.

Add the garlic, onions, and vegetables around the meat.

Pour the beer over all.

Cover and bake for 3–4 hours, until the meat is tender and almost falling apart.

Serve with warm rolls.

A PREVIEW OF *THE COWBOY NEXT DOOR* FOLLOWS.

CHAPTER ONE

Monroe Ranch—Present Day

Hoo boy." Ben Monroe, dressed in his crisp sheriff's uniform, his badge winking in the late-summer sunlight, held his nose as his brother Sam led his roan gelding past him into the barn. "My brother the trail bum. How long have you been up in the hills?"

Sam began unsaddling his mount. "Three weeks. I know I smell. I've been in these clothes for days, and eating dust for miles."

"It's not just the smell. You look like one of those wild mountain men. If your beard gets any thicker, it'll completely cover your ugly face. Not that that's a bad thing."

Sam gave one of his rogue grins. "That's not what the girls at the Hitching Post say."

His brother laughed. Sam's prowess with both a pool cue and the ladies was well known at the local saloon in the little town of Haller Creek. Men and women alike were drawn to his zany sense of humor and his love of a good joke. "If they could see you now, they'd have a change of heart."

"It's nothing that a shower and shave won't fix."

Ben leaned his arms on the stall's door. "What kept you in the hills so long?"

"I offered to handle the herd while Dad and the others caught up on ranch chores"—Sam shot a pointed look at his older brother—"now that one of us has left ranching behind in favor of being a sheriff. You going to lend a hand, or just stand there trying to look important?"

Ben stood a little taller. "You think the uniform makes me look important?"

"Only in your own mind, bro." Sam flung his saddle over the rail of the stall before filling troughs with oats and water. "I'm still trying to wrap my mind around the fact that my big brother is on the right side of the law for a change."

The two shared a laugh.

As Sam started toward the house, he turned. "You coming?"

Ben shook his head. "I just got a call from Becca. She's coming home early, so I'm heading back to town to meet her."

Sam shot him a sideways glance. "You'd think after a year of wedded bliss, things would change. You still rushing home to your blushing bride?"

"You bet." The mere mention of Ben's pretty young wife, Becca, had his grin spreading from ear to ear. "Since we're still in that honeymoon stage, I thought I'd..."

Sam covered his ears. "Stop. Too much information. Remember I'm your brother, not your confessor. Take all that gooey love stuff home, bro."

"Yeah. I'm going. But before I leave I think you should know…"

Sam was shaking his head as he started walking faster. "Not now. I've got the longest shower in history waiting for me. I intend to grab all the hot water before Dad and the others beat me to it. You and Becca should stop by the Hitching Post later. I'm hoping I can lure a couple of suckers from the Murphy ranch to challenge me to a game of nine ball tonight."

"Okay. But before you go inside, you ought to know. Dad hired a housekeeper."

"What?" Sam stopped dead in his tracks. "What's wrong with Zachariah's cooking and cleaning?"

"Nothing. But I guess Mary Pat told Dad about this woman who needed a job. And Dad…"

Sam held up a hand. Mary Pat Healy, social worker, visiting nurse, and teacher for the county, was a proverbial bleeding heart, eager to help every single person in the entire state of Montana. "And Mary Pat asked Dad to work his magic and hire this poor old woman until she can get on her feet."

"Something like that. But…"

"I guess a couple of old men weren't enough for Dad. Now we've added an old woman to keep an eye on." Sam climbed the steps to the porch and pushed open the back door without a pause, leaving his older brother to stare after him with a wide smile splitting his lips.

Once inside the mudroom, Sam paused to pry off his filthy, dung-caked boots before strolling through the empty kitchen to the parlor, unbuttoning his shirt as he walked.

That's when he spotted a small figure headed toward him carrying a huge box.

"What the hell?" His reaction was automatic. No sweet

old lady should be handling something as heavy as this. "Here. That looks like it weighs more than you. Give me that."

He forcibly took the box from her hands and had to blink twice. He found himself looking into amber eyes so wide, they seemed too big for the pretty face that framed them. To his astonishment, it was a pretty *young* face, surrounded by a mane of shiny dark hair that fell past her shoulders. The kind of hair a man could happily get lost in.

The young woman's features went from relaxed to fearful in the blink of an eye. "I don't know what gives you the right to come barging in here, but if you aren't out of here by the count of three, I'll shout down the rooftop. I happen to know the sheriff is right outside."

"I was." Ben's voice came from behind Sam. "Good thing I followed Sam inside."

They both turned to see Ben standing in the doorway. He didn't bother to hide his amusement. "I see I'm too late. You two have already met."

Sam's eyes narrowed. "Okay. What's the joke? I thought you said Dad had hired an old lady."

"That's not what I said. But I guess it's what you heard." Ben turned to the woman. "This smelly cowboy fresh from the hills is my brother Sam." To Sam he added, "Our new housekeeper, Penny Cash."

At the mention of her name, Sam's lips curved into a teasing grin. "Really? Penny Cash? You're making that up, right, Miss...Money?"

"What a tired joke. Believe me, I've heard them all." She looked from Ben to Sam before taking the box from Sam's hands. "Now if you'll excuse me, I'll store these things in the mudroom and finish cleaning out the spare bedroom, which is now my bedroom."

She started to brush past Sam, but he stopped her with a hand on her arm. "Okay. What's a pretty thing like you doing out here in the middle of nowhere, cleaning up after a houseful of men? Are you on the run from the law?"

"No. But you may be the one running if you don't step back right now." She glowered at the offending hand until he removed it. "Mackenzie Monroe knows everything he needs to know about me. If you have any questions, ask him."

Ben slapped a hand on his brother's back. "Better watch out, bro. Looks like she's already made up her mind about you."

She looked Sam up and down, and wrinkled her nose at the offending odor. "As a matter of fact, I have. But I find it hard to believe this trail bum is the brother you and Finn bragged about. The one who charms all the ladies from six to sixty."

Sam puffed up enough to say, "Yeah. They got that right."

She headed toward the kitchen, shaking her head. "Poor things. They must be desperate. I pity them all."

When she was gone, Ben shook his head. "Way to go. I could see she was really impressed." He paused a beat before adding, "Looks like you're losing your touch, bro."

A grin spread across Sam's face. "You think I care what one bossy sourpuss thinks?"

"Hell, yes. I know you too well. You never could resist a challenge. You're going to brood until you find a way to charm her."

"Damn straight." Sam gave his brother a fist bump.

His laughter continued all the way up the stairs.

Once upstairs Sam headed toward the bathroom and stripped off his filthy clothes before picking up his razor. A glance in the mirror had him wincing. He looked even worse than a trail bum.

No wonder the female downstairs was so quick to think he was a dangerous intruder. Her reception had been a shock. He wasn't used to having pretty women treat him like something that crawled out from under a rock. In fact, he'd always taken for granted the fact that women of all ages liked him. His humor and his good looks were all part of his charm. Apparently all that charm was lost on their new housekeeper.

He chuckled as he removed weeks of shaggy beard before stepping under a hot shower.

By the time he'd toweled himself dry and took another look in the mirror, he was feeling smug. Take that, Miss Prim and Proper Money.

His confidence restored, he headed toward his room to dress and enjoy the first family meal in weeks.

"Welcome back to civilization, Samuel." Zachariah York, his lion's mane of white hair framing a handsome, weathered face, looked up from his perfect gin and tonic as Sam stepped into the kitchen.

"It's good to be home." Sam reached into the refrigerator, helped himself to a longneck, and took a long, cool drink.

Mackenzie Monroe clapped a hand on his son's shoulder. "Thanks for stepping in with the herd."

"You know I don't mind, Dad. I can't think of anywhere I'd rather be than up in those hills."

Zachariah shared a knowing smile with Roscoe Flute and Otis Green, who were grinning from ear to ear. "Unless it's in town running the table at the Hitching Post."

Sam chuckled. "Well, yeah. That's a given."

Mac indicated the young woman across the room. "Have you met Penny?"

"We met." Sam studied her backside as she bent to remove a roasting pan from the oven. She was wearing slim denims and a faded T-shirt, her dark hair pulled back in a ponytail, making her look like a high school girl.

She barely gave him a glance before setting the pan on top of the stove and lifting the lid.

If Sam was disappointed that she didn't bother to give him a second look, he was willing to forgive her for the moment. He was content to inhale the amazing aroma that drifted toward him, making his mouth water.

Zachariah turned as Finn walked in carrying his ever-present briefcase stuffed with legal documents. "Ah. Finnian. Just in time for supper."

Seeing Sam, Finn's face creased into a wide smile and he crossed to his brother. "Hey. How're things in the hills?"

"Quiet. How's the lawyer biz going?"

"I picked up another client today." He tossed aside his burden to accept a longneck from Mac. "You know a rancher named Edgar Hanover?"

His father thought a moment before nodding. "Does he have a ranch up on Stony Mountain?"

"That's him." Finn turned to Zachariah. "He wants to take on the county for creating a dam that dried up the branch of the Stony Mountain Creek that feeds into his land."

Zachariah arched a bushy white brow. "I'll remind you, the county has deep pockets, Finnian. They'll spare no expense. You'll be up against an experienced legal team that is kept on retainer for only one purpose—to shoot down the locals who complain about the way things have always been done."

Finn turned to Sam, and the two wore matching dangerous smiles.

Finn took a sip of beer before saying, "I figured as much. That's why I told Edgar Hanover I'd be happy to represent him." In an aside, he said to Zachariah, "And I'm hoping you'll give me the benefit of your expertise."

"Going up against the big guns, are you, lad?" The old man rubbed his hands together. There was nothing he liked better than a chance to step back into the ring and use his years of experience as one of the top trial lawyers in the state. "You have as much of my time and expertise as you want, Finnian, my boy."

They looked toward the door when Ben and Becca walked in, holding hands.

"We were just up in the hills, taking a look at how our house is shaping up. Conway is doing a fine job."

Mac gave a nod of approval. "Conway Miller is a good, honest building contractor. You two hired the best. When does he think you'll be able to move in?"

"Not for another six or seven months. But that's okay. Becca and I are comfortable in the little house in town." Ben looked around. "I'm glad to see we're not too late for supper."

Sam gave a snort of laughter. "Some things never change." He put an arm around his new sister-in-law's shoulders. "I thought Mary Pat was giving you cooking lessons."

Becca nodded. "She is. But only when she's in town, which isn't nearly often enough to suit me."

"Or to suit Dad," Sam said in an aside, causing Mackenzie Monroe to blush.

Sam couldn't resist drawing their new housekeeper into the conversation, hoping to get her attention. "Have you met Penny?"

Becca hurried over to give the young woman a hug. "We met in town, before she came to work here. I hope it's all right that we've barged in on you without warning, Penny."

"You know I'm used to cooking for a crowd. The more the merrier," Penny added.

It was obvious that Penny and Becca had already become comfortable with one another.

Becca reached for a platter. "The least I can do is help pass things around."

As the others took their places around the table, the two young women began passing platters of tender roast beef with garden potatoes and green beans, along with rolls warm from the oven.

When they were ready, Mac suggested they join hands in honor of their missing member, Mary Pat, who always insisted on a blessing whenever she managed to join them.

He smiled as he intoned, "We're thankful for this food, this family, and those who aren't able to be here with us this day."

With murmured words of approval they dug in.

"That was a fine meal, Penny." Mac glanced at the young woman seated across the table.

For the most part she'd eaten dinner in silence, content to let the others carry the conversation.

"Thanks, Mr. . . ." She paused and corrected herself. When Mackenzie Monroe had hired her, he'd asked her to call him Mac. "Thanks, Mac."

"Where'd you learn to cook like that, Miss Penny?"

She smiled at Otis, and it was obvious she felt easy in his company. "I have three brothers. I learned early that the male of the species likes to eat."

"I bet your ma was a good cook, too."

She stared hard at the table. "My mom died when I was ten."

Otis stared helplessly at Mac, who strove to lighten the mood. "Mary Pat said you earned your teaching certificate at the university in Bozeman."

She nodded. "I studied online, and finished college in Bozeman."

Becca put a hand over Penny's. "I went to college there, too. I bet we were there at the same time. Wouldn't it be something if we had mutual friends?"

Penny gave a shake of her head. "I didn't have time to socialize. I carried two jobs while I was there. I worked in a little café mornings, and right after class I worked in a coffee shop off campus."

"And I thought my schedule was tough. When did you sleep?" Becca asked.

Penny gave a short laugh. "Good question. Mostly I went without it. But I didn't mind. Getting my teacher's certification was worth it."

Sam looked over. "If you're a teacher, why aren't you teaching?"

Mac turned to explain. "Penny was brought to Haller Creek by the school board to replace Nancy Carter."

Sam nodded in understanding. "Pryor Carter was telling everyone in town not long ago that he and Nancy were finally having a baby after six years of trying."

"Unfortunately, Nancy lost the baby." Mac sipped his coffee. "She and Pryor have been really shaken by the loss. Her doctor said work would be the best way for her to move on with her life, so she asked the board to keep her job available. The board agreed that they were legally bound to honor their commitment to her, since technically she was still under contract."

Sam glanced at Penny. "But what about your job?"

She shook her head. "I never got a chance to sign a contract, so I had no legal rights."

"Couldn't you teach somewhere else?"

She sighed. "With school already in session, all the positions are filled. The board offered to let me sub whenever one of the teachers needs a day, and I'm happy to do that, but I have a lot of college debt to clear. I need a full-time job, and Mary Pat Healy suggested I come here."

Sam arched a brow. "Not surprising. Mary Pat seems to have a logical solution for every problem under the sun."

Sam's words had Mac nodding. "That's our Mary Pat, all right."

"Do I smell pumpkin pie?" Roscoe's question had Penny pushing away from the table.

Over her shoulder she called, "I think it's cool enough to cut now. I made whipped cream, too."

"I'll help." Sam walked to the refrigerator and removed a bowl mounded with whipped cream. Even before he reached for a spoon, he'd dug his finger in to taste. "I'll be darned. Not out of a can or carton, but the real thing." He dipped a big serving spoon into it and ate it in one big gulp.

Finn chuckled. "That's the fastest I've ever seen you offer to help. Now I know why."

"So do I." Penny fished a second spoon from the drawer and took the bowl from Sam's hands. "After you've licked that one clean, you can put it in the sink. I don't want you passing your germs around to the rest of us."

"Hey." Sam tried to reach over her shoulder with the spoon, but she was quicker and snatched the bowl away.

She shot him a withering look. "If you want a piece of pie, you'd better not try that again in my kitchen, cowboy."

While Sam stepped back, the rest of the family hooted with laughter.

"Guess the lady told you who's in charge, bro."

At Finn's taunt, Sam was forced to drop the spoon in the sink and take his place at the table. But one bite of pumpkin pie smothered in whipped cream had his smile returning.

Penny Cash was bossy. No doubt about it. But the lady could cook. And he was willing to overlook her obvious character flaw as long as he could indulge his sweet tooth on something as good as this.

"So," Finn said around a mouthful of pie. "I guess you must have missed your nights in town while you were stuck up in the hills with nothing but cows for company. Planning on heading into town for your usual entertainment at the Hitching Post tonight?"

Penny's head came up sharply and she regarded Sam with a look of disdain, the way she might study a big, hairy spider.

Seeing the look of disapproval on her face, Sam's first reaction was a slow burn. What gave this self-righteous woman the right to judge him? Just as quickly, he found himself giving a slow, reluctant shake of his head. "That was the plan. But after three weeks in the hills and a full stomach, I've decided I need to sleep in a real bed."

Or did the thought of spending a little more time enjoying the view here at home have something to do with his sudden change of heart?

He saw the rigid line of Penny's back as she walked to the stove and couldn't resist adding, "There's time enough for teaching the yokels the game of nine ball in the weeks to come."

About the Author

New York Times bestselling author **R. C. Ryan** has written more than ninety novels, both contemporary and historical. Quite an accomplishment for someone who, after her fifth child started school, gave herself the gift of an hour a day to follow her dream to become a writer.

In a career spanning more than twenty years, Ms. Ryan has given dozens of radio, television, and print interviews across the country and Canada, and has been quoted in such diverse publications as the *Wall Street Journal* and *Cosmopolitan*. She has also appeared on CNN News and *Good Morning America*.

You can learn more about R. C. Ryan—and her alter ego Ruth Ryan Langan—at:

RyanLangan.com

Twitter, @RuthRyanLangan

Facebook.com

Rocky
Mountain
Cowboy

SARA
RICHARDSON

FOREVER
YOURS

NEW YORK   BOSTON

This book is a work of fiction. Names, characters, places, and incidents are the product of the author's imagination or are used fictitiously. Any resemblance to actual events, locales, or persons, living or dead, is coincidental.

Copyright © 2018 by Sara Richardson
Cover design by Elizabeth Turner Stokes
Cover copyright © 2018 by Hachette Book Group, Inc.
Hachette Book Group supports the right to free expression and the value of copyright. The purpose of copyright is to encourage writers and artists to produce the creative works that enrich our culture.

The scanning, uploading, and distribution of this book without permission is a theft of the author's intellectual property. If you would like permission to use material from the book (other than for review purposes), please contact permissions@hbgusa.com. Thank you for your support of the author's rights.

Forever Yours
Hachette Book Group
1290 Avenue of the Americas
New York, NY 10104
hachettebookgroup.com
twitter.com/foreverromance

First Edition: July 2018

Forever Yours is an imprint of Grand Central Publishing.
The Forever Yours name and logo are trademarks of Hachette Book Group, Inc.

The Hachette Speakers Bureau provides a wide range of authors for speaking events. To find out more, go to www.hachettespeakersbureau.com or call (866) 376-6591.

The publisher is not responsible for websites (or their content) that are not owned by the publisher.

ISBN 978-1-5387-1338-9

To Jenna LaFleur

CHAPTER ONE

In a small town like Topaz Falls, Colorado, the grocery store was the last place you'd want to go if you didn't want to be noticed. But when your diet consisted mainly of Honey Nut Cheerios and you'd run out of milk, you had no choice but to show up at Frank's Market in full disguise.

Jaden Alexander pulled his blue Colorado-flag stocking cap farther down his forehead so that it met the top of his Oakleys. Not that the sunglasses were inconspicuous. They were a custom design, made exclusively for him when the company had courted him for sponsorship six years ago after he'd made his Olympic debut. No one else would know that, though. To other people, he hoped he looked like just another ski bum who moonlighted as a bartender or waiter during the off-season. With any luck, no one in town would realize that J.J. Alexander—dubbed the Snowboarding Cowboy by the media—had come home.

The door still chimed when he walked in, the same way it

had when he'd done the weekly grocery run for his grandma twelve years ago. In fact, it looked like Frank hadn't changed much of anything. The same depressing fluorescent lights still hummed overhead, casting bright spots onto the dirty linoleum tiles. He passed by the three checkout stations, where two bored cashiers stood hunched behind their registers, fingers pecking away on their phones.

One of them looked familiar enough that a shot of panic hit Jaden in the chest. But the woman didn't even look up as he slipped into the nearest aisle, so maybe he was just being paranoid. Death threats on Twitter would do that to a guy. Ever since the accident, going out in public wasn't exactly his favorite thing to do. He'd been ambushed by photographers, reporters, and fans who'd written him off, and he was not in the mood to deal with any public showdowns tonight.

"J.J. Alexander? That you?"

Anyone else and he would've shaken his head and kept right on walking, but he knew the voice behind him. He'd never get away with walking on past without a word. He turned around, and right there at the end of the aisle stood Levi, Lance, and Lucas Cortez. Back in high school, Jaden had bummed around with Levi until Cash Greer passed away. After that, Levi had gone to Oklahoma to train as a bull rider, and Jaden had finally been accepted to train with the U.S. ski and snowboard team.

"Holy shit, man." Levi sauntered over the way a bull rider would—all swagger. "I didn't know you were back in town."

"Hey, Levi." Jaden forced his jaw to loosen and nodded at each of the brothers in turn. "Lucas. Lance." Now, those three had changed in twelve years. They'd all cleaned up. Still cowboys in their ragged jeans and boots, but each of the brothers was clean-shaven and more groomed than he'd ever seen him. Wasn't a coincidence that they all had rings on their left fingers now too. Jaden slipped his sunglasses onto his forehead, grateful the store seemed empty, so they shouldn't attract too much attention.

"Actually, I'm not back." His voice had changed since the accident. These days he had to fight for a conversational tenor instead of slipping into defensive mode. "Not permanently anyway. I'm only here to consult on the new terrain park at the resort." The Wilder family had been looking to expand their ski hill outside of Topaz Falls for a few years now. He'd never been a fan of the Wilder family—no one in town was—but the job had offered him an opportunity to lie low for a while.

"Heard that's gonna be quite the addition up there," Levi said. "I also heard your grandma sold the ranch a few years back. You got a place to stay?"

"I rented a place on the mountain." He didn't acknowledge that bit about his grandma. Hated to think of her stuck in that facility in Denver. He hadn't had a choice, though, once the dementia started. She'd taken care of him—raised him—seeing as how his dad had been a loser and his mom a free spirit who'd rather live the gypsy lifestyle than hang out with her kid.

Four years ago, the roles reversed, and he was the one taking care of Grams. Back then he couldn't do much for her. He was too busy splitting his time between Park City and Alaska, chasing the snow so he could stay in shape. After she'd started wandering off, he'd moved her into the best facility in Denver and dropped in a couple of times a month to visit, even though she no longer knew him.

"Sorry to interrupt, but I need backup." Lance moseyed over. As the eldest Cortez brother, he was serious and stern. He used to scare the shit out of Jaden when they were kids, but from the looks of things, he'd mellowed out. "Jessa didn't tell me there were a thousand different kinds of tampons. I have no clue what to get. Any ideas?"

Uhhh...Jaden looked around, realizing for the first time they were in *that* aisle. The one he never stepped foot in. On purpose anyway.

"There's regular, super, super-plus..." Lucas shook his head as he examined the products stacked on the shelves. "I thought we were buying tampons, not gasoline."

The brothers laughed, and even with the anxiety squirming around his heart, Jaden cracked a smile. "So this is what happens when you get hitched, huh?" Oh how things had changed. Used to be, on a Friday night, he and Levi would drive up to the hot springs on the Cortez's property, share a few beers, have a bonfire, and get to at least second base with whatever girl looked good that night. Now these three spent their Friday nights shopping for woman-stuff.

Levi glared at his eldest brother like he wanted to string him up by his toenails. "We were out for a beer when Lance's wife called with an"—he raised his hands for air quotes—"emergency."

"She was in tears," Lance said defensively. "And quit bullshitting us. If Cass had called, you'd be doing the same thing right now."

That seemed to shut Levi up.

Lucas looked at his brothers with humor in his eyes. "Naomi loves me too much to put me through that."

"Yeah?" Levi shot Jaden a sly grin. "That why she sent you to the store for hemorrhoid cream after Char was born?"

And that was Jaden's cue. There were some things you couldn't unhear, and he definitely didn't want to know anything about having babies and hemorrhoids. "Well, it was good to see you guys. Maybe I'll see you around."

He made a move to slip past and leave them all behind, but Levi walked with him. "Hold up. How're things going?"

The familiar anxiety slipped those cold fingers around Jaden's heart and squeezed. He'd been conditioned. Anytime someone looked at him like that—used that overly sympathetic tone of voice—he wanted to turn and bolt before they could bring up the accident. "Things are fine," he lied. Things had fallen apart after that race. In his life and in his head. Three months later, he still didn't know how to put it all back together.

"I saw the crash on TV."

Yeah, Levi along with the rest of the world. If they hadn't witnessed it during live coverage of the race, they'd seen it in the extensive news analysis afterward.

"You all healed up?"

Did it matter? "Pretty much. I've got a few pins in my arm, but who doesn't?" The joke fell flat, and the anxiety squeezed harder, shrinking his heart in its suffocating grasp.

"Haven't heard much about the other guy in a few months." Questions lurked in Levi's tone and in his eyes. Jaden could see them surfacing.

Had he done it on purpose? Had Jaden intentionally taken out his biggest competition on that last turn when it looked like he wasn't going to win the gold? Everyone had already made up their own answers, so why did it matter what he said?

Breathe. Keep breathing. Never thought he'd have to remind himself to do things like that. "Beckett is still in a rehab facility." Scarred and broken. Still trying to relearn how to walk...

"Damn. Sorry to hear it."

Jaden already knew sorry wasn't enough. Not for Kipp Beckett, not for the reporters, not for the officials. Not for fans of the sport. Not even for himself.

"For what it's worth, I didn't think you did it on purpose." Levi was trying to be supportive, but the fact that he said it at all meant he'd thought about the possibility. Same as everyone else.

"I didn't," Jaden said simply. "I wouldn't." In the replays, it might've looked like he'd lunged into Beckett—who'd been his rival in the snowboard-cross event since they'd both started out—but the truth was that he'd caught an edge and it had thrown off his balance. He couldn't recover. He couldn't stop the momentum that pitched him into Beckett, that sent them both careening through the barriers, cartwheeling and spinning until the world went silent. When the snow had settled, Jaden had gotten up, and Kipp Beckett hadn't. His body lay twisted at an angle, and he was unconscious, maybe dead.

Shock had numbed Jaden to the fact that his arm was badly fractured. He'd fallen to his knees next to Beckett before officials had raced in and forced him away. The papers and news shows and magazines all said Jaden was sneering as the medics tended to him. He wasn't. He was crying.

"I would've taken the silver." If no one else believed him, maybe Levi would. "I didn't care that much." He didn't value the gold more than someone's life. Did he? God, the news reports had made him question himself.

Levi gave him a nod. "Looked to me like you caught an edge. Could've happened to anyone." He clapped him on the shoulder. "Hey, why don't you stop over for a beer sometime? I just finished building my new house. Need to break it in."

"Sure." Jaden said it like he did that all the time—stopped by a friend's house for a beer. But it had been months. Months since he'd had a real conversation with another human being. Months since someone had actually smiled at him. When he wasn't working on the mountains, his days consisted of sitting silently on the back deck with his chocolate Lab Bella sprawled at his feet while he tried to figure out how everything had collapsed.

"What about tonight?" Levi shot a look toward his brothers. "Since my evening got interrupted and I'm now free."

"I've gotta head back up the mountain tonight." They were discussing the possibility of lighting the terrain park for night boarding. "But I'd definitely like to hang sometime. Let me know what else works." Levi was the first person who'd actually heard him when he said he didn't mean for any of it to happen.

Maybe he had one ally in a world full of enemies.

* * *

Up until this very moment, Kate Livingston thought the worst thing about camping was the bugs. No, wait. Actually, the mosquitos in Colorado weren't nearly as bad as she had anticipated. So far she'd seen only one medium-sized spider, which wasn't even hairy like the some of them in L.A. So, before this moment, maybe she would've said the worst thing about camping was the dirt. Yes, definitely the dirt. She could feel it sticking to her skin, grainy and disgusting as she lay swaddled like a baby in the brand-new sleeping bag that still smelled like synthetic fluff.

Another flash of light split the sky above her flimsy nylon tent. Which had cost about $450, by the way. And now the damn thing was sagging underneath the weight of a rain puddle that had collected right over her head. *Waterproof my ass.*

She squirmed to unearth her arms from the sleeping bag and typed in a note on her phone. *Extreme Outdoors Light-*

weight Backpacker Tent—Sucks. Unsatisfied, she underlined, highlighted, and changed the word *sucks* to all caps.

When she'd landed the position as a senior editor for *Adrenaline Junkie* magazine, she had envisioned herself sitting in a corner office overlooking the hustle and bustle of Beverly Hills while she sipped frothy lattes and approved spreads and attended photo shoots with male models who cost upward of a thousand dollars for one hour of work.

But there had been some budget cuts recently, Gregor, her managing editor, had explained on her first day. They weren't working with as many freelancers, and the editor who was supposed to do a gear-test backpacking trip on the Colorado Trail for the fall issue had suddenly quit, so...

Here she was, on an all-expenses-paid trip through hell.

The ceiling of the tent drooped even lower, inching toward her nose. A drop of rainwater plunked onto her right eyebrow right as a crack of earsplitting thunder shook the ground.

Now she knew. She knew that the worst thing about camping was not bugs or dirt but a thunderstorm in the mountains. In fact, she would probably die tonight. Either from getting skewered by a lightning bolt or from a heart attack, whichever came first.

"I went to Northwestern journalism school," she lamented over the pattering rain. After she'd walked out of there with her master's degree, she'd assumed she could have her pick of jobs. But nope. Anyone could call themselves a journalist these days. It didn't matter if they had interned at the *Chicago Tribune* or if they knew AP style or even how to use a fucking comma. If they had fifty thousand followers on their blog, they were in.

Let's just say respectable jobs in the world of journalism weren't exactly knocking down her door. So when the opportunity at *Adrenaline Junkie* had come up, she'd done more than jump on it. She'd immersed herself in it. So what if she'd never actually camped? It wasn't her fault her father was a yuppie attorney and her mother a neurologist. They didn't believe in camping. But she could read all about it on the Internet.

Who cared that the one time she'd felt a surge of adrenaline in the great outdoors had come when she'd lost her Gucci sunglasses in a rogue wave on the beach? She'd never swam that fast in her life. It was a job—a senior-level job—and she could finally move out of her parents' basement and away from her role as the butt of every family joke. Both her older sister and her younger brother had become doctors too. Just to make her look bad.

If only they could see her now.

Bringing the phone to her lips, she turned on the voice recorder. "Day one. The Extreme Outdoors Lightweight Backpacker Tent appears to be made out of toilet paper." She wondered if she'd get away with making that an official quote in her four-page spread. "I've worn a rain poncho that repels water better than this piece of—"

A scratching sound near her feet cut her off. The walls of the tent trembled. Yes, that was definitely a scratching sound. A claw of some kind? "Mary mother of God." The whisper fired up her throat. She wasn't sure if it was the start of a prayer or a curse. She'd have to wait and see, depending on how things turned out.

Scrunching down farther into her sleeping bag, Kate held her breath and listened. There was a huffing sound. An animal sound. A bear? Yes, this definitely called for a prayer. "Oh, God, please don't let it eat me." She squirmed to the corner of the tent where she'd stashed her overstuffed backpack. Yes, she'd read all about how she was supposed to empty the food from her backpack and hang it from a tree in a bear-proof container, but she hadn't actually had the time to find a bear-proof container before she left L.A. Surely bears didn't like freeze-dried macaroni and cheese…did they?

Quickly and silently, Kate dug through the gear until she located her copy of *The Idiot Guru's Guide to Hiking and Camping*. The binding was still crisp. She'd meant to open it on the plane, but she'd forgotten that she'd downloaded *Sweet Home Alabama* on her phone, and God she loved that movie. And Reese. She'd waved to Reese once, across the street on Rodeo Drive, and she'd actually waved back! Well, she might've waved back or she might've been pushing her hair out of her eyes. It had been kind of hard to tell.

But anyway. The bear…

Using her phone as a flashlight, Kate flipped through the pages in search of a chapter about bears while a dark shadow made its way slowly around the tent. "Come on, come on." Hadn't the Idiot Guru thought to inform other idiots what to do if they encountered a bear?

The shadow paused and swiped at the nylon wall.

"Oh God, sweet Jesus." Kate ducked all the way into the sleeping bag, taking the book with her. If nothing else, maybe she could use it as a weapon to defend herself. It was thick enough to do some serious damage. Yet somehow there was no chapter on what to do when a bear was stalking you from outside your tent.

Okay. Think. When she'd first gotten this assignment, she'd read something on the Internet about animal encounters. Was she supposed to play dead? Make loud noises? She fired up the satellite phone again—waiting for what felt like five years for the Internet to load—and searched *bear encounter*.

Big. Mistake. Apparently, bears did eat people. There were pictures to prove it. Adrenaline spurted through her in painful pulses. How could anyone *like* this feeling? Adrenaline junkie? More like adrenaline-phobic. It made her toes curl in and her skin itch. Alternating between hot and cold, Kate crossed her legs so she wouldn't pee in her only pair of long underwear. Lordy, she had to go so bad...

A whimper resonated somewhere nearby. *Hold on a second.* She hadn't whimpered, had she? No. She was pretty sure her voice wouldn't work right now. Did bears whimper? She wouldn't know because the Idiot Guru had left out that critical chapter...

The creature outside her tent whimpered again, softly and sweetly. Kate peeked her head out of the sleeping bag. The shadow was gone, but the whimpering continued.

Holding the sleeping bag around her like a feeble bubble of protection, she squirmed over to the zippered flap that the company had touted as an airflow vent and inched it open until she could see. The rain had slowed some, but it still sprinkled her nose as she peered outside. The shadowy figure of an animal lay a few feet from the tent, still whimpering weakly. But it appeared to be much smaller than she'd originally thought. Way too small to be a bear. It looked more like...a dog.

"Oh no. Poor thing." Kate fought with the sleeping bag until it finally released her. She unzipped the tent's main flap. After slipping on her boots, she slogged through the mud and knelt next to the dog. It was a Lab. A chocolate Lab just like the ones she'd seen playing fetch on Venice Beach. "Are you lost?" she crooned, testing the dog's temperament with a pat on the head. The dog licked her hand and then eased up to a sitting position so it could lick her face.

"You're a sweetheart, aren't you?" She ran her hand over

the dog's rain-slicked fur. The poor love shook hard, staring at her with wide, fearful eyes. "I'll bet you don't like the storm, do you?" she asked. "Well that makes two of us. Come on." She coaxed the dog into the tent. "You can wait out the storm with me." And...seeing as how she couldn't stay out here harboring a fugitive dog..."First thing tomorrow morning, we can head into the nearest town so we can find your owner."

Then she'd find herself a nice hot shower, a real meal that didn't require boiling water on a camp stove, and a plush queen-sized bed where she could finally fall into a dry, peaceful sleep.

CHAPTER TWO

Bella!" Jaden jogged down the hall of his rented ski chalet, hoping to God that his dog was simply hiding under the massive king-sized bed in the master suite.

He tore into the room, flicked on the lights, and hit the floor next to the bed. His heart plummeted. *Damn it.* He should've brought her up the mountain with him tonight. Or at least locked the doggie door so she couldn't get out. If he would've known a storm was coming, he would have. And he would've kept her right by his side. Though it'd been only a month since he'd gotten her from a rescue in Denver, he'd already learned that lightning and thunder sent her over the edge.

Back in the hallway, he stopped at the closet to grab his raincoat and pull on a headlamp and his hiking boots. As soon as he'd heard the first clap of thunder, he'd told the crew he had to get home, but he wasn't fast enough. It had taken him a good hour to navigate the ATV down the steep slopes in the rain, and Bella could cover a lot of ground in an hour, especially if she was running scared.

Jaden slipped out the French doors and onto the back deck. The rain was drizzle now, but thunder still rumbled in the distance. He cupped his hands around his mouth and yelled for the dog again. The echo of his voice sounded hollow and lonely—small in the woods that stretched out on all sides of him. Hundreds of thousands of acres of pine and spruce and clumps of aspen trees. There were jagged cliffs, rivers brimming with snowmelt, and predators—mountain lions and bear. And his poor dog started shaking at the sight of a rabbit crouched in the grass.

Panic drove him down the steps, and he jogged into the woods, whistling and yelling her name. He hadn't counted on getting attached to a dog. Lately it'd been hard enough to take care of himself. He hadn't slept a full night since the accident. Hadn't felt much like eating, either. The lingering depression brought on by the knowledge that he'd ruined someone's life.

But the last time he'd gone to visit Gram, he'd driven by one of those fancy local pet stores. They were doing an adoption event outside. As soon as he'd seen Bella hiding in the corner of the pen, he knew she'd be coming home with him. They had the same struggle. Anxiety. He'd recognized it right away. According to the worker, Bella had been rescued from a farm where they'd found over thirty emaciated dogs that had been abused and neglected. And that was it. Over. Done. No decision to be made. He knew she needed him as much as he needed her.

"Bella!" The wind made his shouts sound so futile, but he had to do something. It killed him to think of her out there in the overwhelming darkness, terrified and cold and running blind. He knew how lonely it was. That's what he'd been doing since the accident—navigating an endless darkness. The dog had been the first light he'd seen in a while. She'd taken the edge off the silence that had consumed his life.

After the dust had settled, friends had stopped calling. Fans had stopped seeking him out. His grandma had started talking to him like he was a stranger. And there were times he felt like he had no one in the world.

But then Bella would come and lie at his feet. She would trot by his side while he wandered the trails in search of freedom from the burden that always seemed to weigh him down. Every morning, she would whine at him from the side of the bed, coaxing him back to life because she needed him.

She needed him to feed her and play ball with her. She needed him to protect her and to show her that there was good in the world. That not everyone would kick her or lock her in a cold, dingy basement or use a chain to strangle her when she peed on the floor out of fright. She still wore the marks of violence on the fur around her neck. It had taken a few weeks for her to trust him, for her not to cower in front of him when he'd call to her. It had taken her a few weeks to realize he wasn't going to hurt her or leave her. And now she was alone again. He'd fucked up.

"I'm sorry!" he yelled. Maybe the wind would carry the sound of his voice right to her. "Come on, Bella, I'm sorry!" Mud slurped at his boots as he tromped straight up the side of the mountain. "I won't leave you out here." It didn't matter if it took all night. He'd rescue her the same way she'd rescued him.

* * *

Amazing how sunshine could make everything look so different. In the radiance of a bright morning, even the piece-of-shit tent looked pretty.

Above Kate's head, the blue nylon seemed to glow with a happy optimism. She turned on the phone's voice recorder and brought it to her lips. "Day two: waking up in the Extreme Outdoors Lightweight Backpacker Tent doesn't suck. It's actually a very pretty color." Maybe she wouldn't write up the tent as the worst creation since tiny backpacks hit the purse market. (Seriously, how could Kate Spade have jumped on that bandwagon?) She was feeling generous this morning. Almost giddy.

The dog licked her cheek. At some point during the night, Jane Doe—as Kate had come to call her after discovering the dog was a lady when she'd taken her outside to pee at four o'clock in the morning—had snuggled right up against her in the sleeping bag. Now they lay side by side, spooning like a happy couple. "You saved me, Jane," Kate murmured to the dog. "You know that?" Today, there would be no bugs or dirt, and she'd get her first real meal since the cab had dropped her off at the trailhead... Wait. Had that only been yesterday? Huh. It seemed like eons ago.

In the sleeping bag, Kate could feel the dog's tail wagging against her leg. "I know, I know. I'm ready too." She glanced at the time on her phone. Seven o'clock in the morning wasn't too early to get up and at 'em when you were in the backcountry. Right? With any luck, she could be sitting in a cute little coffee shop in town by eight o'clock with her new best friend Jane Doe curled up at her feet.

On that note... She shimmied out of the sleeping bag and pulled on shorts and a tank top, which she had to rip the price tags off of since she'd had to purchase all new clothes for the trip. Once she was dressed, she dug out a stale bagel from her backpack and gagged down half before holding the other half out to Jane.

The dog sniffed warily before taking a hesitant bite.

"I know. They're much better toasted and served with flavored cream cheese." Strawberry. Or maybe with just a touch of honey. Kate's mouth watered. "Don't worry, girl. We'll find some real food in town." There had to be a deli or a diner nearby.

Speaking of town...She rifled through her things until she located her topographical map. Not that she had any clue how to read the lines that supposedly told you how steep the terrain was. "But I do know how to find the closest town." She pointed out the small black dot to the dog. "Topaz Falls, Colorado. Sounds like the kind of place that might have a really nice spa, don't you think?"

Jane panted happily.

"All we have to do is head down the trail to where it meets up with the highway; then we'll be home free." Easy enough. She folded up the map, stuffed it back into her pack, and then shoved her feet into the brand-new hiking boots that had given her blisters yesterday. She stood gingerly, stiff from a night on the thin foam pad, which was supposed to be the best on the market. (More false advertising.)

Jane whined as Kate unzipped the tent. Then the dog bounded outside like she couldn't wait to get started. Kate couldn't either. Over her shoulder, she eyed the nylon structure that had taken her the better part of three hours to set up. (The packaging had boasted a twenty-minute setup—what a scam.) Would it hurt to leave it behind? She'd tried it out for one night. And she'd also gotten to try out the camp stove and the sleeping bag and the foam pad and the collapsible lantern. Did one really truly need to spend seven days on the trail with those things to get a good read on the gear? She'd drawn her conclusions in one night—it all sucked.

"Come on, Jane." Kate slipped on her backpack and set

off down the trail, not looking back at the tent. She'd tell Gregor it hadn't survived the storm. That she'd spent the rest of the week building her own shelters out of sticks and logs and leaves. Maybe he'd give her a promotion.

Hiking with a dog was actually fun. Jane would run ahead with her nose to the ground, and then find a stick and bring it to Kate with her tail wagging. She'd toss the stick, and the dog would take off, leaping and running as though this were the best day of her life.

The feeling was contagious. Having company made Kate slow down and actually enjoy the scenery. Yesterday, she hiked the few miles to her campsite with her head down, faltering under the weight of her thirty-pound backpack, cursing the day Gregor had been born. But today she noticed things. Like the way the sun glinted off the new green aspen leaves. And how when she passed a certain kind of pine tree—she didn't know which—the scent of butterscotch would trail in the air.

The mountains were much prettier than she'd given them credit for yesterday. Purple and yellow and white wildflowers dotted grassy meadows that flourished under the shelter of the trees. It was peacefully quiet but not silent. Birds trilled and somewhere water shushed and a pleasant breeze sighed through the thick branches. So basically, if it wasn't for the dirt and the bugs and the thunderstorms, the mountains would be perfect.

They reached the trailhead much faster than she'd thought they would. But then again, she'd never been good at judging distances on a map. The trail broke through the trees and into an open space flanked by the dirt parking lot where the cab had dropped her off yesterday. A few cars sat in the lot but not a soul was around. "Okay." Kate swung her backpack to the ground and found the map again.

Jane trotted over and plopped down panting like her lungs were on fire.

"Just have to figure out which way to go," Kate said reassuringly. Which way had she come from in the cab again? When she'd first looked at the map, she'd assumed they had to go west, but now she wasn't so sure. She stared at those little lines, but they all seemed to blur together. Her head felt a little funny. "Water," she gasped. She'd forgotten. Gregor had reminded her that she had to stay hydrated in the high altitude of Colorado. Letting the map fall to the ground, she uncapped her water bottle and guzzled half of what was left.

"Hi there."

Kate turned toward the pleasant, somewhat shy voice of a woman.

"I noticed you were studying a map. Is there anything I can help you with?"

The woman walked over, and she looked like she knew what she was doing. Her hiking boots and lightweight pants were worn and dusty, as though she headed out on the trail every day. She wore a wide-brimmed straw hat, and her golden auburn hair hung in two braids down her shoulders. The kindness in her eyes instantly put Kate at ease. Jane, too, judging from the way the dog stood and started to wag her tail.

Kate picked up the map, realized she'd been holding it upside down, and turned it around. "I'm trying to figure out how to get to Topaz Falls from here."

Even when the woman frowned, she looked friendly. "That's a good ten miles down the highway." She seemed to assess Kate's attire. "It'd be a long walk. I'd be happy to give you a ride if you want."

Kate pulled her sunglasses down her nose. "Seriously?" She didn't mean to gawk at the woman, but Kate had once stood on the shoulder of the 405 in L.A. with a blown-out tire and cars had whizzed past like she was a statue. No one had even stopped, let alone offered her a ride.

"Sure." The woman shrugged like it was nothing. "We do that kind of thing all the time around here. We get tons of long-term hikers coming through. A lot of them hitchhike into town."

Kate sized the woman up. Normally she'd never get into a car with someone she didn't know, especially in L.A., but there was no way a psychopath could smile like this woman.

"I'm Everly Brooks."

Everly—what an angelic name. "Kate Livingston." She held out her hand for a professional introduction, even though she really wanted to hug the woman's graceful neck. Maybe even give her a kiss of gratitude on the cheek. "I work for *Adrenaline Junkie* magazine and was out doing a gear-test run." Was that what the real adrenaline junkies called it? No matter. "This sweet dog wandered into my camp last night during the storm. So I thought I would head into town to find her owner."

"Oh…" Everly's pretty eyes grew even bigger. "Then you're in luck. My friend Jessa owns an animal shelter just outside of town. I'm sure she'd be happy to help."

"Perfect." Things could not be more perfect right now. Kate could take Jane to the shelter so she could be reunited with her family—a good deed for someone else. Then she could find a place to stay and get a head start on writing her gear-test article from the comfort of a hotel—a good deed for herself. Gregor would never know that she hadn't spent a week out on the trail.

"I'm parked over this way." Everly led her to an old-fashioned Ford pickup truck that was spotted with rust. Kate climbed in, and Jane jumped into her lap as though she knew she was going home.

It took a few tries to get the old clunker started, but soon enough they were on their way, and Kate relaxed against the seat. "Thanks again for going to all of this trouble." Nothing like this had ever happened to her. A complete stranger going out of their way to help...

"It's no problem," Everly said. The truck puttered down a two-lane road bordered by thick, earthy-scented forest on both sides. "So you must do a ton of backpacking with your job, huh?"

Kate startled. "Oh. Yeah. Sure. You know..." She hoped Everly knew because she sure as hell didn't.

"Where's your favorite place to go?"

"Hmmm." She drummed her fingers against her thigh, pretending to mentally compare the many incredible places she'd backpacked. "I guess I would have to say Banff." That was somewhere in Canada. Someone had raved about it at the office last week. Surely it had a lot of trails and scenery.

"Oh my God, I love Banff." Everly's head tipped as though she were picturing it. "Did you do the Consolation Lakes Trail near Moraine Lake?"

"Of course," Kate said, and then quickly added, "It's beautiful."

"I know," her new friend agreed. "It's one of the most beautiful places I've ever been."

"So what do you do?" Kate asked before Everly could get another question in. She'd pretty much run out of ideas for any additional discussion on spectacular backpacking destinations.

"I run a small organic farm and operate a farm-to-table café that barely breaks even." Everly laughed as though embarrassed. "Doesn't sound so great, but I love it."

"Actually it sounds amazing." Kate could picture it. A cute little farmhouse against a mountain backdrop. It sure beat her tiny apartment that looked out on an alley back in Burbank. There were probably animals and wildflowers and the same beautiful aspen trees she'd seen in the forest. "I'd love to see it."

"Sure. After we take the dog to Jessa's, we can swing by my place on our way back to the trail."

Kate shifted Jane so she could see the woman's face. "The trail?"

"Yeah." Eyes on the road, Everly turned the truck off onto a dirt driveway and drove underneath a framed wooden sign that said CORTEZ RANCH. "I figured you'd want to get back to your trip after you get the dog settled."

"Right. The trip." The lonely, miserable, dirty camping trip. There was one problem with that scenario. Kate no longer had a tent. And she seriously doubted her ability to ever find that thing again. "Actually, I might stick around town for a few days," she said thoughtfully, as though the idea had just occurred to her. "Restock on supplies and stuff." Enjoy a few meals, maybe a massage or a day of pampering to recondition her skin. "Do you know of any good places to stay on short notice?"

"Sure." Everly drove them past a couple of rustically elegant houses with wide stained logs held together by heavy steel brackets and accents of stone. The kind you'd see featured in *Adrenaline Junkie* as the perfect adventure ranch destination.

"The Hidden Gem Inn is the best accommodation in town." Her new friend parked outside of what looked to be a refurbished barn. The modest sign above the double doors announced it as the HELPING PAWS ANIMAL SHELTER.

"Jessa's sister-in-law Naomi and her husband opened the inn almost two years ago," Everly went on. "It's a beautiful bed-and-breakfast right in town. Best food outside of the café." She smiled humbly. "And gorgeous. It's a historic home, built during the silver rush, but it's been all redone inside."

Kate could almost feel the warmth of a luxurious shower. The softness of a brand-new mattress. Geez, she was practically tearing up. "It sounds like exactly the kind of place I'm looking for."

CHAPTER THREE

Ditching the tent on the trail was hands down the best decision she had ever made. Kate sipped her high-priced cabernet sauvignon and popped a dark chocolate truffle into her mouth.

Who knew that a small town like Topaz Falls would have one of the best wine bars she'd ever had the pleasure of experiencing? The Chocolate Therapist was something out of a fantasy—all streamlined and modern and classy without crossing the line into pretentious. After meeting with Jessa Cortez and discovering that no one had contacted her about a lost dog, Kate had offered to keep Jane with her—a fostering situation, if you will—while Jessa checked around. It wasn't only that she wanted an excuse to stay off the trail. She happened to love Jane Doe, too, so it was a win-win.

Once that had been settled, Everly had driven Kate and Jane Doe straight over to the Hidden Gem, where Naomi had upgraded her into their best suite at no charge. Then Naomi and her husband, Lucas, even offered her an extra car they currently weren't using, just in case she needed it while she stayed in town to help locate Jane's owner.

It didn't matter what she needed; Kate's new bestie Everly would say, "I have a friend for that."

After Kate had enjoyed an extended time-out in the marble-tiled steam shower of her new suite, Everly had insisted they walk Jane Doe to Main Street so she could show Kate around and they could have an afternoon treat. Her new friend had brought her straight to the Chocolate Therapist, where the owner, Darla Michaels, had hooked them up with the best wine and chocolate pairing that could possibly exist in this world.

"I can't remember the last time I felt this happy." Kate took another sip of wine. She and Everly were sitting outside at a bright orange bistro table—with Jane Doe contentedly curled up underneath. The patio looked out on a downtown area where quaint shops with striped awnings lined the cobblestone sidewalks. Baskets of bright-colored annuals hung from the wrought-iron streetlamps, and the mountains hovered in the background like a beautiful barricade constructed to keep reality out. It was something straight out of a storybook fairy tale, safe and fictional and untouchable. "I might never leave Topaz Falls," Kate told Everly, popping another truffle into her mouth.

Everly laughed. "Watch out. That's exactly what happened to me. I showed up here thinking I might stay a few months, and over two years later, I can't seem to leave."

"I can see why." It wasn't only the mountains and the whimsical small-town charm. It was also the people, all connected, all watching out for each other—and even for the strangers who found themselves in their midst. "I can't thank you enough for—"

"What the hell are you doing with my dog?"

The angry male voice came from behind. Kate turned at the same time Jane Doe shot to her feet, whining and yipping.

A man stalked toward them, his chiseled features locked into a punishing scowl. He dodged people on the sidewalk, looking as out of place as Oscar the Grouch at Disney World.

The dog immediately hurdled the fence and made a beeline for him, ending the dramatic scene with a leap directly into his midsection.

"Bella." The man caught her and knelt, setting her paws on the ground as he wrapped his arms around her. "Jesus, pup. Where have you been? I looked for you all night."

Kate glanced at Everly and mouthed, "Do you know that guy?"

Everly shook her head with a pained expression. Yeah, he didn't seem like a very personable man, but that had never stopped Kate before. She pushed back from the table and stood, calmly letting herself out of the patio's gate before ambling over to where the joyous reunion was still taking place.

"Ahem." She cleared her throat.

The man looked up at her, and immediately the soft relief on his face tightened into anger. Even with the tension that pulled his cheeks taut, there was something vaguely familiar about his features. Though he wore a stocking cap and sunglasses, she could swear she'd seen his square jaw and that exquisite mouth before...

"Why the hell was my dog sitting under your table?" he demanded, standing upright. He was half a foot taller than her, easy, and had broad, fit shoulders, she couldn't help but notice through his T-shirt.

"How about you thank me for rescuing your dog from the woods during the storm last night?" Kate asked cheerfully. No one would ruin this perfect afternoon for her. "She wandered into my camp."

"Your camp?" He flicked his glasses off and swept an irritatingly skeptical look from her head to her toes. "*You* were camping?"

Okay, sure. She would be the first to admit she didn't exactly look the part right now. On the way to the Hidden Gem, Everly had driven past a boutique and Kate had seen this lovely sundress in the window. What could she say? It was love at first sight. The soft pink dress had layer upon layer of delicate, embroidered lace with eyelet trim at the neckline. You couldn't find things like that in L.A. It was both modern and sentimental at the same time. And, since she would be staying in town for a few days, she couldn't resist a few purchases. "Yes, I was camping." Her smile dimmed at the smug look on his face. "In fact, I was on a seven-day backpacking trip," she informed him, glaring right into the man's eyes. They were steely and blue. Whoa. Unmistakable eyes. Famous eyes...

Well, what do you know? J.J. Alexander—disgraced Olympic snowboarder—was walking the streets of Topaz Falls. She knew she'd recognized him!

Kate kept her expression in check. He obviously did not want to be identified, given the hat and the sunglasses, which he'd quickly slipped back on.

"So, what? You were going to keep my dog forever?" he asked, backing down a bit.

"Of course not." She gave him the dutiful smile of a Good Samaritan. "I hiked all the way down the mountain and brought her to the Helping Paws Animal Shelter first thing this morning." And look where that had led her. Right to

Jaden freaking Alexander. He'd hidden from the media ever since a reporter tried to accuse him of assault right after the accident. The accusations turned out to be bogus, but after that, J.J. had disappeared. No stories, no interviews, nothing. And now here he was, standing in front of her like some ruggedly wrapped gift from God. If she could score an interview with J.J. Alexander, she'd never have to go on another backpacking trip again.

"I'm Kate Livingston, by the way." She stuck out her hand, but the man simply stared at it.

He hesitated, obviously not wanting to share his name.

"Your dog is such a sweetheart," she went on to compensate for his silence. He couldn't walk away. Not yet. Not until she figured out an excuse to spend more time with him. "Bella is it? I was calling her Jane Doe. Anyway, she slept in my sleeping bag all night. Curled right up next to me and kept me warm. Didn't you, girl?" She knelt and scrubbed behind Bella's ears.

The dog gave her a loving, slobbery lick across the lips.

Laughing, Kate stood back up and wiped her mouth. "We definitely bonded."

"I can see that." J.J. didn't seem to appreciate it much either, judging from his frosty tone. "Well, thanks for bringing her back." He turned. "Come on, Bella."

"Wait." Kate flailed to catch up with him.

The man stopped and eyed her like he was considering making a run for it.

Humiliation torched her cheeks, but she muscled through it. Typically she didn't chase men down the street, but this was an emergency. "Why'd she run away?"

J.J. seemed to debate whether he was obligated to answer the question. Finally he sighed. "She hates storms. And I'm working long days at the resort. Sometimes nights too. I didn't know there'd be a storm, so I didn't lock her dog door."

Long days at the resort, huh? "Poor thing." Kate petted the dog again, seeing the perfect opening into J.J. Alexander's world. Thankfully, the dog ate up the attention, wagging her tail and whining for more. "When we were hiking this morning, she never let me out of her sight. She seems to get lonely easily."

"Yeah." J.J. watched her interact with Bella. "She's a rescue. Doesn't like being alone."

Kate turned up the wattage on her sunny expression as if an idea had suddenly lit up inside her. "Well, I love your dog, and it just so happens that I'll be in town for a few days, so maybe I could help."

"I thought you were backpacking." J.J. obviously didn't want to take the bait, which meant she'd have to use another angle. Something other than *her* love for the dog.

"My tent was damaged in the storm, which means I'll have to finish out my vacation in town." She nearly gagged on the word *vacation*. Maui was a vacation. Hell, she'd even consider Miami to be a decent vacation. Camping was so not a vacation. "I'd love to watch Bella while you work. Like a doggie daycare thing. I can pick her up in the mornings and spend the day with her so you don't have to worry about her running off."

"That's okay." The man still stared at Kate like she was a lunatic. "She's fine."

"It would be better for her than sitting around a lonely house all day," Kate prompted. If the earlier reunion was any indication, this man loved his dog. So all she had to do was convince him it would be best for Bella. "I'll take her on hikes, and we can play fetch. She can play with my new friend Naomi's dog at the Hidden Gem. Oh, and I bet she'd love swimming in the river at the park."

His torn expression revealed that, yes, Bella did indeed love to swim. What Lab didn't?

"So you'd pick her up in the morning and drop her off after I got home?"

"Yes. I'd love to spend more time with her while I'm in town," she assured him. "You don't even have to pay me." Getting to know J.J. Alexander, aka the Snowboarding Cowboy, would be all the compensation she needed.

* * *

There had to be a catch. Why would some hotter-than-sin woman offer to watch his dog while he worked? For free?

Jaden eyed Kate Livingston from behind the anonymity of his dark sunglasses. She sure didn't look like she belonged anywhere near a backcountry trail. Her silky black hair had that perfect beach-wave thing going on, which he suspected she'd paid good money for. And her skin...it was rosy and flawless. Not lined from the sun like his. Her eyes were the most striking feature about her, though, so dark they were almost black and narrowed slightly in the corners like she had some exotic mix of genes.

His body's swift reaction to her raised his defenses. He'd met women like Kate. All sunny and rosy and completely fake. He'd even had a good time with a few of them, but those days were long behind him.

To get his eyes off the temptation in front of him, Jaden glanced at Bella. His dog had attached herself to Kate's side as though trying to convince him to close the deal. He could see the plea in those sorrowful eyes. *Aw hell.* He was such a sucker. Bella would love having the company. He'd worked almost eighty hours this week, and his poor dog had been on her own.

What would it hurt? The woman—Kate?—hadn't seemed to realize who he was. Bella liked her. And he liked the fact that he wouldn't have to worry about the dog running off again, which would mean he wouldn't have to spend another night tromping all over the mountain searching for her.

Last night had been hell. He hadn't slept at all. He'd hiked until dawn, yelling and whistling and searching until he'd had to go up to work. As soon as the crew had quit for the day, he'd gone home to print some of those lost dog posters he'd seen plastered to lampposts when he was growing up. Which now he wouldn't need.

"So what do you think?" Kate persisted. Yeah. Persistent. That was the only way to describe her. She looked like a woman who had no trouble getting what she wanted.

"I guess it would work."

"Great! Oh, that's so great." A smile made her eyes sparkle. Something about her seemed so young. She was happy; that's what it was. Happy all the way down deep, like Gram used to say.

"We can start tomorrow," Kate said as she hugged the dog again. "We'll have so much fun, Bella! We'll play all day! I'll pick her up at eight. Okay? Make sure to send along everything she'll need for the day. Food, her leash, any toys she'd like to bring, treats."

"Uh…" Jaden blinked at her. Damn Kate had a lot of energy. It felt like she'd boarded a speed-of-light train and he was hanging on the back. "Sure. Okay. That's fine."

"I'll need your address. And I didn't catch your name."

"Jay," he blurted. "My name is Jay." He quickly rattled the address for his rental so he could get the hell out of there.

"Very nice to meet you, Jay." Kate leaned over and gave Bella a kiss on the top of the head. "I'll see you both tomorrow." With a twinkling wave, she sashayed back to a table, where one of her friends was waiting.

"What the hell just happened there?" Jaden asked Bella on the way back to his Jeep. "Did you have to crawl into *her* sleeping bag?" Out of all the sleeping bags in the backcountry, his dog had somehow found the one that held a tempting, aggravating, overly cheerful Disney princess.

"Couldn't you have found some transient guy?" he muttered as he helped Bella jump into the passenger's seat. "That would be a lot less complicated." Something told him he wouldn't be able to keep himself in check forever when Kate Livingston was around. And he'd eventually want to do more than look, seeing as how it'd been a damn long time since he'd had the opportunity. The first sight of her in the strappy little dress had him rubbernecking in a bad way. Not that he'd admit it to anyone else, but that was the only reason he'd seen Bella. He'd noticed Kate first.

Jaden started the Jeep and drove away from Main Street, his eyes sticky with fatigue. All he wanted to do was go home and eat his bowl of Honey Nut Cheerios and then fall into bed. Maybe he'd actually sleep tonight. For once he felt tired enough. But unfortunately, he couldn't go home. Not yet.

"We've got big plans tonight," he announced, trying to muster some enthusiasm.

Bella stuck her head out the window, her lips flapping as she sniffed the air.

"Levi was an old friend of mine. Back in high school. He invited us over for a beer, if you can believe that." Bella probably couldn't, seeing as how they hadn't visited anyone's house since he'd adopted her.

He turned off the highway and onto the familiar dirt road where he used to race bikes with Levi. The Cortez Ranch had gotten a major upgrade since he'd been gone. Originally, there'd been only one house on the property. Now there were four that he could see. Two were newer, one right across from the corrals and one farther up the hill tucked into a stand of aspen trees. That would be Levi's house. He'd described it over the phone but hadn't done it justice.

It wasn't obnoxiously large like the house Jaden had rented near the resort, but it was impressive all the same. Hand-hewn logs stacked one on top of another, stone siding coming halfway up the structure, and a copper roof that must've set him back a good hundred thousand.

Jaden parked the Jeep and let Bella out, taking his time on the stamped concrete stairs that led up the front porch. Stupid that he was nervous. Levi had been pretty mellow at the store, but still...his team had turned on him. When he was winning competitions, they'd become like his family, but after the accident, they'd quit calling, quit inviting him out, quit acknowledging they ever knew him. As his ex-girlfriend and fellow USA team member had reminded him, it wasn't personal. They simply couldn't afford the bad publicity.

His teammates hadn't been nearly as bad as the random strangers, though. The people who had verbally attacked him on social media...and on the streets. It had all made him withdraw from everyone, everything. Social anxiety, they called it. He'd finally looked it up on the Internet.

Bella whined and scratched at the front door, coaxing him onward as usual.

"Yeah, yeah, yeah. I'm going." If it weren't for the dog, he'd probably never get off the couch.

Levi's front door was as grand as the house—stained wood with an inlayed frosted window. He knocked, half hoping his friend wouldn't be around. Maybe he'd forgotten or maybe something had come up—

The door swung open, and Levi greeted him with a hearty handshake. "Glad you could make it."

Jaden kept his grip firm. "Me too."

Bella jumped up on Levi. "Happy to see you too, pooch." He stepped aside. "Come on in."

Jaden walked into an open-concept living room with high arched ceilings, dark plank floors, and a stone fireplace that took up one whole wall. Even being brand-new and so extravagant, the place still had the cozy touches that made it a home—clusters of pictures and books strewn on the coffee table and some of Levi's bull-riding memorabilia on the walls.

"Let me grab you a beer," Levi said, heading for the kitchen on the other side of the room.

"Sounds great." Jaden wandered closer to the fireplace to get a better look at the framed photographs arranged on the mantel.

An image of a blond woman in a wedding dress—Cassidy, he presumed—stood out from the others. She was dancing barefoot in a grassy meadow, laughing, looking past the camera, presumably at her new husband. "That's a great shot." Not posed or unnatural, but spontaneous and full of emotion.

Levi handed him an IPA and studied the picture with a tender expression. "That's my wife." He said it like it still surprised him. "Cass. Remember her? Cash's little sister."

He vaguely remembered, but Cash had made sure that none of his idiot friends had come within a twenty-foot radius of her, so Jaden hadn't known her well.

"She's a nurse in Denver. Working today." He grinned. "Still have no idea how I got her to marry me."

"You lucked out, I guess." That was a joke. Judging from the other wedding pictures, Cassidy looked as happy and in love as Levi. Something told him luck didn't have much to do with it.

The doorbell rang, sending Bella into one of her happy-barking fits. For being so anxious, she sure seemed to like meeting new people.

"Hope you don't mind," Levi said over the noise. "I invited some other friends."

Tension laced up his spine, pulling his back tight. "Nope. Don't mind at all." It was crazy how casual he could force his voice to sound even when that feeling of dread crawled up his throat.

He hung out by the fireplace while Levi opened the door, and Bella greeted the two new visitors with a nose to their crotches.

"Bella, off," he commanded.

She obeyed but whined until they both gave her some attention.

"This is Mateo Torres and Ty Forrester," Levi said, waving Jaden over. "We trained together forever, and now we run a mentoring program when we're not on the road."

"Nice to meet you." He shook each of their hands briskly. Gram would've been proud of him remembering his manners, even when his throat seemed to shrink.

"J.J. grew up on a ranch a few miles from here," Levi told his friends. "We used to raise enough hell that his granny thought about sending him to boarding school."

"Not true." Gram never would've sent him away. "She couldn't get rid of me." He forced a grin. Maybe after enough pretending, it would eventually start to feel real again. "There would've been no one to do the work on the ranch." But Gram had loved him too. The way a mother was supposed to. He'd never doubted that.

"I bet you've got some awesome stories," Mateo said.

"I'm always looking for new material that I can use to humiliate Levi."

Jaden took a sip of his beer and nodded. "I can help you out with that."

"I've got plenty on you." Levi directed the words to Mateo as he went to get more beers from the fridge. He handed them out while the three men compared who had the worst dirt on who.

Jaden stayed out of the conversation. If they'd watched the news in the last three months, they all had dirt on him, and he didn't want to talk about the accident.

Eventually, the pissing match ended, and Levi led them all out to the back deck. Bella followed behind and then trotted down the grass. It seemed his friend had chosen the prettiest spot on the property for his house, right up against the mountain, hidden in a stand of aspen trees. Evening sunlight filtered through the leaves, making everything seem calm.

"House looks good," Mateo said, examining the stone fire pit before flicking a switch to turn it on.

"Yeah. Real fancy, Cortez." Ty kicked back in one of the reclining chairs. "Let me know if you want a roommate."

"Yeah, Cass would love that." Levi pulled two more chairs over and gestured for Jaden to sit.

He had to admit...it wasn't half bad sitting there on the deck with these guys, watching the sun start to sink behind the peaks. It was easier than he'd thought. No questions about the accident. No judgment in their eyes.

"I'm thinking about buying some land so I can build," Mateo said. "Got my eye on a piece of property right on the edge of town. What about you?" He glanced at Jaden. "You sticking around Topaz Falls or you got something else in mind?"

"I'm still deciding." Originally, he'd planned to take off as soon as they'd finished up the project at the resort. He owned a condo in Utah and a cabin in Alaska, but he didn't have a home anywhere. "I guess I wouldn't mind sticking around." The statement surprised him as much as it seemed to surprise Levi.

"That'd be great," his friend said. "Just like old times."

Jaden couldn't resist. "Only now you have a wife who wouldn't take too kindly to you going up to the hot springs to drink beer and skinny-dip with Chrissy...what was her last name again?"

They all laughed.

"Cass would kick your ass," Ty said.

"True statement," Levi agreed. He turned to Jaden. "But seriously, you'd love it here. Small town. Great community. Old friends. You'd be welcome."

Welcome. That one word sparked hope. Maybe Jaden didn't have to live in hiding forever. Maybe he could come back to the place he'd always thought of as home.

CHAPTER FOUR

So this is where a professional athlete went to hide.

Kate climbed out of her borrowed Subaru and walked up the driveway of what could only be described as an ultra-sleek modern take on a ski chalet. The squared structure had been built right into the side of the mountain, constructed mostly of stained concrete and floor-to-ceiling windows, which must've been made from some special type of glass because you couldn't see anything inside.

Standing in front of the heavy glass door, she suddenly felt an agonizing attack of insecurity. Since Jaden had judged her attire yesterday, she'd dressed more carefully for the part she was about to play. Immediately after their encounter, Kate had asked Everly to take her shopping so she could pick out a couple more earthy outfits. Today she wore fitted hiking capri pants with a bright pink moisture-wicking tank top. She'd pulled up her thick, wild hair, taking an extra half hour to make sure the bun looked genuinely carefree and messy. Which it wasn't, of course. There must've been two hundred bobby pins holding it in place. But she'd hidden them carefully. Outdoorsy chicks wouldn't spend an hour on their hair. They wouldn't have changed clothes four times either.

It wasn't that she was nervous to see J.J. Alexander, necessarily. Though the man did have a certain presence that made it difficult to look away. It was more the fact that she had a very limited amount of time to convince him to do an exclusive with her. He didn't seem especially open to interviews at the moment.

But this was it. Her chance for a big story. The story that could make her career. She'd show his personal side. She'd take off his mask for the entire world and dig deeper and deeper until she captured his every emotion, the true heart of who Jaden Alexander was.

"Jay," she reminded herself in a whisper. She had to call him Jay. It didn't bode well that he hadn't even given her his real name, but he would open up. People loved talking to her. She made sure of it. Once, in journalism school, she'd gotten a three-hundred-fifty-pound college lineman to cry during an interview when she'd asked him about his favorite childhood pet.

That in mind, she patted her messy bun into place and rang the doorbell.

Squinting, she watched for a shadow to emerge from behind the glass door, but nothing happened. Tapping her foot, she rang it again. The distant sound of barking could be heard somewhere inside. Within a few minutes, Bella was bouncing and lunging against the door. Where was J.J.? *Jay,* she quickly corrected. Had he changed his mind about their arrangement?

Right when she was about to turn around and stalk back

to the car in defeat, the door opened. Bella hurtled outside, yipping and whining and covering Kate's bare arms with kisses.

When Kate looked up, she nearly fell over, and it wasn't from Bella's weight against her legs either. J.J.—Jay, God, that was going to mess her up—looked a lot different than he had in his stocking cap and sunglasses. His light brown hair was mussed into spikes, and he still had the sleepy eyes of a little boy. Except he was shirtless. And there wasn't anything boyish about his bulletproof pecs and tight abs. Either he did five hundred sit-ups every day or the man had some crazy good genes. Or maybe he had a distant relation to the mythological gods....

"Sorry I didn't answer right away." Drowsiness lowered his voice into a sexy tenor. "I guess I overslept."

"It's no problem." She hiked her gaze up to his eyes. How long had she been staring at his shirtless torso? And more importantly, had he noticed? "I oversleep all the time," she babbled. "It seems like I'm always the last one rolling into work."

His head tilted as he studied her. "What do you do?"

Oops. She had to be careful with questions like that. Lucky for her, he still seemed a bit groggy. "Boring stuff. Really boring." She'd already made herself a vow that she would tell the truth as much as possible. "I edit stuff. Unimportant stuff that no one reads." At least, that could describe her first few weeks at her new job. But once she wrote this story, things would change.

She swept past him and walked into the house before he could fire off more questions. "Wow. This place is amazing. Seriously impressive." A little cold for her taste with the gleaming white walls, uniform leather furniture, and the glossy, seemingly unused kitchen.

"It's the only place I could find on short notice."

Kate made the mistake of turning around to smile at him. He still hadn't put on a shirt, the jerk. "So what did you say you're doing at the resort again?" she asked, running her hand along the white marble countertop in the kitchen.

"Actually, I didn't say." His voice was no longer deep and sleepy. Now it was just dull.

She waited out the awkward silence until he gave in with a sigh.

"I'm on a crew that's helping build the new terrain park."

"Sounds fascinating." She kept her gaze even with his. *Don't. Look. Down.* Or she'd get all weak-kneed and woozy at the sight of his hot body again. She couldn't afford to let Jay make her weak-kneed and woozy. "So you must be into snowboarding, then."

His eyes dodged hers. "I guess."

Wonderful. He was very informative. Getting him to open up and agree to an interview wasn't going to be easy. Good thing she had a whole week. She would have to get creative about making excuses to spend time with him. He didn't seem overly thrilled with the fact that she currently stood in his kitchen. *Well get used to it, buddy.*

Kate turned and started opening the grayish glass cabinets.

"What're you doing?" Jaden walked over and closed one. "Why are you going through my stuff?"

"I'm looking for the dog food," she told him, opening another cabinet. Which was completely empty. "Remember? I'll have Bella all day. I'm sure she'll get hungry. Or did you already feed her?"

After he shook his head, she opened yet another cabinet. Wow. The man had about six boxes of Honey Nut Cheerios stacked above the sink. And he was looking at her like she was crazy? "When's the last time you ate a real meal?"

"I eat." He stiffly marched past her and disappeared into a pantry for a minute. When he came back, he had a dog dish and a bag of food. "She eats twice a day. Once in the morning and once in the afternoon." He shoved the stuff into Kate's hands. "Think you need anything else?" He clearly wanted her to go, and that was probably best since he refused to put on a shirt and she couldn't stop ogling his body.

"Nope. I think this is it. We're good. Right, Bella?" With a bright smile, she turned and headed for the door. "I'll have her home at five o'clock sharp."

Jay followed behind her. "If I'm not here, you can just let her into the house through the garage. The code is one-two-three-four."

She laughed, caught between amusement and a nervous giggle. "Wow. It's like Fort Knox."

He shrugged, tensing those broad shoulders. "Don't have much to worry about way up here."

That was true. Well...the normal person didn't have to worry about much, but J.J. Alexander had just given her the code to his house. Which meant he'd basically handed her an all-access pass into his life.

* * *

Was it just him or were the days getting longer? Jaden shouldered his backpack and started the hike back to the ATV he'd left at the base of the mountain. Eight o'clock. Damn. Late again. Good thing he had someone to watch Bella. Even if the woman happened to be overly chipper and obnoxiously nosy at eight o'clock in the morning. At least all that energy should be good for wearing out his dog. Hopefully Bella had gone to sleep after Kate dropped her off.

"Hey, J.J., hold up." Blake Wilder came sprinting down the hill, and Jaden swallowed a groan. The man had never been his favorite person, but he had to admit—begrudgingly—Blake obviously knew what he was doing. Since the man had taken over resort operations four years ago, they'd almost doubled in size.

Jaden strapped his backpack to the ATV and waited.

"Looks like things are coming together ahead of schedule," Blake said as he approached. "I called out the inspectors for the end of this week. Think we can make it?"

"With the hours we've been putting in? Definitely." A few more twelve-hour days and they'd wrap up this project. The thought didn't thrill him as much as it seemed to thrill Blake.

"You got any idea what you'll do next?"

That question had haunted him for the last few days. "Haven't thought about it much." What options did he have except to go hide somewhere else? Last week, that would've been his first response, but Levi's optimism the other night had made him think twice about picking up and leaving again.

"I'm going to level with you here, Alexander." Blake only seemed to be able to remember people's last names. "I want a bigger focus on snowboarding around here. That's the direction we need to go. And I think you're the guy to get us there."

Jaden couldn't remember the last time he'd laughed, but he was this close. "I'm not exactly well loved in the snowboarding community anymore," he reminded him.

"But you still have a name. You still have the knowledge and experience I need." That was the other thing about Blake Wilder. When he looked at people, he saw only how they could meet his needs. "I could create a position for you here.

Manager for the terrain park. I need someone out here every day during the winter season."

"You're offering me a full-time job?" Was this a joke?

"You're the perfect candidate," Blake insisted. "You'd be responsible for daily risk assessments, inspections, and the maintenance and testing of all the features."

Which meant he'd have to get on a board again. Anxiety skittered through him, headed straight for his heart, and dug in its claws. That's where it always hit him, deep in the chest, poking and taunting and squeezing until the palpitations started. He couldn't even think about getting on a board again.

"The salary wouldn't be what you're used to making. But you'd get full benefits. And there'd be bonuses if you were willing to do some public events to help with publicity."

Public events? Hadn't Blake seen what a train wreck his life had become? Jaden would show up for the public event, and there'd be hecklers and media and the same shit storm he'd been trying to escape. He climbed onto the ATV, ready to start the engine and get the hell out of there. "Thanks for the offer, but I don't think it'll work out." He'd never strap his boots onto a board again.

"Think about it." Blake backed away. "Offer stands for a while. But I'd need a commitment by the end of the project. If it's not you, I'll have to find someone else."

He wanted to tell him he didn't need to think about it. He'd never be able to do it, even if he wanted to. Instead, he gave the man a nod, put on his helmet, and then drove down the mountain.

By the time he made it to his street, the sky was nearly dark, but he could make out a faint outline of a car parked next to the curb in front of his house. Had the media found him somehow? Instinctively, he slowed, but as he got closer he realized it was only a small SUV that looked suspiciously similar to the one Kate had been driving.

What the hell was she doing at his house at eight thirty?

He parked the ATV in front of the garage and cruised through the front door, looking around the empty rooms.

"Hello?" Not even Bella ran to greet him.

Just when he was about to go out front and search Kate's car, he noticed the French doors to the back deck had been left cracked open. He jogged over and slipped outside.

"Oh, good. You're finally back." Kate stood at the grill wearing a white apron and wielding a huge set of stainless steel tongs. "Perfect timing."

Jaden looked around once more to make sure he was in the right house. Yep. It seemed to be his rental. His deck. His grill that she was leaning over. What was he missing here? "What're you doing?"

"Making you dinner," she said as though this were a normal everyday occurrence. "Filet mignon with grilled asparagus." She flipped the sizzling hunks of meat. "Oh! And mashed potatoes with bacon and garlic."

Uh... "Why?" That was the only word he could seem to manage from the fog of shock. He couldn't deny that Kate Livingston was gorgeous. Even more captivating under the soft glow of the globe lights strung overhead. Captivating in a way that triggered his anxiety. For the last couple of months, he'd done his best to feel nothing. It was easier. But she stirred something. A craving that ached all the way through him.

"What do you mean why?" She seemed to laugh so easily. "Okay. I admit it. This is a pity dinner."

"A pity dinner." He couldn't seem to do much more than repeat her.

"All you have in that lavish kitchen of yours are six boxes

of Honey Nut Cheerios." She shrugged and turned back to the grill. "I feel sorry for you. How long has it been since you've had steak and potatoes?"

"Eight years." He hadn't eaten potatoes for eight years. They had too much starch, and he'd had to keep his body fit.

She spun and gaped at him, those standout eyes wide with a look of genuine shock. "Eight. Years?"

"I've had steak. Just not potatoes." But he'd loved mashed potatoes growing up. That might've been his favorite food. Gram used to dump in butter and real cream and fresh herbs from the garden...

"God, really?" she repeated. "Where have you been? In prison?"

"No." But actually, these last three months had felt like exile. Not that he could tell her that.

"Well, I hope you're hungry." Kate walked over to the patio table, which had already been set with dishes and silverware. "Because we have a ton of food. And Darla insisted on sending me home with some wine and truffles." She uncorked a fancy bottle and poured the red wine into two glasses.

Jaden stood right where he was. He had no clue what to make of Kate Livingston. She seemed friendly and innocent. Or maybe that was just the dimples in her smile. Maybe she only *looked* friendly and innocent. Maybe she'd go all *Fatal Attraction* on him any minute. "Why are you here?" he asked again, and this time he wasn't being polite. "Why are you in my house making me dinner?"

Kate set down her wineglass, her shoulders slumping from confidence to surrender. She seemed to think a minute and then turned and walked toward him as though giving up. She stopped a foot away, her mouth no longer smiling. "I'm lonely. Okay?" Her chipper voice had mellowed. "Things in my life aren't awesome right now. I'm not exactly in a place I want to be. And after I saw your house this morning, I figured maybe you were lonely too."

Now, that he could understand.

"Okay, then," Jaden said, taking his place at the table. "Let's eat."

CHAPTER FIVE

Well, what do you know? All those things her mom said about the truth being the best policy were actually legit.

Kate pushed her plate away. As soon as she'd admitted to Jaden that she happened to be lonely, too, everything changed. He still wasn't a Chatty Cathy by any means, but during their dinner, she'd managed to make small talk, and he'd answered all of her questions about the new terrain park in impressive detail.

Unfortunately, he didn't seem interested in talking about anything else, and all the effort she was making to carry the conversation while doing her best to ignore his smoldering good looks was starting to wear on her.

Kate checked him out again. Was it possible that Jay had gotten even hotter as they sat there across from each other? Or was that wine talking?

"Thanks for dinner." Jay tossed his napkin onto his empty plate. There was something magnetic about his eyes when he wasn't so sullen. They were focused and open. Good listening eyes.

Kate looked away. "I'm glad you liked it." It'd been a while since she'd cooked for someone who actually appreciated it. The last guy she'd dated would head straight for the television and turn on the latest football game after they ate, leaving her to do the dishes. But she wasn't *dating* J.J. Alexander. Ha. That would be...ridiculous. She wasn't here to get lost in his magic eyes or sigh with rapture when he smiled, which was so rare that the shock of it made her heart twirl every time.

She was here to get a damn story.

"You seem cold." Jay eyed the goose bumps on her arms.

Cold. Right. Sure. That's what it was...

"Want me to turn on the fire?"

She looked past him to the dark outline of the mountainous horizon. When the sun had slipped behind the peaks, the temperature had dropped about twenty degrees, but she hadn't noticed until he'd said something. A fire already burned low in her belly. "Uh. Sure. Yeah. A fire would be great."

Jaden bent and opened a small door on the side of the table, and as if be magic, flames illuminated the decorative rock piled in the center of the table.

In any other situation, it would've been intimate and romantic, with the stars glistening overhead, the shushing of the wind in the pine trees. But this was an interview. So instead of settling back into her chair and enjoying the peaceful night more than she should, she leaned forward and folded her hands on the table, ignoring the way the fire made Jaden's face glow. "So, Jay..." She smiled, summoning her impeccable small-talk skills. "What do you do when you're not working on terrain parks?"

"In the past, I've competed." His eyes hardened again, as though petitioning her to leave it at that.

Only she couldn't. "You don't compete anymore?" She figured he'd come back eventually, like all those other professional athletes who were mandated to take a short time-out after a scandal but then eventually came back and made their victorious reappearance.

"No. I can't compete anymore."

He can't? That's not what all of the news reports had said. It sounded like his injury had been relatively minor, all things considered. "Why not?"

"I crashed." His face remained perfectly still. There wasn't even a twitch in his jaw. "Got injured."

It seemed she wasn't the only one who excelled at telling the partial truth. What could she expect, though? He didn't know her, didn't trust her. She'd have to earn that over time.

"So what about you?" The fact that Jaden was actually asking her a question obviously meant he wanted to change the subject. "Do you like being an editor?"

"No." Huh. Had she ever admitted that out loud to anyone else? "I mean, after graduate school, I always saw myself doing something different," she corrected. "Something more important."

His eyes softened again as he gazed across the fire at her. "Like what?"

She didn't even have to think. "Writing stories that change the world." That had been the reason she'd pursued journalism in the first place. She could've become a doctor like her brother and sister, but she loved words. She saw power in words. "I wanted to be another Gloria Steinem. A journalist. A political activist."

"So why aren't you?"

Easy for him to say. He probably still had millions of dollars squirreled away somewhere. But she hadn't wanted to fulfill her parents' prophecies that she'd have to live in their posh Beverly Hills basement in order to survive. "I had to find a job." It was more than that, though. It was the rejection. She'd written a couple of pieces, figuring if she couldn't get hired at any of the prestigious publications, she could work her way there by freelancing.

So she'd written a profile about a girl she'd met on the Metro. After seeing her for a few days in a row, Kate struck up a conversation with the young teen and learned that she'd recently joined a gang. Once she got to know her, Kate had written an article detailing the plight of young women in poverty and why more and more are turning to gangs in order to survive.

All total, she'd amassed forty-three rejection emails from various publications, telling her that either no one wanted to read about girls in gangs, or the article wasn't exactly what they were looking for at the moment, or she had a bland writing style. Kate sighed. "According to the rejection letters, I'm not good enough."

Jaden shrugged. "Then you make yourself good enough."

"I don't know how." She'd done everything. She'd aced journalism school. She'd gotten in touch with all of the contacts she'd built over the years. No one wanted her.

"Well, you shouldn't give up."

He'd given up, though. "Why can't you go back to competing, then? Athletes overcome injuries all the time."

"It's more complicated than that," Jaden said, staring into the fire. "And anyway, we're not talking about me. We're talking about you, Kate." He raised his eyes to hers.

She actually shivered when he said her name. At some point, she'd lost control of the conversation, and worse, of her heart. It beat hard and hot and fast. *Shit.* She couldn't do this. Couldn't fall for him. "I should do the dishes." Clumsily, she gathered up their silverware and plates and slipped into the house with Bella following at her heels. Easing out a breath, she carted everything to the kitchen sink.

Unfortunately, Jaden did not head straight for the television set to turn on whatever sports match would be playing in May. Nope. He came right into the kitchen and stood behind her. "I can do the dishes."

"That's okay," she sang as she turned on the faucet. "I've got it." She'd intended to use the few minutes of rinsing and washing to regroup, but it was obvious that she wouldn't be able to recover. She could feel him standing behind her, feel her body being drawn to his...

"Sorry if I said something that made you uncomfortable." Jay reached around her and turned off the faucet.

"Oh no, not at all." She didn't know what to do with the wet plate in her hands. It wasn't anything he'd said. It was the way he'd started to look at her. The way he was looking at her now. Like he saw much more than she'd ever intended for him to see.

"I didn't mean to overstep." He inched closer, his gaze settling on her mouth. "But I think, if you want something, you should go after it."

"Mmm-hmmm." Kate carefully set the plate back in the sink before she dropped it. This was happening. Even with the warning lights of panic flashing behind her eyes, her body was moving closer to him.

Jaden's hand reached for her, fingers gentle against her cheek as he turned her face to his. The touch melted into her, softening her hesitations right along with her knees. Jay looked at her for moment, and all she saw was a man. Not J.J. Alexander, or a snowboarding champion, or a die-hard athlete who'd taken out his competition.

He was a man as caught up in the currents of seduction as she was.

This is a terrible idea. The thought flitted through her mind but found no place to land before Jay's lips came for hers and everything fell silent. The power of him overtook her senses. In the darkness of her closed eyes, she saw sparks of red. She smelled a subtle hint of aftershave—scents of rosemary's spiciness.

A sound come from his throat, an utterance of want, need, hunger.

She answered with a moan when the stubble of his jaw scraped against her cheek as his lips fused with hers.

And the taste of his tongue...It was wine and notes of chocolate, ecstasy in the hotness of her mouth. A helpless sigh brought her body against his, and he held her close in those strong arms as though he wanted to keep her right there. "This is even better than dinner," he breathed, lips grazing her cheek before teasing their way down her neck.

"Better than dessert too." Her whisper got lost in another moan. His lips left a burning mark on every spot they kissed—between her jaw and her ear, the base of her throat, the very center of her collarbone.

"Even better than dessert," he agreed, his voice low and gruff. He raised his face to hers, and that rare smile hiked up one corner of his seductive mouth before he kissed her again, deeper this time, leaving no question that he was taking his own advice and going after what he wanted.

She wanted it, too, so much she was lost in it—the rush of passion and emotion he brought rising to the surface. She could kiss this man forever. Every morning and every night. Every time he offered her the gift of his smile. Except...the word clawed its way through the exhilaration of a first kiss, a potential new love.

Except.

He had no idea who she really was, what she was really supposed to be doing here. The thought rushed in as cold as the mountain air outside, forcing her to break away from him.

Holding her fingers to her lips, she stepped out of his reach, struggling in vain to catch her breath. "I have to go."

"Go?" Jay looked as dazed as she'd been ten seconds ago.

"Yes." She rushed past him before he could touch her again. She couldn't think when he touched her. "I'm late."

"For what?" he asked, following behind her.

"For...book club." She hastily packed up the cloth market bags Naomi had loaned her. There were other things too—the apron she'd taken off outside, the corkscrew for the wine. But she would have to get those later. "Everly and her friends invited me," she said. "It's at Darla's place. I totally lost track of time. I'm so sorry." Before she could make it to the front door, Jay slipped in front of it, blocking her escape.

"I'm the one who's sorry. I think I misread something."

"No. You didn't." He definitely hadn't misread her attraction to him. "This just...caught me off guard." She'd made him dinner to get him to talk to her. Instead she'd ended up seducing herself.

"Yeah, it was pretty unexpected." He seemed to search her eyes. "But I don't mind being surprised once in a while. Do you?"

"No. I don't mind being surprised." Not normally. She loved surprises. But she liked them better when they came without a dagger of guilt stabbed right into her chest.

"Good." He stepped aside and even opened the door for her. "Thanks for making me dinner, Kate. It's been a long time since anyone's done something like that for me."

The words twisted the knife. "You're welcome," she murmured before she slipped out into the night.

"See you tomorrow morning?" he called behind her.

No. She should say no and walk away from this right now. But what would that look like? Her going back to search for her tent and resume her week on the trail? She'd already told Gregor about the detour, and he'd told her to get an interview with J.J. Besides, maybe it would help Jaden too. From what she'd seen in the short time she'd spent with him, he had some unresolved issues surrounding the accident. Maybe talking about them would help.

With that in mind, she forced herself to turn around and even dredged up a smile. "See you tomorrow."

CHAPTER SIX

Kate drove straight to the Chocolate Therapist. Yes, indeed, she needed some serious therapy.

Once again, she'd mostly told the truth. She happened to know her new friends were having their book club meeting tonight, and book club meetings were a great place to talk, right? To get advice on what to do when the subject of what could be the biggest, career-defining story of your entire career ambushes your plans for an interview with a sexy kiss that could've easily led to more. So. Much. More.

With a screech of tires, Kate swerved to the curb in front of Darla's wine bar and hit the brakes, scrambling to get out of the car. The effect of Jay's very capable lips had yet to wear off. Her hands hadn't trembled like this since she'd once mistaken her Uber driver for Zac Efron. He was a dead ringer.

The restaurant sat empty and dark except for a glow coming from a back hallway.

Kate rapped her fist against the glass. This was a disaster. Jay had gone from being distant and unreadable to kissing her in the span of one dinner. And that kiss…it was unforgettable. She couldn't pretend like it didn't happen. The memory of his smile, his lips—softer than she'd imagined they would be—had already burrowed into the section of her heart where her favorite moments lived on forever.

After another hearty knock, Darla finally came jogging out from the back room. The woman happened to be knockout gorgeous. A few years older than Kate maybe, with jet-black hair streaked with red and cut into a stylish pixie. Her skin had that youthful glow women paid good money to achieve, but Kate had a feeling Darla didn't care that much. Her clothes were stylish but subtle, too, as demonstrated by the chic tunic she wore over black leggings and fabulous leather boots. Where did she find those in Topaz Falls anyway?

Kate shook her head. She could not get distracted by a pair of boots right now.

On her way to the door, Darla waved as though they'd known each other for years instead of two days and quickly unlatched the lock. "So glad you could make it!" She waved Kate inside. "Naomi said you couldn't come because you had other plans."

"I did." And they'd been thwarted by a shunned snowboarder who apparently was not the monster everyone wanted him to be. "But my dinner got a little out of hand and I need some advice."

"Then you're definitely in the right place." Darla linked their arms together as they walked down the back hallway. "You don't know how happy I am to see you." She leaned closer. "We were supposed to discuss *Mind-Blowing Intimacy* tonight. Can you believe it?" They paused outside an open door. "Things have really gone downhill around here since Jessa and Naomi got married."

"We can hear you," Jessa called from inside the room.

"It might be good for you to discuss a book on healthy relationships," Naomi added as Kate and Darla walked in.

The coziness of the space instantly put Kate at ease. It was set up like a living room that could've been featured in an HGTV episode. Jessa and Naomi sat on a sagging old Victorian couch while Everly occupied one of two overstuffed chairs on the other side of a rectangular coffee table that looked like it had been made from an old door. The pops of color in the bright paintings on the walls and the polka-dotted pillows had as much personality as the women in the room.

"I'm not interested in a relationship that lasts more than twenty-four hours," Darla informed Kate with a wicked smile. "I'm all for simple, uncomplicated sex."

"Hear, hear," Everly agreed.

"Does that exist?" Kate couldn't help but ask. Because in her world, even a simple kiss came with complications.

"No. It does not," Jessa insisted. "In chapter eight of *Mind-Blowing Intimacy*, it says, and I quote, 'Every act of sexual intimacy leaves its mark on the human soul. Sex does more than bring two bodies together. It also unites their hearts and spirits and intellects, bringing the two into one.'"

"Good Lord," Darla muttered. "She's got the whole damn book memorized."

"It's a very insightful book," Jessa shot back. "Even Lance thinks so. We read it together. He really enjoyed it."

"Ha!" Darla led Kate to the open chair and then wedged herself between Jessa and Naomi on the couch. "I don't think it was the reading he enjoyed. How many times did you and Lance have mind-blowing sex after reading a chapter in *Mind-Blowing Intimacy*? Hmmm?"

Jessa's face turned red. Kate didn't know a woman could blush that much. "That's not the point."

"Lance is no idiot," Everly commented, helping herself to a cookie from a platter that sat on the coffee table. "A chapter in some boring book is a small price to pay for good sex."

"What do you think?" Jessa directed the question to Kate like she'd decided to give up on Darla and Everly. "In your experience, are sex and intimacy mutually exclusive?"

Kate considered the question. Not that she had a ton of experience with either. In fact, her most recent kiss would rank right up there with the most intimate experiences of her life, and she'd only met the man yesterday. How sad was that? "It's probably different for everyone. I'm sure when you're married to the person you love the most in the world, sex feels a lot more intimate." She smiled at Darla to show she meant no offense. "Some people don't want that, but I wouldn't mind having it someday."

"Oh, speaking of sex...how was your dinner?" Naomi asked with an interested smirk.

"Dinner? Who'd you have dinner with?" Everly demanded.

"She made dinner for J.J. Alexander tonight," Naomi informed the room. An echo of girlish excitement went around.

"I heard he was back in town," Darla murmured. "Or at least back near town. Working at the resort. How the hell did you score dinner with him?"

"It's a long story." And it didn't show Kate in the best light. "I'm watching Bella for him while he's working on the mountain."

"Smart move," Jessa said with admiration. "The way to every man's heart is through his dog."

"So did you two enjoy more than dinner?" Darla scooted to the edge of the couch as if the suspense were killing her.

"No." A sweltering blush contradicted her. *Yes, yes, yes.* "Well, kind of. He kissed me."

More cheering ensued, but she muted it with a shake of her head. "It's not good."

"The kiss wasn't good?" Everly asked.

"The kiss was good." So tender and meaningful. Something told her J.J. didn't kiss just anyone. She let her head fall back to the cushion with a sigh. "But I was only having dinner with him so I could get an interview. Except he doesn't know that yet. I was too afraid to tell him I worked for *Adrenaline Junkie*. I wanted to get to know him first. So I wouldn't scare him off..."

"Sounds to me like you got to know him." Darla elbowed Jessa and Naomi with an amused smile.

"So what's he like?" Everly reached over and handed Kate a cookie.

She ate the chocolate chip goodness, still trying to process the last two hours of her life. "He's...different than I thought." She wasn't expecting a snowboarder to have so much depth. Sure that was a stereotype, but in her experience, stereotypes existed for a reason. "And he's definitely a different person than the media made him out to be." Kinder. More thoughtful.

"The media made him look like a bona fide asshole," Darla said.

"Only he's not." Kate was pretty sure her eyes had gotten all dreamy and pathetic but it couldn't be helped. "He's actually a really good person." A little surly maybe, but he'd been through a lot.

"Oh boy," Naomi muttered. "I've seen that look before."

"She's smitten," Jessa confirmed.

Smitten? Despite her current predicament, Kate laughed. She definitely wasn't in L.A. anymore. "I like him," she admitted. "But I also have to get this story."

Her four new friends traded around perplexed glances.

"All right," Darla finally said. "Here's what you should do. Spend more time with him so he'll know you're not a threat."

"But don't wait too long to tell him the truth," Everly added. "And when you do tell him, make sure he knows you have his best interests in mind. That you want to help him repair his image in the media."

"That sounds like a good plan." She had a whole week here, so she could spend a couple more days with Bella. Maybe hang out with J.J. too—on the condition that there was no more kissing until he knew the truth.

* * *

"What do you think, Bella?"

Jaden rearranged the orange gerbera daisies in a vase he'd found stashed in the pantry. The flowers reminded him of Kate. Bright and cheerful, but delicate too. They definitely made a statement on the patio table, much like her. She'd left an impression on him last night with that dinner, and now he intended to do the same by making her breakfast.

The dog took a curious lap around the table, her neck stretching and nose sniffing at the very edge.

"Sorry, pooch. The bacon's for the humans." Jaden pushed the platter of meat and pancakes farther to the center so they'd stay out of reach. After spending so much of her life hungry, Bella had a tendency to get wild about food. "But I promise you all of the leftovers if you behave."

Could he behave? That was the real question. Last night's kiss had stoked something he hadn't experienced in months. Emotion. It'd shocked him to feel something when Kate had looked at him all unsure and shy from across the fire.

The flames had made her face lovely and soft. Then, when he'd gotten so close to her in the kitchen, desire had surged hot and fast, triggering him to act before he could think it through.

Sometimes it was good not to think. He hadn't thought about Kipp or the accident the whole evening. It'd been nice to focus on someone else's problems for a change.

After that, though, he couldn't stay away from her. Kissing her had roughed him up on the inside, chipping away at layers of detachment he'd built until his heart felt raw and exposed and alive again. This morning, he'd woken with a craving for more. Which is why he'd hauled his ass out of bed early enough to make a grocery run so he could surprise her the way she'd surprised him.

The doorbell rang at 7:59. Right on schedule. Bella went crazy, leaping and scratching at the door as though she somehow already knew her new best friend was there to play. "Easy, girl." He gently nudged her out of the way and opened the door.

Kate didn't look as cheerful this morning, but she didn't have to smile to hold his attention. The fireworks between them last night had already changed the way he saw her. She wasn't just an attractive woman anymore. She was downright arousing, especially in a blue hiking skirt that hit midthigh and her white tank top. She'd left her black hair down, wavy and soft around her tanned shoulders. Jaden couldn't look away. Yeah, he was at full attention. "Morning," he finally managed.

"Hi." Her indifferent tone and focus on Bella instead of him dismissed his greeting. "Are you ready for a fun day, Bella? Come on, girl. Let's go."

The dog started for the door.

"Sit, Bella," Jaden commanded in his *I mean business*

voice. She did, but she definitely whined about it. "You can't go yet," he said to Kate. "I made you breakfast."

The woman glared at him the same way she had last night when he'd told her it had been eight years since he'd eaten mashed potatoes. "Is it Honey Nut Cheerios?"

Oh yeah, he'd surprised her. "It's pancakes, actually. And bacon. Fruit." That used to be Gram's special Sunday morning breakfast on the ranch. He hadn't made it since she'd moved into assisted living, but what could he say? This was a special occasion. "Isn't that what normal people have for breakfast?"

Her lips tightened as though she was trying a little too hard to look annoyed. If you asked him, she looked spooked. "I wasn't aware you were normal."

He wasn't. Or at least he hadn't felt normal until she'd pressed her body against his last night. "Have breakfast with me, and I'll show you how normal I am." She was the one who'd made him feel normal, who'd given him the chance to be someone other than J.J. Alexander, the Snowboarding Cowboy.

Kate glanced back at her car. "I don't think I can stay. I have a lot planned for Bella today, so we should probably get going."

"You have a lot planned for my dog?" he asked, making sure his skepticism didn't go over her head. "Like what?"

"Well...you know..." How could he know when she didn't even seem to know? "I'm bringing her to the inn to meet Bogart," Kate said, looking satisfied with herself. "That's Naomi's dog. He's really sweet."

Jaden resisted the urge to smile. "Do you have reservations to meet Bogart?"

"Um...not exactly, but I don't know Naomi's schedule." Kate's cheeks were pinker than they had been when he'd

first opened the door. That was good, right? She didn't seem
to be hesitating because she couldn't stand him. She just
seemed to get nervous around him.

He opened the door wider. "All the food is made. Table is
set." He'd even picked out flowers.

"Okay. Fine." She stalked past him and followed Bella to
the kitchen. "I'll have breakfast with you."

"Perfect. Everything's out on the deck." Jaden led the
way and carefully gauged her reaction as she stepped
through the door.

Kate's dark eyes widened when she saw the flowers on
the table, but she didn't mention them.

They each took the same seat they'd sat in last night. The
ambiance was different, though. Bright and warm and relaxed. Actually, scratch that. Kate's bare shoulders looked
tense.

"Nothing like starting the day off with a good breakfast."
Jaden took the liberty of serving her pancakes and syrup,
along with a helping of fruit and a few slices of bacon before
he filled his own plate. She didn't answer, but silence with
Kate didn't press into him like it did with some people. It
was...easy.

Bella wriggle-crawled her way underneath the very center of the table as though she couldn't decide who would be
most likely to drop her a crumb.

Kate took a bite of the food and chewed slowly. "Wow."
Her face perked up. "These pancakes are incredible."

"Mmm-hmmm." He tried one too. They were light and
airy, exactly the way he remembered. "It's my grandma's
recipe. She always whipped the egg whites forever. Then she
would carefully fold them into the batter."

"They're so fluffy." Kate seemed fascinated, inspecting
them as she cut another bite.

"So this breakfast isn't as painful as you thought." He'd intended the words to make a point, and Kate seemed to take it in stride.

"No. It's not painful at all." The first hints of a smile relaxed her face. "The food isn't half bad. Way better than Honey Nut Cheerios. I'm glad I stayed."

Jaden set down his fork and held her gaze. "Only for the food?" Because he wasn't enjoying the pancakes as much as he was enjoying sitting across from her, sharing breakfast with someone.

"Not only because of the food," she murmured with an unsure glance. "But…my life is a little complicated right now."

Join the club. He seemed to have secured a lifelong membership. "So is mine. That's why it's nice to have something uncomplicated. Dinner. Breakfast." He needed that. Something normal. Another presence in his world. Conversation. He hadn't realized how much he needed it until last night. For some reason, he found it so easy to be honest with Kate. "I like you. Spending time with you is…simple. And nothing in my life has been simple for a long time."

"I like you too." Kate's smile grew, finally resembling that quirk of her lips she'd shown off when he'd kissed her last night.

"So let's not complicate it," he suggested. "Let's have dinner while you're in town. And breakfast. Maybe lunch once in a while. Whatever works."

"That sounds perfect." She poured herself a glass of orange juice. "So what's complicating your life right now?"

A familiar tension crowded his gut. "Let's make a pact not to talk about our complications."

Kate tilted her head as she studied him. "What are we going to talk about, then?"

"Um…" Talking had never been one of his talents. "Our families?" That would be a short conversation on his part. "Funny stories from when we were growing up?" He had plenty of those. "But why don't we start with our most embarrassing moments?" That should be good for a laugh, keep things light.

Kate dropped her head, suddenly extremely interested in her food again. "Um…no thank you."

"Ohhh…you must have a good one."

"I hardly know you." She hastily helped herself to more pancakes, drowning them in syrup. "Why would I tell you my most embarrassing moments?"

"I think you're being dramatic," he teased. "I bet your most embarrassing moment isn't even embarrassing." She'd probably gotten toilet paper stuck to her shoe or something lame like that.

"Oh, it went way past embarrassing," she assured him. "It was humiliating."

"Now I have to know." Jaden refilled his mug of coffee from the pitcher he'd brought out. Though for once he didn't feel like he needed it. He'd slept better last night than he had in months. "I swear I won't tell anyone else."

"Fine." She left a dramatic pause. "My sophomore year of high school, I asked a boy to homecoming."

"That doesn't sound so bad."

Kate narrowed her eyes. "My friends convinced me I should decorate his car. So I skipped our last class and spent an hour covering his beloved Mustang in flowers and streamers and balloons and cute little signs."

"Uh-oh." He had a feeling he knew where this was going.

"Yeah." She crossed her arms and leaned back. "So when the bell rang, the entire school walked out to the parking lot and there I was, sitting on the hood of Tommy's car with a rose in my mouth and this huge, obnoxious, glittery sign asking him to go to the dance with me."

A laugh was brewing. He could feel it starting way down deep. Jaden held his breath so it wouldn't come out.

"When the guy came out and saw me," she continued, "he was horrified. He kept yelling about his car. How could I touch his damn car?"

"Ouch." *Don't laugh. Whatever you do, don't laugh.* It was hard, though, considering she told the story in a way that made him picture every detail.

"He said no, by the way. He said he wouldn't even go to Taco Bell with me."

That did it. Jaden could no longer hold back. But at least she laughed too. "See? I told you it was humiliating. Now you have to make me feel better about myself and tell me yours."

"Right. A promise is a promise." Even though his didn't even compare to the scene she'd just detailed for him. "My most embarrassing moment was in high school too." Wasn't everyone's? "I was in English class screwing around, being loud and obnoxious, and the teacher made me get up to apologize to the whole class."

"I have a hard time seeing you as loud and obnoxious."

"Oh, trust me." Before a couple of months ago, he'd been a lot more outgoing. He'd always preferred to think of it as extroverted and friendly rather than obnoxious. "Anyway, in front of the whole class, Miss Tolbert said, 'You come up to the front of the room right now and tell the class you're sexy. I mean sorry!'" He mimicked the old woman's voice for effect.

Kate did not look amused. "That's it? You're telling me that the most embarrassing moment of your life has to do with you being hot?"

Yeah, he had a feeling she wouldn't be impressed. "Miss Tolbert was a hundred years old. And that's all anyone could talk about for weeks. You should've heard the rumors that went around about us."

"I'm sorry." She shook her head, her sleek black hair swooshing around her shoulders. "That doesn't count as an embarrassing moment."

"Why not?"

"Because it probably made you a legend in your school," she grumbled. "It sounds to me like that was Miss Tolbert's most embarrassing moment, not yours."

Jaden laughed. "I never thought of it that way." But the woman had a point. "If it makes you feel better, I would've gone to homecoming with you."

"Right." She made a show of rolling her eyes. "Sure."

"Why don't you believe me?" Seriously. He would've killed to go to homecoming with someone as intriguing as Kate Livingston.

"You were this big-time snowboarder jock, and I was a newspaper nerd." She huffed. "I highly doubt you would've gone to homecoming with me."

"Maybe I would've surprised you," he said, eyeing her lips. The same way he'd surprised her last night...

"You've definitely accomplished that, Jay." Kate stared into his eyes with a slow smile. "I think it's fair to say I've never been more surprised by someone in my life."

CHAPTER SEVEN

Today's the day, Bella." Kate uttered a heart-cleansing sigh and gazed at the dog, who sat with her ears perked in rapt attention in the passenger seat of the borrowed Subaru. They'd been sitting in Jay's driveway for ten minutes, but Kate hadn't been able to get out and face the man.

"I have to tell him." Time was running out. Over the last week, Gregor had called and texted roughly twenty times, asking how the story was going, checking in to see if she'd finished a draft yet. She'd been putting him off, telling him that Jay had been extra busy so she hadn't collected all the facts yet. Which hadn't been a complete lie. Jay had been extra busy this week. She'd simply neglected to tell Gregor that Jay had been busy with her.

Since he'd made her breakfast that morning, they'd settled into something of a routine. She would arrive at the house around eight to pick up Bella, and Jay would make her breakfast before she and the dog went about their day.

At five, she'd bring Bella back to the house and either pick up dinner on the way or cook something on the grill. They'd sit out on the back deck under the stars, wrapped in blankets while the fire flickered between them, and entertain each other with stories late into the night. He hadn't told her anything about the accident yet, but that was okay because there was so much more to him.

He'd told her about being raised by his grandma, who took over the ranch when her husband died in his early forties, about how she was a better shot than any of the men in the county, about how he hadn't heard from his dad since his sixth birthday, and how his mom moved around the country in an old Airstream trailer, sometimes sending him postcards from wherever she happened to be living at the moment.

Kate had told Jaden things too. She'd told him about the time she'd done an undercover investigation on the recycling efforts at her middle school. It turned out they weren't recycling at all. At the end of the day, everything from the recycling bin got dumped into the garbage, and she'd exposed their deception in the center spread of their extracurricular newspaper.

She'd told him about how, when she'd declared writing as her major in college, her parents, along with her brother and sister, had staged an intervention dinner where they took turns telling her all of the reasons she would fail to find a career. Then she'd told him how her family had been all too happy to reiterate those reasons, along with a hearty round of *I told you so*, when she couldn't find a job.

Those were the real Kate Livingston stories. The ones that hid behind the happy smile. The ones that made her who she was. She couldn't remember the last time she'd shared them with anyone else.

By day three, breakfast had turned into one big flirt fest,

with Jaden teasing her and touching her a lot, placing his hand on the small of her back or brushing her hair over her shoulder when she pretended to be offended by one of his jokes. Dinner had turned into rushing through the food part to get to the make-out portion of the evening, where they'd lie entwined on the couch, kissing with an intensity that seemed to grow stronger every day.

"God, how am I going to tell him?" It would ruin the alternate reality they'd created together. With him, she suspected, escaping from horrible memories about the accident and her finally allowed to simply be Kate. Not a screwup in her family's eyes or an outdoorsy badass in her colleagues' eyes. It had been strange at first, being herself, but she'd started to love the feeling.

Bella yawned with a squeak and curled up in the seat as if she figured they'd be there awhile. Oh, how Kate wished they could be, that she could put this off a little bit long—

The front door of the house opened, and Jay stepped out, looking like an enticing cross between a cowboy and a mountain man in his boots, jeans, and a threadbare gray T-shirt. Even from this distance, his smile summoned hers as he slowly walked to the car.

"Hi," Kate called through the open window. It sounded more like a dreamy sigh than a greeting. Heart thudding in her throat, she scrambled to let Bella out before climbing out of the car herself.

"Didn't realize you were already here." Jaden knelt to pet Bella, who was whining and pawing at his legs like she hadn't seen him for a month.

Kate tried to keep her smile intact. "Just pulled up a minute ago." Now that was a lie.

"Perfect." The man stood, and she couldn't believe how different he looked than he had the first day she'd met him.

His face had relaxed, and his lips loosened into a smile whenever he saw her. Even his posture seemed stronger, taller, and less reserved.

"I want to take you somewhere." Jaden eased an arm around her waist and brushed a kiss along her temple. "I've got dinner packed," he whispered in her ear.

Even with regret and guilt swelling through her, she couldn't resist leaning into his touch, savoring it. Once he found out about her story assignment, he might never touch her again. "Maybe we should eat here. So we can talk." She couldn't tell him the truth in public. The setting for this conversation had to be perfect. They had to be alone.

"We can talk where I'm taking you." Jaden released her and strode up the driveway. "It's kind of a hike, so we'll take the Jeep." He punched in the garage code. Then he walked back to her and took her hand, guiding her to the passenger side and opening the door for her.

He did things like that all the time. Small gestures like moving aside to let her go first through a doorway or always leaving the last bite of dessert for her. In the evenings, he'd walk over and slip her sweatshirt on her shoulders when he could tell she'd gotten cold. Kate closed her eyes as Jaden let Bella into the backseat and then strode to the driver's side and climbed in.

How was she going to do this? She'd rehearsed the words a hundred times. Before she'd pull up to his house every morning, she would say them again. But then he would greet her and kiss her and he was so happy that she didn't want to ruin it. She didn't want it to end.

"You okay?" he asked, backing the Jeep down the driveway.

"Fine," she murmured, close to tears. "Just a little headache." Heartache.

"Here." He reached back into a small cooler and pulled out an ice-cold water bottle. "Water usually helps. It's easy to get dehydrated at this altitude."

"Thanks." Her throat felt raw. She opened the water bottle and took a long sip. She had no idea where they were going, only that it was up. Up the street, then up past the resort, and then up higher still on some lonely dirt road that cut through the wide spaces between trees that Kate assumed were ski runs. Patches of snow still dotted the mountainside, but there was grass too—new and green. Luckily, they didn't need to talk. With the Jeep so open on top, wind whistled between them, which meant Kate didn't have to force the words that churned in her stomach. He wouldn't have heard them anyway.

While the Jeep bumped along, Jaden brought his hand over to rest on her thigh. "Feeling better?"

Nodding, Kate closed her eyes and breathed in the cooling air. She loved the feel of his hand on her, warming her, reassuring her.

After one more switchback, he parked the Jeep, and she raised her head. They were above the trees. There was more snow up here, but she hardly cared about the temperature. The view to her right consumed her. It was endless. A blue-hazed vista of snowcapped peaks hovering above a watercolor of reddish cliffs and green, tree-studded mountainsides that came together in long, lush valleys. There were little round lakes so far off in the distance that they looked like puddles. "This is incredible," she breathed.

"One of the reasons I loved boarding so much." Jaden gave her thigh a squeeze and then got out of the Jeep. "That view never gets old."

He let Bella out and started to rummage through things in the back of the Jeep before meeting her on the passenger side. "It's colder up here," he said, helping her put on a fleece jacket. It smelled like him—like male spice. The same scent that always filled her senses when they were kissing.

Taking her hand, Jaden led her a few steps away from the Jeep, where a large snowfield still smothered the grass. The view once again stretched out in front of them, a painting she wanted to jump into.

"This is the snowfield where I started out," Jaden said. "My buddies and I would hike up here, out of bounds, and we'd board as long as we could. All the way through June some years."

She threaded her fingers through his, holding on to his hand tighter. "You never got caught?"

"Nah. They didn't keep a close eye on things around here during the summer months." He couldn't seem to look away from the snow. "Even as a kid, I loved it. Being out here made me feel so free."

"I bet you miss it," Kate said quietly. She could see it in the sad slump of his shoulders, hear it in the shaky tenor of his voice.

"I almost killed someone." He paused and swallowed hard like the words had the power to strangle him. "A few months ago. At the Olympics." Jaden faced her as though he wanted her to see the pain on his face. "I was trying to take the lead, and I lost control. Plowed right into my rival and took him out."

Kate looked up into his eyes, and she couldn't lie to him anymore. "I know."

"You do?" He dropped her hand and stepped back. The sudden uncertainty in his glare cut off the rest of her words. She couldn't tell him about the article. Not yet. "I kind of put it together. Jay—J.J. You're a snowboarder. You've been in an accident..." He had to realize that she would've heard about it. Everyone had heard about it.

"You never said anything." His expression was guarded, the same way it had been when she'd met him on the street.

Kate eased closer to him, looking intently into his eyes so he would remember she wasn't a threat. "You didn't bring it up, so I figured you didn't want to talk about it."

"I haven't." The rigidity in his shoulders seemed to give way. "Not with anyone. The days after were so intense. With the media, and surgery to reset my arm." He turned back to the snowfield with a blank stare. "Then they told me Kipp had a spinal cord injury. That he wouldn't walk again. And I couldn't function. I couldn't sleep or eat. I had nightmares constantly. Everyone was saying I'd done it on purpose…"

"Of course you didn't do it on purpose." She turned him back to her. God, he was so tormented by it. She couldn't stand seeing him that way, so lost. "Tragedies just happen sometimes. You didn't cause it. You didn't bring it on him or yourself." She took his cheeks in her hands and guided his face to hers. "You are a good person, Jaden Alexander. You didn't deserve this. You didn't deserve to be crucified in the media." But she could change things. She could tell his side of the story. "You need to stop hiding and let people see who you really are. I can help. I can write—"

"First I need to get back on my board," he interrupted, gazing at the snowfield again. "That's why I brought you here. I can't do it alone."

Kate studied him. That was his total focus. Getting back on the board. And yes, he did need that. So talking about the article could wait. "How can I help?" she asked. "You want me to cheer you on? Take a video so you can remember this moment?"

"No." For the first time, he looked amused. "I want you to board with me."

"I'm sorry, what?" This time Kate was the one who

backed away. "As in *snow*board with you?" As in strap a piece of wood or whatever the hell it was made out of to her feet and go racing down a freezing cold snowfield?

Jaden's smile answered the question. That was exactly what he wanted her to do. Which proved he was crazy. The man was nuttier than a five-pound fruitcake. "I can't snowboard," she informed him. "I don't even *have* a snowboard." So there.

"I grabbed one from the rental shop, along with some boots that I think should fit you fine."

Damn his thoughtfulness. "I've never been snowboarding." She eased a few more feet of distance between them. "This might come as a shock, but I'm actually not outdoorsy. At all."

"I know." He approached her, taking her forearms in his hands, and dear Lord his touch wrecked her.

"You do?" she almost whispered. Here she thought she'd played her part of the outdoorsy chick pretty damn well over the last week.

"I kind of put it together." One corner of his delicious mouth lifted higher than the other. "That's one reason you were so eager to help out with Bella, right? Because you didn't want to go back out on the trail to finish your mysterious trek?"

"I hate camping," she confessed. "I hate the bugs and the dirt and peeing in the woods. Oh, and I hate the stupid tents that suck at being waterproof."

Jaden laughed. "I figured." He pulled her close, locking his hands at the small of her back. "But I don't think you'll hate snowboarding."

"I guess we'll find out." For him, she'd give it a try. She'd do pretty much anything to make him happy, to hear him laugh again. Even if it involved adrenaline.

* * *

"I don't know about this." Kate reached for Jaden's arm and peered down at the snow that stretched out below them.

"I don't know about this either," he admitted. What had appeared to be a pristine, sparkling field of snow suddenly looked a lot more like an icy death trap. Now he knew what could happen. He knew he had no control out here. Life could change in seconds if he made one wrong move or caught an edge.

But he also knew that things could be restored, that there could be healing, if he found the courage to seek it out. Kate had reminded him of that. She'd proven there could be light at the end of his tunnel of despair, but you had to work for it. So here he was, slowing inching toward that light, sweating and sick to his stomach.

He'd purposely chosen this spot because it wasn't as steep as some of the other areas he used to frequent, which meant it should be an easy place for Kate to learn. But he couldn't seem to move his legs. Might as well be honest with her. "I'm not sure I can do this." Stay standing. Glide over the snow the way he used to without a thought. Even just the feel of the frozen ground beneath him was enough to trigger the memories of kneeling at Kipp's side, seeing him unresponsive...

Grunting in her cute, soft way, Kate inched her snowboard toward him until she was close enough to squeeze his hands. "You can. Let's do it together." A brave willingness came out in her smile, which meant he couldn't wimp out now. He'd told her everything, and she still looked at him the same way. The ugliness of his story didn't shock her, or overwhelm her, or even make her question his integrity. He'd never been given a greater gift.

"Okay." Jaden locked his weak knees and then held her steady with an arm around her waist. It was awkward with both of them on their boards, inverted sideways on the mountain, but she would need his help.

"First, you want to find your balance." He assumed the position so she could see—weight centered, knees soft.

She emulated his posture. "Like this?"

Taking her hips in his hands, he set her back slightly. "Perfect. How does it feel?"

"Awkward." Her body wobbled. "I don't like having my feet strapped into something."

"You'll get the feel for it." And he would do his best to keep her upright. Maybe that would distract him from the sudden surge in his blood pressure. "Make sure to keep your center of gravity low, then put more weight onto your downhill leg." He let go of her and showed her what he meant, sliding down only a foot so he could catch her or break her fall if he had to.

"Whoa…" Kate eased her weight onto the downhill leg, arms flailing. Somehow, she caught herself and balanced, inching the board down to where he stood.

"You're a natural." He couldn't resist touching her, taking her hands and seeing the color rise to her face.

She looked up at him from under those long eyelashes. "I don't know about that, but this isn't as terrible as I thought it'd be."

"It's not as terrible as I thought it would be either." She kept his mind off the fears. "I meant getting back on a board isn't as terrible," he clarified. "Not being here with you." He eyed her mouth, trying to decide how hard it would be to kiss her when they were both standing on snowboards. "I like being here with you."

She smiled softly at him, still holding on to his hands.

"Thank you for letting me be here. For trusting me." The last words wobbled out, full of emotion.

Screw keeping our balance. He leaned over and kissed her, securing one hand on her forearm to keep her upright and stroking her cheek with the other.

When he pulled back, Kate seemed to be breathing harder, though they hadn't actually gone anywhere.

"So we have to go all the way down to the end?" She moved her gaze down the slope.

It was either that or ditch the boards and hike back to the top. "If you're up for it."

"I guess," she muttered, but she also smiled.

"We'll take it slow." He released her and eased into the board again, sliding it slowly down the hill in a path she could follow.

Kate started out behind him, but her balance was off.

"Low center of gravity," he called.

"I don't know how!" She started to panic, body lurching, her arms flailing, the board going vertical. She picked up speed, coming straight for him.

Uh-oh...

Just before she plowed into him, he opened his arms, catching her against his chest. The momentum knocked them both backward, and Kate landed on top of him.

Bella barked and ran circles around them, as though she wanted in on the game.

Jaden grinned at Kate. "At least I broke your fall."

"Oh my God, you should've seen your face." She shook with laughter, which made him laugh too. It felt good to laugh. Felt good to be out here on the mountain, lying in the snow, feeling this woman against him. There was nothing quite like feeling Kate against him.

When they would lie on the couch after dinner in the

evenings, their legs tangled as they kissed and touched and murmured about how enjoyable it all was, he felt normal and whole. Part of something again. The last time she'd pulled away and said she'd better get going, it almost killed him, but he hadn't wanted to push her. He needed her to want him as much as he wanted her.

Did she? Did that growing hunger gnaw at her the way it did him?

He closed his arms around her. "Will you stay with me tonight? I don't want you to leave."

She propped her chin up on her fist. "That depends…how comfortable is your bed?" She was teasing him again. And damn he loved it.

"The bed is okay. But you should see the tub in the master bathroom."

"Big enough for two?"

"I'd hope so. It takes up half the bathroom." When he first saw it, he'd thought it was a ridiculous waste of space, but now he could see the benefits of having a huge tub.

"Perfect." Kate moved her face closer to his, her eyes full of everything he needed in his life—humor and fun and depth too. She seemed to see so much in him. The good. What he thought had been lost.

"I'd love to stay," she murmured. "I'll need a good hot soak after this little adventure."

"In that case, let's cut this run short and hike back up." He snuck his hand into her fleece coat and felt his way up her chest.

She rolled her eyes in mock annoyance, but her heart beat faster under his palm. "We just got here."

"Snowboarding is overrated." Especially compared to sex.

She wriggled away and maneuvered to a sitting position.

"We can head back soon. But first I want to see you ride all the way down there." She pointed to where the snow tapered off into wet, soggy grass. "You need to finish this run, Jaden."

He loved the sound of his real name on her lips. "What about you?"

"I'll watch. That's how I learn best anyway." She took his face in her hands and pressed her lips to his, brushing them softly, waking him once again. "Go. Alone. Do what you came here to do." She obviously understood how much he needed this, to rediscover peace out here.

He reluctantly stood, surprised to find the dread was gone. There was nothing but anticipation. Starting out slowly, he eased his weight onto his downhill foot, cutting across the mountain before leaning into a turn. Slushy snow sprayed all the way up to his face, cold and familiar. He let himself pick up speed, taking the turns quicker, carving a wavy line into the snow. Wind sailed across his face, stinging his nose the way it always did when he really cut loose and flew.

"Woohoo!" Kate cheered behind him, clapping and whistling. He crouched lower, using the momentum and speed to cut and jump, feeling lighter than he had in three dark months.

CHAPTER EIGHT

They didn't even make it inside the house before Jaden started to kiss her. He moved swiftly around the Jeep and opened her door, taking her hand.

The captivated, aroused look on his face heated Kate all the way to her core.

Seeing him on that mountain—facing whatever demons had chased him through the last few months—had done something to her. She no longer cared about the article. Or Gregor. Or her stupid job as a senior editor. She wanted Jaden. All of him.

Bella scooted out of the Jeep after Kate, barking as though she didn't understand what was happening.

Jaden seemed to ignore the dog. His eyes were intense on Kate's, speaking all sorts of hot, scandalous things without saying a word. He pinned her against the side of the Jeep, kissing her lips, sweeping his tongue through her mouth. Then he pulled back, stealing a glance at her, smiling that private, sexy smile.

Bella wedged herself between their legs and whined.

"It's okay, pup." He reassured her with a quick scratch behind the ears before Kate directed his gaze back to hers by threading her fingers into his hair and holding his face in place so they could take the kiss deeper. So much deeper. His lips were fused to hers with a heat that set her skin ablaze and made her body burn for him. "Inside," she managed to gasp. "Take me inside."

He hoisted her into his arms, and she wrapped her legs tightly around his waist as he carried her through the garage door. Kate was so busy kissing him that she caught only a glimpse of poor Bella tagging along behind them.

Jaden brought her through the kitchen and then the living room, all the way to the master bedroom, kissing her mouth with a recklessness she happily matched.

He paused near the bed. "We forgot all about the dinner I packed."

"Later," Kate gasped. "We can have dinner in bed."

"I love that idea." He carried her across the room and set her feet on the floor just inside the bathroom.

He hadn't been exaggerating. The bathtub in the master suite was enormous. A freestanding rectangle that was tucked into a marble-tiled alcove in front of a large picture window that looked out on the mountain. It was straight out of a fantasy—gleaming white porcelain with a crystal chandelier dangling overhead.

"Holy mother," Kate murmured, staring at the beauty over Jaden's shoulder.

He held her close. "Are you using me for my bathtub?"

"Yes," she said with fabricated certainty. Then she worked her hands up his chest underneath his T-shirt and leaned into him, running her tongue along his neck until she'd reached his ear. "Is that a problem?"

"Nope." He jumped into action, plugging the drain and turning on the water, holding his hand under the faucet to test the temperature.

The running water seemed to spook the dog. Bella scampered out of the bathroom and plopped herself on a cushy pillow next to the king-sized bed. Obviously the dog was not a fan of baths.

Jaden left the water running and came at Kate again, lifting her back into his arms. "It feels so good to hold you," he whispered against her shoulder. He carried her to the king-sized bed and set her on the very edge, standing close enough that she could raise his T-shirt and kiss his tight abs.

His breath hitched each time she pressed her lips to his skin. As she tasted him, his hands smoothed down her hair. He stepped back and took her right foot in his hands, removing the boot, and then her sock, watching her eyes the whole time. He did the same with her other foot, caressing her toes with his thumb until she lay back on the bed, moaning like she was already halfway to an orgasm. "Wow. You're amazing."

"Are you using me for my massage skills?" he asked, running a single finger down the length of her foot.

"Yes," she whispered. She loved the way he touched her. His hands were so strong, knowing and perceiving, taking their cues from the sounds she made, the movements of her body.

Jaden grinned. "Use away." He inched closer and caught the waist of her yoga pants in his fingers, tugging them down her hips, efficiently taking her lace underwear with them. Moving even closer to the mattress, he edged his body in between her legs and leaned over to unzip the coat she was still wearing. He worked slowly, watching her face between long gazes down her body like he didn't want to miss one detail.

Gently, he pulled one of her arms out of the coat and then the other, shoving her jacket aside before securing his hands to her waist under her T-shirt. "You're so beautiful, Kate. Such a good person." The words were almost solemn, as though he didn't think he deserved this, deserved her. But he didn't know.

She cupped her hands on his shoulders, bringing him down to lie over her. "You're a good person too. Strong and thoughtful and funny." So profound in his thoughts, tender in his touch. "I've made mistakes." The biggest one lately not telling him everything the first day she'd met him.

"Mistakes can be forgiven." He slid his hands higher up her rib cage, pulling off her shirt and letting it pool behind her.

"I hope so." She drew in a long, sustaining breath as his finger traced the very edge of her lace bra.

One of his hands eased under her back and popped the clasp, and then he shifted onto his side next to her and pulled the garment away. His gaze swept over her, dark and greedy. Jaden kicked off his own boots, pushed off the bed, and pulled her up to stand with him, pressing her body to his as he maneuvered back to the bathroom. He broke away only long enough to shut off the water, and then he had her back in his arms.

Kate took over, peeling his shirt up and over his head, letting it fall to the floor next to them. She kissed his neck, his chest, sliding her tongue seductively over his skin while she unbuttoned his jeans and pushed them down, taking his boxers with them. "Actually, maybe I'm using you for your body." She stood back to admire him—all that hard, angled muscle tensed into perfection.

"Like I said...use away."

"Oh, I plan to." Keeping him in anticipation, she stepped

into the tub and slowly lowered her body to the water. Resting her head against the side, she closed her eyes. "Ohhhhh."

"That good, huh?" Jaden climbed in and settled his back against the opposite side to face her.

"I can think of something better." She shifted to her knees, opening her legs to straddle his hips.

His chest expanded with a long breath. "You've changed so much for me." He gazed steadily into her eyes. "It's been so long since I've felt anything..."

"What do you feel now?" She ground her hips into his, moving over his erection, feeling it slide against her, slick and hard.

"You." He held her tighter against him. "I feel you. Everywhere. In my head. In my heart. In my arms." He kissed her so torturously slow, as though he wanted to make it last as long as possible. But there was too much passion surging through her, too much want nudging her closer to the edge.

She stilled her body, and Jaden sat up straighter, bringing his mouth to her breasts, nipping and kissing his way from one to the other. Her head fell back, the ache for him driving deeper into her.

He traced his lips up her chest and back to her mouth while his hands caressed her back. He paused and looked into her eyes. "What are you thinking?"

"How much I want this," she murmured. "How much I want you." It had all happened fast but he'd let her see everything, his pain, his heart. Way more than any other man had ever allowed her to see.

Kate stood on weakened legs and stepped out of the tub. Within seconds, Jaden stood with her, kissing her as he slowly eased her backward toward the bathroom vanity. He lifted her and set her backside on the marble countertop and then opened a drawer and found a condom. She leaned over and kissed his shoulder while he put it on. "I need you inside of me," she whispered, tugging on his hips and arching her back to bring him in deep.

Jaden wrapped his arms around her as their bodies came together, moving in a rhythm that loosened her feeble grip on control. He angled his hips on each thrust to graze that magic spot, again and again until she was gasping and throbbing and too close to pull back. Bracing her hands against the countertop, she pushed up to meet his thrusts, welcoming the explosion of sensations as it burst forth inside of her, moaning his name so he knew he could let go too.

"God, Kate, you're amazing," he uttered between jagged breaths. Jaden held her tighter, rocking his body, reigniting her climax until he trembled with release.

He hunched over her, his forehead resting on her shoulder.

"Wow," she murmured into his hair.

He raised his head and kissed her softly, still out of breath. "Wow."

"I'm exhausted." She could hardly hold herself up anymore.

Jaden straightened and took care of the condom before wrapping a towel around his waist. Then he came back and lifted her into his arms and carried her to the bed.

They both fell to the soft mattress, lying side by side. His fingers stroked her bare arm. "I wasn't just saying that earlier. You really have changed things for me."

Kate entwined her fingers with his and brought his knuckles to her lips.

"You're the first person who's bothered to see me," he went on. "No one else cared what happened. Everyone wanted a fallen champion, a villain, so that's what they turned me into."

Kate propped herself up on her elbow and looked at him for a long, beautiful moment. "I see who you really are." And she would make sure everyone else saw it too.

* * *

Waking up had never been Jaden's favorite thing, but it had been especially brutal since February. Most mornings he would've much rather kept his eyes closed than face the world, but not when he had Kate in his bed. Since the sun had come up, he hadn't been able to stop looking at her.

He still held her in his arms, her body curved against his, their legs tangled together. Kate was asleep, her face still somehow just as stunning as it was when she smiled at him.

At some point during the night, Bella had snuck onto the bed and curled up at their feet as though she couldn't stand to be left out.

A lazy contentment weighted Jaden's body. He wanted this. Waking up with someone every morning. Feeling the silkiness of her hair over his arm, feeling her breathe so peacefully against him.

In so many ways, Kate was still a mystery. All he really knew about her was that she lived in L.A. and worked as an editor. But she didn't seem to love it there. He wouldn't either, not with the constant crowds and the paparazzi everywhere. Maybe she'd be open to moving. For the first time since the accident, he could see settling down, sharing his life with someone. And he wanted it to be here in the mountains. At least if he took the job at the resort, he'd have stability, a beautiful place to live where the community had seemed to accept him back. He would have something to offer her.

Kate stirred and stretched her arms. Her eyes opened, and

that gorgeous smile of hers bloomed when she looked at him.

"Morning, beautiful."

"Morning." She wriggled closer and wrapped herself into him.

He couldn't resist playing with her long, soft hair as she laid her head back down and closed her eyes.

"Not a morning person?" he asked innocently.

"Normally I am, but we didn't exactly get much sleep last night." She kept her eyes closed, still smiling.

"Sorry." He wasn't. Not at all.

"I'm not sorry." She peered up at him as though her eyelids were too heavy. "It was the best night I've had in a long time."

"Me too." This whole week had been some of the best moments of his life.

"What time is it?" Kate asked through a yawn.

Unfortunately, he'd been keeping an eye on the clock. He almost lied, but she could easily see for herself. "Nine."

"Nine?" She shot up to a sitting position. "Aren't you late for work?"

He sat up, too, leaning over to kiss her neck. "Yep."

"Then you should go." The words didn't have much conviction.

"Don't want to." He pulled the comforter away from her chest and admired her full breasts. "I'd rather stay in bed with you all day."

Kate lay back down and turned on her side to face him. "Aren't they doing inspections?"

"Mmm-hmmm." He couldn't seem to pry his gaze away from her body.

"Then you need to be there, mister." She pushed at him playfully. "Go. Right now. They won't be able to sign off on everything if you're not there."

Yeah, yeah, yeah. Blake had already sent him three panicked texts. Jaden scooted off the bed. "What about you?"

"Bella and I will be fine. Won't we, sweetie?" Kate reached down and petted the dog's head.

"You'll be here when I get home?"

"Yes. I have some work to do today too," she said cryptically. "But I will most definitely be here when you get home."

"As long as you promise." He pulled on clothes and his boots but couldn't resist going back to the bed where Kate still lay watching him. Her black hair was mussed and gorgeous, her eyes still sleepy and innocent.

"I'll see you later." He kissed her, and she held on to him a little longer.

"Hurry home," she murmured. "I'll make a special dinner."

"Can't wait." He forced himself to leave then, before he started taking off the clothes he'd just put on.

The drive up the mountain didn't ease the ache that had tortured him since he'd left Kate in his bed. When he made it up to the site, Blake jogged over, looking more relieved than pissed.

"Glad you're finally here," he said.

"Sorry. Got a little hung up this morning." Could've gotten more hung up if it hadn't been for his damn responsibilities.

"The inspector is taking some pictures." Blake pointed to a man who was currently sizing up the towrope. "I hope it passes."

"It'll pass." Jaden had no doubt. Every detail had been well thought out and executed perfectly. He'd made sure. That was the only thing he'd had to focus on for the last month. And now that the project was ending, he knew what he wanted to do next. "By the way, I'll take the job," he said to Blake.

The man nodded as though he wasn't surprised. "This have anything to do with the woman you borrowed the snowboard for?"

"Yeah." But it was more than that. "I want to be part of a community again too." He wanted to start over in the same place he'd started out.

CHAPTER NINE

Kate hadn't been this nervous since that fateful day when she'd asked Tommy to homecoming. She finished setting the table and stood back to admire the simplicity.

After the embarrassing car decorating debacle, she'd learned that sometimes subtlety was best, so no balloons or flowers or cheesy *Please forgive me!* signs on the table tonight. No humiliating rejection either. It would be different. She and Jaden may not have known each other long, but he seemed to get her. He would understand why she'd kept certain things from him. And once he read the article she'd written, everything would be okay.

"Right, Bella?" she asked, kneeling to give the dog some love.

Gregor had texted her early that morning to tell her he needed a draft of the article by noon or there'd be serious consequences. "Not that I care about the consequences," she explained to Bella. Writing the article had become something bigger. She'd spent the whole morning pouring her heart into her keyboard, and the words had flowed. She'd likely get fired for writing a personal exposé on what an incredible person Jaden Alexander turned out to be instead of capturing what everyone expected, but it would be worth it.

Sure, Jaden would be surprised, but she could explain everything over dinner. It was a simple meal—lasagna and a hearty Italian salad. She liked to think of this as half an apology dinner, half a makeup dinner. Or at least she hoped they would make up after they had the inevitable conversation she'd been avoiding for a week.

"He'll forgive me," she murmured.

Bella licked her cheek in agreement.

"He'll understand just like you do." Once Jaden read her words, he would see how much she cared about him.

"Hey, gorgeous."

Kate straightened and spun to the French doors. "Hi." The sight of Jaden standing there in his jeans and boots sent a wave of heat crashing through her. "You're home early." She thought she had another half hour to prepare for this.

"We finished up ahead of schedule." He took a step toward her but was blocked by Bella, who wanted his attention first. "The inspector was impressed," he said, giving his dog a pat on the head.

"Well good. That's great." God, she already sounded guilty, and she hadn't told him anything yet.

"I may have gone twenty over the speed limit all the way back here too." He wrapped her in his arms and lowered his mouth to hers. Nope. Uh-uh. She couldn't get distracted now. She had yesterday, but enough was enough. Gently, she pushed him away. "Why don't you sit down? I'll go see if the lasagna is ready."

Without giving him a chance to respond, she hurried to

the kitchen, opened the oven, and peeked under the tin foil. The cheese had bubbled to perfection. *Okay. Whew.* She was really going to do this. Kate patted her pocket where she'd stashed the printout of the article. After a quick explanation of the situation, she'd hand him that right away. Before he could even ask questions. The article would make everything okay.

When she finally carted the lasagna outside, Jaden was throwing the ball for Bella.

"Dinner's ready," she called, setting the casserole on the trivet she'd put out earlier.

"Looks good." He jogged over. "But not as good as you." His gaze slowly trailed down her body. "Maybe we should eat later…"

No, no. They had to do this now. Kate scolded him with a little smirk as she sat down. "We don't want it to get cold."

"Right." Disappointment tugged at his mouth, but he sat too. "So what'd you do today—" His phone buzzed. "Sorry." He dug it out of his back pocket. "Guess I'll turn it off. I've been getting calls from weird numbers all afternoon."

Kate paused in the middle of cutting him a generous slice of lasagna. "Calls?" Her heart glitched. Coincidence. It had to be a coincidence, right? She'd sent Gregor the article at noon, just for his opinion, but it wouldn't go to print for a few more weeks…

"Now I got a text." Jaden was squinting at his phone. "'What's your response to the *Adrenaline Junkie* article?'" he read. He looked up at Kate. "I had no idea *Adrenaline Junkie* was doing an article."

Oh no. No, no, no. Kate couldn't seem to move. Her body had frozen to the chair. Instead of beating, her heart was zapping in her chest. "Oh God."

"I know." Jaden rolled his eyes. "They've left me alone

for a long time. Why are they all of a sudden interested again?"

Tears flooded her vision as she stared at him wide-eyed. "I'm sorry. Jaden, I'm so sorry." Regret burned through her, thawing the shock, letting her move. She got out her phone and went to *Adrenaline Junkie*'s website. Sure enough, her article had been posted on the blog, and it already had 14,253 shares on social media.

When she looked up, he was staring at her. "Why?" His voice hollowed as though he was afraid to know. "Why are you sorry?"

"I wanted to help." She dug the folded papers out of her pocket. "To tell your side of the story."

"Wait." His eyes narrowed into that distrustful glare she recognized from before. Before he knew her. Before he'd kissed her. Before they'd made love. "You sent them an article about me?"

"No." *Don't cry.* She couldn't let herself cry. "I work for them. I'm a senior editor there."

"What the fuck?" He pushed away from the table and stood. His eyes had hardened like he didn't want her to see the pain behind his anger.

Kate stood too. "I printed out the article so you could read it. I was going to show you tonight. I had no idea they'd post it today. It wasn't supposed to go to print for a couple of weeks." As if that made any of this better.

Hand trembling, she handed him the papers, but he ripped them into pieces and tossed them into the wind. "I can't believe this. You played me. You never told me you worked for *Adrenaline Junkie*."

"I was afraid to." She eased a few steps closer to him, but he backed away. "I knew you wouldn't even talk to me if I told you where I worked."

Jaden shook his head. Closed his eyes. When he opened them, the anger had been replaced with indifference. "Go. Get out."

"Wait. No." He hadn't even read the article yet...

"You got what you wanted out of me." His jaw went rigid. "Now you can go."

"I'm not like that." He knew her. He knew the real Kate Livingston almost better than anyone else. "I don't use sex to get stories." She inhaled, calming the desperation in her voice. "I really feel something for you, Jaden. And I think you feel something for me too."

"I don't." His tone was as dull as his eyes. "I feel nothing for you."

The apathy in his gaze tempted her to look away, but she refused to give in. "Nothing? Really? Because you said all that stuff. About me changing things for you... about wanting to trust someone again."

"And you proved I can't trust anyone."

No. She'd proved that he could get back on his board. That he could come out of hiding. That he could feel something again. He just needed to remember that connection they'd built. "I'm sorry I didn't tell you about *Adrenaline Junkie*. I should have. But spending time with you wasn't only about the story for me."

He studied her for a minute, as though trying to judge her sincerity. "Why did you offer to watch my dog?" he finally asked. "Did you know who I was when we met on the street that day?"

Before she even answered, she knew she would lose him. But she couldn't lie. "Yes."

"And you saw an opportunity to use my trauma to your advantage."

"No," she whispered. "I didn't know..." How deeply

he'd been wounded by all of it. How it haunted him so much. "I never meant to hurt you. I only wanted to help. If you would just read the article—"

"You're the fakest person I've ever met." Anger simmered beneath the words. "You're worse than the reporters who ambushed me on the streets." Jaden turned and strode down the deck stairs, heading for a trail worn into the tall grass at the edge of the forest. "Bella, come." The dog looked at Kate and whined.

"Come, Bella," he commanded again.

Head down, the dog trotted across the yard to follow him.

Kate wanted to follow him, to force him to read what she'd written about him. She'd put her heart into that article. But it was too late. She'd lost him.

Before Jaden disappeared into the trees, he glanced at her over his shoulder once more. "You need to be gone when we get back."

* * *

If Kate had learned one thing about the women of Topaz Falls, it was that they were always prepared.

When she pulled up at Everly's adorable café on the outskirts of town, Jessa, Naomi, Darla, and Everly were all there to greet her. They ushered her into the old converted farmhouse where they'd already claimed a booth, and they were armed with enough comfort food to feed a whole cast of brokenhearted rejects from *The Bachelor*.

"We've got chocolate and scones and muffins and wine and brick-oven pizza," Darla announced.

"We wanted to cover all our bases," Jessa added, patting the open seat next to her.

"Thanks." Kate slumped into the booth, unable to look

any of them in the eyes. She'd given them the gist of what had happened with Jaden via text so she wouldn't have to relay the story in person.

"It's a great article," Everly said, pushing a plate across the table. "Very heartfelt."

"Has he read it?" Naomi asked quietly. Her baby girl was sleeping contentedly in a wrap secured around her shoulders, and she obviously didn't want to wake her.

"No. I printed it out for him but he ripped it up." Kate winced at the sting the memory brought.

"Well that's dramatic." Darla popped a truffle into her mouth.

"I'm sure he'll calm down when he reads it," Jessa offered.

"I don't know." His eyes had been cold and dull. Not full of feeling like they were when he'd looked at her before. "He has every right to hate me." Though she hadn't exactly meant to, she'd tricked him. He was right. She'd seen an opportunity, and she'd selfishly pursued it, never considering how it might hurt him. Or her. "I should've told him a long time ago." Like her new friends had recommended. They could all be sitting there saying *I told you so.*

"It seems like people are really connecting with the article, though." Everly glanced at her phone. "Up to 24,953 shares already. It's going viral."

Yeah, she'd heard. On her way over, she'd called Gregor to have a few words with the man about posting something before she'd approved it, but he'd been too busy counting hits on their website to care much.

"So what are you going to do now?" Jessa asked, cutting a slice of pizza into petite bites. "Head back to L.A.?"

"I don't have much to go back to. I quit my job." She hadn't planned to, but when she was talking to Gregor,

Jaden's words had echoed back in her head. *You're the fakest person I've ever met.* He was right. She didn't want to be a fake anymore. Even if it meant she had to slink home with her tail between her legs and move back into her parents' basement for a while.

"In that case, you can stay in Topaz Falls." Naomi's excitement woke the baby. She quickly stood to sway Charlotte back to sleep.

"Yes!" Everly, Jessa, and Darla whispered in unison.

"Stay?" She had a feeling there weren't a ton of jobs for unemployed writers in a small town like Topaz Falls. "But I have to work."

Darla's face brightened. "I've been thinking about hiring a manager so I can have a little more freedom to pursue my hobbies."

Everly grinned. "She means so she can have more time to date."

Darla ignored the snickers. "You'd be perfect management material," she said to Kate. "You're friendly, a good communicator, detail oriented..."

"Not to mention gorgeous," Jessa added. "That'll be good for business."

Kate looked from face to face with another round of tears brewing. "It sounds incredible." She had never fit anywhere. Not really. Not in her scholarly, overachieving family, not in her job. And here were these women she'd met only a week ago making a place for her.

"We're not fully booked until July." With Charlotte back to sleep, Naomi slid into the booth across from Kate again. "So you can stay at the inn for another month until you find your own place."

"And if you need more time, I've got an extra bedroom," Everly chimed in.

"Wow." A job, a place to live. But more importantly than either of those things, it came with the most generous, lively, compassionate friends she'd ever met. "Okay. I'd love to stay."

Excited squeals woke the baby again. Naomi stood and swayed while Darla poured everyone a celebratory round of prosecco.

"Cheers!" Jessa held up her glass, and they all clinked away.

"I can't believe I'm moving to Colorado." Maybe Jaden would stay too. Maybe after time, he would give her another chance to prove to him that he could trust her with his heart.

"And you won't have any problem building a freelance writing career now," Jessa pointed out. "Not after the article goes viral."

That was true. With all of the exposure the article was getting in the mainstream media, she'd have a more recognizable name. "But that's not why I did it."

"Of course not." Everly reached over and squeezed her hand. "But maybe now you can focus on the kinds of things you've always wanted to write. You'd be great at profile pieces. Diving past the surface to really capture someone's heart."

Gratitude welled up in Kate's eyes once more. "Maybe I'll start with a profile on the extraordinary women of Topaz Falls."

CHAPTER TEN

Secluded Mountain Cabin on 30 acres! Exceptional privacy! Hidden driveway!

Jaden clicked on the real estate listing that promised the escape he needed. *Perfect.* The place was in No Man's Land, Canada, which sounded like paradise right now, considering it had been almost three days since that article had gone viral and the influx of calls and texts from reporters all over the world hadn't even started to slow down. Some paparazzi idiots had even camped out at the end of the street just waiting for him to leave.

At the moment, moving out of the country looked like a pretty damn good option. Except Canada might not be far enough away. Maybe Siberia...

Bella slunk into the office with the same forlorn posture she'd moped around in since Kate had left three nights ago. Didn't matter that Jaden had taken the dog on two hikes a day via their secret trail out back, or that he'd thrown the ball for her, or even that he'd given her extra treats. She still gave him those sad, pathetic eyes every time he looked at her.

"Come here," he said through a sigh. The dog trotted over. Was it just him or did she look more guilty than sad this time?

Bella came and sat at his feet, and sure enough, she had something in her mouth.

"Drop it," he commanded.

The dog complied all too happily. Didn't take him long to figure out why. It was a hair tie. Kate's hair tie. The one Jaden had tugged on to free her soft, long hair when she'd spent the night with him, when it felt like nothing could damage the connection they'd built.

Except for lies. Those could pretty much destroy anything.

The ache that had taken up residence in his gut sharpened. "You've got to get over her, Bella." Yeah, sure. He was telling Bella. Not himself for the thousandth time. "I know it's hard being here." Seeing as how this is where the three of them had played house for the better part of a week. "But we'll move on."

He scrubbed his hand behind the dog's ears until she leaned into him with a purr-like growl. "I'm looking for a place to go right now. We can start over." Again. He was getting pretty damn good at it. "Then it won't be so hard to forget." And yet he already knew how that logic worked. He hadn't seemed to forget either one of his parents, even though they'd pretty much abandoned him the day he was born.

Jaden turned back to the computer screen. What choice did he have, though? When he and Kate were messing around about her using him for his bathtub and massage skills, he had no idea how much truth hid inside those jokes.

While he'd been thinking about a future with her, she'd been carefully taking notes on his story so she could expose him to the masses. How could he have been so stupid?

A sound outside the window forced him to leave that question unanswered.

Bella's ears perked.

Awesome. Just what he needed. The paparazzi sneaking around his backyard. Jaden shut his laptop and crept along the office wall, staying just behind the curtain. He almost laughed when he peered out and saw Levi Cortez tromping across the back deck like some kind of criminal.

The dog saw, too, judging from the mad swing of her tail. Bella scratched at the window, barking and whining at the prospect of company.

"Easy, girl." Jaden nudged her out to the living room, where they met Levi at the French doors. "What're you doing here?" he asked as he let him in. He had a feeling he already knew.

Levi sauntered past him in his cowboy's gait. "Haven't heard from you for a while. Figured I'd check in. And I saw the photographers outside, so I came around back." The man sat on the leather couch in the living room and leaned back like he had all day. Bella followed him, nosing his hand as though she'd been starved for attention the past three days.

Jaden stood where he was. "You could've called."

"I have called. You haven't answered."

Yeah, he hadn't even looked at his phone in a good twelve hours. After getting a text that had asked if he planned to marry Kate Livingston, he'd thrown the damn thing in a drawer. But Levi wasn't here to simply check up on him. And Jaden had had enough bullshit for one week. "Why are you really here?" He positioned himself in the chair across from the couch so they were facing off.

Levi grinned. "You haven't had the pleasure of meeting my sisters-in-law, Naomi and Jessa. But they're about as obstinate as a bull that's lost his balls. And they happen to like Kate. So here I am."

Jaden shook his head to stop Levi right there. "You're wasting your time," he informed his friend. "I can't stay here now. I've already found a place in Canada. You have no idea what it's like to have to hide in your house."

"So quit hiding. Who cares if they take pictures or write more stories?" Levi leaned forward, resting his elbows on his knees, still casual but also more determined. He obviously still had that stubborn streak. Typical bull rider.

"According to Jessa and Naomi, Kate's pretty broken up about everything."

"She's good at pretending." Jaden knew that for a fact. He'd replayed every scene of their tryst in his head. Every kiss. Every story she'd shared. Not once had he suspected she'd turn on him. That was the worst part. After everything he'd been through, he'd become an expert at sniffing out ulterior motives, and she'd completely snowed him.

"I get why you're pissed off," Levi said. "But it seems to me you used her too."

The anger that had only started to recede churned again, growing bigger, stronger. "How do you figure?"

The edge in Jaden's voice didn't seem to faze Levi. He simply shrugged. "When we talked on the phone last week, you told me you didn't think about the accident when Kate was around. So you used her as a distraction. Or did you screw her that night for *her* benefit?" The obvious sarcasm confirmed Levi already knew the answer. It also confirmed that word about him and Kate had gotten around Topaz Falls faster than Jaden could've dreamed.

"I guess that's it, then. We were using each other." That

wasn't how it felt, though. He hadn't intentionally used her. It wasn't about the sex for him. It was that he thought she'd made the effort to see him. The real him. The one no one else cared to notice.

"She wasn't using you." Levi sounded so sure, but how could he know? He hadn't been there. He hadn't seen how good Kate was at drawing information out of him. How she'd lured him into telling stories that she'd probably written up in the fucking article.

"Maybe she was using you at first," his friend acknowledged. "But that's not why she wrote the article. Have you even read it?"

No. He hadn't been able to stomach the thought of staring at her words. Words that had been taken from him without his consent.

His silence must've spoken for him because Levi nodded. "You really need to read it. Hell, it almost made me choke up."

"I can't read it," Jaden said simply. He'd read plenty of articles that had torched him, and he hadn't cared. But Kate's words would matter more.

"Guess I'll have to read it to you, then." His friend shifted and pulled his cell phone out of his pocket. "At least the good parts."

"No thanks—"

"'When I first met J.J. Alexander,'" Levi interrupted, "'I saw what the rest of the world had seen—a cocky, bitter, fallen hero—'"

"You can stop now." Pain roiled in Jaden's gut. He knew her words would sting.

"Sorry. I shouldn't have read that part. It gets better." Levi turned his gaze back to the phone. "'After spending a week with him, I realized I was wrong. We were all wrong. J.J. isn't bitter or closed off or arrogant. He's wounded, haunted by regrets just like the rest of us. In one split second, his board caught an edge, and that tragic accident didn't only change Kipp Beckett's life, but it also changed J.J.'s life forever. He hasn't been able to escape it. He thinks about Kipp every day.'" Levi glanced up at him. "See? She's obviously trying to help, to get people to see your side of the story."

"I don't need people to see my side of the story." He hadn't made excuses for any of it. The accident might not have been intentional, but it was still his fault. It was all on him. "The article will only make things worse." She'd put him back in the same spotlight he'd been running from for months.

"There's more." Levi bent his head and went back to reading. "'Instead of exposing Jaden as a disgraced athlete like I had intended to do in this article, I fell for him. I fell for his subtle wit and his thoughtfulness and his profound depth. I fell for the way he loves and protects the dog he rescued from abuse and neglect. And yes, I even fell for his emotional scars because they are what make him so real. In one week, I discovered that J.J. Alexander has more empathy and strength and compassion than I ever will.'"

Her words roused hope, but he couldn't quite hold on to it. "Maybe she wrote it that way on purpose." Everyone wanted a good love story. "Maybe she wanted it to go viral so she'd have a recognizable name." What if she didn't care about him at all? No one else except for Gram ever had. Not his parents or his teammates. When he had been competing and winning, everyone had wanted to stand by him, but after he had fallen, he stood alone.

Levi shoved his phone back into his pocket and glanced around, a sure sign he was changing his approach. "Growing up, you and I didn't exactly have the greatest example of what love should look like."

"That's an understatement." When your parents left, love pretty much looked like abandonment. Levi knew that as well as he did.

"I was like you for a long time," his friend said. "Happy with a hookup here and there. But everything was different when I reconnected with Cass. It didn't matter what she did to me. How angry she got or how many times she pushed me away. I couldn't let her go. Not because I wanted anything from her either. I just loved her."

Jaden stared out the window. Had he ever just loved anyone? He didn't know how.

"Look…" The first signs of frustration showed in Levi's narrowed eyes. "I'm not as good at this lecture thing as Lance is. All I know is, I couldn't picture my life without Cass. I guess you need to decide if you could have feelings like that for Kate. Or for anyone. Maybe not now, but someday."

The feelings were already there. That's why he hurt like this. Somehow, the last two days had been lonelier than all twenty-four years of his life before he'd met Kate because now he knew what he was missing. "I already screwed it up." Jesus…had he really told her she was the fakest person he'd ever met? It wasn't only the words he'd used, though; it was also the venom behind them. She'd never forgive him for treating her that way.

"Believe it or not, I have some experience in begging a woman for forgiveness." Humor returned to Levi's voice. "But before you can ask for it, you've got to get yourself in a better place so you don't need a distraction anymore. Or things will never change."

The words were like stones sinking into his gut. Nothing would ever change if he didn't work for it. He'd put too much on Kate. It couldn't be her responsibility to pull him out of the pit he'd been living in. It shouldn't be. She deserved more. "I did use her." He cared about her, too, but that didn't change the facts. He'd only wanted her there because she made him feel something. She'd given him the courage to face the mountain again. All that had mattered was what she could offer him.

"Well, my work here is done." Levi stood and gave Bella a good scratch behind the ears before he opened the back door. "We've got a poker night at my place next Tuesday if you're up for it."

Jaden simply stared at him. How could he think about next Tuesday right now?

"You can let me know after you get this shitshow cleaned up," Levi said with a grin. Then he slipped out the back door, leaving Jaden to sit and wallow in his own stupidity.

Seeming to sense his misery, his dog walked over, sat down, and laid her head on his knee.

"Damn, Bella." He rested his hand on her head. "How are we gonna fix this?"

* * *

The Craig Hospital gift shop was stocked with flower arrangements, stuffed animals, and inspirational books and plaques. Jaden wandered down an aisle past shelves of trinkets inscribed with clichéd messages: *Get well soon! Healing thoughts and good wishes!*

The sentiments turned his stomach sour. What could he say to Kipp? What could he bring him that would make any of this better? He'd been trying to figure that out for two days, and he still had nothing.

Hands empty, he ducked out of the gift shop, dragging three months of guilt along behind him. When he'd emailed a request to visit Kipp in the hospital, Jaden fully expected him to decline, but he hadn't. *Come on by anytime,* Kipp had written. *I'll make sure you're on the list.*

It was surreal walking down the hall now. He'd imagined this place would look like a dungeon—dark and depressing—but windows everywhere let in the bright sunlight. Two young women pushing themselves in wheelchairs rolled toward him, chatting and laughing like they were in the hall of a high school. They smiled as they passed, and somehow he found a smile too. They looked happy. Healthy. He hoped the same was true for Kipp.

Jaden continued down the hall, following the directions to the rec center where Kipp apparently spent most of his afternoons. The room looked nothing like he imagined. There were low Ping-Pong and pool tables and a huge television screen mounted on the wall with video game consoles lined up underneath.

"What's up, Cowboy?" Kipp wheeled himself over, a Ping-Pong paddle sitting in his lap. He looked...the same. From the bandanna tied around his head to the sturdiness of his broad shoulders to his confident grin.

The sight stung Jaden's eyes. "You look...good." He didn't mean to sound so shocked, but all of the mental images he had of Kipp were still from those first few days after the accident when the media had plastered pictures of him being loaded into the medevac.

"I feel good. Just kicked Jones's ass in a game of Ping-Pong." He gestured to another man in a wheelchair who'd moved on to the Xbox. "You want to be next?" Kipp asked with that signature spark in his eyes. Without waiting for an answer, he wheeled over to the Ping-Pong table and brought Jaden a paddle.

He almost didn't know what to do with it. "You want to play Ping-Pong?"

"Hell yeah. I'm undefeated." Kipp trucked to the other side of the table and got into position. "Zeros," he said one second before he nailed a killer corner shot that Jaden of course missed.

"I wasn't ready." He wasn't ready for any of this. He hadn't even told the man he was sorry yet.

"Better get ready, Alexander. Because I've had a lot of time to practice." Kipp found another ball on the floor nearby and rolled back to the table. "One–zero." He served another zinger that whizzed by Jaden's right shoulder.

"Wait. Hold on." Jaden set down his paddle. "I didn't come here to play Ping-Pong. I came here to tell you I'm sorry. I'm sorry you got hurt and not me. I'm sorry I'm not the one sitting in that chair." It could've been him. "You don't have to pretend this is easy." He got that Kipp didn't want his pity—Jaden wouldn't want pity either—but the man's life would never be the same.

Kipp rolled his eyes as though he'd been dreading this conversation as much as Jaden. "It's not easy," he acknowledged. "But I've had three months to process things. At first I was as pissed as hell about it. Some days I still am. But I've also learned my life isn't over. Hell, I've already been invited to be a commentator for the X Games next year."

He should've been competing in those games, though. Jaden didn't say it. Kipp already knew what he'd lost. Somehow he seemed to be on the road to accepting it. So why couldn't Jaden? Why couldn't he release the guilt? "You let me know if you ever need anything." Maybe that would help. If he could just do something for Kipp, maybe he could forgive himself. "I'll be there for you. I'll help you out however I can."

"You don't have to be sorry, J.J. I've seen the footage." His old rival mocked him with a smirk. "It's not your fault you're not as good on a board as I was."

Same old trash talk from one of the greats but this time Jaden didn't return fire. He couldn't. "I should've pulled back." He'd been moving too fast, too recklessly. He'd wanted to win. That was the truth of it. If he'd backed off, the accident never would've happened.

"I would've been offended if you had slowed down," Kipp said. "We competed. We're athletes. That's what we do." The man's expression sobered. "The last three months have sucked but I've got a lot going for me. That's what I want to focus on now. The future."

And that's what Jaden would focus on too.

CHAPTER ELEVEN

Welcome to the Chocolate Therapist." Kate greeted the older couple with the same enthusiasm as she had greeted every other couple and family group and friend group that had walked through the doors for the last nine hours.

Her feet, which were stuffed into her favorite pair of black Manolo Blahniks, ached like a mother, but even the pain couldn't dim the excitement of day four in her new life. All within less than a week of the big falling out with Jaden, she'd managed to fly home, pack up her apartment, and say farewell to everyone before she'd driven straight back to Topaz Falls.

When she'd driven into town, the sun was setting over the mountains in a fiery red welcome. So far it felt like this place had always been her home. Even with long days of learning the wine and chocolate business, the shininess of her new venture still hadn't dulled.

"Would you like a table?" she asked the couple, gracefully withdrawing two menus from the hostess stand. "Or would you prefer to sit at the bar?"

Darla appeared behind her. "I can take over, Kate. Your shift was over a half hour ago."

"That's okay. I'm having so much fun." Even with achy, swollen feet, this was better than going back to her room at the Hidden Gem to spend the evening by herself. Despite the homey decorations, loneliness echoed between the walls.

"All right." Darla drifted back to the bar. "But at least sit down after they're seated."

Ignoring her friend, she turned back to the elderly couple.

"We would love a table near the windows, dear." The woman appeared to be in her early seventies with white wispy hair and jewel-like blue eyes.

Her husband was a head shorter than her and just as adorable with a rim of frizzy gray hair around a shiny bald spot. "There's something going on down the street, and we'd like to see how it turns out."

"Of course," Kate sang. "Right this way." Ignoring the pinch in her toes, she led them to a quaint table for two that looked out on Main Street. Darla had been right. She was good at this. Good with people. They always smiled at her, and even though she'd only been working here for a few days, she'd managed to defuse three grumpy patrons' complaints and had them all smiling and laughing again within a matter of minutes.

"Here we are." She tucked the menus under her arm and pulled out each chair with a charming smile, patiently waiting until the couple had gotten situated before she handed them the wine and chocolate list.

Instead of opening his menu, the man craned his neck as though trying to see down the street. "Any idea why all that trash is piled onto the car out there?"

"It's not trash, Gerald," his wife corrected. "It's sweet. There are flowers and streamers and balloons..."

Kate choked on a gasp. Flowers. Streamers. Balloons. On a car...

She tried to keep her hopes smothered under practical logic, which had never been one of her strengths. Jaden hadn't returned any of her emails or calls. After a few days, she'd stopped trying.

"It's so pretty," the woman went on. "I saw the man fixing it all up nice. He was tying heart-shaped balloons to the door handles, the sweetheart."

Sweet Lord...

Those darn hopes threw logic to the wind and sent her heart sky-high. Bracing her hands on the table, Kate leaned forward as far as she could without bumping her forehead on the glass. Each beat of her heart thumped harder when she looked down the block to where she'd parked her car earlier. Sure enough, it was covered.

"Oh my God." It had to be him. No one else around here knew that story.

"Um...your waiter will be right with him...I mean you," Kate stammered to the couple. The happiness burning in her eyes made her voice all weepy. She steadied herself against their table once more and pulled off her shoes, letting them dangle from one hand as she hurried toward the door.

"Are you all right, honey?" the woman called.

"I will be." As soon as she saw him—as soon as she felt his arms wrap around her—she would be. Kate ran down the sidewalk barefoot, her pencil skirt surely making her resemble a waddling penguin, but she didn't care. It was such a lovely sight, her car covered in orange. There were gerbera daisies and orange hearts cut out of construction paper, and yes, even heart-shaped balloons. But she couldn't see the front yet. Would Jaden be there? Had he really forgiven her?

"Pardon me," she mumbled, bumping her way past people.

When she finally broke through the crowd that had gathered, her knees gave. Jaden was sitting on the hood of her car with the stem of an orange gerbera daisy between his teeth.

"Look at you…" She stumbled off the curb, nearly incapacitated by the tears and laughter, sure that the happiness of this moment could fill a whole lifetime.

"Hey, gorgeous." He somehow managed to annunciate perfectly, even with the daisy in his mouth.

The crowd around them grew, pressing in on both sides of the street. Both locals and tourists snapped pictures and selfies on their phones. He hadn't tried to disguise himself. No hat. No sunglasses. Just J.J. Alexander sitting on the hood of her car. None of the attention seemed to bother him, though. He stared steadily at her as she crept closer. "What're you doing?"

"I'm asking you on a date." He took the flower out of his mouth and dropped it on the hood and then reached for her hand. "Kate Livingston, will you go on a date with me?"

"Hell yes, she will," Darla called from behind her. "How about right now? We can set up a nice private table in the back."

Murmurs of approval went around the crowd. Someone even clapped.

Kate shushed everyone with a frantic wave of her hand. This moment was a scene straight out of her dreams, and she didn't want anyone to intrude.

"I'm sorry I was such an ass." He eased off the hood and stood across from her. "I'm sorry I didn't hear you out. I'm sorry I ripped up your article."

"Awww. I'll go on a date with you," some woman yelled from the other side of the street.

"No." Kate put her hands on his broad shoulders to make sure this was really happening. "I mean yes. Of course I'll go on a date with you."

Jaden lowered his face to hers, her favorite grin in the entire world flickering on his lips. "Now?"

"Now," she confirmed.

The crowds parted. Cell phone cameras followed their every move as they huddled together and hurried back to the Chocolate Therapist, ducking through the doors so they could leave the rest of the world behind.

"Back here, you two." Darla quickly ushered them down the hall to the room where they met for book club. She'd already had the waitstaff drag in a small round table, two chairs, and a vase with a single orange gerbera daisy she must've swiped from the car.

God, these women. They had the best and biggest and brightest hearts she'd ever seen. "Thank you." Kate brushed away her tears as Darla gave her a wink and disappeared, closing the door firmly behind her.

They both sat down.

"You're crying." Jaden took her cheeks in his hands, using his thumbs to wipe away the tears.

"You humiliated yourself out there." All for her. "That'll be all over the news by tonight." People were probably tweeting and Instagraming and Facebooking the pictures right now.

"I don't care." Something had changed on Jaden's face. The day she'd met him, it had borne the lines of tension and stress, but now his features seemed softer. Relaxed. "I'm tired of caring what everyone else thinks. Except you." He slipped his hand under hers and held on. "You were right. There is something between us. Something...special. Something I've never had with anyone else."

Kate closed her eyes, letting those words soak in to heal all of the wounds he'd inflicted before. She looked at him again, wanting him to cut away that last bit of uncertainty that still dangled from her heart. "What changed?" she whispered. "You were so angry..."

"Yeah." A sigh slipped out. "Levi pretty much put me in my place. Told me I'd better get my head out of my ass and figure things out before I lost you for good."

"Levi, huh?" She smiled, thinking back to Jessa and Naomi's secret little side conversation at Everly's café the day she'd told them what had happened.

"Yeah, Levi." His smirk confirmed her suspicions. "He reminded me that I had issues to work on too. So I went to see Kipp."

Kate tightened her grip on his hand. "That must've been hard. How is he?"

"Still in rehab." Jaden threaded his fingers with hers, and the power of it, the intimacy of that gesture, heated her eyes again.

"But I spent the afternoon with him. He's exceeding the doctor's expectations. He's even taken a few steps with a walker."

"That's great news." For Kipp and for Jaden. No wonder his appearance had changed so much. He'd been set free.

"I read the article too. Actually, Levi read it to me." Jaden brought her hand to his lips and kissed her knuckles, sending an electrical charge all the way down to her toes.

"I'm sorry I betrayed your trust." She'd been waiting to say those words for over a week, but before now, something told her they wouldn't have done any good. "I should've told you. Right away. But I was afraid you'd keep me out. And I loved being with you."

"I loved being with you too," he murmured, leaning over the table until his lips were nearly touching hers. "I think that's why I lost it when I found out about the article. It was an excuse to bail. I figured you'd turn out to be like everyone else." His gaze shied away from hers. "I haven't exactly had much commitment in my life."

She kissed him, hopefully taking away any lingering doubts about her feelings for him. "I meant everything I said in the article."

This time his eyes stayed steady on hers. "I know."

"Levi said you were thinking about moving away." God, when she'd heard that, she'd had to excuse herself so she could cry in the bathroom.

"I was seriously considering it," Jaden said. "Until he reminded me it wouldn't help. I want to stop hiding. I want to make you happy. I want to focus on the future instead of the past."

She rested her forehead against his. "Me too."

Just as his lips brushed hers, the door swung open.

"Don't mind us." Darla traipsed in, followed by Everly and Jessa and Naomi, all carrying something different. They set down truffles and a bottle of wine and glasses and small china plates.

"Carry on," Everly said, herding the others toward the door.

"Those truffles are strawberry-filled dark," Darla called, fighting Everly's hold on her.

"The perfect aphrodisiac," Jessa added before Everly shoved her outside.

"Happy date night!" Naomi said with a sly grin.

Shaking her head, Everly waved at Kate and Jaden once more before closing the door.

Jaden laughed. If she could bottle up that deep throaty

sound and listen to it every night before bed, she totally would.

"Levi wasn't kidding about their persistence."

She leaned in to claim the kiss she'd never stop craving. "Sometimes true love takes a village," Kate murmured against his lips.

And they seemed to have found theirs.

ACKNOWLEDGMENTS

Thank you, dear readers, for spending more time in Topaz Falls. I hope you are enjoying this town and these characters as much as I am. It's impossible for me to express how grateful I am for your notes, comments, reviews, and mentions. Your support keeps me going.

As always, I am so thankful to the team at Forever for allowing me to live my dream and write more books. You all continue to amaze me! With each project I learn more from my brilliant editor, Alex Logan. Thanks for everything you do to make me look good.

I will never be able to thank my family enough for their patience and perseverance, especially while I was writing this book under such a tight deadline! Will, AJ, and Kaleb, you will always have my heart.

ABOUT THE AUTHOR

Sara Richardson grew up chasing adventure in Colorado's rugged mountains. She's climbed to the top of a 14,000-foot peak at midnight, swum through Class IV rapids, completed her wilderness first-aid certification, and spent seven days at a time tromping through the wilderness with a thirty-pound backpack strapped to her shoulders.

Eventually Sara did the responsible thing and got an education in writing and journalism. After a brief stint in the corporate writing world, she stopped ignoring the voices in her head and started writing fiction. Now she uses her experience as a mountain adventure guide to write stories that incorporate adventure with romance. Still indulging her adventurous spirit, Sara lives and plays in Colorado with her saint of a husband and two young sons.

Learn more at:

www.sararichardson.net

Twitter @sarar_books

Facebook.com/sararichardsonbooks

Ready for more cowboys?
Don't miss these other great Forever romances.

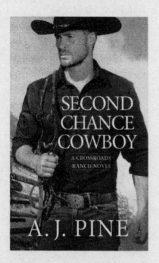

Second Chance Cowboy
By A. J. Pine

Once a cowboy, always a cowboy! Jack Everett can handle work on the ranch, but turning around the failing vineyard he's also inherited? That requires working with the woman he never expected to see again.

Cowboy Bold
By Carolyn Brown

Down on her luck, Retta Palmer is thrilled to find an opening for a counselor position at Longhorn Canyon Ranch, but she's not as thrilled to meet her new boss. With a couple of lovable kids and two elderly folks playing matchmaker, Retta finds herself falling for this real-life cowboy.

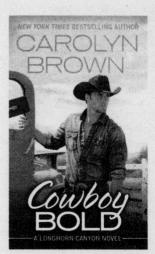

Look for more at: forever-romance.com

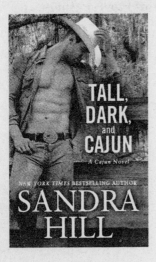

Tall, Dark, and Cajun
By Sandra Hill
Welcome to the bayou where the summer is hot, but the men are scorching! Sparks fly when D.C. native Rachel Fortier meets Remy LeDeux, the pilot with smoldering eyes angling for her family's property. He'll need a special kind of voodoo to convince Rachel she was born for the bayou.

Cowboy on My Mind
By R. C. Ryan

Ben Monroe has always been the town bad boy, but when he becomes the new sheriff, Ben proves just how far he will go to protect the woman he loves—and fight for their chance at forever.

Be sure to follow the conversation using
#ReadForever and #CowboyoftheMonth!

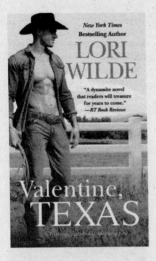

Valentine, Texas
By Lori Wilde

Can a girl have her cake and her cowboy, too? Rachael Henderson has sworn off men, but when she finds herself hauled up against the taut, rippling body of her first crush, she wonders if taking a chance on love is worth the risk.

True-Blue Cowboy
By Sara Richardson

Everly Brooks wants nothing to do with her sexy new landlord, but, when he comes to her with a deal she can't refuse, staying away from him is not as easy as it seems.

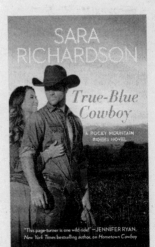

Look for more at: forever-romance.com

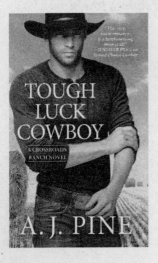

Tough Luck Cowboy
By A. J. Pine

Rugged and reckless, Luke
Everett has always lived life
on the dangerous side until a
rodeo accident leaves his
career in shambles. But life
for Luke isn't as bad as it
seems when he gets the
chance to spend time with
the girl he's always wanted
but could never have.

Cowboy Honor
By Carolyn Brown

Levi Jackson has always
longed for a family of his
own, and, after rescuing
Claire Mason and her
young niece, Levi sees that
dream becoming a reality.

Be sure to follow the conversation using
#ReadForever and #CowboyoftheMonth!